I0680976

Protectorate Trilogy: Book 2

Cobalt City Blues

Nathan Crowder

These things they flow as blood must flow
Dust to dust and wind must blow
You can die before you get old
But me, I'm going to live forever.
125 MPH
(Sullivan/Heaton/Harris) 1987

1st Revised edition
1st Printing

Direct all orders to:
Timid Pirate Publishing
509 N. 85th St. #14,
Seattle, WA 98103

www.timidpirate.com

Printed in the United States of America
First Revised Printing: October, 2010
ISBN 978-0-9830987-0-6

Note from the Author

I love heroes. I graduated from Greek mythology, Robin Hood and King Arthur to the four-color spandex crowd as I got older, but I never lost track of my roots. Naturally, I gravitate towards people who like that epic level of storytelling. I gravitate towards role-playing gamers who like a heavy dose of story and character with their dice rolling.

Cobalt City was born a shared sandbox shortly after the dawn of this century. Its inception was innocuous, just one more setting for a role-playing game with family. Based around the lives of super-heroes living in a generic New England city, the game took on a certain richness, attracting friends as additional players. The bulk of the heroes in these pages were created by friends and family, hashed out in magical evenings of temporary art and shared creativity. Those stories fired my imagination, and sadly, were never written down. When the game ended, victim to conflicting schedules, distance, and the myriad of life changes that accompany adulthood, the sandbox sat quiet – for a while. But the characters refused to remain silent.

It always felt wrong to me that super-heroes were only for comic books. With the exception of novelizations of established comics and George R.R. Martin's brilliant *Wild Cards* series, no authors wrote those characters as the spiritual successors of mythic heroes we all grew up with. *Cobalt City Blues* captures and shares some of that magic. It is a tribute to my friends, the creators of these characters, and gave me a chance to tell the one, big story I never got around to sharing with them. They gave me these bright stars, and I gave them voices. And that brought Cobalt City to life, even for readers who had no previous association with the characters or their earlier adventures. Thus a series, and a universe, was born.

I would like to dedicate *Cobalt City Blues* to the people who made it possible -- to Kathleen "Wild Kat" Crowder, Andrew "Knockabout" Warren, Jennifer "Velvet" Fermon, Catherine "Worm Queen" Warren, Sean "Gallows" Hamilton, Ian "Archon" Hamilton, Ed "Stardust" Johnson. This one is for you.

Nathan Crowder
October 2010

Prologue

Cobalt City - March 27th, 1931

Simon left Camilla alone with her needle and her junk. Curled up there on the bed in the small apartment they shared, a stone's throw from 70th, it was too much for him to handle. The false euphoria on her face, the sticky, sweet smell of her skin – no. It brought back unpleasant memories, and he had to get out for a while. Simon saw too many friends fall victim to the siren call of opium during the Great War. He couldn't bear to watch the woman he loved wrestle with the same demons. But Camilla made her position abundantly clear early on, back when she had agreed to become his lover. And she had reinforced that position in dozens of heated arguments. She had habits, and if Simon loved her he would have to accept her -- flaws and all. But it didn't mean that he had to watch, which was what compelled him out onto the streets, towards the club. On the bright side, it would give him the chance to get a jump on a new arrangement.

Simon Floyd would give anything for Camilla's young, laughing beauty, with skin like polished mahogany. He had in fact given everything. He still couldn't understand the American attitudes about race. They seemed to find no problem with having a colored girl on the side, but it had to be discreet. To be seen in public, in polite company, could easily ruin a man. Simon knew that for certain. It had all but ruined him. At least his band understood, half of them being black themselves.

He told himself that his family back in England would be as forgiving as his band mates. But then he pictured the quiet Devon streets, the pale faces and hard eyes hidden by working class grime so thick it might as well be tattooed. No. They never approved of anything he did, from joining the Royal Navy to moving to America to pursuing a career in music. Simon had been a constant source of disappointment. This was no different. At least his parents were now dead and Simon only had his brother Charles and Charles' thick, cow-eyed wife to let down now.

Camilla understood him. She of the dark skin, dark eyes and dark gods, possessing the light bayou accent, light, birdlike laughter, and light touch. She made all the mocking glances and words worth putting up with, even the lost friends, the refusal of most clubs to book his mixed race band, and the tiny apartment in the Bohemian neighborhood swarming with rats and roaches. Even when people

1

laugh behind their backs on the rare occasions when they went out, calling them the darkie and the limey, Camilla made it all worth it. When he slid into the sheets beside her in the still hours of morning, nothing else mattered.

He stepped off the lift on the Marco Polo Hotel's fourteenth floor just after noon, and headed across the broad marble floor of the foyer to the door of the Oriental. Half-John, the silent, distant-eyed doorman let him in with a distracted nod. Once inside, Simon slid quickly around the edges of the dim, opulent interior of the rooftop club, heading for the curtained stage. It was empty now, and quiet except for the sounds of prep work in the distant kitchen, but he didn't want to risk an encounter with the contemptuous club manager Antonio Morigi. If Mr. Morigi were there somewhere, he would most likely be in the back office near the kitchen, and Simon desperately wanted to avoid him. He was certain that if the manager had his way, the band would have to find another steady gig. Steady work was hard to come by these days.

If not for the club and hotel's owner, Nicholas Anduscal, Simon would not be there. The big-hearted owner had approached Simon after the first set he and the combo had played in a small dive several weeks ago. In wafts of peppermint-scented breath, he told Simon that it would be in his best interest to speak with Mr. Morigi at the Oriental the next morning. Never one to pass up a potential booking, Simon did just that, and was delighted when the reluctant-looking manger signed them to an extended four nights a week engagement.

Just about every night, Mr. Anduscal sat in his private booth at the back and listened to the set. He also ate peppermint Starlight mints by the bowl, a habit that had earned him the moniker Peppermint Nick. Skitch, the drummer, once joked that the club owner, probably all of his employees too, were mobsters. It was a suggestion that Simon had immediately laughed off. Not all successful Italian business men were criminals.

On the darkened stage, Simon carefully folded his faded gray topcoat and put it, along with his hat, out of the way on Skitch's stool behind the drum kit. Then, with pencil in hand, he began looking over the Gershwin tune he had rearranged roughly over coffee and hash in the White Spot Diner hours after hearing it for the first time. He was pretty sure he could make it work with his small combo, and if Camilla found herself lucid enough to sing again, then he might get the band back to its full glory. Smiling at the thought of his lover at the top of her form and on stage like when they met two years ago, he readily lost himself to the music in his head. The better part of an hour passed as he scribbled. Off-stage in the dining area, the staff worked and swore and shouted in Italian, but he was able to shut it out without even thinking.

Simon was so caught up in his work that only the sound of footsteps running up the stairs to the stage brought him out of his focused mindset. Pencil held between his teeth, a page of sheet music in each hand, he turned to the curtain just in time for the gunshot which stopped the running figure dead in his tracks -- a silhouette on the red velvet.

For a long second, there was no sound but for Simon's eyeteeth indenting the soft wood of the Ticonderoga #2 while he stared at the expensive loafers visible under the bottom of the velvet curtain.

Then two more shots, and the meaty body of Antonio Morigi fell through the curtain, hands curled on the red velvet in a death grip. The club manager spun as he fell, taking the barrier between Simon and the rest of the club with him, throwing a sliver of bright light across the stage and piano.

Once again, the room was frozen in silence.

Simon was reminded of an incident during the Great War, when his ship had been badly damaged and low on ammunition. They were out on the North Sea, heading for home with the German Destroyer Freya closing on them swiftly from starboard. And then the fog rolled in. Before the guns could sound, before Simon and his friends and shipmates could be sent to the bottom of the sea as little more than blood and twisted metal, the miracle happened. The fog that settled upon them was like a great wet blanket sent by God himself. Visibility was reduced to mere feet. A lifetime growing up on the English shore and he had never seen a fog so absolute. The captain cut the engines and ordered the lights doused. One hundred and thirty-two men, proud sons of England all, held their breaths and waited. At one point, Simon swore that he felt the Jerries pass by so close that he could stretch out from the railing and touch their hull, but he didn't dare try for fear that he was right.

As Simon sat on the stage, his eyes adjusting to the sudden light, he hoped that another fog would roll in, and suppressed a nervous giggle. In the muted light of the dining area, he could barely make out Peppermint Nick seated behind his customary table, Half-John standing next to him with a pistol still smoking in his hand. He could hear the two of them having a muted conversation in Italian, but wasn't paying enough attention to understand what was being said even if he could breach the language barrier.

Instead, Simon turned his mind to getting out of there alive. The stage was placed so that to make it to either the club doors or kitchen, he would have to get past Half-John who had, at his count, three bullets left. He didn't like the odds. And who was he to be dodging bullets anyway? No, if he wanted to make it out of this alive, he would have to be careful. Nick had always professed to like him, right? Maybe he wasn't in any real danger after all.

"It is very unfortunate that you had to be here to see this, Mister Floyd," the thickly accented voice said from the back of the room. He unwrapped another peppermint, one-handed, with practiced ease and popped it into his mouth.

Simon's voice sounded small in his own head. "I didn't see anything, Mister Anduscal."

"That's very good of you to say, Simon. Can I call you Simon?"

"Of course." Simon became nervously aware of the dryness of his mouth.

There was a thick, sweet smile in Nick's voice. "I like you, Simon, regardless of your reputation and some ugly rumors to the contrary. I believe you have ethics, and that is very important to me." He leveraged himself out of the booth and walked to the edge of the stage. Half-John kept pace with him, gun still at his side. "With a better sense of ethics, Tony here might not have run into in the dilemma that he found himself in."

Simon nodded sympathetically, showing he understood the burdens Nick had to endure with such disloyal employees. "Yes. And now that you've dealt with the problem, I might as well excuse myself and fetch a late lunch."

Nick held up a hand. "Now, let us not be too hasty." His rings glittered in the light. Half-John raised his gun.

Simon put his heartbeat on hold for a few seconds, tightly coiled, waiting for the gunshot. When the fatal bullet failed to come, he allowed himself to relax a little and found that he had closed his eyes and that Nick and company had stepped the rest of the way up onto the stage.

"You got yourself a girl, don't you?" Nick said. "A Negro girl, used to sing with you before she started riding the horse...what is her name again?"

Half-John chose that moment to pipe in. "Camilla." Maybe his half-there persona was all just an act. It was possible that he was observant as well as crazy, which Simon always felt made for a lovely combination. "She runs with that nigger voodoo crowd other side of the highway, in the south-side of Karlsburg."

Simon felt his hands flicker and tighten into fists despite himself. He sized up the towering gunman. He figured he might as well have been carved out of particularly unattractive granite. Attacking him would be suicide. Despite the years in the Navy, Simon wasn't a fighter and he knew it. He was a musician, and if he wasn't careful, a dead musician. But he saw something in Peppermint Nick's eyes at the mention of voodoo. Something he hadn't expected. Fear. "Voodoo?"

"Yes," Simon thrust out his chin, suddenly confident that the superstitious old man would be afraid to touch him.

Nick looked nervous. "You mean with zombies -- the walking dead and whatnot." His voice was flat, his emotions poorly hidden as wheels turned in his head.

"Zombies and everything." Simon hoped his tone sounded sincere and ominous, neglecting to mention that for all Camilla's talk, he didn't believe in it himself. Her quaint superstitions were a crutch, not unlike her habit, but he let her have them both and never criticized them.

Before him, Nick still had on his thinking face while he sucked hard at the candy in his mouth. "Christ, but we can't have none of that." Nick turned on his heel and started back down the steps. Half-John did not move. "Damn, that's going to complicate things a little."

"Do I still get to kill him?" The gunman sneered. He watched Simon with the compassion of a shark, and the pianist was certain that Half-John had planned this. He had, after all, let Simon in. He had to know that he was still there. And he had waited until Tony was on the stage to shoot. It started falling into place for him. Camilla had never cared much for Half-John, but she talked to him regularly when she came to the club to hear Simon's band.

And she always had a fresh supply of dope after that. Simon wanted to believe that she picked it up somewhere on the street, or from one of her friends in Karlsburg. But if Nick and Half-John were truly the mob figures they now appeared to be, how likely was it that Nick's right-hand man had been the supplier for the heroin? And there could be any number or reasons for Half-John wanting Simon out of the way if that were true. He felt like an idiot as the scales began to fall from his eyes. Simon hadn't considered the man a friend, but he had never considered him an enemy undermining his happiness before, either! Rage boiled up inside Simon, and he began to plot how best to realize his revenge against the doorman.

"Well, we can't have him walking around as a zombie now, can we!" Nick mused.

"Certainly bad for business." Simon smiled tightly. His eyes stared daggers at the doorman. *And by that, I mean your drug business, you bastard.*

"Ok, Johnnie, here's what you need to do," Nick rubbed his temples. "After you kill him…"

"What?" Simon watched his plans for revenge freeze stillborn. Nick shot him a sympathetic look that turned his blood cold.

"After you kill him, take him down to Leo at the Silent Rest. He owes us a few favors, all the business we send his way. See to it that the limey gets cremated."

Half-John raised the gun with an icy, reptilian smile. Simon found that he could not move, not even to blink.

"I'm sorry, Simon, but loose lips and all that," Nick gave a dismissive wave. "I liked having you around. You really brightened up the place. In fact, we might just keep you around. I've been meaning to do something with the space behind the bar. What you think, Johnnie? You think our Simon would look good in red?"

"Without a doubt." Half-John seemed to be sizing the pianist up carefully.

It didn't make any sense to Simon. "A suit?"

"An urn," the gunman smiled.

Simon was so worried about how Camilla would handle the news of his death that he never heard the shot that killed him.

Camilla woke several hours later to the sound of loud knocking. She looked at the time and realized that she had not even noticed Simon leaving. When she went to the door, she was surprised to find Skitch there smelling of cheap liquor. He had Simon's coat and hat in hand. They had been found when the rest of the band had shown up for their set. Neither Camilla nor Skitch were ignorant of who Peppermint Nick was. Hell, she bought her drugs from Half-John, even though she couldn't stand him on a personal level, with his hungry eyes and veiled innuendos. Only poor, sweet Simon, with his stubborn insistence to look past stereotypes, had failed to see the successful businessman with the colorful nickname and well-muscled and twitchy friends as the mob kingpin that he was.

No one had admitted to seeing Simon at the Oriental, and when Skitch found the hat and coat with the untouched wallet inside, the band knew to stop asking questions. They could find another pianist, possibly in Chicago or up in Harlem. Dex, the saxophonist, had family up Harlem way. Camilla was welcome to join them, Skitch told her.

But Camilla refused to run, refused to be afraid, refused, in the end, to let go of the sad-eyed Englishman who had looked past her demons and seen her potential. Still shaky with anger and tears, she ushered the nervous drummer out of the apartment. With a focus and clarity she hadn't felt in months, she cleared room in the middle of the floor. She went to the roof and took a dove from one of her neighbor's cages, and used its blood to draw her symbols on the cracked wood floor. Candles lit, offering waiting, she let the Loa overtake her.

When she awoke with the taste of blood and rum in her mouth the next morning, she knew her call had been answered. With aching muscles, she scoured the floor clean and got rid of all evidence of her act. By now, she told herself, her and Simon's revenge would be well underway. And now that he had risen from the dead to destroy those who had wronged him, he would return to her -- back where he belonged.

The inevitable passage of time flowed more slowly for some than others. But flow it did. Camilla's magic, while powerful, could not forestall what was to come – only preserve something that had been.

Camilla never moved from the apartment, waiting with quiet and patient faith for Simon to come back to her. She died with a needle in her arm in November of 1938.

Half-John suffered an accident when he fell into the concrete foundation of the Forbidden Palace Hotel in Quayside in April of 1941. The only witness to the accident pushed him under the wet concrete with a pole. After taking over John's job, he enlisted in the Army when Japan bombed Pearl Harbor eight months later. He died a hero on the beaches of Iwo Jima.

Peppermint Nick was also killed by a rival, gunned down in the back seat of his car while it parked outside his girlfriend's house. It was December of 1946, and both the girlfriend and the gunman were convicted; her of conspiracy to commit murder and him for murder in the first. He went to the chair. She went to a women's prison upstate where she served out almost four years of her sentence before being overtaken by pneumonia.

And so it was that when the red vase behind the bar of the Oriental was broken during a robbery, Simon found himself touched by the sun for the first time in over seventy years. He was not happy about it, having spent over seven decades of confinement, trapped with his own twin voices of cowardice and doubt in what used to be his head.

He looked out over the city that had changed, but not so much as he had. A swirling cloud of ash animated by dark, Voodoo magic, Simon took the shape of the invisible man when he concentrated. From a distance, he could almost pass as normal…top coat, hat, glasses. But he would never be normal again. Life was full of disappointment. He had, in fact, expected everyone to have rocket jetpacks by the end of the century. It was yet another disappointment.

If not for the charity of Katherine Wilde, the new owner of the Oriental, he would have had nowhere to go.

In the end it was time, not Peppermint Nick, that took everything that he could hope to call his own.

Especially his revenge.

Chapter One

The man who had just robbed the jewelry store was a step above the typical suburban nightmare. Not only huge, black and angry, he also possessed bullet-proof skin and the strength to lift a train engine over his head. And then there were the dogs. There were three in all -- each dog twenty feet tall at the shoulder, looking as though they had been badly painted with a spray can on an alley wall and then brought to life. As their master stepped out to the curb, they rejoiced by overturning an old Honda hatchback and batting it around like a wounded squirrel.

Simon approached from above, cascading down the molded concrete façade of Boyleston Jewelry Exchange as a waterfall of gray ash. He surveyed the scene quickly and was outraged by the ignorance of his target. It was one thing, he reasoned, to put your name on the back of your jacket. Athletes did it all the time, and the very expensive red and white leather jacket this criminal was wearing certainly had the look of a football warm-up jacket. But there was no excuse for incorrect spelling.

He hit the ground behind the jewel thief softly. No one would have been able to hear him over the sound of the dogs playing and the alarm from inside the jewelry store anyway, but practice makes perfect. Simon thought himself back into his human form and tapped soundly between the "Blak" and the "Dawg" on the jacket before him. The big man spun around and glared down at Simon Floyd. "If I may be so bold," Simon said politely, "You really should consult a dictionary before committing unfamiliar words to writing. Poor spelling reflects badly on your intelligence."

Blak Dawg looked momentarily confused. The three dog-type things turned their massive, blocky heads on the side as if they were confused as well. Good, Simon thought, got them thinking. That should buy some time for the others.

Simon watched the hulking criminal size him up, seeing him as an easy target. Appearances could be deceiving, however. A casual observer would see Simon only as a slight man in a fedora, gloves, and top coat, his head wrapped in bandages. Glacier style glasses covered his eyes. No flesh showed, at least not living flesh. All that was left was ash, held together by some sense of self-image. Without that sense of self he would be only…what? Simon shuddered to think of the possibilities.

9

Blak Dawg howled at him. "Yo, English! I'm gonna enjoy killin yo pasty, gray ass!"

A massive fist, wrapped in one of those silly, fingerless weight-lifting gloves thundered towards Simon's head. There was a time when he would have made some effort to duck. Funny how death changes a man, he thought as he let the fist pass through the cloud of particles that were making up his head at the moment. Unimpeded, the fist passed cleanly though, leaving Simon's head whole, but not as well defined as before.

He shouldn't have felt the blow. It had been a long time since he had felt *anything*, but somehow, a trace of the impact had managed to bleed through. While it wasn't enough to put him down, it was certainly concerning. Simon flowed backward, his legs turning cloud-like to get him out of range of any follow-up attack. He located his Protectorate communicator swirling around where he once had a liver, and directed his voice into it. "I trust I shall not have to deal with this miscreant alone?"

"Hang on, Mister Grey," he heard Stardust's voice buzz, "the cavalry is on the way!"

Knockabout took this opportunity to chime in as well, his Swahili accented English as smooth as twelve-year old scotch. "Draw him out into the street if you can. Let us please try to minimize the property damage this time."

Simon turned his whole body to a low cloud and rushed through Blak Dawg's legs to the hind feet of one of the giant dogs. As the huge thug turned to follow, he was surprised to find that Simon was not alone.

With a speed that always amazed Simon, Stardust zipped past Blak Dawg, hitting him with an energy-laced punch as he flew above the sidewalk at full tilt. While his teammate curled around for another pass, Simon saw a chilling, gold-capped smile spread across their opponent's face. The dog-things turned and began ripping ineffectually at Simon's wraith-like form. "Congratulations, Stardust. I think that might have tickled him."

"Tickle my ass!" Stardust sounded a little hurt at Blak Dawg's stubborn refusal to lie down.

Simon tried not to smile. "I'd rather not."

Knockabout chimed in from the rooftop of an apartment building across the street. "Allow me to slow him down a bit." Clad in an expensively tailored black suit, the erudite African felt the flow of gravity around Blak Dawg and flexed. In an instant, the gravity weighing on the leather-jacketed menace increased exponentially to the power of ten. It was enough to leave just about anyone pinned to the ground gasping for breath and unable to move.

The sidewalk under Blak Dawg's feet cracked, then crumbled to dust, and he sank to one knee, as if he had suddenly found himself walking in heavy snow and lost his footing. He grunted, a dark rage burning in his eyes, as Stardust picked up speed for another pass.

Half distracted by the attacking dogs, Simon almost didn't see it coming, but even forewarned he wasn't anywhere near fast enough to react in time. As Stardust drew closer, a sly look passed across Blak Dawg's face. It was a trap. And there wasn't anything he could do about it.

Once again, Stardust's energized punch did little to stagger his foe, and at the last second, a meaty fist lashed out and grabbed Stardust by the ankle. It did not seem likely that he would let go willingly. The brilliant millionaire inventor had been snared cleanly, and based on the punch Simon had intercepted moments ago, he knew Stardust would not be able to get free on his own.

"He's strong enough to shrug off the gravity. I might have to take this fight inside," Simon said. "Do we have someone to watch the dogs if this doesn't work out?"

Like an answer to a prayer, he heard the shout of "Worms to me!" as the Worm Queen made her appearance with the rest of the team, teleported by Gallows into the middle of the dog pile. A fifty foot worm the pale blue of glacier ice slid into existence, and its master, in a black body suit accented with colorful worm-like squiggles rode regally atop its head into battle. Simon didn't envy the dogs.

Considering the situation handled, Simon drove his ash form at Blak Dawg's face, forcing his way past the gold teeth and strong tongue into his lungs. As distracted as he was trying to rip Stardust apart, Blak Dawg didn't even to think to fight back against the unexpected tactic. It only took a few seconds for Simon to lay claim to his passenger. In a weaker person, Simon would be able to force the air out, making his target quickly unconscious, but he was confident that this tactic wouldn't work in Blak Dawg instance. The massive jewel thief had already shrugged off too much physical abuse, and seemed, in fact, to thrive on it. No -- something else was called for here.

Simon let his consciousness disconnect from his sense of body and a whole new world opened up. It was a dark, indistinct realm of firing neurons, where thoughts drifted by like seas of kelp. In this place, only his own strength of will and his target's sense of will existed. In here, Simon was the 800 pound gorilla. Without 70 years of existential self-reflection to back him up, Blak Dawg didn't stand a chance. Simon took control of the lout's body and looked through eyes that were not his own. He was thrown, as he had come to expect, by a moment of vertigo, suddenly taller by over a foot. Someday, he told himself, he would get used to the sensation of wearing someone else's body, but he wasn't certain if that knowledge was comforting or disquieting.

The first thing he noticed upon taking control of Blak Dawg was the burn of a deep scratch along his right forearm and that Stardust was gone. He didn't feel Wild Kat's weight on his back through all the gravity that Knockabout had piled on, but he knew she was there. Right on cue, he felt one of her razor sharp claw pierce the alloy strong skin on his neck just enough to draw blood. She wasn't supposed to be there. He could tell that by looking at the big clock in the window of the jewelry store.

"Didn't you have a lunch date?" he asked her, his voice low. He had gone to great lengths in coaching his good friend Manuel de la Vega to be a little more active in his pursuit of the enigmatic Katherine Wilde. But every time he thought that progress was being made, something came along to derail it. He didn't understand why. They were both exceptionally busy people, but their mutual fondness for cat monikers and their desire to put on leather and inflict pain on criminals made them a perfect match. If only they could see that themselves.

"Mister Grey has him," Simon heard Wild Kat say in to her communicator as she released her hold. She saw Simon's communicator on the ground and swept it up in one perfect, graceful motion, handing it back to him. It had most likely been scraped out of the ash by Blak Dawg's teeth or nostrils. Simon fit it into Blak Dawg's ear so that he could be back in communication with the rest of the team.

"Can you do something about the dogs?" Archon asked from his perch next to Knockabout. Simon turned his attention to the fight happening before him, and saw that the dogs were still going strong. Worm Queen and her gigantic ice worm were wearing down one, while the blue cloaked powerhouse named Velvet tag-teamed another with Stardust. The final dog was trying to sink teeth into the incorporeal Doctor Shadow, his magically blackened hair making his albino skin even more striking while he assailed the dog with telekinetic blasts.

With the leather-jacketed Gallows teleporting bystanders out of harm's way, it looked as thought his teammates had matters well in hand, but a quick resolution would prevent any further damage to the surrounding property. Simon groped blindly around for the "controls," looking for some command to make the dogs vanish. In his searching, he found something else entirely.

There, deep in the most hidden recesses of the self, back where Blak Dawg would never have known to look for it, Simon found magic.

Being a creature of magic himself, Simon had become adept at sniffing it out in the past year. Blak Dawg's powers were not magically derived. He had been the unfortunate winner of some genetic lottery, perhaps bitten by a radioactive junkyard dog. But no magic. Most certainly not magic. And yet here it was. And what Simon found even more fascinating, was that the traces he picked up had been hidden. If he had not taken this intrusive course of action, possessing the dog-loving strong man as he did, there was no doubt that this little secret would have remained buried. Someone had gone to great lengths to do something to Blak Dawg. They had gone to greater lengths to keep their involvement hidden.

This, Simon realized, was more Doctor Shadow's area of expertise. Simon may have been living, or more accurately, dying the magic lifestyle for the last seven decades, but the good doctor had been around for over 4,000 years. And Archon, with his encyclopedic knowledge of just about everything might be able to help decipher this mystery as well.

"I can't shut them down. They appear to be acting on their own impulses now that their master is out of touch." Simon shook the head of the massive jewel thief. "And I think I found something in his brain worth of a deeper look."

"No problem," Knockabout responded, looking at the printout from Archon's handheld computer. "Archon shows these things are inorganic, solid energy constructs, so I can deal with them myself. Everyone get clear."

It took little more than a thought and ten seconds before Knockabout shut gravity off on the three dog things. They left the atmosphere in only a few minutes, falling upward with comically confused looks on their misshapen faces. Knockabout lost track of them after that. Worst case scenario, they were in orbit chewing on a satellite, but Archon was confident that they vanished as soon as Blak Dawg lost sight of them. The failed jewel thief was cuffed in power shackles by then, allowing Simon to relinquish control. But power shackles made it impossible to call up more playthings.

And the Protectorate had a mystery to unravel.

Chapter Two

"I do not think our work is done here," Mister Grey said into the communicator. A strong breeze blew up the street, blurring him slightly around the edges. He stood on the sidewalk and watched as Blak Dawg was loaded into the back of an armored police transport in stony silence. It was difficult to convincingly talk tough when being arrested, and he wasn't going to waste the energy trying.

Worm Queen, Knockabout, Gallows, and Archon had already left the scene, each with their own full schedules and cover identities to maintain. Doctor Shadow had turned invisible shortly after the fight was over and could be anywhere. He could be in the shadows watching, waiting for something to happen, or he might have simply flown home and put on some tea. Mister Grey remembered being the most mysterious member of the team and almost missed it. That left himself, Velvet, and Wild Kat to give statements to the police while Stardust did an aerial patrol.

Stardust's voice chimed in on the communicator. "Security cameras didn't show him having backup other than the dogs. I've just finished reviewing the footage."

"How did you get the tapes so quickly?" Wild Kat's whisper was loud enough for the communicator to pick up and amplify but not so loud that the half dozen police nearby could hear her say anything.

A few hundred feet above the scene, Stardust hovered, watching the police lights strobe in the shadows of the street as file download bars scrolled past in his view screen. "The jewelry store security cameras are wireless and transmit to a digital recorder somewhere in the back office. I would have to be real close to pick up what the cameras were transmitting, but harvesting the footage off the recorder itself was a piece of cake. I'm sending a copy to our mainframe for analysis."

Mister Grey dissolved and then reformed in the mouth of an alley fifty feet from the crime scene. He watched the door of the police transport as it closed with a hiss of pressurized air before it rolled off into the crowded streets. "It need not have been someone present. But I strongly suspect that our friend there was the beneficiary of some kind of...enhancements. And they were magical in nature, which doesn't make any sense to me."

The haunting voice of Doctor Shadow rolled from the shadows behind Simon. "And you are certain of this?"

14

Velvet, finally finished giving her statement to the police, took this opportunity to chime in. She had recently gone over the subject's file back at The Keep as part of her probationary period training. "Blak Dawg isn't magic. He's strictly post-adolescent mutation, and while the origin of his powers is open to debate, I'm fairly certain that we can rule out a bunch of guys with pointy hats, wands, and old books. No offense, Doctor."

"None taken." There was a trace of amusement in Doctor Shadow's voice. "But while our new friend's powers might be scientific or genetic in nature, this magical signature bears some further investigation. It might not be an enhancement we're looking for. Perhaps it is only the after-effect of a mind-influencing spell -- something that spurred him into action. But we should rule nothing out."

Mister Grey ran through the fight in his mind, finding the bits and pieces that seemed, to him at least, to reinforce his concern. "Blak Dawg should not have been able to hurt me. Yet when he punched me, I still managed to feel the force of the blow. He may talk a big game but he isn't strong enough to do that, I am quite certain. There is something going on -- something that seems to have given him an edge. Finding out what isn't my specialty, Doctor. That falls to you. Look deeply enough into his psyche and you shall find it, I promise you."

Doctor Shadow made no expression, his eyes void as he seemed to gaze through Mister Grey. "Wild Kat, could you secure an interview with our subject?"

Wild Kat headed towards the detective in charge of the crime scene, having already decided that if Simon felt Blak Dawg warranted a second look she wasn't going to question it. She whispered into her communicator, "I'm on it," seconds before reaching Detective Engels.

Mark Engels had been on the force for only a few years, having transferred up from a small town in Pennsylvania when his wife got a nursing job at Mercy Hospital. He had read about people like Wild Kat and Velvet in the pages of *Cape and Cowl Quarterly*, mostly at his doctor's office. But he had never had to deal with them on a professional level before. Like most cops, he walked a fine line between resenting the spotlight that shone on these so-called heroes, and thanking God that he didn't have to do the things that they put themselves through daily.

As Wild Kat walked up to him, he was struck by the panther-like grace of her step, and the razor-sharp claws poking from the fingertips of her gloves. Her full and wavy auburn hair was cut to just above her collar. Her eyes were emerald green and slitted like a cat's, and her ears sat too high up on her head and were just slightly pointed. In her black leather corseted ensemble, she was many men's fantasy and had proven to be many men's nightmare as well.

Detective Mark Engels felt his mouth grow dry. "Was there something I could help you with, Miss…um…Kat?" He felt deeply and immediately stupid.

"Detective, I would like the suspect to be made available to answer some questions for us." There was a faint purr in her voice that she knew most men had a difficult time resisting.

"No," said a voice with authority. Mark was more than a little surprised to find that it had been his own voice. "We have him red-handed. Anything not by the book from this point on, and we risk letting him walk on a technicality. You can be present at any questioning if his lawyers agree to it, but not before then."

Wild Kat smiled, looking shocked that he would suggest the Protectorate was overstepping their bounds. "We aren't going to ask him about the robbery or anything that would jeopardize your case. But we have reason to believe that he can lead us to someone else."

"Not good enough for me to risk losing this collar." Engels smiled. Blak Dawg. Collar. These heroes weren't so tough.

"Did you see how big his dogs were?" She angled in for a different approach. "I don't have the exact comparison data in front of me, but they appeared to me to be bigger and stronger than when last sighted. The same goes for Blak Dawg himself."

From high above the street, Stardust took the hint and sent a command to the base mainframe to compile and download any information they had on Blak Dawg. Down Below, Engels was unimpressed. "So the old dog learned a new trick." Engels almost chuckled. Another gem of a line, and still Wild Kat wasn't even smiling. Probably didn't like cops. "New tricks or no, it isn't going to change anything. He's a cheap thug and he will always be a cheap thug."

"But the person he can lead us to…" she began.

"…is none of my concern." Engels cut her off. He turned and started to walk away when she stopped him with two words.

"Jeremy Red."

Detective Engels stopped and an involuntary chill went up his spine, as if a shadow just passed between his soul and the sun. He didn't turn, wanting to conceal just how strong of an effect that name had caused.

"If this person taught Blak Dawg a new trick," Wild Kat

continued, "Imagine what would happen if he took an active interest in Jeremy Red?"

Even in rural Pennsylvania, the Jeremy Red murders had made news. Mark Engels was certain that there were parts of the world, deep in the jungles of Brazil, perhaps, where the only American names people recognized were Mickey Mouse, Michael Jackson, and Jeremy Red.

Three years ago, that wouldn't have been the case. Then, Jeremy had just been another troubled student at a local public school. And then overnight, he became one of the most powerful mentalists in the world. He hadn't asked for the power -- hadn't been prepared -- and was dismayed to discover that he couldn't turn his new abilities off. It only took four days for the constant assault of every thought in a three mile radius to drive him insane. He responded by creating an illusory world that encompassed the size of a football stadium, trapping and disorienting everyone caught inside the field of influence. Using comfort images and memories taken from their minds, he kept them placid. And then one by one, he began to methodically end their lives with an old rip and tear can opener. All so he could get some peace and quiet. In the end, the city had to send in robots to drug him into unconsciousness.

Since that day, Jeremy Red had been locked up in the Fermi Institute for Mental Health. Every psionic dampening drug and piece of hardware known had been brought to bear to keep the lines between Jeremy's consciousness and the rest of the world crisp. But it wasn't quite enough, and those working at the hospital were only too aware that sometimes thoughts bled through. People across the country had lost sleep wondering what would happen if Jeremy Red were to get out.

Engels half-turned towards her. "You won't ask our prisoner about the robbery?"

"Not a word." She neglected to mention that Doctor Shadow would most likely be doing most of the questioning with telepathy anyway. The laws were somewhat more ambiguous on that, but it wasn't anything their subject could detect, and they weren't looking for anything that could be used for prosecution anyway.

"And you agree to have a police witness with you?"

"Agreed."

Detective Engels straightened his tie as he thought it over. He knew he didn't have any options now. He had to cooperate, and there was no way around that. But he had to make sure that the uniform cops didn't see his decision as buckling to the will of the capes. "He's being taken to the 16th for processing. I'll call ahead and let them know to expect you." He expected a thank you at least but would have to get used to disappointment.

Wild Kat was already gone, having raced up the side of the jewelry store to the roof and then away, off in the direction of the 16th. Mark realized that he was holding his breath and let it out in one long sigh. Then, with a trembling hand, he plucked his cell phone out of his pocket and hit speed dial. After a few rings, his wife answered. "Hey, baby," he said, still a little breathless. "You'll never guess who I just talked to."

Two blocks away and moving fast, Wild Kat was coordinating her own investigation, while Velvet tried valiantly to keep pace behind her. "Doctor Shadow, I want you and Velvet in the interrogation room. I want two lines of questions, one verbal, one mental. Find out what's in his head. Stardust, can you spare an hour or so to crunch data?"

"I'll reschedule my massage and meet you at the station."

From the darkness of the alley Doctor Shadow worked a simple spell that lifted him into the air after his companions. "I picked up an address from Blak Dawg's surface thoughts as he was being detained. It could lead us to wherever he was hiding."

Wild Kat chose to delegate in the interest of expediency. "Simon?"

"I can cover that one. I will call in if I find anything of interest," Mister Grey agreed. Doctor Shadow downloaded the address telepathically, and Mister Grey left the alley as a cloud of dust without being seen by a soul.

Booking and processing Blak Dawg ended up taking over an hour, but Stardust had managed to clear up the rest of his afternoon and no one else had to be anywhere. It was no surprise to anyone when Mister Grey called in with his scouting report of the address he had been given long before the others were allowed to see the prisoner.

The address corresponded to a small rental house up in Morrison. The three champagne glasses in the sink indicated that there had been at least two other people there with him the night before, both wearing lipstick. A Styrofoam container of half-eaten beef chow mein from some takeout place called Li Ho Fooks was sitting in the fridge along with another bottle of champagne. Two empty bottles of the same expensive vintage lay on their side on the counter. The mirror on the coffee table had been sucked clean of any cocaine, but the rolled up $100 bill in the carpet next to it hinted that Blak Dawg had been living the rap video lifestyle.

There was no one else in the house, but Simon was certain that

Blak Dawg had been staying there for at least a few days. The clothes in the closet were evidence enough of that, unless Frankenstein's monster was in town and had developed a taste for pimp clothes.

At the police station, the others listened to Simon's report, not finding much of any use. Then their escort showed up to take them to the interrogation room and its adjoining gallery. It was time to have a chat with Blak Dawg himself.

A quick refresher from his police file revealed that his real name was Edward James Dawkins. He was twenty-six years old and had a BA in economics from Cobalt City University. He had been a late bloomer, being the shortest and skinniest kid in his class until the summer of his fifteenth year. Both parents lived in Cobalt City. His mother was a pharmacist and his father managed a small electronics store. He had lived, for the most part, a typical suburban life. Then, possibly to help pay for school, he had turned to a life of crime, selling his services to anyone needing a little bit of muscle and attitude.

Yes, Blak Dawg's life was full of contradictions. Katherine Wilde pondered them as she looked in on the interrogation. Stardust stood next to her in the small observation gallery, while a police detective she had just met stood on her other side. His name was Leo Kukoch, and he smelled like hummus and red onion masked by several sticks of cinnamon gum. There was also a faint hint of Red Lotus perfume on his lapels, possibly from a suspect or a midday indiscretion. His own scent was Aqua Velvet, but he hadn't used any for two days. She wished that the ventilation in the small room was better so that she wouldn't be so overwhelmed by the smells, or for the detective to leave so that she could abandon her feline form, effectively shutting down her enhanced senses. At least Stardust's armor had air purifiers which left him smelling mostly neutral with a hint of lemony freshness.

On the other side of the one-way glass, Velvet paced around the shackled prisoner asking questions, her steel-like hands clenched within long, deep-blue velvet opera gloves that matched her floor-length cape and cowl. Her confident manner, military precision, and reputation for being a scrapper contributed to her intimidating presence, and was part of why Stardust had recommended her to the team. While she worked the prisoner verbally, Doctor Shadow levitated in the darkest of the four corners and peeled Blak Dawg's memory like an onion. It was an effective combination, Wild Kat knew, and virtually guaranteed to get results. But the need for this inquiry troubled her.

It was Stardust who broke the relative silence of the observation gallery. "Like duck hunting with a cannon."

19

Detective Kukoch looked pointedly at him. "What the hell are you talking about?"

"The reading from his restraints show a 40% increase over the last time he was detained. With that kind of power rating, why is he knocking over small time jewelry stores?"

"Maybe he was looking for some quick bling-bling." The detective turned back to the questioning.

That Kukoch, Katherine thought. What a poet. The information did back up Simon's earlier observations, however. "When was his last arrest?"

Stardust got the information fastest. "He was brought in just a few months ago, on January 22nd for aggravated assault. No charges. But his power index was the same as it's been for two years. I've sent the data to Archon to analyze and corroborate."

Kukoch seemed impressed with the speed which Stardust came up with the answer. "You must know this guy pretty well. Is he in your rogues gallery or something?"

Stardust and Wild Kat didn't reply. There was no point in telling their escort that the onboard computers in Stardust's helmet had hacked into the police database. The detective probably wouldn't find it amusing. No, the truth was that that they had never given Blak Dawg any thought at all. He was just a hired thug, after all. Even to them. Where he came from, why he did what he did, even his real name, until now, none of it had mattered. Maybe, Katherine thought, that's what landed him here in the first place.

Inside the interrogation room, Velvet and Doctor Shadow finished with their questions. Blak Dawg looked smug, but Katherine suspected that it was just an act. He might not have said anything, but that didn't mean that Doctor Shadow hadn't found what they needed. The nod the ancient sorcerer gave through the mirror as he floated out the door showed that he had gotten something, at least.

Doctor Shadow's voice appeared in Stardust and Wild Kat's head. "I have a name. It is not much, but it is something."

What is the name, Katherine thought.

"Augustus Dei."

"It reminds me of an argument a friend and I had back in college." Stardust hadn't moved and was still looking through the mirrored glass as officers came in to move Blak Dawg. "Picture going back to when the Europeans first colonized North America. Now, give guns to the natives, anyone willing to fight. Does that change history? I used to think so, but I've changed my mind since. Just because they have high tech weapons doesn't mean they know how to use them, right? Until they change their tactics, educate themselves on how to use these new tools they aren't any better off than they were before. I see Blak Dawg in there, all beefed up and he could hit, I don't know, a mint or something, and the first thing he does is rob a jewelry store, like nothing's changed."

Wild Kat gave their subject a lingering glance as he was led out. Her voice was pensive. "I fought him before."

"Really?" Stardust tried not to sound surprised.

The door closed and he was gone, but something of him lingered there, just a memory floating in the ether. "It was a robbery. He was working for someone else at the time. He was the one who woke up Mister Grey."

The gallery fell into silence as the two heroes pondered the significance of the odd coincidence, and Kukoch pondered his next coffee break.

Chapter Three

After observing the questioning of Blak Dawg, Stardust flew several patrols of Cobalt City. His mere presence in the sky had been shown to reduce crime rates by a few percentage points, even without doing anything. With his armor's sensor array on high alert and the computerized data filter interpreting incoming signals, he could focus on the sensation of flight while he dictated his analysis and report of the Blak Dawg power-reading anomaly. His onboard computer transcribed and filed it away on the hard drive. His wife Elizabeth's pre-recorded voice signaled him when the file was ready to be transmitted, and he made a low pass over The Keep to download the report. The paperwork done for the night, he performed a tight turn around city hall and raced home.

The building Jaccob had picked to be Starcom Industries headquarters in Cobalt City was a bargain. The fact that a recent interstellar invasion attempt had destroyed the top three of the eighteen floors of the mid-town tower had considerably reduced the price. But a fixer-upper was a perfect opportunity to add a highly customized five additional floors to one half of the rebuilt roof. These he turned into a private lab and living quarters for himself and his family. It was a cutting edge sanctuary; Stardust would have it no other way.

The nineteenth floor security portal of his building was accessible only by air, and the two-foot thick alloy door would not unlock without an encrypted electrical signal from Stardust's gauntlet. The signal changed on a schedule hardwired into his helmet and the door itself. Stardust placed the palm of his gauntleted hand on the reader next to the door. A beam inside his helmet read Jaccob's iris and released the signal to unlock the entrance. Maybe the security protocols were a bit obsessive, but Stardust was only one of a handful of public identity capes in the city. And security was next to Godliness in his book.

For the sake of his family's safety, it had to be.

He made his way to the changing room on the 20th floor via what his ten-year-old son Michael had dubbed the "Hamster Tube." Elizabeth had brought down his Stanford sweatshirt and a pair of stonewashed jeans he had just broken in a few days ago. The neatly folded change of clothes sat on the corner of a big, black sarcophagus. Jaccob pressed a recessed button and a deep, fitted drawer slid out, lit from within by a blue light. There was a man shaped indentation in the blue gel-like material, with thin, coiled wires around the edge of the cabinet. Stardust pulled off the helmet and fitted it into place in the drawer. He did the same with the rest of his armor, stripping down to socks, lycra shorts, and a Dexter's Laboratory t-shirt his daughter had gotten him for his birthday. With quick, sure motions, he plugged wires from the cabinet edge into concealed ports in each piece of hardware and began downloading the day's flight data for later evaluation. Innovation never rests, he thought as he closed the drawer for the night.

Jaccob pulled on the sweatshirt and pants and found, lying in wait beneath them, a letter from his children's school. He knew even before opening it, that it couldn't be good or even neutral news. A letter of accomplishment or notice of an impending open house would never have made its way down to the changing room. He unfolded the crisp, bond paper with the Franklin Academy letterhead and read slowly.

> *Dear Mr. and Mrs. Stevens,*
>
> *It has been brought to my attention that your son Michael is having problems turning in homework in several of his subjects. I have spoken at great length with his teachers about the situation, and they have all told me that his test scores which have been, up until now, exemplary, have begun to slip noticeably. His mounting missing assignments have compounded this situation to the point where Michael is in danger of failing Math, Science, and History, with English suffering to a lesser degree.*
>
> *Michael is a gifted child. He would not be attending this institution otherwise. His Advisory teacher has looked into this curious decline in performance, but has not found its cause.*
>
> *We had hoped that the academic warning letter we sent home three weeks ago would encourage you to take a more active role in his schoolwork. Unfortunately, we have seen no improvement in test scores or missed work. If the situation is not remedied soon, we will have no choice but to hold Michael back for another year.*
>
> *Thank you for your attention to this matter,*
> *Headmaster Marlon Whitney*

Jaccob read the letter through twice and it still didn't make sense. What academic warning letter? He hadn't seen anything from the school since the last parent night newsletter last month. Elizabeth was so involved with the children's schoolwork; she would have seen a notice of falling grades.

On the third reading, something hit him. They "sent" a letter home. Not "mailed" but "sent." Sent how? He got a sinking feeling as he went up to the 6,000 sq. foot penthouse. He found Elizabeth in the kitchen, scraping pork chop bones off a dirty plate into the trash. Michael scurried out of the media room and up to his room, without offering even a wave of hello. He must have known something was up. Come to think of it, his son had been quiet and furtive for the past few days. Elizabeth heard him come in and put the last plate in the dishwasher, turning with her serious face. "You read it?"

Jaccob greeted her with a quick kiss, then looked at Michael's red high-tops vanishing the rest of the way upstairs. "I read it." He sighed wearily. As if almost getting split like a wishbone by Blak Dawg hadn't been enough of a headache for one day, he thought. "You never saw a warning note, did you?"

She shook her head, a lock of her long, blonde hair falling across her face. Jaccob hooked it with his index finger and tucked it back behind Elizabeth's ear. "Has everyone finished dinner already?" He looked in the direction of the kitchen.

"Just the kids. I wanted to wait for you."

He kissed Elizabeth on the nose. "I want to talk to the boy first." In the media room, their daughter gasped and grew very still. She knew that her dad only used the phrase "the boy" when Michael was in trouble, and she wanted no part of it.

Jaccob found Michael in his room hard at work on a math worksheet, while a holographic night sky twinkled on the ceiling overhead. He stood just inside the doorway watching his son, not saying anything. He knew Michael had heard him come in and waited for his son to break the uncomfortable silence. While he waited, he watched the fake stars on the ceiling, once again amazed at how real the scene looked. When an associate of his, a genius in large area holography, had offered to decorate the kids' rooms, Jaccob had originally resisted. Memories of a Bradbury story he had read as a child where misbehaving kids had holographic lions eat their parents and psychiatrist made the idea uncomfortable. But they had finally agreed on ceilings for the two bedrooms. His daughter had flying ponies with wings. At least it wasn't flying lions.

"I heard you caught Blak Dawg today." Michael continued to feign intense interest in his study of fractions.

"You did, did you?

Michael shrugged. "It was on the news."

"Ah," Jaccob walked further into the room and sat on the bed near his son. "That's not really what I wanted to talk to you about." He could see that Michael was biting his lip a little.

"I know."

"So, let's talk about what's going on at school. You start."

Michael sighed and fiddled with his pencil. Stardust had witnessed so many interrogations that the stalling techniques of a ten year old, even his own ten year old, were no match for him. He waited it out, knowing the truth was close to the surface.

"My teachers can't find my assignments that I turned in," Michael began, "I don't know what happened to them."

Either Jaccob or Elizabeth checked his homework every morning, just to make sure it was up to standards. The homework was being done. It just wasn't being turned in. "Are all of your teachers losing your homework?"

The hesitancy of the answer was almost proof enough. "No."

Jaccob pushed further. "And are they losing anyone else's homework?"

"I don't know." Michael was close to tears and afraid to even look at his dad. Jaccob let the silence sit between them for a few seconds before moving on, letting his silence show that he knew Michael was lying and that he was disappointed.

"Your mom and I know you're doing the work. Why aren't you turning it in? Help me understand, okay?"

Michael shrugged and kept his eyes on his desk.

"Ok, how does this sound? You can either tell me, or I can go get a sock puppet from your sister's room and you can tell it."

A fragile smile flickered across Michaels face, like a moth in a hurricane. He looked up at his dad. "Not the puppet. Anything but the puppet."

Mock menace entered Jaccob's voice. "Then you have to tell me what's going on or it's puppet city for you, mister."

Michael had lost, and he knew it. "I don't like my school."

Jaccob watched closely, looking for something deeper. "It's a good school. You really liked it when you first started there."

"I don't have any friends."

That didn't make any sense to Jaccob. "What about Opal? I thought you were friends with her. She went out for pizza with us just a few weeks ago."

Michael's voice grew weak. "Yeah, but she's mad at me right now."

"And why is that?"

"Because I'm not turning in my homework. She says that I'm trying to get left behind."

"Is that true?" Jaccob gently prodded.

Michael picked at the ragged edge of a page of paper torn from a spiral notebook. "Maybe. I don't know. I just don't want to be there anymore."

"Because you don't have any friends. You told me that part."

"And because of Bart Rice," his son added. Jaccob had heard the name before, but couldn't attach any significance to it other than the fact that he was in Michael's class.

"What about Bart?"

Michael was on firmer ground here, and his face was set with stony certainty. "He's a dingus."

Jaccob fought between being shocked at his son's swearing and laughing at how long it had been since he had heard anyone say "dingus." The good parent won out, and he didn't even crack a smile. "What did I tell you about using that kind of language?"

Michael looked confused for a second as he recalled the lecture. "Um, not where mom can hear?"

"Exactly."

"But she's not here," Michael sounded a little worried now that his mom might have heard him.

Jaccob lowered his voice to a conspiratorial whisper. "I think you underestimate how much trouble you are in. She's probably right outside the door. Now tell me what your problem with Bart is."

Michael became guarded again, turning back to his worksheet. "I don't want to tell you."

"Well, I'm afraid that you are going to have to tell me, Michael." Jaccob let loose with an exaggerated sigh that he thought sounded fatherly.

Michael's voice had gone quiet again. "But it's about you."

Uh-oh, Jaccob thought. "Now I have to know."

"Please don't make me…" Michael pleaded, tears coming to his eyes.

"Michael, you have to tell me, especially if it's about me."

"Bart says that you're gay." Michael locked his eyes on his desk.

Ah. The other shoe had dropped. The Stardust armor was shiny, golden, and flashy. The meteor fragment that powered it created a sparkling, golden glow. The combined effect was, as a columnist in Seattle had put it, "fabulous!" His assistance in stopping a series of hate crimes in that city had made him a hero of the gay community.

26

He had also saved a charter jet of rabbis and a high profile black basketball player. But for some reason, no one ever thought of Stardust as Jewish or black. He had hoped that revealing his identity as a happily married, multi-millionaire family man would satisfy the media's curiosity.

For the most part it had. Sure, he was a hero of the gay community. He was a hero in a lot of communities. He was, after all, a hero. It was in the job description. But he looked at his wonderful, gifted son and saw how he was suffering. He had forgotten how cruel ten-year-old kids could be. It was an unfortunate part of human nature.

"You know it isn't true, though," Jaccob said.

Michael nodded. "I know. But he just makes me so mad. I hate him."

"I can see that. But even if it were true, which it isn't, of course, there isn't anything wrong with it."

"Except that you and mom wouldn't live together anymore and I'd be caught between you all the time, and I've have to make new friends when mom moves to Indiana, and…" Michael rushed on breathlessly.

"Whoa, cowboy! Slow down there! Where is all this coming from?" Jaccob was a bit stunned. Michael didn't answer, but the specifics sounded eerily familiar. "Have you been watching the Lifetime channel?"

Michael nodded sullenly.

"Okay, no more docudramas for you, young man." Jaccob laughed. "And I'll make you a deal."

Michael looked up from his desk suspiciously. "What?"

"Get your missing assignments turned in and get at least a B average and next year we'll home school you." Jaccob managed to suppress yet another smile. He had been considering it for safety reasons anyway, but making it motivation couldn't hurt.

"Why not pull me out now?"

"Because Stevens men don't run, Michael. Ignore Bart. Keep your back straight, and don't be afraid to stare him in the eye. Those who hold truth in their heart cannot be stung by the lies of tyranny."

Michael's brow furrowed. "Who said that?"

"I don't remember," Jaccob admitted. "I read it in a comic book somewhere."

Michael pondered the deal. "What if I don't get a B average?"

"Then you stay at the Franklin Academy." Jaccob made his way to the door. "And next interview the Protectorate does, I kiss Knockabout full on the lips."

Michael's eyes got as wide as saucers. "I'll get B's."

"Get a few A's too if it isn't too late." Jacob left the room.

Elizabeth had set the small glass-topped table in the kitchen nook for the two of them, and the aroma of rosemary pork chops and apple stuffing drew him to his seat. The media room was silent, the television and lights off. Jaccob pointed towards it with his thumb as he joined his wife at the table. "What happened to…"

"She's taking her bath." Elizabeth smiled.

"Really?" Jaccob looked around to make sure his daughter wasn't hiding behind the curtains, waiting to surprise him.

"Really. She saw that Michael was in trouble and decided to make a play for the coveted favorite child position."

"Smart kid." He took a bite of stuffing and then quickly edited himself. "Not that I have a favorite."

"The other one is smart too." They ate in silence for a few minutes. Jaccob hadn't realized how hungry he was until he smelled dinner. "So you got things sorted out?" Elizabeth finally said.

"We have an understanding."

A sly smile appeared on his wife's face as she intently cut her pork chops. "I've heard that this Bart Rice kid is a real dingus."

"You were right outside the door, weren't you!" Jaccob stared at her in amusement.

Still smiling, she shook her head. "I was plugged into the home security network. I got most of the conversation with sound and digital video without having to leave the kitchen. If anyone has doubts about your masculinity, they should just ask me." She winked at him, laughing the suspicions off as easily as the first time they had surfaced.

He laughed with her and finished up the last of his chop.

Turning more serious, she set down her silverware and looked Jaccob in the eye. "I saw the news this afternoon. They got hold of video from a traffic camera down the street. Not the best footage, especially with those big dogs getting in the way all the time."

"No real injuries, though. It was more of a nuisance than anything. People had to take some time off work because of it."

She pointed a menacing finger in his direction. "Tell me something I don't know. I've been waiting for you to sign off on that feasibility study before I okay the contract for the Indonesian satellite project."

"I'll take care of it before bed."

Elizabeth lowered her finger and smiled. He had been promising to sign the study for a week, but had kept forgetting. "Good. It's on your desk." She stood and began clearing the table.

"I'm just glad no one got hurt today. That Blak Dawg character looked tough."

Jaccob smiled and shook his head. He looked over towards the stairs. "No harder than raising a ten year old boy."

Chapter Four

Simon Floyd wasn't worried about odd coincidences. He was, instead, possessed by the most intense stage fright he had experienced since his first concert at the age of six. That first audience, consisting of his mother's old-before-their-time Dover housewife friends, was a far cry from the eighty-odd paying customers who had turned out to see him and his combo this night. No, the swirling crowd of strangers that floated beyond the floor lights was here to see a freak show. Was that what he was reduced to? Having to fight his way back to respectability because of some unfortunate events seven decades ago?

His eyes were fixed on a small table in the front with a little white "Reserved" card. Several such tables dotted the front row, but most had filled already. This table, this lone two foot across table with the four vacant seats, was his only hope of getting through the night.

Where are they, he wondered. He knew that Katherine and Manuel had made other plans. He had, in some small way, taken a hand in making those plans. But Marcus had made it back into town a few days ago and had been eager to see the rest of the gang. And Anna and Edirin were looking forward to doing something that didn't involve beating up on people wearing spandex. Even Velvet, who had yet to reveal her real name to anyone except for Stardust, had made clear her intent to attend, using the last of the four comp tickets he had set aside. But now it was minutes before showtime, and his friends were nowhere to be seen.

He knew his combo was tight. They had been rehearsing in secret for almost two months, and they weren't trying any new material, just old standards. Bobbie Spellman on drums was young but gifted, in his last year of classes at a community college in Quayside. Bobbie's friend Prescott played bass and had left a college rock cover band to play with the combo. The three of them worked very well together once Simon learned to trust his musical instincts again. Jazz was not the same beast as when he died, but just that constant evolution of the sound had attracted him to the music in the first place. He had saturated himself in how the sound had evolved over time and had almost become overwhelmed, but he couldn't let himself give up. Maybe he was trying too hard to hold on to his past life. He could recognize the desperation in the effort. That didn't mean he was going down without a fight.

For a vocalist, Prescott had recommended his aunt Anne. She

had sung professionally thirty years ago in a tour of dives, blues bars, and roadhouses throughout the south. She knew the material, and her voice had seasoned well. The husband who made her give up performing had died years ago, and like Simon, she desperately longed for a return to the stage lights. She watched Simon watch the crowd from backstage in the intimate Colonial Club and said nothing.

"Bigger crowd than I was expecting," Simon said, seemingly aware that he was being observed. Anne stuck a cigarette in her mouth and tried to keep her hand from shaking while she lit it. "You look nervous."

"Yeah, maybe," she said looking away. She took a deep drag, felt the mix of tobacco and menthol smoke scratch the back of her throat. "It's been a long time since I've done this."

"No longer than me," Simon said softly. He didn't bother to turn around, his attention and hope focused on the white card on the empty table out front.

"Hey buddy, we haven't missed anything yet, have we?" said the youthful voice of Marcus Castile. As the fourth person to wear the mantle of Huntsman over the last half century, he had been the first to join the Protectorate when a short-term replacement for the missing Icons was announced. His legacy status brought a degree of credibility that the new team desperately needed, but recent events had led to a brief vacation. He was young, still a teenager, and a period of soul searching was to be expected. Simon liked him, despite the youth's seeming inability to relax. Young people shouldn't be so serious all the time; but wasn't everyone except Doctor Shadow younger than him these days?

"A few more minutes and you would have missed our entrance," Simon said. "I trust the others are with you?"

"Snowflake is dropping them off in style. Rented limo. Very discreet," Marcus laughed. It sounded like the sabbatical had done him some good. The young archer had been so somber after their trip along the Coil. Witnessing a shadow war spread through multiple alternate realities and facing down an avatar of rot was a tough ride to buy a ticket for. The fact that Marcus was willing to put on the cowl again after that was a testament to his strength and maturity. "Edirin said Anna didn't have anything appropriate to wear, so they had to pick up a new dress. You know how he is. He has style in his blood, I think."

Much relieved, Simon moved from the curtain and straightened out his tie. To minimize his freakishness, he had decided to dress formally rather than create a formal look out of his ash self.

He hoped it didn't make him appear *more* freakish. It was the first time he had tried wearing clothes in over a year, and he found it surprising how well they fit. Then again, with more or less perfect control of his body shape and size, he could have made anything fit like a glove.

By the time the Simon Floyd Combo took the stage, his friends were seated with drinks in their hands. Marcus was drinking milk as always. The introductory applause was polite, and the emcee introduced him as Simon, and not as Mister Grey, as instructed. While the two were not officially one and the same, it was the worst kept secret in Cobalt City. He didn't need a secret identity like so many of his teammates. It wasn't like he had a normal life. And it wasn't as though he could pass himself off as normal even if he wanted to hold down a job and rent an apartment. But he felt it was important to keep his accomplishments as a pianist separate from his work as a hero. He often wondered if Stardust, the only other member of the team to be "out," felt the same way.

Simon acknowledged the applause with a polite nod as he sat at the piano. The others took their positions and sounded a few notes to shake out the jitters while the clapping died down. Then, with a smooth four count, they launched into a simple arrangement of "Is You Is Or Is You Ain't My Baby."

They had decided to stick to early 40's jive music: Louis Jordan and Cab Calloway numbers for the most part. Retrospection on Simon's part had determined that those tunes suited the style of his band the best. This was only a test run after all. If things went well, word would get out. Then they could attract a few horns and expand the sound a bit. Simon had been listening to a lot of Stan Getz and flirting with the idea of finding a percussionist and working in some Bossa Nova, but one thing at a time. Camilla would have loved it. First time out, however, it paid to keep it simple and wow them with the basics.

And wow them they did. Bobbie and Prescott were as solid as ever, having played with each other for several years. That's the key, Simon thought. A good rhythm section is the heart of any band. And Anne simply sizzled, pouring out thirty years of pent-up frustrations in every word. And Simon, well, he was a hero by circumstance, but he put his soul into being a musician. The crowd was won over by the time they hit "What's The Use Of Getting Sober (When You're Gonna Get Drunk Again)" and it was only the third song. As they closed their first set with "Jack, You're Dead," the verdict was unanimous: these cats could swing.

Simon stood and took a slight bow as Anne announced the

end of their first set and the twenty minutes until the second set. The applause was thundering for an eighty seat venue, and Simon couldn't help but smile. Then he saw who Marcus was talking to back by the bar, and his smile collapsed.

Camilla.

It had to be her. The way she moved, her smile -- even through the glare of the footlights, it had to be her. As Simon stared through the standing crowd, he saw her put a delicate hand on Marcus's arm as she laughed. Simon froze, uncertain of what to do until he felt a hand on his own arm. He saw without giving the appearance of turning his head, that Bobbie was steering him off stage, smiling wildly.

"Man-oh-man!" the chunky drummer said, "That beats playing in the halftime marching band at the Colonial Bowl any time!"

Numbly, Simon allowed himself to be led to the backstage where Bobbi re-hydrated with some sports drink. Prescott was already there, sipping on a longneck of some local micro-brew called Anubis Red Ale. Anne was talking excitedly at all three of them while she took a sip from a bottle of water. But for all the chatter, Simon couldn't hear a word.

Camilla was here. How could that be? He made some excuse that he didn't even hear himself say, and went down the narrow, dim hallway and out the back door to the silent alley behind the club.

"Marcus, can you hear me in there?" he said into the communicator. There was no answer. "Protectorate one, this is Mister Grey. Over."

"Mister Grey, this is Protectorate one. What can we do for you?" came the neutral voice of one of the staff dispatchers. Simon thought his name was Sandy, but although he could put a face to the voice, he was stymied for a name.

"Do you have Velvet, Knockabout, Worm Queen, or Huntsman online?" Simon said. He heard the click of a keyboard over the communicator. He wished he didn't have to do it this way, but to go down into the crowd, to approach the table of his friends would compromise their secret identities. That was something he could never do. Not having a real life of his own made him respect the real life of his friends that much more.

"None of them are online now, but Velvet has her beeper on, so we can call her in," the guy who could be Sandy said.

"Beep her and patch her through to me when she calls in," Simon said. He surveyed the alley, empty except for the occasional rat. Pacing on the narrow stair, he could do nothing but wait.

The back door to the club opened and Anne stuck her head through. "Everything okay out here, chief?" she said, her concern evident on her face. Ah, forever the caretaker, that woman.

"Just checking my messages," Simon said, forming a smile. "I'll be back in a minute."

Anne didn't look convinced, but figured it was none of her business. The door closed and he was left alone until his communicator hummed again.

"This is Velvet. You buzzed me?" she said in hushed tones.

"Marcus was just talking to someone back at the bar..." he began.

"Dark skinned, green dress, vintage cut..."

"Yes, that was the one," Simon said. "I might have recognized her. I need to speak with him, but he appears to be offline."

"I'm the go-to girl tonight," Velvet said, her shrug evident in the tone of her voice. "Is this woman a potential criminal?"

How to approach this, he wondered. How to not give away too much while still resolving the issue. Truth, he decided, was usually the best policy. "If it's who I think it is, she's supposed to be dead."

"She looks good for a corpse, but that explains the vintage dress," she said. "Where are you now?"

"Out back."

"I'll send him out," she said, and then the signal was lost.

While he waited, Simon poked his head back inside to encourage the band. Everyone was in high spirits, but obviously concerned by their pianist's mood. A few jokes, a few smiles, a quick check of the clock, and things were smoothed over. "One more quick call to make and we can go out and try to top ourselves," he said with what he was pretty sure looked like a wink. Bobbie and Prescott bought it, but he could tell, despite her brave smile, that Anne knew it was a front.

"Don't take too long, and don't go saving the world. You're supposed to be off the clock tonight, remember?" she said.

Simon smiled and returned to the slight chill of the spring night air, not surprised to see Huntsman waiting there in full costume. The alley lights glinted off the chain mail under the deep green tunic. "I heard you needed to speak with me?" he said, his steely voice giving no indication that underneath that famous cowl was a seventeen-year-old child of privilege.

"The woman you were talking to, the one in the green dress, did she give you her name?" Simon said.

"The one right at the break?" Marcus said.

34

"That would be her."

"No, but she did say she knew you."

A chill gripped Simon Floyd, and he stepped closer to Huntsman. "What else did she say. Be specific."

"You're starting to creep me out, Simon," Marcus said, a hint of his youth peeking through the exterior.

"I'm a little creeped out myself," Simon said softly. He backed up slightly.

"I figured her for an agent, or maybe a fan. She said you and the combo were sounding great," Huntsman said. "She said she was there on the behalf of someone who could really help you out. Hey, maybe she's a rep from a record label?"

"Did she say who she was representing?"

"She didn't say," Marcus said. He reached into his tunic and pulled out a business card as utterly black as the space between stars. "But she gave me this. She said with such good seats, I might be able to get it to you."

Simon reached out and gripped the card lightly by the edges.

"But I don't know what good it will do you," Marcus added. "Looks blank to me. Black business cards. Classy, but a poor printing choice unless you use the right inks."

Simon nodded. Marcus would know all about printing, since his family owned the city's oldest publishing house. But blank? Hardly. The card radiated magic. While Marcus would never be able to notice something that subtle, whoever gave him the card knew that Simon would pick up on it. Subtle but not invisible, the card read "Augustus Dei" followed by a phone number in an area code that he didn't recognize.

"Did she say anything else?" Simon said, pocketing the card.

"Now that you mention it, as she was leaving, she just looked at me and smiled and said 'He'll make Simon's dreams come true!' Crazy, isn't it?" Huntsman said, a hint of a bemused smile appearing beneath the cowl.

"You have no idea," Simon said. "Did you notice if she stuck around?"

Huntsman shook his head. "No, she bailed as soon as she gave me the card."

Hm…curious. A mystery for later, he decided. Right now he had to go do the second set. Two magical mysteries in one day. Could it be a coincidence? It was possible. *Anything* was possible.

"Thank you, Huntsman," Simon said as he prepared to go back inside. Then he dropped the official tone and said in a conspiratorial whisper. "Did you enjoy the first set?"

"It was good," he said carefully. "I just don't get jazz, is all."

Simon paused. "But you came anyway?"

Huntsman smiled broadly. "Of course I came. It's what friends do."

"So noted. I'll see you at work."

Huntsman nodded and watched Simon return inside. See you at work, he thought. How could he tell Simon? Yes, he was back in town, but he still wasn't sure if he wanted to go back to the Protectorate. His family had such high expectations of him. He had taken a semester off from school and now he had so much catching up to do. As the fifth person to wear the mantle in the last hundred years alone, he already had so much weight on his shoulders. Did he really want to add to that stress? After all, he had seen that same stress drive his father to addiction and the brink of suicide. Did he want to take the same chances himself?

The Protectorate was supposed to be short term--a stopgap measure, to protect the city until the Icons got back from their mission in space. But it had been a year, and there was no sign of their return. Everyone held out hope that they would be back eventually, but what if they weren't? Did he really want to commit himself to long term?

The applause from inside signaled the start of the second set. He checked his watch and realized how late it was getting. He triggered his communicator and sent a private transmission to Velvet.

"You coming back, kid?" she said. "Your milk is getting warm."

"I have a lot to do. I have to be getting back home. Give Simon my apologies."

"What about the milk?" she said.

"It's all yours," he said with a laugh that he hoped sounded happier than he felt.

"You got it," Velvet said, signing off and signaling the waitress for a double of Kahlua.

Chapter Five

"Explain to me again why we're doing this?" Gallows said.

Doctor Shadow turned from the unassuming front door of Louis Malenfant's house and looked calmly at the Protectorate's tattooed teleporter and Archon, the resident expert in just about everything. "Because it must be done," the ancient mage said. "And as we have had little luck finding information on Augustus Dei, it is time to pursue more...unorthodox sources of knowledge."

"Yes, of course, but I believe what Gallows is trying to say is, why us?" Archon said, hands thrust deeply into the pockets of his suit jacket.

"Ah," Doctor Shadow said, his eyebrow raised slightly. "Because you are untainted."

"Because we're rookies?" Archon said, a trace of resentment slipping unbidden into his voice.

If Doctor Shadow detected Archon's displeasure, he showed no sign of it. "No. Because you are untainted. You have never been in the presence of the Mirror of Shadows." He telekinetically raised the demon-faced knocker on the door and then let it fall. The sound echoed faintly through the interior of the house. He was prepared to knock again when the door opened.

Standing in the foyer was an unassuming man in his late forties, hair thinned to an unattractive widow's peak, his belly straining the buttons at the front of his lavender dress shirt. Louis Malenfant looked unsurprised to see his unusual visitors. He opened the door wider and stepped aside wordlessly to let them enter.

The foyer was honey-colored wood, well worn by years of traffic. The white walls were unadorned and stark. Doorways on either side opened up to similar rooms; bare floors, bare walls, no furniture.

"You just move in?" Gallows said, looking around.

"I don't use the downstairs much," their host said, his eyes shifting nervously around the foyer, refusing to settle on any of the guests for long as he headed for the stairs. "Too close to the ground."

That's why they call it the ground floor, Archon thought, but was polite enough not to voice it. This Malenfant was clearly a nut. He had done his homework on their host before making the trip over. Malenfant claimed to be an occult researcher, and had a long record of dubious claims to his name. He also had a medical record as long as his arm, including being institutionalized as a delusional schizophrenic.

The name Malenfant meant bad child in French. During the height of
the Sun King period of France, it was unheard of punishing the
children of royalty, so they instead punished someone else in their
place. Thus the name was passed down. Louis was the latest in a long
line of whipping boys and scapegoats. Archon almost felt sorry for him.
With his weak chin and quivering lips, the shifting eyes, Malenfant
looked like the victim he was bred to become.

Following their shuffling host, the trio arrived on the much
more lived-in second floor. Here, texts and handwritten journals
covered the floor like a deadfall of leaves. Shelves lined every available
foot of wall space, each packed to overflowing. Archon bent and
reached for one of the books, an antique-looking folio written in
French, surrounded by pages of notes in an illegible scrawl. The text
was obviously a play of some kind, not the kind of thing he expected to
find worthy of such intensive study by an occultist.

Malenfant stopped Archon's hand with a hastily shouted "No!
Not for you!"

Archon retracted his hand and said nothing. There was more
than a hint of madness in their host's eyes. While he had little reason
to fear this lunatic, something was going on here that he didn't
understand yet. Why else would Doctor Shadow find it so important
that the three of them come here at such a late hour?

"You aren't here to talk to me, are you?" Malenfant said, the
certainty in his voice making the question rhetorical.

"Will he speak with us?" Doctor Shadow said.

"About?" Louis said, a finger toying idly with the button on his
shirt cuff.

"Augustus Dei."

Malenfant's eyes shot up at the mention of the name, a visible
jolt close to a spasm coursing through his body.

"Not here," he said as he hurriedly ushered the trio into what
looked to have once been a bedroom. The windows to the small room
were bricked up, and the hardwood floor was scorched in several
places, is if torches had been ground out against the boards.

Archon felt Doctor Shadow touch his mind, and knew that he
had done the same to Gallows. "Whatever you do," they were told by
the ubiquitous magician, "if you see a black circle, about eighteen
inches across, do not, I repeat, do not look into it."

Before Archon had a chance to respond, he saw the world
ripple outward from Louis Malenfant as though all of reality was a
pond that had a big pebble dropped into it. And when the ripple
passed, they were standing not on flame-touched wood, but on stone as

ancient as time. Alien stars stared down at them like a million, blazing yellow eyes. Most importantly, their laughable host had been replaced by someone, or perhaps something, far less easy to ridicule.

Standing before them in multi-layered robes was a figure just over seven feet tall. The robes were the yellow of jaundice, of nicotine stains on infant fingers, of disease, of corruption. It was the most unholy color Archon had ever seen in his life. Atop the figure's head was a helmet of bone, ornately carved, which swept back like a tusk, two, maybe three feet in length. A silver chain with charms and small ornaments ran from the peak of the helm to a yellow veil that obscured everything on the dread face but for the milky white eyes. Archon felt the sudden impulse to bow, to kneel before the weight of his invisible but undeniable gravity. He took strength in Doctor Shadow's unwavering stance, and the sound of Gallows popping his gum.

"Cool," his fellow rookie said.

"Why do you seek out the one known as Augustus Dei?" the figure said in a distant voice that sounded like several voices compiled into one.

"He is in Cobalt City," Doctor Shadow said.

The voice of the ancient, Egyptian sorcerer didn't sound so creepy by comparison, Archon noticed.

"Indeed," their host said. He turned and walked from the room. With the wave of a thin, long-fingered hand, he motioned them to follow.

Wordlessly, they followed him across the black stone floor to a giant bridge. Looking back, Archon noticed that they had been in a tall, square tower. The bridge seemed impossibly high, and he realized that it crossed a street of some kind, invisible in the darkness below. Ahead stretched rooftops and walkways, an ancient city as large as any he had ever seen. Lights shone behind shutters in hundreds of windows, but he saw no one else, no movement of any kind. The wind howled off an enormous lake, glimpsed through a gap in the buildings, but no other sound was evident. A ghost city on a dark lake. Lovely.

"So you know this guy?" Gallows said. His voice was barely loud enough to carry over the sound of the wind. "You've heard of Augustus Dei?"

"I am aware of him," their guide said, his voice clear despite the wind, though no higher than a whisper. A slight sibilance in his tone made the inside of Archon's ear itch like an insect had flapping wings in his ear canal. They were led into a wide hall with a high, vaulted ceiling. Their host turned to face them again. "I am curious, however. How did you discover his presence in your city?"

"He had dealings with someone who came to our attention," Doctor Shadow said.

"Ah," their host said knowingly. He said nothing more, and the great hall filled with an uncomfortable silence. Outside the wind howled, and minutes passed. "I see you brought new friends with you," the yellow figure finally said. "Do you wish them to be baptized by the mirror?"

From the back of the room, a black disk of uncertain size floated free from the wall and began to advance towards them. Archon closed his eyes tightly and hoped that Gallows had done the same. It suddenly occurred to him where he was and what their host was. Thought to be a myth or a dark fiction dreamed up by the delusional and desperate, this could be no other than the fabled King in Yellow.

"No!" Doctor Shadow said. His black cloak floated up about him, snapping and animated by telekinetic winds of his own creation.

"Then why did you bring them?" the thing that had replaced Malenfant said. His voice was smooth and seductive, coaxing Archon to open his eyes. They remained tightly clenched. The voice had a rapist's smile in the tone, the voice of the first serpent, the voice of Judas as he kissed Christ goodbye. Archon couldn't control the chill that raced along his spine, but he was able to keep his head down, his eyes closed.

"I brought them here because there are no hooks in them, because they are untainted," Doctor Shadow said. His voice was strong, a rock for them to hold on to in the raging undertow of their host's presence.

Then suddenly the assault of ego was gone, and the four of them were simply standing in a large room in an alien land. "You may open your eyes," Doctor Shadow said in their minds.

Doctor Shadow's cloak had stopped its undulations. Archon looked at his friends and noticed that, despite the earlier display of bravado, Gallows had swallowed his gum. The black disk was back on its mount far across the room, and Archon shared a nervous smile with Gallows, wondering again why the hell Doctor Shadow insisted on them coming along.

"This Augustus Dei you seek is nothing like you poor mortals. You can never hope to truly understand him," the King in Yellow said. "He is like me in many ways, a singularity if you will."

Doctor Shadow nodded. "In what way?"

Their host motioned towards the black disk on the back wall. "He doesn't reflect," was all he said.

"What does he want? Why did he contact Blak Dawg?" the

40

mage pushed.

Their host's laugh sounded like out-of-tune church bells. "Didn't you pull that from his mind like a rotting tuber this very afternoon? Has your time wandering among the mortals dulled your skills, great sorcerer?"

"Blak Dawg knew nothing of why he was approached. A stranger made him an offer of assistance. I saw merely a name and a face but nothing else. If there was more, it was either well hidden or removed before I got there."

The figure pondered this for a second. "This much I can tell you, although I am forbidden from meddling in his affairs. Augustus Dei wishes to make people happy."

"Well, he's doing a bang up job of it so far," Gallows said.

"One person's happiness is often someone else's horror," their host said. "I believe Sondheim said it best in *Into the Woods*. 'Wishes come true, not free'."

"I have more questions," Doctor Shadow said.

Their host waved a hand dismissively. "I have no more answers for you. I have humored you this one time because of your assistance in securing the Mirror of Shadows, but do not presume to think I owe you more than your due. Ask Augustus Dei your questions if you must have answers."

"Where can we find him?" Archon said.

The yellow robed figure pulled himself up to his full height, and the wave of presence rolled off him again. "Oh, worry not, insect. He will find you."

The ripple hit them again, and they found themselves on the street in front of Malenfant's home. Archon checked his watch and noticed that over three hours had passed. Neither Malenfant or the King in Yellow were anywhere to be seen.

"Well, that was informative," Doctor Shadow said.

"Thanks a lot for the ticket to the horror show, Doc. Mind telling us what the hell that was all about?" Gallows said. His skin took the appearance of a black, star-lit field for a second, and all three of them appeared on the roof of The Keep. Archon entered in his lengthy security protocol and the hangar bay opened.

Doctor Shadow made his way down into the hangar bay and headed for the elevator. The others followed, waiting for an explanation. It wasn't until the elevator doors closed and they began their descent into the building's sub-basement that the enigmatic mage spoke.

"Archon, you are familiar with alternate realities, correct?" he said.

"I imagine we were just in one. Kind of a first for me," Archon answered.

"But you understand the theory," Doctor Shadow continued.

"Well, according to research done with quantum physics, they have been able to prove mathematically that an electron faced with two choices will, rather than choose between the two, choose both," Archon recited. "The theory is that there is a universe where the electron went left and another universe where the electron went right. But I fail to see the relevance."

"The relevance is that they are very much real, arranged in a rough coil – some above, some below, some adjacent. And in these universes, there are an infinite number of Doctor Shadows; an infinite number of Wild Kats. And so on. My only other encounter with Louis Malenfant – my first with the Protectorate -- involved an artifact, a powerful mirror that, in many ways, is more like a fractured lens. Those reports are not available to probationary members, so it is no wonder you are unfamiliar with it. But you have passed that period and should have access to the black files now. The mirror is a secret best protected at the highest levels. And it is something that you both saw with your own eyes this very evening."

"The one you helped him secure," Archon said, "The Mirror of Shadows."

"Do not dream that giving it a name diminishes its power. It has dozens of names, but none do justice to its true nature. It has the ability to open connections between alternate realities, alternate identities."

"When you dealt with Malenfant before, did you deal with your alternate selves at all?" Gallows said.

The elevator dinged as they reached the bottom floor. The Doctor led them towards the computer room. "Not directly, no. And we were fortunate in that we didn't deal directly with our opposite selves – our spiritual antithesis, essentially -- which we saw reflected in the mirror. From what little we saw, it is possible that they are as different from us as day from night. For a few, haunting moments, the lens showed us all something we could have gone the rest of our lives without seeing. It was enough to make Huntsman take an extended leave of absence, but I believe it marked and affected each of us in some way."

"But Archon and I were untainted," Gallows said. "That's why you wanted us there."

"Yes," Doctor Shadow said, a trace of amusement in his

otherwise dark voice. "You both acted as my anchor, otherwise I might have come under the influence of the lens in some fashion."

"And here I was thinking you were protecting us from the Yellow King," Archon said.

"Oh, I was," the Doctor said, sitting before one of the computer terminals. "And I'm impressed you knew his name, considering you have not read the file. The Yellow King is not to be trifled with. We protected each other tonight. Let us leave it at that."

"You said there were an infinite number of variations on us, but this Yellow King said he was different. What do you think he meant when he said that he and Augustus Dei were singularities?"

"In an infinite universe, there is only one Augustus Dei," Doctor Shadow said. "Malenfant is similar but not the same. There were no mirrors present in his home, perhaps you noticed? Malenfant does not reflect, nor does he cast a shadow."

Archon thought back. He hadn't noticed at the time, but Doctor Shadow was right. In the library room, only the three from the Protectorate had cast shadows.

"The reason he doesn't reflect or cast shadows," Doctor Shadow went on, "is that he and the King in Yellow are each other's shadows, each other's reflections. Malenfant is tied here, with the King tied to the lost city you saw tonight."

With deft keystrokes, Doctor Shadow pulled up the current case file and updated it with what they learned from Malenfant. Archon pulled up a chair himself, deciding to go through the file on the first appearance of the Mirror and the Yellow King. Gallows put in a new stick of gum and chewed it solemnly, a question forming behind his eyes.

"So when you looked into the mirror, you just saw another version of yourself?" the teleporter said. "I don't understand why that was such a big deal."

"Then perhaps you should read the report yourself," Doctor Shadow said. "That night we stared into the abyss. And the abyss stared back."

Chapter Six

Manuel de la Vega had been horrified to find that Cobalt City was overrun with chain coffee stores when he moved there several years ago. It was like a cancer. He should have expected as much; they even had the inexplicably popular coffee franchise in Mexico City where he used to live, but only tourists drank there. Well, tourists and anyone desperate to feel American. Shortly after settling into his routine as a homicide detective, he began a systematic exploration of the several independent coffeehouses in the city.

He found Schrodinger's Cup deep in his third week and never went anywhere else again. It was close to the Cobalt City University, and only a block from the north edge of Lafayette Park. Not only was their coffee the best in town, but their Mexican hot chocolate, made with Ibarra bittersweet chocolate, was every bit as good as his parent's housekeeper Angelica used to make when he was growing up. He would have moved within a few blocks if he could. Manuel felt that strongly about good coffee.

But property was too expensive in that part of town, and he needed a lot of space, what with needing a secret headquarters and everything. In the end, he had found several floors in the Hollow. A strip club occupied the lower two floors, and the third floor he kept vacant as a buffer zone from the heavy bass of the club noise. His garage and workshop were on the fourth floor, and he lived on the fifth. The freight elevator was secure, and opened on an alley across from the long, windowless wall of a converted movie theatre. He was the only one who used the elevator, so it was no problem keying a coded remote to get him in and out quickly and unnoticed. He felt as strongly about his secrecy as he did his coffee.

Manuel had taken the monorail most of the way to the coffeehouse, just as he always did. He had decided to take the non-threatening approach with his wardrobe, going with a lamb's wool sweater in a neutral color under a cocoa-colored suede blazer. Pinwale cords to compliment the blazer and loafers topped off the look. Very metro-sexual, he thought. He hoped Katherine would be impressed.

Katherine, of course, said nothing about the new wardrobe. Missy, the perky barista who knew his coffee drinks by heart, shook her head sadly as she handed the two mugs of steaming coffee across the bar to him. "You're wasted on Miss Park Avenue there," she said in a conspiratorial whisper.

Manuel smiled at her and took the mugs. "She has hidden talents," he said, winking. Missy had the good manners to blush and get back to making coffee as he carried the drinks over to the small table and comfy, mismatched chairs. "She likes me," he said, motioning towards the espresso machine with a tilt of his head.

"I can see that," Katherine said drolly. She had paid attention to her wardrobe as well, but had tried to keep it subtle. Her moss green mock turtleneck was silk and fit like a second skin. Her black skirt was cut just high enough to be scandalous in more refined company. And her knee-high boots were worth over seven hundred dollars. Not that she really noticed the price tag. When you have as much money as Katherine Wilde, you don't really look at price tags unless you're buying an airplane.

They sat in awkward silence for a few minutes, nursing their hot mugs. Katherine had secretly been having her personal assistant fetch coffee from Schrodinger's ever since Manuel had introduced it to her several weeks ago. She would have gone herself, but worried that if Manuel ran into her there he might get the wrong impression. But she couldn't bring herself to get second-rate coffee anymore. Manuel de la Vega really did know where the best coffee in the city was, even if his passion for it bordered on obsession.

"So," Manuel said, watching the nearest occupied table fifteen feet away where a student with an MP3 player pored over Cliff Notes for *Canterbury Tales*. "Have you heard from the kids recently?"

Katherine sighed, reminded suddenly of what had been a mostly frustrating phone call from the Tesla twins out on the west coast just the other day. "Xander got the grant to further develop that synthetic muscle tissue, but Tamika turned down the Martin-Lockheed contract."

"So what was it?" he said. "Not enough money or schedule conflict with the hero gig?"

"I almost wish that was the case. That I might be able to understand a little better. And to be honest with you, I don't know why it bothers me so much. It's not like they're family or anything."

"They were on your first team. That's better than family. So what happened?" Xander and Tam were good kids, despite their propensity for finding more trouble than the Bobsey Twins.

"She's taking time off to focus on her band," Katherine said. She made no effort to hide the despair in her voice. "And I know it's stupid for me to be upset about something so minor. I shouldn't let it affect me. It's silly."

45

Manuel smiled and took a sip. He remembered Tam's band. It was a five piece steel pan ensemble, and while it didn't exactly pack the house in New England, the west coast was a whole other market. And they were actually pretty good. "I don't know," he said. "It isn't that silly."

"Great," she said with a laugh. "The guy who races motorcycles and fights crime dressed up as a cat telling me what's silly."

Refusing to give ground, and overlooking for the moment that he wasn't the only one at the table with a cat motif, he pressed on, his eyes on the prize. "I mean, think about it. Your first team was just you, the twins, and Simon. That's pretty defining."

"Ah yes," Katherine said, shaking her head at the mention of Simon's name as if he were just one more problem child. "Simon. I guess that's why we're here, isn't it?"

Manuel smiled and took another sip. "I'm here for the company and the coffee, Miss Wilde. But now that you mention it, I do wonder how his concert is going."

"That's right," she said. "I thought you were going to go to that!"

"I was. I was really looking forward to it, too," he said, putting his mug on the table. "He and I sat around and talked about his band for over an hour at my place the other night, listening to a Stan Getz re-master I picked up. But you know what happened?"

"I thought you backed out," she said.

"No," he said, leaning in intently. "You backed out. So he gave my ticket away and practically forced me to ask you out to coffee instead."

"How romantic. Practically forced you?" she said, a sardonic smile playing across her face. "Did he have a gun to your head?"

"You know what I mean. He's very..." Manuel snapped his fingers trying to connect with just the right word. "He's very *Parent Trap*."

"You've seen *Parent Trap*?" she said, mildly incredulous.

"They had Disney movies in Mexico, for your information. And I loved Haley Mills very much when I was younger."

Katherine shook her head. "I always hated Haley Mills."

"Really?"

"Really."

"Por que?"

Katherine shifted uncomfortably in her seat. "I always hated her accent," she confided. "I always suspected that it was fake. And she was too damn cheerful."

"Yes, I can see where the animosity comes from now," he said. "It is all very clear to me."

They shared a laugh and turned back to their coffee.

"He keeps trying to get me to join the Protectorate," Manuel said suddenly. He sounded so serious that Katherine thought he was making a joke, but a quick look into his eyes told her that he was concerned.

"What did you tell him?" she said.

"That I wasn't really a joiner."

"Ah."

"Yes," he said. "Ah. I don't think it was the answer he wanted."

Katherine mulled it over. No. It would definitely not have been the answer Simon wanted. "All this and then the Blak Dawg mystery..." she said. She suddenly felt tired, despite the caffeine.

Manuel sat up straight, his curiosity piqued. "What mystery? I heard at the station that it was a clean arrest."

"There is more to it than meets the eye," she said. She finished off her cup then set it down, running her finger around the rough, earthenware handle. "We're looking into it."

"You know if there's anything I can do to help, you just have to give me a call, right?" he said. He was so sincere. She discovered that she was smiling despite herself.

"Well," she said, standing, "you can walk a lady home."

Manuel bolted the rest of his coffee, not leaving any to go to waste. He had priorities, after all. They were almost out the door when the pretty, tattooed bike messenger girl swooped in upon them and looped her arm around Manuel's waist. She kissed him hard on the mouth before he knew what was happening, and remained latched onto his waist. She was young, maybe eighteen, with a lithe, muscular frame. Her bare midriff shirt, little more than a jog-bra, really, seemed to frame a black tribal, bug-like tattoo around a pierced navel. And she looked vaguely familiar to Katherine, which she found to be the most maddening part. Manuel, she noticed, at least had the decency to look shocked. But he didn't push this little vixen off quickly enough either.

"What's shaking, sugar daddy?" the messenger girl said.

"Do I know you?" Katherine said, trying to figure out why she looked so familiar.

"I don't know. Are you one of my mom's bridge friends?" the little tramp said with a scarlet smile.

"Um, Katherine, I don't..." Manuel said.

"Save it for another time," she said as she stormed out. "If

47

there is another time, that is."

Katherine was halfway home before she figured out who the messenger was. When the Protectorate first formed, she had made the initial roster, but washed out mere minutes into their first conflict. Psychic feedback had knocked her out for the better part of an hour, if she remembered correctly. Katherine couldn't remember her real name, which was a shame because she was a reserve member of the team under the name of the Libertine. She thought briefly about turning back, but didn't want to face either of them right now. It's not like the Libertine knew that Katherine Wilde was really the Protectorate's Wild Kat. What would she even say to her? It wasn't like she and Manuel were dating.

Or was it?

It wasn't until she was in front of her television with a pint of double fudge brownie ice cream that she realized she had been crying.

Chapter Seven

Manuel stood on the sidewalk out in front of Schrodinger's Cup and watched as Katherine stormed away. It was not the first time he had seen a woman walk away from him with anger in her step, but it bothered him more. Manuel knew enough to realize that going after her right now would not help his situation. He instead turned to the young woman still clinging to his waist and stared into her pale, green eyes. "I suppose my first question should be, 'Do I know you?'" Manuel said.

"We have never met," she said, batting her eyelashes at him. "Not officially at any rate. You helped me with the bank robbery down in Cannonade three weeks ago."

Something didn't make sense. Robbery wasn't his beat. He worked Homicide. But he did remember the robbery. He replayed the memory across his mind's eye. First Colonial Savings bank, just before closing three weeks ago, a group of five men in rubber monkey masks walked in with automatic weapons and walked out again with two large bags of money. They were met by the Libertine, resplendent in her flowing bottle-green silk robes and highly polished red lacquer mask painted with arcane symbols. He arrived on the scene as Gato Loco and...

Wait! An alarm went off in his brain.

She must have known that he was Gato Loco. All the effort at concealing his identity, and somehow this woman was bringing it all down around him. "You must be thinking of someone else," he told her confidently. "I work homicide, not robbery. Perhaps you're thinking of Engels? He's a robbery detective..." Behind him, the baristas chased out the last of the late night patrons and locked the door. Missy looked over the girl on Manuel's waist and glared. The messenger stuck out her tongue, then led Manuel down the street, steering him by the elbow. "I'm not thinking of anyone else. I see the truth of who you are, and don't worry, I'm not going to out you."

"And you would be the Libertine, I hope?" he said.

"Got it in one," she said. "You are a detective. Anyway, I read your mind just to be sure when you were in there with her royal cattiness."

"You know Kat?" he said carefully. He submerged any thought of Katherine as far as he could. He wasn't sure if the Libertine knew who Katherine really was, but if not, he didn't want her finding out through him.

"The chilly socialite and patron of the arts Katherine Wilde?" the Libertine scoffed. "I read the society pages. Old money, holier than thou, and now, apparently slumming it with a spicy Latino cop."

"Maybe the cop likes chilly socialites," he said.

The Libertine laughed and patted him on the shoulder. "Oh, please! You deserve so much better than that. Anyway, she'll just break your heart when she gets tired of you. That kind always does. Good enough to bed but not good enough to wed."

"Well, aren't you the jealous one."

"Maybe," she said with a shrug. "Or maybe I don't like heiresses. I'm very class conscious."

As they passed through the shadow between street lamps, Manuel noticed that the Libertine had changed her appearance from bike messenger to masked avenger of evil. He raised his left hand to his face and saw that he was wearing his black Gato Loco leathers. At least it looked that way. The weight of his clothes hadn't changed, and he didn't feel his helmet, but a quick glance at his reflection in a store window showed it upon his head. Clever. Now he could conduct business as Gato Loco without compromising his identity as Manuel de la Vega. Unless it came to a fight, that is. Without his suit, he was essentially powerless.

"Awful formal clothes for a social call," he said.

"You want it to be a social call?" she said, pressing closer to him.

"No," he said. "I'm not feeling very social right now."

"Well, it isn't social. It's business," she said. He detected a pout in her voice, but couldn't see it behind the expressionless red mask. "You have never been a member of the Protectorate, have you?"

"No," Manuel said.

"I was," she said.

"Really?"

"For one day," she said. "Actually, for less than three hours. Then we faced our first fight as a team, and I went unconscious less than ten seconds in. I decided to shift to the reserves for a bit, get a little more training under my belt. I've been in the reserves for a year, and there isn't any sign that I'm being moved up into the majors, you know? Did they ever ask you to join?"

"Officially? No."

"Bet that stings, huh?" she said. He recognized the tone in her voice. It was classic "good cop" sympathy, as real as crocodile tears.

As a cop, he would know. "I mean, you had worked with two
members of the Protectorate back before, when they were the
Mysterious Five. But when Mister Grey and Wild Kat got invited to
the big show, you were left behind."

Manuel shrugged. He had thought about it before. He would
be lying if he said otherwise. But he had never let it bother him. "I'm
not that much of a team player. Is this going somewhere, miss? I was
hoping to get to bed early tonight."

They had stepped into the north edge of Lafayette Park, and
gravel crunched underfoot as they walked. She stopped and let go of
his elbow. "How many members does the Protectorate have on their
active roster?" she asked suddenly, all business.

"Nine. Well, ten if you count Huntsman who should be
rejoining the team when he gets settled back in."

The Libertine's eyes flashed behind the narrow slits in her
mask. "He's already settled in. Just moved into a loft over on Ditko
Street in Cannonade."

"And whose mind did you read to find this out?" Manuel said.

"I told her," said a voice from the branches of a large tree near
the path. "I told her when I sought her out."

Manuel wished for a second that he had the low light filters
from his helmet, but then Huntsman dropped gracefully into the light
from a thick oak branch overhead. "So that brings the roster to ten,"
Manuel said, still grasping at why he had been maneuvered here.

"Yeah, but ten members in one group, in one city? Doesn't
that strike you as a bit top heavy?"

Manuel couldn't believe what he was hearing. Huntsman had
been around off and on since the forties. There was no telling how
many people had worn the mask, but he was an institution, a legacy.
"Aren't you a little young to retire?"

Huntsman laughed. So did the Libertine. Ok, Manuel
thought, still don't know what the hell is going on. Come to think of it,
the Libertine was a legacy hero as well. The first one had vanished in
the wake of the McCarthy hearings, but he had been around for a
while. This one was, at the very least, a spiritual successor...same
powers, same theme, despite the obvious gender differences and the
variation of the older costume's color scheme.

Huntsman seemed to sense Manuel's confusion. "It isn't like
that. I've been gone a few months and the Protectorate moved on
without me. I didn't ask them to keep my seat warm for me, and I'm
glad that they filled up the ranks. To be honest, it was a little too big of
a group for me anyway. I was always struggling to find my place. Now

I might have found a way to find my place."

"I'm listening," Manuel said.

Huntsman smiled. Manuel knew the smile. The last time he'd seen it, he had almost been sold storm windows. "Well, it's a work in progress, but I'd like to offer you the opportunity to get in on the ground floor…"

"I'm not really a joiner," Manuel said.

"That's true," the Libertine said. "He just told me a few minutes ago."

"But Gato Loco was a member of the Mysterious Five," Huntsman corrected.

"You know, that's a common misconception. You see, the funny thing about the Mysterious Five…" Manuel began.

"…was that there were only four members," the Libertine finished.

"Right," Manuel said. "I worked a few cases when it suited our purposes. But we weren't a team, more like a loose alliance, a network."

"And that worked out pretty well, didn't it?" Huntsman said. "Well enough that when the city looked for a temporary replacement for the Icons, the two most…visible members of the Mysterious Five were tapped to build a replacement team. I know. I was there at the beginning."

So that was it, Manuel thought. A recruitment drive, but not the kind he was expecting. Rebuild the Mysterious Five? The idea was crazy. But now he understood why the Libertine had driven Katherine away to get to him. The Five had been her group, and while the Libertine might not be able to make the connection, Huntsman sure as hell could. The last thing he would want would be Katherine Wilde finding out that someone was getting ready to pick up her baby and run with it, especially at this early stage.

No, it would never work. And even if it did, how would Katherine react if the Protectorate lost their only legacy hero? Not only that, wasn't Libertine also a legacy? And stealing two capes from the roster was one thing. Taking the moniker of a team that used to be hers was a more dangerous form of poaching. How would she feel if he, the humble, Mexican, leather-clad vigilante, chose this new team over the Protectorate? Well, after tonight's interruption, she would probably applaud the decision, but how long would that last? How long before she began spiteful litigation, or worse, killed them in their sleep. Ok, he admitted, that was just crazy talk. But the litigation, maybe a cease and desist order…well, it wasn't outside the realm of possibility.

The Mysterious Five had been effective, he admitted. It hadn't put any great demands on his time, but allowed coordination with other heroes who would probably be working the same case anyway. The idea was dangerously tempting. It would break Katherine's heart, however, and ruin any chance of the two of them getting together. But still...dangerously tempting. He noticed that Huntsman was watching him intently, and only hoped his smile didn't show from beneath the illusion of helmet that the Libertine was projecting. It would spoil his poker face.

"The Mysterious Five worked just great," Gato Loco found himself saying.

Huntsman smiled. It seemed to be the answer he had hoped for. "Do you think she'll let us use the name?"

"Do you want to ask her?" Manuel countered. He was started to get a little excited about the idea, and that bothered him. Sure, it was crazy. But so was dressing up in black leather with a helmet that looked like a yowling cat head. He could do crazy. It was in his name. "Don't count me in. Not yet. It's a big step on a lot of toes, and I'm not sure I want to do it yet. But I will consider it. Who are the other two members you have in mind to round out the five?"

The Libertine smiled slyly. "No other members, but I'm tempted to talk to Kara Sparx and see if we can have her robot Lumien on loan for special occasions. We won't be a team, just a loose alliance, a network. And we can fill in that network with more specialized heroes when and where we need to."

"But keep it under your hat for now," Huntsman cautioned him. "Wait until I talk to Wild Kat."

"As far as I'm concerned, ese, I wasn't even here this evening," Manuel said. "But just to be clear, when are you going to talk to her?"

"I hear there's a meeting tomorrow, and she's most likely expecting me to be there," Huntsman said. "But I should probably wait until later in the day. I don't want to spring this in front of the whole group."

"But you're going to the meeting, right?" Manuel said.

"That would give the impression that I've returned to the team," Huntsman said.

Huntsman's age was showing, Manuel noticed. He had watched the young archer face down intergalactic killers armed with only a bow and arrow, never flinching from duty, never hesitating or showing fear of any kind. But the act of confronting Katherine about wanting to leave the team and start his own group, and suddenly he was just a seventeen-year-old kid. "Take your time," Manuel said. "It can wait a few days."

Chapter Eight

It had been a long day and Edirin Okoloko was glad when Snowflake dropped him off at the corner of his Parkside condo. Having his workday interrupted by the jewelry store robbery was nothing new, and he had been close to the scene anyway. And he had been looking forward to the unveiling of the Simon Floyd Combo since he had been told about it two weeks ago. But the drama and mystery that accompanied the concert he could have done without. Unanswered questions were piling up, and he didn't like that. First thing in the morning, he was going to have to download everyone's progress reports and start putting pieces together. It would cut into the research time he had set aside for his project at work, but it couldn't be avoided.

He said hello to the always-smiling doorman, and made his way up in the elevator. Three floors away, he sensed the vibrations and heard the hushed voices in his condo. Four, no five people were waiting for him, one of them sitting in his favorite chair near the living room window, the others hiding in what would be the darker corners. He would have to do something about his lighting design some other time. He was just glad he checked ahead. It pays to be prepared.

The talking had stopped by the time the elevator deposited him on the 12th floor, but he had heard enough. They had been speaking Swahili. The one in the chair had an accent, not native born, possibly from somewhere in France or Belgium, or one of the many African countries that still used French as a state language. The hidden four were to wait until the signal was given. That was good, Knockabout thought. It would buy him time.

He inserted his key, jingling the key ring to let them know he was home, gave it a twist, and opened the door. The lights in the tiled foyer went on as the motion sensor picked up the movement of the door. His alarm beeped at him, and he raised an eyebrow almost imperceptibly as he turned it off. Curious, he thought. They turned the alarm back on behind them. That narrowed the list of possible guests considerably.

He tossed his keys into a beaded gourd on the ledge between the foyer and the spacious living room and pinpointed one of the four sentries. A subtle push with his mind, and the gunman's specific gravity increased enough to immobilize him without doing damage to the lovely hardwood floors he had installed three months ago. Before the gunman could tip anyone off, Knockabout also dampened all sound from that corner. He stepped into the room and did the same to two more hiding around the corner of the rattan-fronted entertainment center. As he made a show of reaching for the light switch, Edirin caught the fourth hidden guest behind the potted palm in the corner and froze and silenced him as well.

As he expected, a voice from the big leather chair by the window stopped him before his hand touched the light switch. "Don't bother with the lights, Master Okoloko. I have taken the liberty of removing the bulbs."

"To what do I owe this unwelcome intrusion, DuChant?" Edirin said.

"I'm flattered you remembered my name," the thickly accented voice said.

"I remember the name of my uncle's dog, but it does not mean I like him."

DuChant laughed warmly at the insult, not moving from the chair as the two considered each other across the darkened room. "You cannot be too surprised to have me finally pay you a visit, can you?" DuChant said.

"One does not generally expect the head of a foreign secret police to break into their home in the dead of night."

"Well, I knocked, but you weren't in. I felt you would not want me waiting outside, you being so charitable. Anyway, we both know that you aren't just anybody, are you?" his guest said. "You are a natural resource, wrongfully taken from glorious Kingdom of D'habu. You have repeatedly refused polite invitations to return home. Now it is necessary for me to extend the invitation personally."

Knockabout noticed a hint of ambient light flicker off something in DuChant's grasp. He suspected it to be a knife. The head of the secret police was well known and rightfully feared for his love of knives. When the new king had taken the throne several years ago, everyone had expected DuChant to be replaced or even exiled. After all, he had been blamed for every mysterious disappearance for almost two decades, from legitimate threats to the kingdom to the peace activist Totende of the Elusive Step, a folk hero throughout most of the countryside. The new king, N'Kala, was a reformer and nothing like his father before him. But when the young prince sat upon the Antelope Throne and took the sacred spear, DuChant somehow retained his job. And while it was true that the brutal official's activities had been greatly curtailed, there were many a true son of D'habu who would have loved to see DuChant dragged through the streets and left to the dogs.

"Natural resource?" Edirin said, his voice like steel. He was careful not to let DuChant get to him, distract him, make him forget the guards in the corners of the room. If he let them slip, for even just a second, his advantage here was compromised. "I am a free citizen of D'habu. No laws barred my emigration here."

"You speak only truth, of course, but you know the laws regarding the sacred metal are exceptionally strict. And we cannot be expected to overlook the fact that you possess several pounds of that metal."

Edirin sighed. He had always known that somewhere down the road they would try to use this against him. "Almost forty ounces of the sacred source, yes. But we both know full well that the metal is so imbedded in my body that it can never be removed. King N'Kala was aware of this when he allowed me to leave the country."

"But you were always expected to return. He has been most patient waiting for this, but time has gone by and still you disappoint him," DuChant said. Edirin could hear the smile in his voice, could see the light play across the edge of what he was now certain was a dagger.

This was all wrong, Knockabout knew. Two years ago, foreign powers had arranged an international incident that had required King N'Kala's attention at the United Nations, and once out of the country they staged a coup to put someone more flexible about granting mining rights in the Antelope Throne. It was only the timely intervention of Knockabout that had held D'habu together long enough for N'Kala to return and restore order. The two of them were not friends, of course. Kings had no friends. But there was an understanding, a certain degree of mutual respect. It could not be the king's will that brought DuChant here; if it was, then something was horribly wrong back home.

Edirin reached out and felt DuChant's personal gravity. He tried to crush him with a few hundred G's, but it was like pushing on a strong spring. No matter how hard he worked the gravitational field around DuChant, no matter which direction he tried to manipulate it, something confounded his efforts. He noticed a faint beeping coming from DuChant, and his guest laughed softly.

"That beeping tells me that you have tried to use your ill-gotten powers on me. As you can no doubt tell, your powers will not help you here."

Ah, but I know about your lackeys, and I have them tight, Knockabout thought. He tried to zero in on the subtle beeping and found it originated on DuChant's belt. How fascinating. He slid off his jacket and draped it carefully across the arm of his sofa. "You do realize that I have no intention of letting you walk out of here, don't you?" he said to DuChant.

With a flick of his head that Edirin took to be the signal for the four hidden thugs to attack, DuChant whipped his dagger straight at Knockabout's heart. Knockabout sapped the kinetic energy from the blade before it had crossed even half of the distance between them, and it fell harmlessly to the nineteenth century Persian carpet. The thugs of course did not move, could not move, but Knockabout didn't want DuChant to have a chance to figure out something was wrong. He charged across the room and caught the sadistic head of the secret police as he was standing from the chair. They collided on the far end of the carpet and went crashing to the ground.

DuChant was one of the most feared men in D'habu. He was the boogieman, a story mothers used to scare misbehaving children into doing their chores. He was a torturer, an assassin, a butcher, with a small army of loyal, brutal assistants. None of that would help him here. He was alone, and his skills were useless in a clutch. If only he had done his research a little more diligently, he would have realized that before Edirin gained super-powers, before he moved to the capital city for college, when he was just a child playing in the dust of a small village, he was the best wrestler for hundreds of miles in any direction.

As DuChant twisted, trying to get to hidden weapons, trying to work his way free from his opponent's grasp, Edirin swiftly and surely countered every move, improving his hold with each second. He was even able to maintain his concentration on the four gunmen as they watched, helplessly. It took less than a minute for Knockabout to pin the assassin completely, and even less time to find what he was looking for. Just as his hearing had told him, the gravity winder was on DuChant's belt. He reached down and pulled it off, tossing it onto the sofa for further study.

"You cannot thwart the will of D'habu forever," DuChant grunted. There was defiance in his tone, not the fear that Knockabout had hoped for. Men like him didn't scare easily. He would have to change that.

Knockabout put his mouth up next to the pinned man's ear and whispered harshly, "If D'habu needs me, have King N'Kala give me a call. He knows where I can be found. But I do not work for you, DuChant. I never will. So leave, and say hello to the old king for me. You will be seeing him soon." Then, with one smooth motion, he rolled onto his back while he shut off DuChant's gravity. Thus unencumbered, Knockabout launched the assassin out the big plate glass window, increasing his kinetic force as he did so to get him as far from the side of the building as possible. DuChant hung there for a while, looking down twelve floors to the busy street below, his gravitational equilibrium perfectly balanced. Knockabout held him in his thoughts as he sapped the four gunmen of their kinetic force and sent them out to join their boss one at a time.

An unseasonably chill breeze came whistling through the shattered glass. Knockabout casually slid his jacket back on, plucking a bit of lint off the lapel as he did so. He activated the communicator and had dispatch put him through to Snowflake. "You haven't reached Morrison yet, have you?" he said.

"Just dropped Velvet off, and then Worm Queen wanted me to stop so she could pick up coffee, so I'm sitting double parked a few blocks away while she gasses up," the Protectorate's driver said, sounding worn out and cranky as always. "Did you know this crappy chain place is open 24-7?"

Knockabout went about packing an overnight bag, not forgetting about his guests floating out in the space between buildings. As he passed the window, one of them raised a gun in his direction. A quick wave of his finger and a sudden two-foot drop made him put it away quickly. "If it wouldn't be too much trouble, could you swing back by? I should be in the street in a few minutes."

"You forget something in the car?"

"I'm having unexpected repairs done at my place," he said, standing in the window. "I'll be needing the use of my rooms at The Keep for a few days."

"You got it," Snowflake said. "Be there in five."

Edirin turned back to the unresolved problem spinning listlessly fifteen feet from him, panicked looks in the four pairs of eyes behind their stocking masks. Duchant looked smug, his curly brown hair combed back, turning silver at the temples, the long scar across his right cheek livid. He didn't look so frightening in person. Growing up, Edirin had always expected the boogieman to be taller.

He released his claim on his prisoners, and watched as gravity grabbed them in its hungry embrace. Ten feet from the ground, he caught them again. He was pleased to notice that all five of them had screamed on the way down, at least a little. He projected his voice down next to their heads, as if he were standing next to them. "I pray you remember this encounter the next time you decide to try something as monumentally stupid as threatening me in my own home. I will not be so forgiving again."

He waited until the street was clear and let them drop the rest of the way to the ground. Cursing ensued as they limped quickly to the alley and were gone. Edirin was fairly certain he hadn't seen the last of DuChant, but he wasn't too worried about it. There are always dangers around every corner, are there not?

He stepped out onto the curb just as Snowflake screeched around the corner. The driver kept hidden behind the tinted window while Edirin loaded a small suitcase and a hanger bag into the trunk. Anna opened the door from inside and offered him a steaming paper cup.

"I heard we were coming to get you and went back and picked up a chai latte," she said.

"Soy?"

"Always," she said.

"Not tonight, thank you," he said, remembering how the chai at the place she frequented was usually far too sweet for his tastes.

"You want a chai, Snowflake?" Anna said through he partition.

The limo's panda-like driver looked over his shoulder. "Or what, you're going to throw it out? Great to know I rate right above the garbage."

"Never mind," she said, setting it into a cup holder in the back.

"I didn't say no," he said. "Hand it over."

She handed the steaming cup over the back seat. "You can pay me back for it later," she said.

"Pay for it? Five seconds you were going to throw it away. I'm doing you a favor taking it off your hands. Now buckle up."

Any protests from Anna were cut off as the loyal driver rolled up the heavy dividing glass between the front and back seats. She sipped her coffee and glared through the glass divider at Snowflake. "You know," she said finally, "it makes me wonder why anyone bothered advancing him up the evolutionary ladder in the first place."

Knockabout shrugged as he watched the city go by outside the window. The streets were almost empty. Every alley held a shadow, every shadow a secret. So different from D'habu, yet at the same time so similar. "Snowflake? The lab that did the experiment figured that if pandas were more like humans, they would be less likely to go extinct. It was declared a failure shortly after turning out Snowflake, of course."

"Humans tend to be more pleasant," she grumbled, resigning herself to being screwed out of yet another cup of coffee by the panda.

"Not all humans," Edirin said. "Some humans are not very pleasant at all."

Chapter Nine

The rest of the band had closed down the room, letting appreciative audience members buy them drinks. But Simon didn't drink and wasn't in the mood to be patted on the back. Marcus hadn't returned after the set break as expected, and Edirin and the others had congratulated him over the communicator as they left at the end of the second set. Simon carefully removed the tuxedo and left it on a wooden coat hanger backstage. He left without telling anyone goodnight.

He had spent too much time alone, clad only in the ashes of a prior existence to be comfortable there. Unburdened of unfamiliar clothes and the suffocating jubilation the rest of the band felt, he turned into a cloud of ash and lost himself in the quiet streets. Cobalt City was not the city that did not sleep, for if you do not sleep, you cannot dream. While there was the requisite scattering of all-night eateries or 24 hour coffee kiosks, the streets were all but abandoned not long past midnight. Only the bar closings at two in the morning brought any semblance of activity, with waves of cabs prowling the streets like a swarm of giant, nocturnal beetles. By three in the morning, the city was well on its way to sleep, dreaming a Cobalt City nocturne. Mister Grey stood watch over them, all of them, saints and sinners and everything in between, alone but for the stars and his own brooding thoughts.

He didn't know where his wanderings were taking him until he got there. He stood, a cloud billowing around his feet, in the second floor hallway of an old walk-up apartment building. Simon hadn't been here since his death. Despite the advancing years, he had been afraid that the apartment was still here, unchanged. Try as he might, it was difficult to shake the feeling that Camilla was still inside, angry at him for being gone for so, so long. Maybe it wasn't crazy to be afraid of ghosts. After a fashion, he was a kind of ghost himself. And hadn't he seen her for himself just this very night?

The hallway had been painted and carpeting put in to cover the stained and gouged floorboards. But those improvements had been decades ago, and constant wear and tear made the building look even worse than when he lived there. Somehow, this building, this whole neighborhood, had missed out on the gentrification boom experienced in other parts of the city. While the theatre district prospered only two blocks away, the Hollow died slowly, year by year.

Here was the line, Simon realized. He had been fighting it since being freed from the urn behind the bar of the Oriental. His strength of will was phenomenal, but there were still some things he knew he couldn't face. He had researched what had happened to Camilla, read the microfilms in the library of her sad and lonely death. But it was still just a report; still just words on a screen. In his head, in his heart, something of her would always be waiting for him just behind the scratched, white door to this tiny apartment. And with every tiny mote of his cremated body, he knew that crossing the threshold would destroy those illusions. And then Camilla really would be gone forever. Nobody but the damned were eternal.

He couldn't bear that loss again. Not that final loss. Camilla was, he realized, the last thing connecting him to what he used to be: human. But he wasn't exactly human anymore. He was…what? An anomaly? An echo of a more innocent time? The restless undead? A memory that refused to be lost? The last, fading note of a sad, sad song? He didn't even know anymore. Despite all that he had seen and experienced, or perhaps because of it, he was afraid of looking too closely, afraid that a moment of self-realization would destroy him.

It was the irony that made him want to cry. In wanting to save him, Camilla had, instead, damned him forever. "Why did you do it?" he found himself saying, desperate for answers he could never have.

"Because I was selfish," said a long familiar voice from the other side of the door.

Simon pushed himself up against the scarred wood, seeping around the edges, but a harshly whispered "No!" from Camilla stopped him short.

"You can't see me," she told him, her voice dripping with sorrow. "You can't come in."

"But why?" he said. Mister Grey massed at the borders, filled the cracks between the door and frame, but didn't press further. Her voice, for it truly was her voice, had denied him access, and he had no choice but to honor that, no matter how painful.

"We don't live here anymore, love," Camilla said. Her whisper cut through the door as if it were cheesecloth. "A single mother and her three children are here now. They are asleep, but I can't take the chance of waking them up. I would fade if they saw me, and I don't think I could come back again."

"Then you have to come out," he pleaded softly, suddenly concerned about waking the apartment's occupants.

"I can't, Simon," she said. "There are rules. More than I ever imagined. I'm sorry, but it has to be this way."

Simon weighed the cost of breaking rules he was unfamiliar with, and pulled back to a more human form, entirely on his side of the door. "Was that you at the club?"

"Yes," Camilla said, "and no. It was a fragment, discarded at a time of desperation. But the reward of seeing you play again...I would do it all over again."

"I don't understand."

"I didn't understand at first either," she said. "I didn't understand why you didn't come back to me. I waited, Simon. I waited and I prayed and I raged and I doubted. I tried every avenue I could find to discover what had happened to you and how you had become lost to me forever. That was how I met him."

"Augustus Dei," Simon said.

"He was able to determine that my original spell had worked and that you still lived, after a fashion, but that you were confined," she said. "I was told that I had made you immortal, but that by the time you were released from wherever you were, I would be long gone. I was desperate. And he offered to make me a deal."

"How much did you get for your soul?" he said, a chill creeping up a spine he no longer had.

"Simon, I was raised in the bayou, with the Loa around me every moment of my life. I know when a devil is offering a deal, and it wasn't like that," she said, confidence strong in her voice. "All I had to do was get his business card to you, to make introductions. But I didn't realize how long I would have to wait. Augustus Dei is big mojo, Simon. I don't think there is any limit to what he can do. He didn't even blink when I told him how he could help me. In exchange for getting you his card, I got to see you play one last time. And I got to speak to you one last time. To tell you..."

She paused. Simon feared, for a moment, that she was gone. Maybe someone on the other side of the door had woken up, had seen her. Maybe she was gone, and what she had come back to tell him would forever be a mystery. "Camilla?" he said softly, his face pressed flat against the door.

"You were my rock. My beautiful white knight," she said, the tears back in her voice. "And I treated you so badly. I saw the look in your eyes every time I picked up the needle. It killed me a little bit inside, knowing that I was too weak to stop, knowing that you loved me too much to break the stupid rules I made you swear too. I couldn't fight the need. I was just a poor, stupid, selfish junkie, but you treated me like a queen. No matter what people said, no matter how they treated us, treated you, you never stopped loving me. And I couldn't be bothered to put down the needle. And then, when fate conspired to take you from me, I somehow managed to make matters even worse. Oh, Simon. I'm so sorry. That's all I came back to say. I'm sorry for everything."

Simon found that he was crying tears of ash. On the other side of the door, there was a long sigh, and then nothing. He called out to Camilla again, but there was no answer. By the time he had seeped under the door, no sign of her remained. It was if Camilla had never lived there at all.

He made his way to The Keep across rooftops. It was the super-hero kind of thing to do, but mostly he just didn't want to be seen by any curious night owls who might still be out and about. He arrived at the front gate and stepped through, letting the cold, alloy bars part his body like stones in a stream. Reclaiming his human form on the other side, he walked up the broad path, past the fastidiously maintained lawn, to the double security door. Usually open during the day for visitors to the public first floor of the building, including the gift shop and trophy room, it was locked now, the access panel lit from within by a soft, golden light.

Simon punched in his seven-digit code and heard the beep. "What fools these mortals be," he recited while the scanners read his voice signature and his ambient energy pattern, comparing it against the profile attached to the number he entered. With Simon now registered as on-site, the door hissed open and sent a signal to the computer to open any other doors in the facility for him with a simple voice command. The security protocols were simpler for others, most requiring a retinal scan, palm print, or biometric scan. He had none of the above. Devising a way for him to verify identity without creating a security loophole had given Stardust a headache for days until he had invented something to do the job.

Deciding not to wait for the elevator, Simon took the stairs, reaching the third floor living quarters in seconds. When the Icons had used the building, the third floor had been guest quarters. The building still echoed with their presence. Simon had never felt entirely comfortable there, as if he were desecrating a grave, a ghost in someone else's tomb. It was why he and Wild Kat had never taken the name of the Icons themselves. They still held out hope that the team they were there to replace would eventually come back. Perhaps that was why Simon couldn't bring himself to use the regular living quarters. It was too much of a reminder that he was merely a squatter.

It had been over a year now. Simon still felt like a squatter.

He made his ways into the spacious apartment he had taken

over. Simon had accumulated a large music library since moving in, the compact disks stacked neatly on top of a small stereo. A baby grand piano had been squeezed in, replacing the sofa that the room had come with. He had no need for a sofa. He did no entertaining. Nor did he need the bed in the bedroom. He never bothered to go in there anymore. He didn't sleep, so why bother? So why was the door open now?

Drifting silently over, Simon peered into the room. It was vacant, just has he had left it, the bed undisturbed, no movement, not a single sign of life. Nothing but a tidy, blue bedroom, with his tuxedo laid out on the bed for him. He closed the door and decided to put aside his current concerns and bury himself in the reports of the day's activities. He desperately needed to get caught up. Since leaving the rental house he had been sent to investigate he had heard nothing but for Stardust's confirmation that Blak Dawg was indeed more powerful than before. Certainly, someone had found out more by now. He made ready to go to the computer room to pull up the reports, but stopped, inches from the door.

His tuxedo, laid out on the bed for him.

He had left it back at the club, and was going to ask Snowflake to pick it up the next day. He remembered it clearly.

Simon went back to the bedroom door and swung it open slowly. It was his tux. The same vintage cut, the same mother of pearl cuff links that Katherine had given him as a good luck gift. Simon glided over to the bed and checked the breast pocket and found what he feared would be there. The simple, black card that read Augustus Dei and listed the unknown phone number stared up at him like an accusing lover.

Mister Grey knew that he should ignore it and get back to work. But he couldn't put down the card. The final, posthumous exchange with Camilla still cut too deeply. It would probably mark him for a long time, he knew. Letting go of emotional baggage had been more difficult since his death. One last performance, one last conversation, and all her benefactor wanted her to do was pass along his business card? To cheat death, if only for a moment, for something this capricious, maybe this Augustus Dei was as powerful as Camilla claimed. So why was it that Simon had never heard of him before?

And how had his tuxedo found its way home?

Simon flipped the card around in semi-solid fingers, watching the low bedroom lighting play off the embossed gold ink, likely visible only to him. Augustus Dei hadn't asked for her soul. It could have meant any number of things. Maybe, Simon hated to suggest, Camilla had already bargained her soul away to one of her voodoo gods. He had no way of knowing. He had never given her religion its proper due, but that was before it had brought him back from the dead. Things like eternal damnation tended to put things into a bit of perspective, he felt.

He was dialing the number on the card before he realized he was doing it. His fingers paused, poised over the last number on the bedroom's cordless handset. Simon fought the urge to hang up and go do paperwork. His obligation to Camilla won out and he pushed the last button. To his amazement, there was a ringtone on the other end. He also heard another sound from the living room, an insect-like buzzing, on then off then on again. Handset raised to his head, he started back towards the living room to investigate.

As he passed from one room to the other, the buzzing stopped, while at the same time, the ring tone on the handset stopped. Simon Floyd stepped into the living room, a warm "Hello," heard in stereo, over the phone and from the stranger standing next to his piano with the cell phone to his ear.

The stranger was unassuming, in early middle age with dark hair cut short and styled without looking overworked. He was wearing a black suit, perfectly tailored, over a black shirt with a red silk tie secured with a Windsor knot. His blue eyes sparkled, and his teeth were perfect when he smiled at Simon. His build was perfectly average in every way, but his crisp posture made him look taller, broad shouldered. He flipped closed his cell phone and the phone in Simon's hand went dead.

"Sorry for the dramatics," Augustus Dei said. "It has become somewhat of a habit of mine. I can't pass up a chance at a grand entrance."

"Well, considering that this is one of the most secure buildings in the country, job well done," Simon said, tossing the phone onto the bed in the other room. "I understand that you've gone to a great deal of trouble to secure an invitation."

"Not a great deal," Augustus Dei said. "The truth is, your situation interests me."

"I interest you enough for you to approach Camilla over half a century ago?"

"No. She sought me out. That's how things work. The rules, if you will. I have to be invited."

"And she invited you, and you helped her, but then from her cause to mine…" Simon said.

Augustus Dei walked to a heavily padded chair and sat down.

He had a martini in his hand. It hadn't been there a second ago, Simon was certain of it. "Camilla told me about her situation. I checked it out, and what I discovered intrigued me," Augustus Dei said. He took a sip and nodded in approval. Apparently, the martini was perfect in the way only imaginary martinis are. "In exchange for helping her out, I wanted an introduction. I knew you weren't going to be gone forever, so I froze a fragment of her in time. I figured you would come back, and eventually perform again. If not, then I couldn't fulfill my end of the bargain. When you took the stage, the fragment I set aside activated and everything else followed."

"I don't mean to pry...well, yes, actually, I do mean to pry. Why go to all the trouble?"

"You have a unique situation. I enjoy helping people with their unique situations. When you've been around as long as me, it's easy to get bored, and something like what happened to you, well, it isn't an everyday occurrence," he said. "It really is that simple. I want to see what I can do for Simon Floyd."

"I would have to be a fool to make a deal with the devil," Simon said, his voice chilly.

"I would certainly hope so," Augustus Dei said, toasting Simon for his forward thinking. "But if he does make you an offer, at least give me the chance to match it. After all, you did call me first."

"By which you mean to say that you are not the devil."

Augustus Dei looked insulted. He took out one of his business cards, read it, and then returned it to the depths of his jacket pocket. "The card says Augustus Dei, Simon. I know you can read or you wouldn't have dialed the number, right?"

The dead pianist sat at the piano and nervously tapped at the keys. Camilla worked with dark voodoo gods for her entire life and she had trusted this Augustus Dei. And he had given her, Simon admitted begrudgingly to himself, everything she had asked for, asking almost nothing in return. "Camilla said you could do anything," he said.

"Not anything," the black-suited figure said, sipping his drink. "But just about anything."

"Please explain."

Augustus Dei seemed to roll the explanation around his head for a few seconds before answering. It was an act, and Simon could tell. He had given this speech perhaps hundreds of times. He would have had to. The thing was to keep it looking fresh, like Simon was the first one to have the foresight to ask the question. The pianist let him have his game, waiting patiently. After all, he wasn't going anywhere. "Say, for example, that you wanted Camilla back. I could do it,"

Augustus Dei finally said.

Simon froze, considering the possibility.

"But," the stranger said, raising a cautionary finger, "Her soul has already moved on and her body has been in the grave for a long time. Yes, I could bring her back, after a fashion. Any monkey's paw could do that, but would you really want that? In short, I can't reverse time. But other than that, I can work around most anything. I'm very adaptable."

"So you couldn't give me back my body," Simon said. No Camilla, no chance at returning to a normal life, anyone he wanted revenge against decades gone, was there anything left to ask for?

"I didn't say that," Augustus Dei said.

Simon looked into his guest's eyes for some hint of betrayal, some punch line. But if there was one coming, he could not see it. "You can make me flesh," Simon said.

"Of course. A simple transmutation," he said with a dismissive wave of his hand. "Are you sure you don't want tons of money or maybe unequaled success for your band? I know people in the recording industry. We go way back."

"And what would you ask in return?"

Augustus Dei looked at Simon intently, concern in his eyes, "Are you sure that's all you want? I have a lot of power at my disposal. I did tell you, didn't I? Maybe King of France? I could do that."

"You heard what I wanted. What is your price?"

Augustus Dei sighed. "Yeah, no one ever wants to be King of France anymore. Let me think about it." He finished his martini and stood. He paced a bit, doing calculations in his head. Finally, he shrugged and stopped pacing, leaning against the piano. "Well, like I said, it's a very simple procedure. I don't have a cost for that kind of thing. I mean, isn't losing the powers your ash body grants you cost enough?"

Simon hadn't considered that. He would have to quit the Protectorate. But, he reminded himself, he wasn't a hero. He was a pianist. Circumstances made him what he was, and now he had a chance to change those circumstances. "I'll have to quit the team."

"I would think so. I mean, it's not like they have a piano bar in this dump. You think you could do that, though? Walk away from the hero's life?"

"Yes," Simon said, surprising himself with how little he hesitated.

"Well, I think to be fair to your friends and not give them the shock of their lives, I should add, I should wait until after you've told them before I do anything."

Simon went to the wall computer and checked the team's schedule for the next few days, and noticed that a reminder had been placed for a team meeting at nine, less than five hours away. The whole team would be there, most likely to welcome Huntsman back. It would be a perfect opportunity to announce his retirement. "I tell them, and then it's done?" he said.

Augustus Dei took a folded contract out of his inside breast pocket. He flattened the heavy, white bond paper on the top of the piano. "We have a deal, Simon Floyd," he said. They shook hands, and then Simon signed on the dotted line.

Chapter Ten

Snowflake had not bothered to check the schedule for the day. Generally, when his services as the Protectorate's driver or pilot were required, it wasn't something that showed up on his "do-list." After a long night of tossing and turning from the sugar and caffeine of his late-night chai, the last thing he wanted interrupting his pleasant dreams involving a well-known, bikini-clad TV personality was the heavy, metallic "chung-chung-chung" of the roof doors opening. His dream ground to a halt, and he came storming out of the bunkroom just off the hangar bay door, a Hello Kitty sheet wrapped around his waist just in time to see Stardust and Gallows appear.

"Are we the first ones in?" Stardust asked, as if he didn't notice the sheet.

Snowflake blinked at him, checked his watch, then blinked at Stardust again, his sleepy-headed confusion fighting his innate surliness. "Do you have any idea what time it is? Why the hell don't you use the front door?"

"Um, because I flew over…" Stardust began.

"Next time fly to the front door, why don't you? How can a panda get any sleep with that damn roof hatch grinding open this early in the morning!"

"I can look at the door," Stardust said, "Maybe make it a little quieter?"

"This isn't about the door, armor-boy! Remember that next time you need me to drive you somewhere then ply me with liquid crack," he growled, heading back to his bunk.

"What the hell was that all about?" Gallows said as the bunkhouse door slammed shut.

"I have no idea," Stardust said. He was starting to understand why the mechanic and EMT had moved out of the bunkhouse several weeks ago, however. "I always thought that pandas were supposed to be, I don't know, mellow."

"He is mellow," Gallows said, pushing the button for the elevator, "at least when you compare him to the Yellow King."

"Doctor Shadow took you guys to the fright night, then?" Stardust said as he waited for the elevator. "So what did you think of him?"

"About which one: Malenfant or the Yellow King?"

"Both. Either. I don't know," Stardust said with a shrug. The

70

elevator arrived and they both stepped on, the doors hissing closed behind them. "I didn't have to spend much time with the King in Yellow, and most of the time with Malenfant, I couldn't figure out if he was crazy or really tuned in to the mysteries of the universe. Magic bothers me that way. I can't regulate or control or measure it, so it leaves me a little groundless. When we found the Mirror of Shadows, I tried to analyze it in my lab and...well, let's just say I'm never doing that again. Plus, I've had my share of wand-wigglers take a shot at me and mine the past year or so, so I might be biased in that regard."

They began their descent to the secure sub-basement meeting room. "Did you ever think that magic was just another kind of science, and since you don't understand how it works, it looks, well, magical to you?" Gallows said.

"Maybe. I mean, don't get me wrong here. Last thing I want is to start rumors that I'm against all magic and magicians. I get along with Doctor Shadow and he's as magic as they get. And Simon, well, he's a creature of magic, right? I get along with him great, despite the fact that he can't really go out and get a beer with the guys. But Malenfant...he makes me uncomfortable. Worse, I think he likes making people uncomfortable. It's like he operates in a world all his own," Stardust said, staring straight ahead as he tried to put words to what he felt like the first time he had met the yellow-robed entity. "And the Yellow King...I don't like the way he looks at us."

"Like the way we look at an ant or something," Gallows said, remembering what the Yellow King had said the night before.

Stardust's hand flashed out and hit the "Elevator Stop" button. Instantly, the brakes gripped the sides of the elevator's guide rail. "What made you say ant?"

"That's what he called us last night...no...insect. That was it," Gallows said. He wished that Stardust wasn't wearing his helmet. It was so hard to read his reactions through the visor.

"The first time we dealt with him..." Stardust said, "Did you read the report about his involvement with the Mirror of Shadows? For that matter, whose version of the report did you read?"

"I read the condensed synopsis. The one the computer compiled from all the individual reports. I figured it would be the most objective," the teleported said.

"Most objective, but not the most concise. What the compiled report glosses over is that the entity who set everything in motion with the mirror had a strong bug affinity. She claimed to be the daughter of Worm Queen and Mister Grey. Now we know that isn't possible, because Simon is dead and about as infertile as a guy can get because of it. And the two of them don't really socialize much anyway, with each other or anyone else for that matter. Are you still with me?"

"Haven't lost me so far, chief," Gallows said, putting a stick of gum in his mouth.

"Now, the Yellow King claims to have been summoned to protect this mirror of hers centuries ago by some sorcerer on Earth, to keep her away from it, basically. Apparently, it happens to be her one, central artifact of power. So with her being all insect focused, and him treating people like insects, it's all connected. It's all about her and the Yellow King and the mirror. It's all one big connection."

A moment of awkward silence passed between them as Gallows mulled it over. "This has to do with the Kennedy assassination, doesn't it?"

Stardust sighed and let the elevator continue its descent. "I know it sounds crazy, but this Yellow King is more than he pretends to be. Magic," he said, shaking his head. "I don't trust it. I would advise you to do the same."

When they got to the secure meeting room, they discovered Wild Kat, Knockabout, Archon, and Doctor Shadow were already waiting for them. Wild Kat sat in her customary seat, a half-eaten breakfast roll on a small plate before her as she intently read the imbedded computer screen in the table. Knockabout and Doctor Shadow were puzzling over the large, pink box of pastries while Archon explained again what they all were.

"...round one is an apple-cheddar roll, and the long one is the cinnamon-cardamom braid," Archon said patiently, smiling at the others as they entered. "I know we usually have donuts, but since it was my turn I decided to do something a little differently. And since there is this great Russian bakery near where I jog..."

"Zarkhov's?" Gallows said.

"Ah yes, you've been there with me before, haven't you?" Archon said.

Gallows teleported to the pastry box and scooped out a sticky-looking braided sweet bread. "Where's the coffee?"

"It was Wild Kat's turn," Doctor Shadow said, unemotionally. "And I watched H.P. Blavatsky make piroshky several times, and she never saw the need to make the carrot and cabbage ones look like carrots."

"Did you get the coffee from the same place as last time?" Stardust said, placing his helmet next to his seat as he contemplated breakfast. "You know, the place over near the park?"

"I delegated to Anna this morning," Katherine said. She

sounded tired and more than a little distracted, but kept her eyes on the monitor before her as she read updates. "She's bringing a tea and coffee cart from the commissary instead."

Within minutes, Worm Queen and Velvet rolled a service cart loaded with coffee pots, creamer, hot water, and tea bags into the room. Everyone selected pastries and beverages and made their way to the conference table where they busied themselves with reports of the previous day's events and water-cooler talk of Simon's premier concert.

The minute hand tickled the nine o'clock hour and Wild Kat did a quick head count. She turned to Knockabout, the only one sitting near her who had been at the concert the night before. "You saw Marcus last night, didn't you?" she said. "Did he say anything about not coming to the meeting this morning?"

"Not to me," Edirin said. "We spoke of the meeting, so I am certain that he was aware of it, but I don't recall him committing to anything. He seemed a little distracted."

"It isn't as though we are desperate to have him back, is it?" Velvet said. She hadn't met young archer before the concert, and was mostly familiar with his exploits from years of press coverage. She had joined the team the same day as Archon and Gallows, more than a week after Huntsman had gone on his sabbatical. She had never worked with him, and was finding it hard to understand why they needed him back.

"He still has a communicator," Wild Kat said. "As long as he has one, it's assumed that he's still on the team. But he's been avoiding the subject since he got back. I just want to know his status."

"This is more than just needing his communicator back, however," Knockabout said. "We need to know if he's going to answer if called. If we can't depend on him being there when we need him, it's better for all of us if we know now."

"How about we put him on the reserves until he makes a point of coming in and talking to us about it?" Stardust said. "That way he won't pick up general radio chatter, and if we put out an all points emergency notice he will at least be informed."

"Should we put it to a vote?" Worm Queen said.

"By show of hands," Wild Kat said, "Who thinks Huntsman should be put on active reserve?"

Seven hands went up, with Knockabout abstaining. The motion was carried.

As Stardust made a note to change Huntsman's communicator code, Wild Kat looked around the table again and noticed that Mister Grey had not shown up yet either. Strange, she thought. She had taken his presence as a given for so long. He was never late without letting her know, and the fact that he wasn't here concerned her slightly. She tried not to let it show. Maybe he had heard about the incident at the coffeehouse between her and Manuel, and had gone to Manuel to try and smooth things over. It was possible but not likely. There was little chance he could have found about it so soon, and he usually came to her to start damage control anyway.

"Has anyone seen Simon?" Katherine asked the group.

"I know he's onsite," Knockabout said. "He was whistling in his quarters when I passed by on my way to the meeting."

"Whistling? Simon? And you're sure it was him?" Wild Kat said. She had known Simon longer than anyone, and she had never heard him whistle. Without lips or teeth, she didn't know if it were even possible for him to whistle.

"Mister Grey, are you still on grounds?" Doctor Shadow said into his communicator. The conversations around the table died as they waited for an answer, which was reassuringly quick in coming.

"Please accept my apologies for tardiness. I had matters of a personal nature that required my attention, but I just got off the lift and should be there in seconds," the erudite dead man said.

Wild Kat thought that he sounded tense, perhaps a bit nervous beneath the pleasant tone and English accent. Her own family was not long removed from England, and she was still very adept at peeling through the veneer of civility patented by the British.

True to his word, Mister Grey strode through meeting room doors only a few seconds later. Unlike the others, he did not waste time with coffee and pastries and instead went straight to his seat. "Once again, I offer my apologies. I trust that I have not kept anyone waiting for long."

"You missed a vote to put Huntsman on active reserve," Katherine said, watching Simon closely for some hint of reaction. She saw nothing.

"Was it close?" he said.

"Almost unanimous," Archon said.

"Well then," Simon said, placing his hands flat on the surface of the table before him. "It hardly matters how I would have voted. But I would have abstained, and would like to do so, retroactively."

He already knew, Katherine thought. Did he talk to Marcus about his team status last night? Was there more going on? And why was she getting the feeling that Simon was only half-engaged with this conversation to begin with?

"On other matters, I believe that a powerful figure has made

74

its presence known in Cobalt City," Doctor Shadow said. "For those who have already read my addendum to the Blak Dawg report, this will not be new information, so please indulge me. I was able to determine during questioning that Blak Dawg had contact with someone by the name of Augustus Dei…"

"Augustus Dei?" Simon said, leaning forward in his seat. Doctor Shadow fixed him with a calm yet unsettling gaze. Wild Kat feigned disinterest as she watched the silent exchange. The others might not have noticed, but Simon was unmistakably shaken by the name Augustus Dei.

"You are familiar with the name then, Simon?" Doctor Shadow said, arching an eyebrow.

"Through other circumstances, but yes," Simon said. "Please continue and I might be able to illuminate somewhat from what I know."

"Indeed. This Augustus Dei is a power broker with a well-hidden trail. I believe, and Stardust and Archon's mathematical and scientific comparisons should bear this out, that he was able to amplify Blak Dawg's powers, making him a much more serious threat."

"Why?" Velvet said. "What does he get out of it? Did he get Blak Dawg's soul or something?"

"Well, his powers are magical in nature, so bargaining for a soul was my first assumption as well, but there is no evidence to support this supposition," Doctor Shadow said. "I am only familiar with his dealings in this case. Perhaps if we knew of more of his bargains, we could determine a pattern."

"But he's definitely a bad guy?" Stardust said. "I mean, if he helped Blak Dawg, isn't that aiding and abetting?"

"He also helped Camilla," Simon said, slowly.

All eyes turned to Simon. Everyone knew the tale, even the newest members. It was very common knowledge but it was never discussed. Only Katherine, Edirin, and Jaccob had talked to Simon about Camilla, and those conversations had been short and awkward.

"When did he help her, Simon," Katherine said, afraid of what the answer might be. "Was it in 1931?"

"Oh! No! Certainly not," Simon said, surprised at the thought. "Unfortunately, she did that - this, I mean, on her own. No, she sought out his help years later when she was trying to find out what happened to me."

"And Augustus Dei told her where you were?" Worm Queen said, fascinated that there was more to this little tragedy than anyone had been willing to discuss.

"He didn't know where I was. But he knew that I was immortal, so eventually I'd turn up again. He was able to ensure that she saw me one last time."

"The woman who spoke to Marcus last night at the Colonial Club," Velvet said. "The possible dead person you were all hot to talk to him about."

Simon raised his chin, defiant of the phantom tears he wanted to shed. "That was Camilla. She asked to see me perform one last time and to speak to me one last time."

"You talked to her?" Katherine said. Well, that explains how he knew about her deal with Augustus Dei at least. "What did you talk about?"

"It was intensely personal," he said, his back straight. "I have no wish to discuss it. Suffice to say, Augustus Dei was able to freeze a fragment of her in time to fulfill her wish. And before you ask, no, he did not take her soul in return."

"Then what was the cost of her services?" Doctor Shadow said, his voice hauntingly crisp.

"An introduction," Simon said, his eyes on the table, no, on his hands lying flat on the table surface. "He desired an introduction to me, actually."

There was a silence around the table as it sunk in. It was Katherine who finally asked what everyone else was thinking. "Simon, what did you do?"

"I met with him, of course," he said, his tone suddenly conversational with a hint of fragility. "It was the...polite thing to do. And he said that he could help me."

"Is Camilla..." Edirin started.

"She's gone," Simon said, unable to hide the sadness in his voice. "She has finally done what she needed to do, said what she needed to say. She has moved on. But Augustus Dei can give me back something else that I've lost."

"What did he promise you?" Doctor Shadow said, rising to his feet.

"My flesh. My humanity. I will lose my powers, of course, so I would like to take this opportunity to tender my resignation," Mister Grey said, barreling forward. It had the ring of a speech he had been practicing, waiting for the right opportunity to present it. He stood and slowly, deliberately, removed his communicator and placed it on the table before him. When he released the high tech plastic ear-bud, his fingers took on the sudden crispness of the solid.

The transformation had begun.

Archon had been sitting directly to Simon's left at the big table, with Stardust on Simon's other side. Both of them could clearly see the ash ripple and dance before it settled into a solid, flesh form. The naked skin was still a soft shade of grey, but there could be no argument. It was solid. Archon could tell at a glance, that while human and solid, the flesh was most certainly dead, with a texture that looked like foam rubber.

At about the same time that Simon made the realization that he had been screwed, Archon drew, what appeared to him, to be the obvious conclusion. Simon had been promised his humanity and his flesh, but could not be returned to life. Not in the way anyone thought of life, anyway. He would be little less of an outcast now than he had been before. The ash continued to condense, reaching his torso, racing down his spine and up to his head while Simon howled, falling to the ground and writhing, trying too late to prevent the change. Velvet and Gallows stood, wondering what they could do. Inexplicably, the other members of the Protectorate sat and did nothing.

Suddenly, Gallows became aware of someone else in the room with them, a dark-haired man in a black suit with a Bloody Mary in his hand. He had somehow stepped out of the corner of the room when no one was looking, and while he didn't look particularly frightening, his innate calm and the simple fact that he shouldn't be there were immediate red flags for the teleporter. Gallows couldn't even teleport into the building as a member without some kind of alarm going off.

Gallows and Velvet moved closer to Simon, whose transformation was all but complete, the suffering subsiding. And still, the other members of the Protectorate did not move. But Velvet could see that they weren't frozen in time or paralyzed. There was something going on *inside*. While Simon went through a painful external metamorphosis, something was happening to the others. She saw Gallows looking over her shoulder and followed his gaze to see the exceedingly civil Augustus Dei.

"Is it everything you hoped for Simon?" Augustus Dei said. "It is your request, your wish, your desire to a tee. You know I could not undo what had been done. I had made that abundantly clear. But there was another you, wasn't there? I couldn't undo what had been done. So instead, I decided to make a switch. A simple transmutation."

Suddenly Archon understood it all, thankful that he had reread the reports the other night. He looked down at Simon Floyd as the resistance reached its end, and knew that it wasn't Simon anymore. No, over there they had other names. This was Lazarus now, not

Mister Grey. And if Augustus Dei had somehow managed to swap out the minds of those tainted by the Mirror of Shadows, then perhaps Simon wasn't the only one feeling a little...different.

A look into Edirin's eyes just the other side of the table confirmed his worst suspicions. Where once sat one of the noblest people he had ever met, was instead a tyrant, a dictator, a devil made flesh. He was no longer Knockabout. Archon was confident now that he was in very, very big trouble.

From the looks on the faces of Gallows and Velvet, they could tell that something was wrong as well, but probably didn't know just how bad things were going to become very soon. "Gallows," he said pointing to Velvet, "Evac pattern three."

Before she could mount a protest, Gallows had grabbed Velvet by her heavily armored gauntlet and popped her away. The sudden activity stirred the others into movement, and Wild Kat, or whoever was in her body now, was at his throat in less than a second. Lazarus stood, and draped himself in Augustus Dei's offered jacket. "Who the hell is this?" Lazarus said, his accent fainter, but his voice stronger, somehow colder.

"Your pale reflections have made new friends," Augustus Dei said. "They have not been touched by the mirror. When you came through, they had no reflection to get caught up in your wake."

The technocratic fascist who wore Jaccob's skin put on his helmet and patched into the base computer. "Gone. Both of them are off property already. That tattooed freak has a long range. It would have been handy to know that they had a teleporter in their little clubhouse."

"They might ruin everything," Wild Kat's voice said, inches from Archon's ear. Her claws scratched his throat with each nervous swallow he made. "But he can ruin nothing if I kill him now. Not if I eat him."

"I don't have a problem with that," Knockabout said, obviously distracted by the weight and cut of his expensive suit. He kept raising his arms to his side and rolling his head about, getting used to the constraints of such clothing.

There was a sudden burst of activity as Gallows popped in at several points in rapid succession, looking like a strobe light, punching at Wild Kat just enough for her to let go of Archon. On his last appearance, the teleporter grabbed hold of Archon's sleeve and popped him out as well.

Worm Queen stood and moved next to Lazarus. The look she gave the zombie Englishman would have made a necrophiliac blush.

"Well," she said, her voice dripping with sarcasm, "that certainly could have gone better."

"And so it comes to pass that I have delivered you into this world, as promised," Augustus Dei said. "My part of our bargain is now complete."

"All this and we only have to give you the freedom to seek out new contacts?" the Egyptian necromancer in Doctor Shadow's body said. "Your price is a fool's price. There is no profit in this for you if all the world will soon be ours anyway."

Augustus Dei smiled and took a sip of his drink. "Not everything is about profit," he said. "I just want to see people get their heart's desires." He went to the door and opened it, on his way to find a nice place to watch the coming festivities. "You see, making people happy is its own reward."

Chapter eleven

"So do you have a theory for what the hell just happened in there?" Velvet said, looking pointedly at Archon. They were crouched with Gallows beneath a water tower on the roof of a Parkside high-rise condo. Archon had their communicators spread out before him and was rapidly disarming the tracking feature built into each one.

"I don't need a theory," he said, not raising his eyes from his work. "Augustus Dei pretty much blurted out everything while Gallows was getting you out. Now I know how Nancy Drew feels."

"He used the mirror somehow, didn't he?" Gallows said, watching the sky in the direction of The Keep for signs of pursuit, however futile that would be if Doctor Shadow chased them.

"If you mean the Mirror of Shadows, I thought that was locked away safe somewhere," Velvet said.

"True, but not before most of the team was reflected in it," Archon said, rewiring the last connection. "It's done. Go," he said to Gallows. A second later, they were looking at the downtown skyline from a tree-shaded bluff in Regency Heights. "Somehow, the fact that they had been reflected in the mirror left them vulnerable or drew his attention. The three of us were unaffected because he didn't know who we were. For now, that's one of our few advantages, and one I don't plan on giving up. I need access to a computer, and preferably not my own. They might already have my home address."

"I can get us in at Starcom. I want to pay a visit and take care of some security issues anyway," Velvet said.

"How does the front lobby suit you, Miss Daisy?" Gallows said with a cocky smile. Before she could answer, they were standing in the middle of the big flashing star in the middle of the tasteful five story lobby of Starcom.

Their sudden appearance made several of the half-dozen employees heading to the elevator yelp with surprise. The two security guards standing near the reception desk didn't even blink, although it was difficult to tell behind their Ray-Bans. Velvet strode to the desk, flipping her midnight-blue cloak back over her shoulder dramatically. "We need to see Elizabeth Stevens. Immediately."

The stunned-looking receptionist, a former Miss Creamed Corn from Iowa named Lovette, picked up her phone and dialed, having to go through two secretaries before finally handing the phone over to Velvet. "Liz, we have a situation. I'm downstairs with Archon and Gallows and we need to meet with you now."

Velvet nodded tersely at Elizabeth's reply and handed the phone back to Lovette. A few quick words were exchanged, and then the phone was on the cradle, with Lovette authorizing the two security guards to issue gold security passes to the three Protectorate members.

Before heading to the elevators, Archon asked the security to notify them immediately if Jaccob showed up. They nodded, confused. Jaccob never come in through the front door.

Elizabeth waited for them just off the elevator on the top administrative floor. She was alone but still masked her concern over the sudden visit behind a façade of professionalism. "Is everything alright with Jaccob?" she said.

"We don't know," Archon said, "None of us may be particularly safe. Is there a nearby terminal I can use?"

"Of course," Elizabeth said. She led them into her spacious office and motioned Archon towards her large desk made of burnished copper and what looked like beveled, frosted glass. She motioned the others to a pair of comfortable black leather sofas surrounded by potted ferns. She sat in the middle of one of the sofas, one leg folded beneath her, back straight, unyielding.

"Elizabeth," Velvet began, hands clasped before her as she sat, "a few minutes ago, we were attacked at the Keep. We have reason to believe that someone has swapped consciousness with the other members of the team, including your husband. You aren't safe here until things get straightened out."

Stardust's wife stared across at them, carefully absorbing everything before she made a decision. It was something Velvet had always liked about the CEO of Starcom. She had come to know Elizabeth pretty well earlier in the year during some very lucrative private security for the family.

"This is one of the most secure buildings in the city," Elizabeth said, "and I'm not entirely defenseless myself. What makes you think that I am in danger here?"

"Because the person who might have taken over your husband is an evil version of him from another dimension," Gallows said, not content to sit and watch any longer. Confusion wrestled with concern on Elizabeth's face, and confusion won out.

"Velvet, is this regarding the black mirror thing Jaccob told me about?" she said.

"From what little information we have, yes, we think so. I know it sounds crazy, but if you won't lie low yourself, could you at least find somewhere safe to send the kids for a few days?" Velvet said, her voice calm and even.

"I can arrange for them to be picked up after school and taken somewhere. I have a cousin in Boston who has a daughter Michael's age. She's been trying to get us to visit for months."

"And are you going with them?" Velvet said, already knowing the answer from the look in Elizabeth's eyes.

"Jaccob started this company," she said, "but I make it run. There is too much going on for me to get away right now. We've finally gotten our foot in the door on the European market. After tomorrow's meeting with some German investors, I could slip away for a few days. But not until then, and certainly not for long."

"In the meantime, you should have Stardust's codes locked out," Velvet said.

Elizabeth stood and the others followed suit. Gallows looked over at Archon and noticed that he was standing as well. "Are you finished over there?"

"I've been finished," Archon said with a trace of a smile. "I even had time to check my investments and put in a few buy and sell orders."

Once the elevator doors were closed and they were on the way back to the lobby, Archon pulled out his PDA and activated a program. "There we go," he said, "we can talk freely now."

"What did you do?" Gallows asked, trying to get a look at the screen of what he was certain was more than just a PDA.

"I made myself and anyone within ten feet of me pretty much invisible to electronics. Don't stray too far and we should be fine," he said. "I also managed to get into our computers back at the base and lose our personnel files, so any secrets shall remain secrets. I did the same to the Starcom computer just to be safe."

"Doesn't Stardust have security against that kind of thing?" Gallows said.

"He certainly does! It took me almost thirty seconds to get past it."

"If I had known you were going to run ahead of schedule, I would have asked for total building access to Starcom in case we need it later," Velvet said.

Archon smiled and held up his hand in a "wait" gesture, then reached into his jacket and pulled out what looked like a video rental card. He slid it into a slot at the top of his PDA, tapped the screen with his stylus, then handed the card to Velvet. It was a video rental card. "Total access," he said, still smiling. "And on Tuesdays, you get two for one rentals at fifteen locations across the city."

She slid the card into a concealed pocket in her cloak. "Okay. On to the next order of business: there are three of us and six of them."

"Plus, Wild Kat is scary enough when she isn't being evil," Archon said, touching his recently threatened Adam's apple reflexively. "And the others are pretty tough as well. One on one, I don't think we can take them. We need reinforcements."

"Who do we have available from the reserves besides Huntsman?" Gallows said.

"I have Libertine's contact info," Archon said. "But Kara Sparx is in Los Angeles and has Lumien with her, so count them out."

"What about Gato Loco?" Velvet asked. "Can we contact him?"

"Only Simon and Wild Kat know how to do that," Archon said. "He values his privacy. Plus, he's not really a member of the reserves."

"And he would be out of his depth," Gallows said, who had never liked the leather-clad biker.

"So we only have Huntsman and Libertine available?" Velvet confirmed.

"There are a good half-dozen solo operatives around the city. Some are more visible than others, some are the kind of powerhouses we could use here, some stop muggers. But I can't find any of them reliably – not without exposing ourselves to the false Protectorate. So it looks like those two are all we've got right now," Archon said as the elevator doors dinged open and the three of them walked out across the lobby to return the now-redundant gold security passes.

"Let's go get them then," Gallows said, taking the address from Archon. A second later, they were on the roof of an old brick apartment building in Cannonade, with ivy crawling up the walls and Reggae music pounding from the windows of the room below. The tattooed teleporter smiled, walked to the edge and inhaled deeply. "Someone started burning the ganja early," he said.

Archon took a slight whiff and isolated each of the separate scents he detected. "No. I believe what you are smelling is sandalwood incense, Italian roast coffee, and if I'm not mistaken, a frosted strawberry toaster pastry."

"No one likes a smartass," Gallows grumbled. "I hear Bob Marley and…"

"Toot and the Maytalls," Archon corrected with a sly smile. Gallows glared at him. Archon didn't back down. It was like they were a duo again, out fighting crime without all the trappings of a big super team. Eventually, Gallows turned his head and smiled slightly.

"Oh yeah," he said. "I forgot they recorded this first. I was always more of an Ini Kamoze fan myself."

"Here come the hotstepper!" the two of them said in unison. Velvet stood and watched, shaking her head. They were all doomed.

"Anyone care to explain what they are doing on my roof?" a hard, female voice said from behind them. They turned and saw Libertine floating menacingly a few feet off the roof, her cloak flapping in a telekinetic wind.

"We're here to offer you the chance to return to active duty," Velvet said.

"I see," Libertine said, looking over the trio. "And they sent the junior varsity to tell me instead of using the communicator? You understand if I'm suspicious."

"The communicators are not secure at the moment," Archon told her. "Until I recode the frequency, we're better off not using them at all."

"So what's with all the cloak and dagger from the cape and cowl set?" the young psychic said, gliding a little bit closer.

"The rest of the team has been swapped out with evil pod people," Gallows said.

"Really?" she said, looking to the others for confirmation.

Archon shrugged. It was a pretty concise, if not entirely accurate, way to sum up the morning's events. "Minus the pods, of course, but essentially, yes. We need to gather up what forces we have before they start clearing out perceived threats."

"So you three are it?" she asked, scanning the sky for signs of Stardust and the street for signs of anyone else.

"And we need to find Huntsman as well," Velvet said. "He was an active member for long enough that they might see him as a major obstacle. And they probably know where to find him already. If the communicators were secure, we could just call him, but he doesn't always have it on, especially since he hasn't returned to active duty yet. Do you know him well enough to be able to find and contact him telepathically?"

Libertine wondered just how much to give away. Did they already know that she and Marcus had been talking? He had moved into a building only a few blocks away, and none of them had known. Did she really want to be the one to tell them? "I believe I can reach him, but it may take a little time. Where would you like him to meet us?"

"Are you sure you wiped out our records?" Velvet asked

84

Archon. He nodded, almost insulted that she had to ask. Velvet wrote down a quick address overlooking Lafayette Park and handed it to Libertine. "And ask him to come in street clothes, but bring his work clothes with him. We might be getting dirty before the day is out."

Libertine nodded and searched for Marcus' mind, connecting to him almost immediately. While she was in his head transmitting the message, she realized that he had been thinking about some girl he had met on his recent road trip. She considered altering his memory, making him angry or ambivalent, or even wiping this girl from his memory altogether, but finally decided that it would be wrong. She sighed inwardly, and tried not to read any more of the young archer's thoughts. He told Libertine that he would join them after lunch with his family, and said he would leave his communicator turned off in case anyone tried to trace it. She closed the link and opened her eyes.

"He will join us early this afternoon. And he has turned off his communicator," she said.

"That would be a good idea for you as well," Velvet said.

Libertine nodded, deciding it wasn't worth mentioning that she hadn't bothered turning her communicator on for over a month. "So evil pod Protectorate, huh? Is this of the alternate universe variety?"

"Yes," Archon said, "Are you familiar with the phenomenon?"

"I share some memories with my predecessor, and he traveled the Coil. That and I watched a lot of *Deep Space Nine*," she said. "How much do we know about their duplicates?"

The others looked to Archon, who had done the most recent reading on the subject.

"Doctor Shadow did some research on the matter once he became aware of the duplicates. His information is far from exhaustive..." Archon said.

"Just the highlights," Libertine said.

"Stardust's counterpart is a technocrat in the Pacific Northwest. He has his own feudal fiefdom. He goes by the name Deathstar."

"Lucas is going to love this one," Gallows said, smiling slightly.

"Yeah. Well, he conducts business somewhere between Lucas, Gates, and Attila the Hun. He's a bad character."

"Ok, what about Knockabout?" Velvet said. Of all the Protectorate's members, he was the one she perceived as having the most raw power.

"In the other world, he goes by Sundiatta. He never left D'habu, killed the standing king, and took over the Antelope Throne for himself. He's a conquering warlord, and has most of sub-Saharan

Africa under his thumb. His only real competition is Doctor Shadow's duplicate, Shade," Archon went on. "Shade is a powerful necromancer who comes out of somewhere in Egypt every few centuries on a campaign to take over the world. Doctor Shadow had a hard time getting much more than that. But the necromancer part is enough to make me nervous."

"Tell her about the happy couple," Gallows urged.

"The happy couple?" Libertine said.

"Mister Grey and Worm Queen," Archon said. "Or Lazarus and Lenore, over there at least. He's a big time mobster, and she's his…companion. They're the only ones in the parallel Cobalt City that we know of."

"And he's still dead over there?" Libertine said.

"Lenore doesn't seem to mind," Gallows said.

"Moving on," Archon said, not comfortable lingering on the gruesome twosome for too long, "that leaves Wild Kat. Over there she goes by Rakshasha. The deadliest of predators, her name alone inspires terror throughout India. No reliable information on her, either, unfortunately."

"And now they are all over here in Cobalt City," Velvet said. "And only we know about it. Everyone else assumes that the Protectorate are here to keep them safe. And all that's standing between them and the rest of the world is us."

"The junior varsity, as you so eloquently put it," Archon said. "We need all the help we can get."

Chapter Twelve

Katherine Wilde was a mutant by choice. At the tender age of twenty-two, she had sought out the world's expert in experimental gene sequencing and genetic grafting. Dr. Sri Patyaloo ran his clinic on a small island two miles off the eastern coast of India, where people didn't ask too many questions. She flew out to Calcutta where she met with him three times to discuss the procedure.

The first meeting felt like a disaster. The small, balding man had pursed his thin lips as he looked over her medical records and her written proposal for what she wanted done. When he was finished reading, he tossed it back onto the small mosaic table between them dismissively. "Everyone wants to pass as cats," he said. He looked at Katherine as if she were beneath his notice.

"I don't want to look like a cat," she explained patiently, "I want the essence of a cat. I want the speed, the agility, the leap, the claws, and only you can do that." She had done her research. If Dr. Patyaloo refused to handle her request, then her chances of horrible complications went from 15% to 63% and the chance of less severe side effects was almost absolute.

But Sri was noncommittal. He stood and told Katherine that she would have his answer in a few weeks. In the meantime, he suggested that she enjoy her vacation. She figured then that her quest was over.

She stayed in Calcutta for three weeks and enjoyed it despite herself. Her grandfather had been born in India and had lived there until he was twenty-five. She had grown up reading his journals, and enjoyed seeing firsthand all that she had read about. But she wanted to experience more of what she had read. Her grandfather, much to the disappointment of the rest of the family, had been an adventurer. Those tales of thrilling escapes, intrigue, and danger had fueled her imagination as a child. To the rest of the family, he was a black sheep, held responsible for the death of Katherine's aunt Lucy when she tried to follow in his footsteps. But to Katherine, Kimbal Wilde was a role model. It broke her heart when he vanished somewhere in China during her first year of primary school.

She hadn't expected Dr. Patyaloo to agree to take her on following the initial meeting. But when Katherine returned to her hotel after a three-day trip to see the ruins of an old palace up river, she found a message waiting for her at the desk. The brief message, handwritten in clear, sharp penmanship on crisp, linen paper said that he believed that he could do as she requested. He advised her to call as soon as she arrived to arrange a second meeting to go over the details of his proposal. She called him from the lobby and scheduled a meeting over tea the following day.

The second meeting had been a total change of pace. Dr. Patyaloo was pleasant, cheerful, and excited about the possibilities of a human-feline splice. But as he presented Katherine with folders of information detailing what he was thinking of doing and getting feedback on the customization she wanted, Katherine thought she detected an undercurrent of fear in his manner. She wasn't sure if she was imagining his nervousness, but she saw something there, in the corners of his eyes, in how he kept whetting his lips. Something had frightened him enough to change his mind.

At the third and final Calcutta meeting, she arrived at the same restaurant with a briefcase full of money as requested. She exchanged it for a series of forms, which she signed and returned. The doctor told her to return to her hotel and check out. A car would be sent for her shortly. True to his word, ninety minutes later, she was on the way to her destiny.

It wasn't until months later that she found out how close she came to returning home empty-handed. One of the doctor's earlier patients had become a friend of hers, and since he worked security on the island, he was in a position to know all kinds of interesting things. Jerry the minotaur man said that two weeks after meeting with her, Dr. Patyaloo was ready to turn down Katherine's request. But late one night, a stranger showed up on the island and confronted the doctor in his study. Sri was unharmed, but incredibly shaken up. He insisted the island be searched, but no trace of the intruder was found. Dr. Patyaloo threw himself into preparing for Katherine's transformation the very next morning. When asked about the change of heart, all he told Jerry was "I don't wish to incur the wrath of the Wrecker of Engines."

It was the first time she had heard anyone mention the Wrecker of Engines since she was a child, and it shook her to her foundation. So, old Kimbal Wilde was still alive after all. And he was apparently keeping tabs on his favorite granddaughter. The last time she saw him, it was late in the evening on her fourth birthday. She woke to see him standing over her bed, his featureless white mask staring down at her, his black long coat dripping with rain. Even as a half-forgotten memory, it still filled her with fear and fascination. He left her with a small wooden trunk full of journals, each volume bound in weathered leather, and jammed cover to cover with his tiny, precise writing. Even though he didn't speak, it struck Katherine as if he were saying goodbye.

She never told her parents about the visit, about that last birthday gift. Even at the age of four, she knew her father would never approve. And it wasn't as if anyone would notice the small chest. Her room was large, cluttered with a curious mix of toys and odds and ends from around the world. She couldn't remember a single instance of her parents entering her room, for any reason.

The journals infected her, made her want more than the safe, predictable life of privilege she was hurtling towards. Her grandfather put her on the path of an adventurer. And when that path seemed in jeopardy, he had made his presence known and smoothed over the obstacle. She wasn't aware of any attempt to contact her. Respecting his privacy, she made no attempts to find him, however much his abandonment stung.

Between the interview, the multiple medical procedures, the rehabilitation, and the training she underwent to understand her new abilities, she spent close to a year in India. She and the kind-hearted minotaur grew to become good friends, and for perhaps the first time in her life, she felt like she was where she belonged in life.

That changed when terrorists attacked the island. Patyaloo's experimental research was seen as an abomination against God by certain fundamental terrorist groups in the area. In reaction, thirty-four highly armed militants made the short trip from the mainland determined to kill anything that moved. They succeeded in destroying the lab and its years worth of test data. And, in a fashion, they killed Dr. Patyaloo.

But the attack exposed something that no one, not even his closest associates, had suspected. The good doctor was not entirely human himself. Upon his death, his body burst into flames, and a new Sri Patyaloo was reborn full grown. And this time, he was not the forward-thinking and frequently distracted geneticist. With rebirth came a new personality, and perhaps shaped by his death at the hand of terrorists, he became a terrorist himself. The damage the fanatical militants did to the island was nothing compared to the violence Patyaloo himself rained down.

Declaring war on an imperfect humanity, he turned his early patients into soldiers. Some embraced the change, drunk on the power of being able to unleash their abilities in new, destructive directions.

Jerry had been a pacifist and a social worker serving in the Peace Corps when Dr. Patyaloo had recruited him for an experimental procedure. Jerry said the doctor saw something in him, an untapped potential. He felt that the changes the doctor made in him would allow him to help people in ways he had only dreamed of until then. Jerry didn't want to sign on with the doctor's new crusade.

Dr. Patyaloo made an example of him. It took hours for the minotaur to die, and there was nothing Katherine could do to save him. Instead, she swam to the mainland. She didn't much care for water before her modification, but she hated it now. Maybe it was the cat in her, or maybe it was the association with Jerry's death, she couldn't tell. When she made landfall, she made her way through the jungle to the nearest city where she arranged for transportation home.

Katherine had moved to Cobalt City, not only because that was where the heroes went, but also to distance herself from her earlier life. There were so few things worth remembering fondly in it. As much as she loved India, she had never gone back.

Not until now, that is.

There was no denying that India was where she had found herself transported. The calls of the birds, the vine-covered trees, the distant banana plantation, the ruined temple she found herself sitting in: all undeniably India.

And worse, the body she was in was not her own. Close, of course, but not entirely the same. The big, pointy teeth were new, for instance.

Instead of the black leather corset and matching lace-up leather pants, she was wearing some kind of orange silk body wrap that fit like a jog bra, leaving her finely haired mid-section exposed above the thong and a loincloth combination around her waist. Not a bad look if you were going for the cover girl on some bad sixties sci-fi novel. This had to be Rakshasha's body, she reasoned. Nothing else could explain the combination of similarities and differences. Well, nothing else other than a heavy-duty illusion, or some other kind of induced hallucination.

Wild Kat had read Dr. Shadow's addendum to the report, with its mention of the King in Yellow and the Mirror of Shadows he protected. She had been prepared on some level for a confrontation of one kind or another with her reflected self since its discovery. But swapping places with Rakshasha had never been part of the equation. Judging from the evidence before her, however, that was precisely what had happened. And somehow, Simon's deal with Augustus Dei had been the key.

Scanning her surroundings, she saw the outer walls of a building about two miles away on a hilltop. She had to start somewhere, and at least there she might be able to narrow down her location. Katherine set off at a healthy trot, not so fast that she couldn't look out for hidden dangers, but still much faster than most things traveling by foot.

When she thought about it, she should have seen this all coming. She was closer to Simon than just about anyone other than Manuel or the Tesla kids, and with the twins gone and everything going on, or more accurately, not going on between her and Manuel, Simon had a lot of alone time on his hands. The fact that he didn't even sleep compounded issues. She knew Simon kept busy, what with band rehearsals and fighting crime, but didn't he need more than that? Didn't everyone? Had she given Simon's boredom and isolation that much thought before?

She had never had a friend who was dead, or in Simon's case, undead. Weren't the undead supposed to be dark, brooding loners? Or were they simply dark and brooding because they were alone? Maybe all a vampire really needed was a hug and a cup of tea to just "get over it." She had tried, she knew she had, to reach out to Simon, but somehow acting if he were alive and, well, normal, had just made things more awkward. He couldn't exactly go out to dinner and not get noticed. He didn't even need to eat, so why would he go out for dinner in the first place? With the exception of Stardust, everyone else could have some semblance of a normal social life, and Stardust at least had his family to go home to.

Wasn't it only natural that Simon should want his life back? And how desperate would he really have to be to not read the fine print? Katherine was certain that he couldn't have known the result of his bargain with Augustus Dei. She had seen his reaction when Dr. Shadow mentioned his name. It made her wonder what was going on back home. It also made her wonder where Mister Grey was now and if he was happy, if he even knew what had happened.

Her reverie was cut short a few hundred yards short of the big, stone building on the hill when three gunshots sounded from the undergrowth. She sensed their trajectory with a combination of sound triangulation and raw, feline instinct and went low. The bullets passed harmlessly overhead, one of them creasing the fur across her back.

Two of the gunmen broke and ran when their shots missed. Smart, since she had been headed in their direction anyway and would have been hard-pressed to miss them. The third gunman stayed in place, hidden by the broad-leafed elephant ear plants, but she heard him chamber another round, so she had an idea where he was. Wild Kat turned on the speed and disabled the first shooter almost before she could think about it. The second shooter veered to the right, and she took him with a pounce, crouching on his back, her claws extended. She had to remind herself that on this world just because someone was shooting at her, that didn't necessarily make them a bad guy. Rakshasha was a killer, a man-eater, the terror of the sub-continent. But safety first, she decided. She punched the shooter in the back of the head, rendering him quickly unconscious.

Now, time to deal with the third shooter. Wild Kat stalked through the undergrowth, and saw an unobstructed path from her to the rear of where the shooter had positioned himself. But there was something else. She could pick up the scent of fresh dirt. Someone had been digging. And there were branches missing from a tree a few yards away, the wounds still fresh. Someone had gone to the trouble of building a pit trap, probably to catch her. It was kind of quaint. But she didn't feel like playing around anymore.

Katherine picked out the shooter by the smell of sweat and gunpowder and leapt the distance easily. When the inevitable shot came, she was able to contort around the bullet and still stick her landing, though this body felt slower than she was used to. One quick claw lashed out and ripped the rifle from the hunter's grasp. The second set of claws retracted, and she cuffed the blonde, hard-faced target into unconsciousness. Slower, she thought, but stronger. That was valuable information.

Katherine searched him quickly. He was a professional hunter. She knew the type. In among his spare ammo and survival tools, she found a waterproof pack with his German passport and other travel documents. In among those, she found a small ad clipped from a mercenary magazine. It promised ten million in U.S. currency to the person who could kill Rakshasha in the ultimate test of hunting skills. An address in Calcutta was provided to contact for details.

How wonderful that someone out there thought she was the most dangerous game. This wouldn't make things any easier, she thought. Katherine took the ammunition from all the guns and finished the trip to the nearby building a little more carefully than she had started.

It took Katherine a while to recognize where she was once she got there. The last time she had been here, the palace had been in ruins, deserted. But someone had gone to great efforts to restore it. Perhaps in this world, it had never fallen into disrepair in the first place. She knew Rakshash lived here. If Katherine had not fled India herself, she might have done the same. True to her instincts, the guards on the wall above the door shouted to get it opened as soon as she stepped into view. Ah, a nice home and lackeys. This Rakshasha knew how to live. Too bad she was a bloodthirsty murderer.

As she made her way through the lushly gardened front courtyard towards the main building, she was aware of every eye on her. The guards, the gardener, no doubt everyone who worked here, was terrified of her. What should she tell them? "Hey, I'm not the cannibalistic tyrant you used to know. Let's all sing campfire songs!" No…that wouldn't work. It was probably best not to say anything. Instead, she trusted her instincts to lead her to living quarters. Maybe a shower or something would help get rid of the alien smell of this new body, a scent she could only assume was a product of her all-meat diet.

She found the opulent bedchamber after only a few tries. But she was completely unprepared for what she found there.

Seated on a heavy wooden box seat, enjoying the approaching sunset with a bottle of tequila, was Jerry. He was still a minotaur, and he looked unsurprised to see her. He was wearing only jeans, his brick-red back bare and covered with long, parallel scars. Claw marks. Her claw marks. "The hunt went well, I take it?" he said, a cruel smile on his broad face.

"No complaints," she managed to say. "One of them built a pit trap."

His eyes widened in surprise. "Really? That was nice of him to keep you guessing like that."

"I thought so," she said. She almost meant it.

"I have a group of Japanese sport hunters flying in next week," he said, turning back to the sunset. "Nothing until then, so you might as well relax for now."

He arranged the hunts, put out the ads, brought in fresh meat for Rakshasha. Of course he did. If she had never left India, if Jerry had not died, if she were a psycho, it all made sense in a twisted kind of way. She remembered what she could of the other Protectorate's dark reflections. None of them had gone to Cobalt City, not once they had powers. In her world, you went to Cobalt City to be a hero. But over here, you didn't have to travel far to be a monster. Maybe, she thought, that was the case everywhere.

"Oh, and we'll have to make arrangements for another serving girl," Jerry said, not taking his eyes off the pink and purple clouds.

"Really?" she said, trying to sound disinterested.

"She refused me. I had to…correct her," he said. There was no emotion in his voice. No anger, no passion, no regret, nothing. It was the most chilling thing she had ever heard. "I kind of let go and lost control of myself. You know how I can get. Anyway, they finally got the mess cleaned up about half an hour ago, so you can use the bathroom again without slipping around too much."

Katherine maintained her composure, but she was still glad that Jerry wasn't watching her. She wasn't sure how her reflection would have reacted to the news, and she didn't want to tip him off that there had been a change. Jerry's skin was hard as granite, and she didn't want to force a stand up fight if she could help it. There were too many variables. One being that this wasn't Jerry. Not really. The pacifist minotaur she knew was dead. He had been dead for a long time. Careful to keep her step casual, she went and stood behind him.

"Jerry?" she asked.

"What is it, babe?" he said, turning languidly to face her, his breath heavy with tequila.

Her claws were only four inches long, but they were long enough. With lightning fast speed, she drove one finger deep into Jerry's brain through his left eye. The minotaur barely had the time to register surprise or some sense of betrayal before he died. Then his body jerked, and collapsed without a sound. "I'm sorry," she said, choking back a tear she knew she shouldn't shed, "I thought you were someone else."

Wild Kat went to the bathroom and cleaned up. She felt the bile rising over the execution, shaking with the release of tension, with the pain of having to lose Jerry a second time, at the cruel irony of her having to be his executioner. She sat there on the sparkling clean tiles until the sun had finally set, and then went off to find a computer.

Her eyes avoided the window box and its grisly occupant, but the smell of death was already heavy on the air. Katherine had to shift back to her human form as she searched for what she needed. Finally, she found an office of sorts behind a huge teak door concealed underneath silk wall hangings. The computer with its satellite uplink enabled her to find most of what she wanted within half an hour. With the scale of villainy perpetrated by her team's shadow selves, it wasn't hard to find them. She considered finding some way of e-mailing Edirin or Jaccob, but wasn't certain of her relationships on this world, and didn't want to run the risk of exposing them to a spying underling.

No, if there was any way out of this, it lay with Doctor Shadow. The ancient magician was the best chance they all had of getting home, and he could only be reached in person. Ruling over an undead army in a kingdom of eternal night, he would be found in the Valley of the Kings in Egypt. No one who entered the "land of the sunless sky" came out alive. At least that was the general opinion. But she wasn't just anyone. She just hoped that she wasn't the only one who had been swapped with their evil counterpart. If Shade she found

Shade there instead of Doctor Shadow, they were both in for an unpleasant surprise.

Rooting through the desk, Katherine found several sets of keys and an envelope full of money. She decided the expensive SUV would be the best choice for a long overland excursion, especially if she took several spare containers of gasoline. She took the keys and money into the bedroom where she endeavored to find clothes more conservative than the harem girl outfit she was now wearing. It was not easy going. Rakshasha, she decided, liked trashy clothes. She was at least able to find a pair of lycra shorts and a blousy top that didn't scream "jump me!" Probably something Rakshasha wore to watch peasants being tortured. She decided to keep the silk torso wrap. It had taken a little getting used to, but now that she had a little fur on her belly, she preferred having the wind blow through it.

On her way out, she stopped a servant who would not look up from the floor as if the secrets of the universe were etched on the pavement stones. "There is a mess in the bed chamber," she said, trying to sound cool and imperious. "See that it is cleared up. And do not expect me back for a while. I am going out of town."

"When will mistress be back?" the hunchbacked old servant said.

"Never," she said, "if you are lucky."

She left him there to puzzle it out. By the time she was out the gate, they would no doubt find Jerry slumped over dead. If they had a lick of sense, they would all be gone by morning. And if wishes were horses, she thought.

By then she hoped to be far away from this place. It had been her second trip to India. It looked to end like the last one, with her fleeing across the border to the west. But she refused to see it as a pattern. This time it was different. This time, she planned to leave the planet altogether.

Chapter Thirteen

Tensions were running understandably high at The Keep. The staff suspected that something was going on, but had no idea what. There was something in the way the Protectorate inspected the building, almost like it was new. And Snowflake was surprised when he woke to see a confused Worm Queen standing over him, looking at him like she had never met him. She had a jet-black worm about four feet long coiled around her neck like a slimy feather boa. Its head section was pulsing slowly, disconcertingly, and Worm Queen herself had a thousand mile stare.

"You are Snowflake," was all she said.

"Last time I checked," he said, more than a little disturbed by the suddenness of the encounter. "Is this about the chai? I'll pay you back. I promise. Just…just let me find my pants."

"Your money does not concern me," she said. She took one more quick glance over the inside of the bunkroom and, perhaps finding nothing else of interest, she turned on a heel and left.

Once she was out of the room, Snowflake pinched himself to make sure he wasn't still asleep. It hurt, and would probably leave a bruise under his fur. The fact that this was not a dream was not comforting. He got up and locked the door, and, as an afterthought, jammed a chair under the handle. It wouldn't help if any team members really wanted in, he realized. But it was all he could think of at the moment. So much for going back to sleep, he thought.

A few floors below, Jaccob chased the two staff techs out of the lab so that he could take a closer look at his armor. He was dismayed that the gauntlet blasters had no disintegrate setting. How was he expected to disintegrate things and people without the right weapon systems? He had, however figured out the helmet interface and had learned how to activate the tracking feature on the communicators. Only one signal was picked up outside the building, and he keyed a handheld tracker to the signature. The new and improved Wild Kat had taken it from him, determined to track down the escapees before they tipped off any of the local "heroes."

Sundiatta and Shade were avoiding each other, each wanting to maneuver for a bigger piece of the world then they had conquered back home. While the mage locked himself away to project his consciousness over Egypt to survey the situation, the other one had taken over the computer room downstairs to monitor everything he could get on West Africa. Both of them had already lost track of their primary objective, and that was to locate and neutralize any potential resistance before they lost the element of surprise. Jaccob hoped that after a quick world civics lesson, they would take care of business.

Lazarus hadn't left the conference room. He stood like a statue, eyes closed. When his lady-friend asked what was wrong, all he would saw was "I'm not alone in here." It was probably for the best if he didn't go out much in public for a while anyway. Of all the ones replaced, Lazarus had undergone the only obvious physical change. Explaining his suddenly fleshy status could provoke unwelcome questions.

At least the worm girl was on board with the program. She had called up some kind of brain worm that was letting her read minds, and had taken off to get the lay of the building. She had found the labs, and the living quarters, and had picked up enough of the staff's thoughts to keep them from getting too suspicious. Jaccob would have liked to evacuate the building, but it was a bad option. Didn't want anyone wondering what was going on in the Keep. Restricting access of sensitive areas was enough to give them room to move while still giving them privacy.

Jaccob was keeping his eyes on the prize. And he was keeping his eye on his back, too. He had come this far on his own, and the idea of trusting this group of power-hungry competitors was not in his nature. Had Augustus Dei not approached him with new worlds to conquer, he wouldn't have considered this alliance for a second. Trust was a weakness. And this Jaccob Stevens was anything but weak. A quick retrofit of the armor, a few disintegrator beams, and he could reinvent himself. People did it all the time. And maybe he could ditch the name Stardust, call himself something cool like, for instance, Blackstar, Synistar, or Starfury. Hmm…Starfury. He liked the sound of that. Maybe he could put some heat beam eyes into the visor. That would be cool. He grabbed a drafting pad off the worktop and started looking at design options.

He was so intent on solving power coupling issues, that he didn't even hear the door open behind him. "Stardust," he heard the freaky worm lady say. He immediately lost focus on the circuit relay he had visualized.

"It's Deathstar," he said, then he smiled and shrugged, jotting down what he could remember of the relay on the drafting pad. "At least it's Deathstar for now."

"No, it's Stardust," she corrected him. "And you should call me Worm Queen, not freaky worm lady."

Jaccob looked up and saw the thin, black worm coiled around

her neck. The worm's head pulsed as if it could tell he was watching it. He felt a lump in his throat, and he tried to keep a reign on his thoughts. He didn't know Lenore...check that...Worm Queen that well, but he did seem to remember that there were very few limits on what her worms were capable of. The raw potential made him nervous.

"Sorry," he said. "Worm Queen. What can I do for you?"

"The three who escaped," she said. "What did you find of them in the computer?"

"Nothing," he said. "There were no personnel files on any of them. There were a few case reports written by someone called Archon, and a few written by someone called Velvet. One of them called the teleporter Gallows, and I found some references to him, and guess what? He's a teleporter. But as for write-ups on capabilities, power descriptions, weaknesses, favorite movies, it's all a big blank."

"Or the files have been purged," she said.

Jaccob shrugged, "I jumped on looking for the data pretty fast, but after reading a few of Archon's reports, he might have been smart enough to get in and sabotage the records. There might have been some kind of failsafe put in the system for just this kind of situation. I don't know. But the records are gone, so we're working in the dark. I suspect that he's disabled the tracking devices on the communicators as well. I was only able to find that one signal."

"So three renegades, but one signal," Worm Queen said. "Then who is Wild Kat tracking?"

"Who?"

"Wild Kat. Rakshasha?" she said, her voice crisp.

"No idea. It's probably a trap," he said. "Or it could be someone else who has a communicator, someone we don't know about yet, who they haven't been able to contact."

"And if it's a trap?"

Stardust smiled. "Then whoever laid the trap is in for a nasty surprise. They have one big, scary, pissed-off kitty heading their way."

Worm Queen shared his smile. It was a pleasant image. She had no love for Wild Kat, seeing her as the Alpha female in this small group, but the idea of tearing into some unsuspecting local warmed her heart. "Then it's a win-win, isn't it?" she said.

"I can't argue with that," Jaccob said.

She seemed coy, like she was toying with him, like she knew something he didn't. Worm Queen lingered in the doorway, watching him, waiting for him to figure it out. Out of the corner of his eye, he kept seeing the pulsing head of the black worm, and it was making it very difficult for him to concentrate on the armor upgrades. Finally, he couldn't take it anymore. "Was there something else?"

"Have you read your own file yet?" she said, a sly smile on her lips.

"No. Is there anything interesting?"

"Well, everyone knows Jaccob Stevens is Stardust, and he lives here in Cobalt City," she said.

"Does he have his own house or does he stay in the clubhouse with the rest of the good scouts," he sneered.

"He has his own building," she said. "Starcom Tower, just uptown a bit. Very successful business doing communications technology from what I could figure out."

"What an idiot," Jaccob said. "Doesn't he know the real money is in weapon technology?"

"And he has a family."

That was a surprise. "I have a family?"

"A wife and two little grubs," she said, a mocking tone in her voice.

"A wife, huh?" he said. "Is she a looker?"

"Not my type. Blonde, perky, too pink in the cheeks, you know?" she said. Oh yeah, he remembered. She likes her boyfriends a little less ambulatory.

"Well what do you know?" he said, putting down his pencil. "Maybe when I finish up here, I should go home and pay wifey a visit."

"How very Norman Rockwell of you," she said as she slithered out of the room.

Jaccob Stevens wasn't the only one in Cobalt City thinking about relationships at the moment. Across town, Manuel had been trying to call Katherine on her cell, but finally decided that she had turned if off. Huntsman had told him about the morning meeting, and it was likely that she wouldn't want to be disturbed. But that was hours ago, and she still hadn't returned any of his messages. He couldn't blame her for being angry, but she had to understand that he had done nothing wrong. Surely, she would be able recognize Libertine. She was a reserve member of the team, after all.

But noon was fast approaching. No calls. Manuel was getting desperate. He was considering revealing one of his biggest secrets to Katherine. He sat in a deck chair on the roof of his building in the Hollow, watching the clouds roll in, turning his secret over and over in his hands. It was a Protectorate communicator.

He wasn't supposed to have one, but Simon had given it to him just in case. You never could tell when an emergency would arise and it would be all hands on deck. But he noticed that Simon hadn't given one to any of the other solo heroes in the city. And he was pretty sure that Simon hadn't told anyone else about the gift.

If he used it to contact Katherine, there was no doubt that she would answer. But there would be hell to pay. Not only was it a misuse of emergency channels, but it also revealed that he had betrayed her trust. In the end, it would most likely do more harm than good. If he could just be patient, wait for her to return his calls, maybe run into her at Schrodinger's Cup, then they could work it all out. Things had been going so well. Best not to mess things up further, he thought.

But still, with the communicator, he could talk to her now...

Stupid idea, he knew, but there it was.

He tucked the communicator into the breast pocket of his mocha-colored suede over shirt and pulled out his cell phone again. No harm in leaving another message, was there?

And then, without warning, Wild Kat raced up onto the roof of his building, like an improbable dolphin breaching. She landed on the edge of roof and stared at him in confusion with a small device blinking in her hand. Manuel cancelled the phone call and tucked the phone back into his pocket.

"Katherine," he said, not expecting to see her so soon. Not even in his most optimistic scenarios.

"Yes," she said cautiously.

"Listen, about last night, there was a misunderstanding..." he began.

"You have a communicator?" she said, cutting him off as if she hadn't even been listening. She checked the device in her hand again.

Oh shit, he thought. She wasn't here to talk to him. This wasn't a reconciliation. She was investigating a security breach. He should have guessed when she came racing up the side of his building rather than calling or using the elevator like a normal person. Like he really knew that many normal people, he reminded himself. "Yeah, about that. I know I shouldn't have one, but Simon thought in case of an emergency I might be needed," he said quickly.

"Simon," she said. She took a short step towards him and tucked the blinking device into her belt.

"Mister Grey, whatever, he gave it to me. Recently, I might add, so it's not like I've been concealing anything from you. It just hadn't come up yet."

Wild Kat turned her head slightly to the side, sizing him up. There was something in her eyes, something new, something...predatory. He noticed her nostrils flare slightly. Was she *smelling* him? Had some kind of switch flipped? He had to admit, it wasn't an entirely frightening prospect. "Mister Grey must have a very high opinion of your power," she said finally.

"Power?" he said, feeling his ears grow red. Great. Now I'm blushing, he thought. *Muy* macho. "Not my power so much as my skills, I suspect."

"You are very...skilled?" she said, a slight smile, her predatory gaze kicking into a new, unexpected gear.

"Well, I don't mean to brag, but...wait. Aren't you angry with me?"

"I don't know," she said. "Should I be?"

"No," he said quickly. "It was just when you didn't return my calls, I was, well, I was a little worried that through a little misunderstanding, that I had made you angry."

Wild Kat closed on Manuel, circling him, looking him over closely. He felt the hairs on his scalp tingle, and seconds later, she drew a claw lightly across the back of his neck. "You and I, we are close, aren't we?" she said in his ear, her voice husky with a hint of a purr.

"I'd like to think so," he said, trying to keep cool. "But we could be closer if you'd only let me in."

It was strange hearing himself say that. Him! Manuel de la Vega, the Latin playboy! True, it wasn't the first time he had used that line, but it was, however, the first time it had not just been a line. Maybe he was growing up. As long as he didn't have to give up his action figure collection, maybe it was worth it.

He didn't know what had come over Katherine. Maybe it was jealousy. Maybe the realization that she might have him stolen from her before things got off the ground, the threat of another super-heroine being interested in him tipped her into action. He didn't know. But he liked the change. It was nice being the hunted and not the hunter for a change.

"You could provide me with an interesting distraction," she said, snaking a claw through his dark, slightly curly hair.

"I'm not just some piece of meat," he said. He tried to make it sound light, but he knew it came off as a little defensive. Was that all he was to her? Maybe the observations of Libertine and his barista friend were not far off the mark. Was he only a fling? And was that what he wanted? No, he thought. Certainly not. Not in this case at least. He was in danger, he knew. It wouldn't' take much for him to be in over his head emotionally. Wow! Now he knew how his former lady-friends must have felt. And maybe that was it. Maybe Katherine wasn't really interested in him. Maybe she wanted to teach him a lesson, treat him like she imagined he had treated all his prior dates. It made a twisted kind of sense.

He was never going to understand women, he decided. Maybe he should just get a dog. Something small, though. And short haired. He didn't want to deal with heavy shedding or something that would chew up his leather furniture.

"Mmmm…a piece of meat," she said, her eyes sparkling. "That would be okay too."

"You know, that doesn't really turn me on," he said. But strangely, he found that in being objectified, his body had betrayed his pride and was, in fact, being turned on right that very moment. "Okay…maybe it does. So what do we do now?"

"Would you come to the Keep so that we may continue this?" she said while placing her hand on his chest.

"I could do that," he said. "Do you mean now?"

"Don't keep me waiting," she said, going to the edge of the roof again. She winked at him. "Keep me waiting and you will be punished."

She disappeared over the edge at top speed and raced off in the direction of the Keep.

Yeah, he decided. He liked this sudden change in Wild Kat. Deciding that since he was off shift for the evening, he might as well put in some crime-fighting hours after dark, he changed into his Gato Loco costume before leaving. As an afterthought, he took his police handcuffs with him. He knew a few guys on the force who used them in their off hours. And if there was the possibility of punishment, it was best to be prepared.

Wild Kat was back at the Keep before Gato Loco was even finished tucking his handcuffs into a pouch on his belt. Arranging for a visitor pass for her guest was more complicated because she had not thought to ask for his name. That would have made the conversation a bit more awkward, she realized, but it would have been handy. Fortunately, once she told the receptionist that she was expecting a special friend and that he was to be allowed access up to her quarters immediately, a light went on in the receptionist's eyes. Gato Loco and Wild Kat had been the Ross and Rachel of the Protectorate for weeks. Of course they weren't dating, but they both wore black leather, liked cats, and beat up criminals. It was a very small community. Mindy, the receptionist told Katherine that her friend would be ushered right up and winked knowingly. When the charade was up, Katherine would kill Mindy herself. It would be fun.

Chapter Fourteen

Finding the special door into Starcom Tower had been a piece of cake compared to opening it. If he hadn't been wearing the key designed to fit the lock, Jaccob would have never gotten in. Even with the hardware to access the system, it still took him seven minutes and twenty-four seconds. He hated to wait. Waiting was for the weak. But thankfully, breaking into highly secure buildings was second nature. A coordinated program of corporate espionage had made him the man he was today, though in another world. If not for his nefarious ways, he could have never turned a major northwest city into his own, personal Camelot. You didn't become the undisputed technocratic ruler of the west coast by playing nice. And you didn't get there by waiting, either.

But any violent impulses that waiting bred in him diminished when he saw the lab spaces hidden behind the highly secured portal. Stardust may be a doofus, but he was a smart doofus. He had been somewhat dismissive of his host's inventive genius after his first pass at the armor, but seeing all the works in progress in the lab changed his mind. With all the modules ready to begin testing on the suit or in other devices, it would take him days to reverse engineer everything he saw.

He was so excited by all the toys that he almost forgot why he was there. A picture of a stunning blonde with a great smile above a workbench reminded him. "Elizabeth," he said, touching the black aluminum picture frame with gauntleted hands. She looked just like a girl he knew in college. She was so smart, such a gift for business administration, that he had to have her. They only went out on a few dates, and things were going okay. But at that time he only wanted her for her mind, and she wanted something else entirely. She saw him as a meal ticket. He was no one's meal ticket. He had her kidnapped and downloaded her personality and skill set into his recently developed experimental software. Now he still had her for her mind.

He couldn't remember what happened to her physical body. He was pretty sure she was in an institution somewhere, but couldn't remember which one. Not that he cared, really. She was just a shell now anyway.

But this Elizabeth was no shell. It would be a nice change to play house. Maybe he could get a home-cooked meal now and again, too.

He found the stairs to the living quarters and made his way up, stepping out into the softly lit foyer. Across from him was the elevator, and the small antechamber opened up into the living room off to his right. The apartment was lit from the midday sun outside, but the tinted glass cut down the glare dramatically, making the room warm without being hot. He made his way through the ground floor, looking for some sign of life in the kitchen, dining room, media room, and study, but found no one. Shouldn't Elizabeth have a pot roast on or something? What the hell good was it having a wife if she couldn't have dinner on the table when he came home. Admittedly, it was still early in the afternoon, but it didn't look like any preparations had been made.

He opened up the refrigerator and couldn't even find any beer. It was shaping up to be one of those days. He did uncover a few brownies and took them. Jaccob flipped up the visor and walked around the first floor again, taking it all in while he snacked. He was getting brownie crumbs on the nice carpet, but he didn't let it get him down. Accidents happen.

Into the media room, he ran a finger across the selection of DVD titles, amazed at all the titles he didn't recognize, but even more amazed at the ones he did know. He wondered if every fragment of reality had some version of *Weekend at Bernie's*. He also wondered what the hell a "Scooby-Doo" was and why someone would make a movie about it.

"Honey," he called softly as he made his way to the second floor. "Your tin soldier of love is here. Come out, come out, wherever you are."

The second floor had a pair of kids' bedrooms with cool holographic ceilings. When he had the time, he was going to have to figure out how those worked. But as much as he liked the bedrooms, he was disappointed to find no kids in them. He even checked under the beds and in the closets. Maybe school wasn't out yet, or maybe the little ankle biters had soccer or something, he thought. But the silence made him wonder.

The stairs to the top floor opened to a small indoor pool and spa done in a grotto theme. A canopy of some transparent but alloy-tough material provided the roof for the pool area. He had considered coming in through there instead of trying to hack the security, but a density reading from his onboard systems showed him how futile that would be. Plus, the sight of Stardust trying to blast his way into his own house was likely to raise some eyebrows.

The spacious master suite was off the pool area, and he was beginning to think it was empty as well, until he noticed a seam in the back of the walk-in closet. He ran a quick space management routine, and realized that there was a ten by ten room back behind the closet. A panic room. Of course there was a panic room. And much to his disappointment, it was on a shielded system with a manual lock, so he would not be able to override it from the outside. He found the fiber optic camera and stared daggers at it. "You know, it would be a lot easier on you if you didn't make me wait. I've already had a really long day."

"It's about to get longer," said a hard, female voice behind him. Stardust turned and saw the woman who had escaped from the conference room earlier in the day. She was standing in the doorway to the bedroom, the hood of her cloak low, her hands clenched at her side.

"Hey there, cupcake," he said. "You'll just have to wait your turn. I'm dealing with the missus just now."

"You'll deal with me now or I'll open you like a tin of deviled ham," she said. She didn't move from the doorway, but he was pretty sure she could close on him fast. Not fast enough to avoid getting shot at, but still, pretty fast.

He realized his visor was still open and hoped he didn't have brownie crumbs in his beard. He didn't want to look stupid while he was kicking this little cookie's ass. "I'm afraid you've made a mistake. I live here. I'm going to have to ask you to get out of my home before I call the authorities."

Velvet smirked, calling his bluff. "Feel better getting that out of your system?"

"Just stating the facts," he said, enjoying the charade. "You're an intruder on my property. I believe I have the right to eject you by force if you resist," he said. To emphasize his point, he flipped down his visor and warmed up the weapon systems. He really wished he had found time to finish the disintegrator beams, but beggars can't be choosers. There was always tomorrow.

"And I'm working security for your wife," Velvet said, not giving an inch. "I'm responding to a domestic disturbance complaint. I think I have to ask you politely to leave the premises and cool down before this situation escalates."

"I don't feel like leaving," he said. He looked her over carefully. High-density readings in her gauntlets, mixed density reading on the cloak, but nothing that looked like it would present a problem. And she had run so quickly this morning.

"That's okay," she said, clenching her fists, "I don't feel like being polite."

"So we're at an impasse," Jaccob said, squaring off.

"Unless you intend to cooperate," Velvet said. "Personally, I'm hoping you'll resist."

He didn't answer. Instead, he fired off a deadly pair of bolts from his gauntlets. One seemed to glance off the fabric of her cloak, but the other shot hit her square in the chest, sending her sprawling at the edge of the pool.

She didn't get back up.

He waited, watching closely, his gauntlets raised for another blast, but nothing happened. Jaccob took a few steps closer, but still nothing. He popped the targeting cursor over her prone figure, and scanned for life signs. Nothing. How anti-climactic, he thought.

Jaccob had figured on an easy fight. I mean, she was only a woman, but this was pathetic. He took a few steps out of the bedroom onto the pool terrace and felt something crunch under his foot. As he watched, the image of Velvet shimmered and disappeared.

There was a sudden, slight impact on the middle of his back and his armor started powering down. "Tag, bitch," Velvet said, standing in the shadows just beyond the bedroom door. She had sneaked up behind him and distracted him with a cheap hologram. He wasn't sure what she had put on his back, but in seconds, his armor batteries were down 50% and falling fast.

He tried to override the power drain, but there was an external device causing the problems, and it couldn't be shut down remotely. And while he was trying to figure a way around the problem, Velvet was wasting no time. She landed a series of punches squarely into his face and kidney. Both were protected by armor, but she focused her attacks into strong, precision blows. Without his power at full, he was considerably slower, and hitting him was a whole hell of a lot easier. With that in mind, she was able to sacrifice some of her considerable skill for a boost of her already impressive damage. He would definitely bruise, and she might even loosen up a tooth or two if the assault continued.

Two more punches landed while he was planning an exit strategy, staggering him back towards the edge of the pool. It was no good, he thought. A few more blows like that, and the fight was over. In the armor, she would be able to keep up with any break he made for the exit several floors down. And with the water of the pool behind him...

And that's the answer, Jaccob realized. He took a quick step and fell into the pool, letting the water wash over him. The suit was designed to handle the depths of space. It had contained atmosphere. A little water wasn't going to hurt it. The same couldn't be said for the device the cloaked harridan had sucker-punched him with. It shorted out almost immediately.

From under the surface of the water, he watched the suit's power reading climb slowly. Velvet was not going to join him in the pool, or she would have done so by now. With his indefinite air supply, and her cloak weighing her down, the advantage was clearly his. But she was waiting out there. He could see her through the water, just beyond the lip of the pool. He fired off two shots, but her cloak easily deflected both. This has turned into an unpleasant stalemate, he thought to himself. And if I try to force the fight and she has another one of those power-draining devices on her, I'm right back in the drink, he thought.

No home-cooked meal was worth this. Jaccob took a density reading from around the walls of the pool and looked for the softest spot. His luck held, and he was able to find a relatively thin area of the outside wall near the back of the grotto. The gauntlets unleashed a blazing firestorm of destruction, and he flew towards the damage as fast as his propulsion systems would allow. Two more blasts right as he hit the wall sent him soaring out into the afternoon sky almost twenty floors up amid a shower of concrete and chlorinated water.

There was no way for Velvet to follow, and she had to content herself with watching him fly off empty handed. And maybe the damage he had caused making his escape would serve to alert some of the city's independent heroes that something was rotten in the state of Denmark.

"Does it look like he's coming back?" Elizabeth said over the apartment's intercom system.

"Not immediately, but I suspect that he might make a return trip before too long," Velvet said. "I would like to recommend, yet again, that you find somewhere else to sleep tonight."

The door to the panic room hissed open, and Elizabeth came out, still shaking slightly. She had donned a suit of armor that resembled her husband's, but even a cursory glance showed it had no offensive capabilities. And it didn't appear to make Elizabeth feel any safer. "I could have taken care of myself, you know," she said, her chin raised.

"If you say so," Velvet said, her eyes on the retreating silhouette of the Stardust armor.

"This suit comes equipped with force fields. They would have protected me," Elizabeth said. A note of defiance tinged her voice.

Good, strong, determined Elizabeth Stevens, Velvet thought. Master of the business world. Nothing can scare her off, and she doesn't need anyone's protection. Velvet remembered it all vividly from her brief security contract. "Would your force fields have protected you from that?" she said, pointing to the huge hole in the wall of the swimming pool, through which the last of the water was draining.

"Yes," she said. But Velvet could tell that she wasn't so sure.

Velvet turned and looked at her evenly, her voice calm. "Then what would you like me to tell your children if he comes back and your force fields *don't* protect you? What would you like me to tell Jaccob when he gets back and finds out what someone did to you wearing his body?"

Elizabeth stared in horror at Velvet, her eyes wide and brimming with tears, her jaw trying to form words that she could not find. Finally, the shock of her situation, and her responsibility to her children kicked in. The tears broke free, but a hint of the sensible businesswoman that Velvet had come to actually like rose to the surface.

"I suppose I should pack a few items quickly and meet the children at my sister's," she said.

"Good idea," Velvet said, watching the now distant Stardust vanish into the gathering clouds. "I might not be able to come and rescue you again."

Chapter Fifteen

Long before he had adopted the name Seth Umbra, long before he made the decision to take an active, visible role in the world as Doctor Shadow, he had another, ancient name. When a life spans thousands of years, names become like the shell of a lobster, outgrown, discarded, and never reflected upon again. And so it was with great confusion that he found himself looking over a scene that could have happened thousands of years ago. Below the black sky of perpetual shadow, the Valley of Kings bustled with activity, and he stood on the high balcony of an opulent suite of rooms overlooking it all. He wondered, for just a second, if he had gone back to the height of the Egyptian empire, but no...the living quarters were sleek, like something out of an issue of *Modern Architecture* from 1960 where Dean Martin would have been very comfortable. And who would have put a penthouse apartment in a tomb, anyway?

Stationed just inside the suite doors stood a contingent of eight well-appointed skeletons, their dry bones polished to a high luster. As he approached for a further inspection, their heads turned and tracked him, their finger bones clicking like beetles on the hilt of their swords. They made no move to attack him, but it was clear to him that they registered his appearance. So they weren't just for decoration, he guessed. As a precaution, he turned invisible, but their hollow eye sockets stayed on his form, even as he floated soundlessly above the polished stone floor, first one way then another.

Lovely, Doctor Shadow thought, undead warriors who can see the invisible. He could tell that he was going to like it here. He returned to the balcony, and let his gaze pass through the ancient stones. A few minutes of careful observation confirmed many of his worst suspicions. The bustling crowd below and within the building was all skeletons. Some hauled blocks of stone while working on new construction; others were armed with all manner of weapons. These marched in a tight, protective cordon around what had once been a tomb. But the Valley of the Kings was a tomb no longer. It was a city of the dead, a necropolis unlike any he had encountered before. And it was the seat of power to his own dark opposite, the being of pure evil that called itself Shade.

And this Shade seemed to have the same aversion to light that he had been cursed with. Softly glowing hieroglyphs ran in two rows, one just above head level, the other at waist level, and provided all the light he could ever need. The sky was a dome of shadow that blocked out even the harshest rays of the midday sun. The fact that the shadow shield still stood was testament to Shade's sorcery. A spell with that large an affected area and an apparently perpetual duration did not come cheaply. But with enough time concentrating, enough preparation, the right ritual, a dedicated and ancient mage could do just about anything. And that was one thing that Shade and Doctor Shadow had in common above all else: plenty of time to make the impossible happen.

This was the nature of alternate realities, Doctor Shadow knew. The further away from the point of deviation, the further apart the two alternatives were. Unwelcome in the land of the dead because of sides they took in an ancient war between gods, he and Shade were effectively immortal. Thousands of years living their own lives, each act taking them further away from center, all their powers derived from their studies, there was no telling how much they differed. Doctor Shadow didn't believe in polar opposites. Not when there were so many variables. But he could not deny that his darker self had seemed to master arts that Doctor Shadow found to be abhorrent.

Necromancy was a perfect illustration of that split.

As he prowled the halls, he realized that the hieroglyphs contained the personal history of the body he now occupied. While the story it told was by no means objective, it was more than he had been able to find out on his own. Starting near the front door where the vigilant skeleton guards watched his every move, and quickly winding deeper into the spacious suite, Doctor Shadow began to unravel the enigma that was Shade.

Under a different name, Shade had spent thousands of years sealed inside the Valley of the Kings as punishment. He had turned that time to his advantage and used his confinement as an opportunity to study the darker arts. When tomb raiders released him in 1002 AD, he poured forth with a black vengeance not seen since the fall of the Egyptian gods. Each death swelled the ranks of his unholy army as he spent almost two hundred years scouring the world for knowledge. Then, with a massive library of arcane texts and scrolls, he willingly sealed himself up in the Valley of Kings again.

The world thought that they were done with him, but they were wrong. Every few hundred years or so, Shade reappeared, spreading his shadow across the land like the wings of the angel of death, always on the lookout for more knowledge, always keen to remind the world why people feared the night. In 1933, he declared his research at an end, and he sought to conquer the world with his undead army. If not for an Austrian occultist named Hitler, Shade might have done just that. But using a combination of Kabalistic magic and powerful artifacts, the diminutive occultist and his team of specialists had driven him back to the Valley of Kings.

Shade spent decades licking his wounds, but he had one advantage that his nemesis did not: time. Eventually Hitler died, and the wards he placed were diminished. And once again, Shade began his plans of conquest. But this time, he was more cautious. The world had seen the birth of new, powerful beings, others like him who had risen above the herd of cattle who could, in time, challenge his place as rightful ruler of the world. He bade his time and kept tabs on this new plague of superhumans. Knowledge was power. He would rise again, and this time there would be no more surprises.

Doctor Shadow took it all in, this strange alternative history, and wondered how much was fact and how much was self-promotion. He passed from stone room to stone room, each with furniture that would make an antique dealer's heart beat out a Keith Moon drum solo. At the end of Shade's narrative, he found himself in what he could only call the map room.

Adjacent to the front parlor and the library, this small room was packed with tables stretched along all the walls. The entire civilized world was represented on realistic maps that looked like the world cut into rectangular sections and reduced to scale. Some that Doctor Shadow took to be covered in dust or spider-webs turned out instead to be covered in wispy miniature clouds. The maps radiated magic, as well they should. Each was part model, part satellite map, and updated continually. It was like a child's train set times a million. Doctor Shadow could barely tear his eyes away.

A center table featured North Africa and the Mediterranean in a greater scale. A dome of shadow covered an area hundreds of miles across, centered on the Valley of Kings. He reached out to touch the dome and was not overly surprised to see information display in glowing, magical text. Troop strength and placement was featured along with borders and supply centers and enemy troop locations and dozens of other menu options. "A computer," Doctor Shadow said, the pieces fitting together more naturally now as he realized that yes, it was a computer. Bulky, definitely, and extremely limited in its application, but there could be no denying it. Shade had constructed a tactical computer using magic. "Oh, I have to have one of these," he found himself saying.

The shadowed area he understood to be the core of his expanding empire. Outward in all directions, his area of conquest stretched, with provisional governors administrating in his place in key areas such as Fez in Morocco, and Jerusalem, Istanbul, and Kabul as well. Wherever it was hot, miserable, and life was hard, Shade had endeavored to make it harder. Doctor Shadow's fingers played about the map, pulling forth bits of information, getting a feel for the world he found himself temporarily trapped in. Down along the southern border of Sudan, a large army was massed, led by a warlord named Gravas Tet Amon whom Doctor Shadow had seen executed over five hundred years ago. He wondered if the warlord had been executed here too, or if he had drunk from the poison chalice of immortality as well.

Doctor Shadow's fingertip slipped across the dimly illuminated border and confirmed that Shade was not the only empire builder on this continent. Sandwiched between the shadow states of the necromantic mage and the ocean, another kingdom had grown to occupy everything else north of the Namib Desert. It was a recently expansionist country, only a few years into its objective of conquering all of Africa, and it had its own troops massed on the border across from the troops commanded by Gravas Tet Amon.

He knew immediately. It was D'habu, Edirin's homeland. It had gone from reclusive, technologically superior kingdom to expanding empire. Shade's army was dead set to roll in and leave no stone standing, and there was nothing Doctor Shadow could do to stop it.

A chaotic clatter sounded from a few rooms away, and the enigmatic mage put the problem of battle-lines on hold to investigate. The walls between him and the noise were like glass as he turned his gaze outward. There, near the front door to the suite, the skeletons had begun fighting amongst themselves. There was no motivation, no sensible reason that he could see, but a disturbing theory occurred to him, settling coldly in his gut.

He became incorporeal and drifted down, out into the permanent night of the Valley of Kings. All around him fights had begun to break out among the skeleton army. Small at first, these conflicts quickly grew from two person scuffles to outright street war involving upwards of a hundred skeletons in a single skirmish. The sounds of battle, of whistling spiked chains swinging through the air, of splintering dry bones, of heavy iron mauls crushing skulls and ancient stone echoed off the towering, carved walls.

"Well, that should resolve at least one problem," Doctor Shadow thought, as he returned to the suite where the two remaining chipped warriors hacked and thrust at each other, their companions already reduced to piles of inert bones. With telekinesis, the mage picked up a heavy-looking table and sent the final two guards to join the fate of the others with only a few quick blows. He pushed the bones into a neat pile in the corner to keep them out of the way. Then he double-checked to make sure that the door to the outside was securely barred and locked. No point in letting his guard down now, he decided.

Working deeper and deeper into the suite of rooms, Doctor Shadow was able to find a small sanctuary perfect for his purposes. He sat on a pile of saffron-colored pillows and let the emptiness overtake him. It was time to work on one of his other problems. He had some idea where Edirin should be, and that would be the closest location of the transported members of the Protectorate. Communicating with him was of utmost importance.

Doctor Shadow was certain that he alone had not been transmuted into this other world, into this other body. Why take the effort to exchange a powerful sorcerer and leave untouched his equally powerful associates? The economics of scale dictated that as many people as possible would be caught in the area of effect. Since the exchange was with his reflected self, then the Mirror of Shadows was a factor in some way. And if the mirror was a factor, then Archon, Gallows, and Velvet were most likely untouched. That was important. It would give him a link back home if he should need one. But while he could breach the dimensional barriers with but a thought, the challenge was not to get home, but to get everyone returned back to their own bodies.

And he was disappointed to admit that he had no idea how to go about doing that.

But at least he could endeavor to get the transplanted members of the Protectorate together again. From there, they could explore their options in more detail. The fact that Shade's standing army was self-destructing should make everyone's travel to the Valley of Kings far more convenient.

He pushed his telepathic range further than he was accustomed, and with determination born of thousands of years of practice, he managed to make telepathic contact with Knockabout.

"Are you nearby, Doctor?" Edirin said, "Or is this a long distance call?"

The corner of Doctor Shadow's mouth twitched up in a reflexive smile. That was what was missing around here, he realized. Skeletons don't make the best conversation partners. "Consider it very long distance. But at least it's not a trans-dimensional call."

"And that answers my next question," Knockabout said.

"I could not help but notice that we have inherited a border dispute."

"Yes," came the reply, "And tensions are running high. The general in charge of your troops has made many enemies down here. I don't think I could stop this war if I wanted too. Your troops are positioned to make a move on the borders in the dead of night, finishing with a skeletal cavalry charging the flank from the south."

"And you know this how?" Doctor Shadow said.

"The old fashioned way," Edirin laughed grimly, "The most technologically advanced nation in this part of the world, if not the entire world, with all of its resources turned towards the purpose of conquest. There are surveillance devices and weapons that push the boundaries of what I recognize as known science from back home."

"It should even the odds. I've seen your troop strengths and a complete overlay. The general Shade put in charge is named Gravas Tet Amon. He was an expert in that terrain several hundred years ago, and I imagine he's only gotten better since then. He will probably hit your artillery with something nasty, silent, and undead long before you see the main army move. I would venture something wraith-like, probably descending from the bluff above the mortar emplacements."

There was a silence on the other end of the connection, and Doctor Shadow could sense that Edirin was looking over his own reports and maps. "How did you know where the mortars and artillery were placed? Those are so hidden that they don't even show up on our sensors."

Doctor Shadow laughed, "The old, old fashioned way," he said, "with magic."

"Is your situation secure?" Knockabout said, turning back to their primary dilemma.

"Nothing but skeleton underlings here, and they are so busy destroying themselves that there should be nothing left by the time the rest of the team gets here."

"That sounds good. I imagine most of the others would think to seek you out first, anyway," Knockabout said. "What kind of control do you have over your forces?"

"Control of the undead is achieved only through training. In this area, I have none, which I believe is why there is infighting among the troops. I believe the army you have standing across your border is under the direct control of Gravas Tet Amon. I am certain I could bully him into standing down, but a sudden change of plans might not sit well with him."

"Don't worry about Tet Amon," Knockabout said.

Doctor Shadow could sense a cold anger in his teammate. Reflexively, he probed a little deeper and saw the carnage that Shade's undead general had done to the border and surrounding lands. He didn't know how Edirin had become so intimate with the details of the conflict, but he could not deny that there was a strong, personal interest in his thoughts. "You will be taking care of him yourself," the ancient mystic said.

"There is a valley on the edge of the hills to the north of here. When the sun rises, it kisses the edge of the bluff and a warm red glow falls upon the people who live there. It looks as through the stones themselves blaze with the light of a loving God. No one who sees the sun rise in that valley for the first time fails to be moved to tears. The people who live there do not have much, but they are well cared for, loved by each other, secure in the knowledge that they live in a sacred place, happy in the presence of a sacred metal that they know lies beneath those hills."

Knockabout paused, but Doctor Shadow could tell that he was not done. He waited patiently, seeing the valley as his friend described it. He had never been there, but he knew what it looked like. There were countless places like it in the world. Some were verdant plains, some lush, rolling hills, some even harsh, wind-scoured mountains. It was a place called home. There was nothing more beautiful.

"Three nights ago, Gravas Tet Amon led his troops to that valley," Edirin said. "He butchered the women, the children, the old men, and fed them to his unholy army. The rest he killed and turned into his own troops. Thousands of people, Doctor. Thousands dead for a war they didn't chose."

"These are not your people, Edirin," Doctor Shadow told him.

"But are they not still people? Our counterparts here are evil, and even the normal people all across the planet seem more willing to follow their baser instincts. I have surveyed the history since arriving. I am not naïve about the innocence, or the possible lack thereof of those who died there, but the land is neither good nor evil. And it cries out for vengeance."

"The risks inherent in this kind of action…"

Knockabout cut him off. "I am aware of the risks. But I urge you to consider that my counterpart here is a ruthless, unconscionable dictator, with a pack of violent generals beneath him just waiting for the moment when he looks weak, vulnerable to a coup. We are not going to be here forever, Doctor. And I see an opportunity to leave this world better than we found it."

"Understood," Doctor Shadow said. He heard an

unexplainable clattering sound in a distant hallway, and felt his
concentration waver. "I will see you in the Valley of Kings shortly.
Good luck."

"Thank you. To yourself as well," Knockabout said.

With the audience over, Doctor Shadow let the link between
himself and Knockabout fade into nothingness. The clattering sound
reached his ears again, this time closer, accompanied by a scratching,
rasping echo. More skeletons, he thought to himself. Surely he would
have heard the door being broken open. He turned his body
incorporeal and went in search of the disturbance.

Not more skeletons, he discovered, but he almost wished it
had been. Shade's undead army was self-regenerating, but with their
master gone, their regeneration was chaotic at best. The remains of the
eight guards had reformed into one, singular bone monstrosity, limbs
jutting from impossible angles, fused to each other. The end result was
almost too big for the hallway, and was not even remotely recognizable
as once human.

"Well," Doctor Shadow heard himself say, "This is certainly
unexpected."

Thirty seconds later, a large carpet wrapped around a mass of
struggling bones swept off the high balcony of the Valley of Kings. It
smashed enthusiastically to the hard stone, where, moments later, the
broken pieces of bone rolled off to begin the regeneration again.
Doctor Shadow watched from the balcony, torn between concern and
amusement.

By the time the others showed up, the entropic bone golems
below might be one, unwieldy entity, too large to act under its own
weight. Or it might be a huge, incredibly dangerous threat. Only time
would tell. He would have to keep close watch on the situation.

If nothing else, it would keep his mind off Knockabout's
troubles.

Chapter Sixteen

Edirin sat stoic on the Antelope Throne, reading situation reports on translucent, floating energy screens. Guards and advisors had been around when Doctor Shadow shared a telepathic conference with him, but he had masked his reactions by appearing intent on the maps and numbers scrolling by before him. Now that the contact was gone, he was better able to focus on the task at hand.

The files Sundiatta had compiled on those he considered enemies were concise, filled with the obsessive detail of a paranoid schizophrenic. If the security protocols on the files hadn't been keyed to his voice signature and biometric scan, Edirin didn't believe that he would be reading them now. Sundiatta had seen enemies everywhere. Judging by how he dealt with people he deemed a threat, he was probably not incorrect in that view. In cracking down on imaginary enemies, he had no doubt created new ones.

In D'habu, *his* D'habu, Knockabout had worked with a team of individuals with powers similar to his own, called the Kuwinde, the Hunt. Those same individuals had been made an example of after an attempt on his life that he suspected but never proved originated from them. Their powers had been negated, and they had been placed in a cage with a descending ceiling. Five pounds were added every few minutes. Sundiatta did not stop adding weight until long after the ceiling was flush with the floor.

His own friends, his own allies, some he had known and worked with for years, reduced to a bloody smear in the course of one beautiful afternoon, while the public was forced to watch at gunpoint. That was the kind of lunatic who now inhabited Edirin Okoloko's body back home. He couldn't get back soon enough.

Never mind that the lion skull helmet and lion pelt cloak were a major fashion faux pas. Certainly, Sundiatta had to have something in his wardrobe that didn't look like it came from a Tarzan comic book. From here Edirin was headed to the Valley of Kings, and he was fairly certain that there would be no Brooks Brothers along the way.

A thin, dark suited man who kept his gaze carefully lowered shuffled purposefully into the room and stopped near the base of the throne's dais. He bowed deeply and did not straighten. "Most glorious of warrior kings, your generals await your orders."

Knockabout had read the files on his generals, and not one bore a name he recognized. He was not surprised. Sundiatta had been ruthless in eliminating anyone from his past who might know something about him. But in trying to conceal any indications of weakness, he had instead revealed what could, if properly used, be turned into a major flaw. Sundiatta was incapable of trust. Edirin pondered how best to put this information to use as he nodded for the steward to bring in the generals.

The three generals arrived with a degree of respect that bordered on fear. Two of them were Hutu from nearby Rwanda, brothers who had personally butchered hundreds in that nation's ethnic cleansing a decade earlier. They had been discovered piling the severed feet of the dead inside a church to settle a never-ending competition as to who was the bigger thug. Banjoko and Kidjo had so impressed the conquering Sundiatta with their capacity for violence and total lack of ambition that he folded them into his own army immediately. The third general was Emil Al-Aswan, an Egyptian expatriate by way of Morocco. He had led a damaging campaign of terrorism and guerilla warfare against Shade's army in the Atlas Mountains for two years before being forced to retreat. His skills and instincts in fighting the undead were daunting, and Sundiatta had seen him as too great an asset to overlook.

All intelligence on Al-Aswan showed him to be the wild card. He had no strong loyalty to Sundiatta or the Antelope Throne. He fought only to damage Shade's expansion, and if that avenue became closed to him, Edirin had no doubt that Morocco's Lion of the Atlas would be gone in a heartbeat. Emil's steady black eyes revealed nothing as he stood next to the eager-to-please Hutu brothers. Edirin wondered what was going on behind those eyes; what kind of analysis the terrorist had made of him.

"Your men on the Northern front are at the ready, I trust?" Knockabout said in a tone that he hoped inspired full attention.

"They are ready to repel anything that Shade's dog throws at us!" Banjoko replied with gusto.

"Good, because there has been a change of plans," Edirin said as he waved the shimmering computer screens away.

The brothers looked at each other confused but afraid to ask what these new plans entailed. Emil looked straight ahead, saying nothing. He might as well have been dead on his feet for all the emotion he showed.

"Gravas Tet Amon will assail the artillery before sunrise. I don't intend to give him the opportunity," he continued.

"We attack," Emil said.

"We attack," Knockabout agreed.

"We will push them back to their whore's son of a master in

the Valley of Kings!" Kidjo bellowed. He and his brother slapped their fists into their chests, thrilled at the prospect of bloodletting.

"When we are done, there will be nothing left to return to Shade," Knockabout said, letting his voice boom off the superb acoustics of the throne room. The brothers stopped their posturing, but he thought he saw, for just the slightest of seconds, a smile flit across the corner of Al-Aswan's mouth. Interesting, Edirin thought. He let the change of tactics sink in for a moment before dropping the final bombshell. "And I will be directing the battle myself," he said.

Knockabout didn't wait for their protests. He suspected that his counterpart wouldn't have either. And this wouldn't have been the first time Sundiatta led the troops on the battlefield, so he didn't expect any suspicion or resistance. Only the foolish would resist the will of Sundiatta. He strode purposefully from the throne room to the hangar, glad that he had memorized the route earlier. He let his generals trail in his wake, jaws flapping in mute protest.

A short high-speed trip in a jet that would have looked more at home on Tattooine than in Africa took them to the hills and high bluffs of the impending battle. Banjoko and Kidjo went quickly to check on their respective troop readiness, while Emil lingered for a moment on the improvised landing pad. "You should go and prepare your troops for the offensive," Knockabout said.

"They are already prepared," Emil said with a distracted air.

"They are prepared for a defensive action," Knockabout said. A look passed between them, a calm certainty thick in the heavy air. "Unless you did not listen to my original orders, that is."

Emil Al-Aswan made a great show of appearing disinterested. He looked out over the light of hundreds of portable heating units, towards the shifting darkness of the border and waved his hand dismissively. "I listened to your orders," he said, a tinge of respect in his voice that was not reflected in his manner. "But I trusted that you would, in your infinite wisdom, see the advantage of a full and decisive victory here."

Knockabout eyed him in silence for a moment. Was he playing some kind of odds or did he have some insight that Sundiatta, in all his paranoia had somehow missed? "There is more to you than your reputation suggests, Lion of the Atlas," he said, finally.

"And you as well," Emil said over his shoulder. He clicked his heels together and walked out into the darkness to issue final orders to his troops.

In only an hour, an army of thousands was readied, with orders passed from generals down to foot soldiers.

Knockabout settled into the floating viewing platform, confident that Gravas Tet Amon had no significant ranged weapons. Zombies and the like couldn't be trusted with rocket launchers, and even if they were, Knockabout had dealt with worse with the Protectorate. He had pored over his battle plans until his head hurt. Admittedly, it hadn't taken long. This really was more Archon's area of expertise. Well, everything was Archon's area of expertise, actually, but planning a battle on this scale? It was beyond the computer simulation he had seen Stardust playing while on monitor duty a few months ago. No simple tanks and infantry here. He doubted that there was a simulation for high-tech mobile infantry and guerilla soldiers with flamethrowers versus a wide range of the undead.

And what he found most difficult was not just that he needed to win, but that he needed to keep it close. It was important that both sides be decimated by the conflict. He couldn't risk either side going on a rampage through the countryside following a victory. Innocent people would be the victims there, not soldiers. No, it was important that this battle had no winners. And having Emil as an added unknown made the planning even more difficult.

But Edirin knew that contemplating who would be better suited to manage the affairs of this battle was a waste of time. The fact remained that Archon was not here. He could trust no one in this time, in this place. He had to be self-reliant. And regardless of how difficult this current set of circumstances was, he had faith in his own abilities. This battle would turn out the way he needed it to, even if he had to send everyone involved into orbit.

Suddenly, Emil's voice came to him crisp and clear through the observation platform's speakers. "Enemy troops trying to make a silent advance from the east have been picked up by our scouts. We have confirmation that they are using Wraiths. Very dangerous, hard to spot, but not particularly smart if that is any comfort. My men are ready to engage. What are your orders?" Emil said, his tone already presuming the answer.

"Encircle and eliminate, then begin the counter-offensive," Knockabout said. He then contacted Banjoko and Kidjo and told them to launch their offensive. It was still the dark hours before dawn, and conventional night vision options were ineffective in this kind of situation. The undead were all at ambient temperatures, making heat vision impractical, and with all the weapon flare, starlight lenses showed just overpowering flashes of bright light, making them useless as well. But Sundiatta had come across a solution, elegant in its simplicity, chilling in its conception.

A swarm of drone planes, each a little smaller than a motorcycle, swooped out into the front lines of Shade's army and dropped their payloads. These incendiary charges provided an explosion of light and heat bright enough to see the full might of the force arrayed against them while, at the same time, setting over a thousand of the enemy on fire. The burning bodies of the enemy troops would provide the light for the rest of the battle. And if the fight stretched on and the flames grew dim, another squadron of drone planes lay in reserve. Brutal, callous, it was the calculated act of a commander who did not wish to rule, but only to destroy.

Shade and Sundiatta deserved each other, Knockabout thought to himself - not for the first time.

At the mouth of the verdant valley, the two forces clashed. Edirin kept the hovering command platform within view of the front lines and enemy command tent as best as possible, but he refrained from watching the battle itself as much as possible. "These are not my people," he whispered, focusing on the numbers that scrolled by on the display panels. "These are simply numbers." But he couldn't believe the lie, not enough to stop the involuntary knots in his stomach. True, perhaps, that they were not his people, and they might have embodied most of humanity's worst traits, but they were still people. And he was sending them to die. At the end of the day, what kind of person did that make him? He had no answers.

Live reports showed that Emil had eliminated the Wraith contingent with minimal losses of his own and was now moving into a flanking position with the possibility to strike at the command area. He checked the maps against his data and realized that Emil was out of position. The Lion of the Atlas was improvising—or, worse, this had always been his plan. He was going to devote the bulk of his forces to destroy Gravas Tet Amon instead of committing them to assist Banjoko's troops on the eastern line.

He believed that it was chaos theory that warned against trying to micromanage big situations, but he considered that he just might be remembering Jeff Goldblum's character in *Jurassic Park*. Either way, it was time to get his hands dirty to try and force the outcome he wanted. Knockabout created a force field around himself, straining to push the edge of the bubble to encompass the entire command platform. With the metal imbedded in his body vibrating from effort, he managed to push the field well out to a respectable distance. With constant thoughts towards maintaining his protective bubble, he spurred the platform over the field of battle towards Gravas and Emil, hoping that he would not be too late.

Flying only fifty feet above the battle, it was more difficult to depersonalize the experience. But at least the closeness allowed him the luxury of being able to focus on small groups, making him effectively blind to the scale of the conflict. For that, he had the numbers. And with a careful eye on those numbers and a frequent mental focus on the force field, he was able to affect the tide of many fights, draining or enhancing kinetic potential of troops as circumstances dictated. The shifts of kinetic potential lay in his mind like an image of pluses and minuses, red and green dots, a minefield of contradictions to the laws of physics. He held them in his mind like a favorite memory lest he loose his grip on the reins, bringing the natural law of physics crashing back in.

He was feeling better about the possible outcome as he passed over the last vestiges of the melee and closed on the secondary conflict. Emil's men were greatly outnumbered, but their experience in fighting the undead was evident. The Lion of the Atlas himself stood at the forefront of the battle, and his men rallied around him as he waved his flaming sword and pushed them onward. All around him, the swift-footed zombie warriors fell like wheat. Despite the odds, Gravas looked to be in real trouble. But then the dread general himself made his appearance in the fray and the tide turned again.

Gravas Tet Amon was hundreds of years old. Unlike Doctor Shadow, he had not aged well. His skin was pale, lifeless, and had fallen free of the bones in several places, allowing unsettling glimpses at leather-like muscle tissue or bare ribs beneath flowing robes. He wielded no weapon, but his hands pulsed with dark energy, and every living man he passed within ten feet of withered and died in mere seconds.

Knockabout knew immediately that he had to shut the undead General down or it was all over. He reached out and tried to find some purchase on the personal gravity of Tet Amon, but, to his dismay, the general had no mass. He had never tried to extend his abilities to affect something in an incorporeal state, and wasn't sure if it could be done. He strained to find something. Even the incorporeal had to exist on some level, perhaps as a wavelength, composed entirely out of energy. And gravity had power over energy, didn't it? Couldn't he use that somehow? The metal fragments in his body vibrated hard enough to move from tingling to searing pain, but it was like trying to grab a bead of mercury.

Less than a minute after entering the battle, over half of Emil's force had wilted or broken ranks and run only to be cut down by the reinvigorated zombie army. If something didn't change soon, the battle

122

would be over and Gravas Tet Amon would burn a swath clear through to the ocean, killing and consuming everything in his path.

There had to be some other way, something he was missing. From the relative safety of the observation platform, Edirin watched the grim specter of death itself wade through the army towards Emil Al-Aswan, talking, always talking…wait. Talking? Knockabout focused his attention, listening intently to Gravas, and realized that the general was not giving orders or reporting back to someone else. While he couldn't understand the words, the tone was universal. Gravas Tet Amon was praying.

There was nothing left to try, Knockabout decided. He had seen others who used magic, and while he wasn't familiar with how it worked, he did know that some of them had to vocalize their will to make their powers work. A limitation to be sure, but it frequently granted them access to greater powers. He reached out with his mind and killed all sound in the area. For over a hundred feet in all directions from Gravas Tet Amon, there was no sound. Those still living could not even hear their own breath or the heartbeat in their ears. The silence was total. It was absolute.

The result was spectacular.

To a man, the zombies faltered, looking around confused. Emil's troops, never one to look a gift horse in the mouth, pressed the advantage, laying waste with biblical fury. Gravas Tet Amon screamed. He shouted. He raged and flailed, but all to no effect. The black fields around his hands vanished. And when a stumbling zombie fell against him and knocked him back, Edirin had all the proof he needed that the undead general had returned to the physical world.

Knockabout allowed himself a smile. "Say 'goodnight', Gracie," he said as he released the silent, confused commander from the bonds of gravity. Gravas Tet Amon rewarded him with a horrified expression and several five-century-old curse words in a foreign tongue as he began to fall upward. His speed picked up the further he fell, and Edirin waited until he felt the undead mage settle into a nice, high orbit where he would be unable to hurt anyone. Only then did he let go, sentencing Gravas to an eternity high above the land he once sought to destroy, unable to die, and with no air to carry sound, unable to extract himself from the awkward situation he now found himself in. Knockabout felt that to be a fitting end.

He turned his attention back to Emil and the battle before him and realized that it was already over. Knockabout set down the command platform in a field of corpses and took stock. Checking the displays before him, he realized that although Kidjo had been killed,

Banjoko had rallied the troops and eked out a narrow victory as well. But the victory was not as narrow as Edirin would have liked. Already over a hundred bloodied warriors whooped and cheered, full of bloodlust, looking for the next fight. With no enemy left to fight, the countryside was going to be a dangerous place.

"My men will take care of them," Emil said, stepping up onto the platform with Knockabout. The blood-splattered warrior looked back towards what remained of Sundiatta's army, and Edirin wondered just what was meant by Emil's simple statement.

"And now we go to the Valley of Kings," Emil said, a sly smile on his face.

"My army is in tatters. To march them across the desert into the land of eternal shadow would be their death," Knockabout said carefully.

"Not the army. Us. You and me."

Knockabout looked Emil over again. There was no question this time, just a matter-of-fact certainty of what would come to pass. "And why would we do that?"

"Games do not become men like us," Emil said. "The air is thick with destiny. Surely you can feel it too. This is what will come to pass. How long did you really think you could continue to fool me?" he paused and leaned close to Knockabout, staring seriously into his eyes. Knockabout could smell a hint of oranges beneath the blood. Emil was deadly intense. "You, my friend, do not belong here."

Edirin said nothing, but looked at his panels again. The numbers of troops crept lower as Emil's troops went from man to man doing what had to be done. True to his word, they were being taken care of. By morning, there would be no one left breathing in the valley. "If I do not belong here, then where do I belong, oh Lion of the Atlas?"

"Back on the other earth," Emil said with a chuckle. "The one we both come from."

Chapter Seventeen

Jaccob Stevens could still taste the Russian pastry and coffee on his tongue when he suddenly found himself sitting in a hot tub overlooking fog-wreathed pines and a stunning view of pre-dawn Lake Washington. An untouched Bloody Mary was at his fingertips, and he found, to his surprise, that he was completely naked. A thought started fighting its way through what he could only assume was either extreme fatigue or a hangover, something he hadn't experienced since college. Magic. Magic had screwed him over again.

Leaving his drink on the side of the tub, he got out and wrapped himself in a white towel as soft as a supermodel's airbrushed skin. H was moderately familiar with the view, on the eastern side of Lake Washington, with the northern part of the city of Seattle barely glimpsed over the hill. It was prime real estate by anyone's standards. To build anything here would have required a fortune. Gauging by the layout of the house as he padded wetly across red, Mexican tiles, it was a fortune well spent. The house was opulent, without being ostentatious. State of the art security and electronic components, quality hardwoods, butter soft, nut-brown leather on the sofas and recliners, one wall twenty feet high made of river rock, the living space was a tasteful blend of high tech and natural material. But all the interior designers in the world couldn't hide the fact that it was soulless, empty, and cold. Half an hour of wandering didn't uncover a single other person in the entire 10,000 square feet.

But he did find a pair of pants and a silk t-shirt, which were a great comfort. He was starting to get chilly. A handful of pictures on the dresser confirmed his worst suspicions. He was through the looking glass, or evil world as he liked to call it. His reflection in the silvered lenses of $800 sunglasses confirmed that instead of a full beard, he had a goatee not unlike Spock in the episode "Mirror, Mirror." He was not amused. He put on the sunglasses and went to look for the garage.

Strange, he thought, to be the evil Stardust and not have armor lying about anywhere. There wasn't even a workshop in evidence. It ran contrary to what little he had been able to find out about his doppelganger. However the garage, when he found it, quashed any suspicions that Deathstar or whatever he called himself, was all hype.

Yes, there were a few quarter million dollar cars that didn't surprise him too much. But there was also a hover bike and three suits of armor hanging from ceiling racks like sides of beef, with cables and conduits galore leading off to generators and diagnostic equipment. Jaccob almost forgot about his predicament for a few minutes as he inspected the hardware. This, he realized, was the real sanctum sanctorum for Deathstar, not the fifty million dollar home.

One suit, in shades of blue, seemed to have been designed specifically for deep-sea work. He recognized elements of the design from a water-based villain he had helped capture before joining the Protectorate. Some of the tech was so directly cribbed that Jaccob was certain that it had been reverse engineered from the original.

The second suit was silvered, with engine systems, life support, and high-G thrusters that could only be used in deep space environments. He couldn't even guess the suit's range, but based on the linguistic software loaded into the suit's memory, contact with multiple alien cultures had been logged.

But it was the third suit that gave him pause. Shades of cloudy black and gray, it seemed to swallow light. Top-of-the-line data link and decryption software, a massive storage drive, photo-sensitive composite armor to render the suit invisible, sound baffles on the thrusters, a sensor suite that enabled the wearer to look through walls and see on a wide range of spectrums, it was the ninja of battle suits. Then he inspected the weapon systems and realized how accurate the metaphor was. The suit was designed not only to move silently and pilfer information, it was also designed to kill. The gun mounted along the right arm fired razors using a silent, magnetic propulsion system offering a subsonic targeting system. Using a variation on sonar, someone wearing this suit could cut the wings off of a mosquito in total darkness.

And the lunatic who designed this armor was wearing his skin, a world away with his wife and children. "Oh God...Elizabeth," he whispered.

There was a slight whir as cameras pivoted and irises contracted. "How may I assist you?" Elizabeth's voice said from a speaker mounted near the armor racks.

Jaccob was so startled that he dropped the voltometer that he was holding. It skidded underneath a worktable, unbroken, as Jaccob regained his composure. "Elizabeth?" he asked the speaker. "Where are you?" There had been no sign of her anywhere in the house, no sign of anyone other than himself, actually.

"I am on floor seven, suite four, of your Seattle campus," she said.

There was no emotion in her voice, he noticed. No additional information had been offered, just a simple answer to a simple question. He began to fear the worst. "How are you doing?" he said, his stomach tightening.

"All systems are operating within design parameters," Elizabeth said.

Well, on the bright side of things, at least if he was dealing with Elizabeth as an operating system interface instead of an employee, she wouldn't be asking uncomfortable questions. But the nagging question of where the real Elizabeth was wouldn't go away. He could already tell that he was going to have to solve that particular mystery before he went home. "How do I get to the Seattle campus from here?"

Unexpectedly, the hovercycle started up and began to float in its charging dock. "GPS marker downloaded to Deathstar One," Elizabeth said. "Daily reports will be waiting on your desk when you arrive."

Jaccob went over to the cycle and inspected it quickly. It was big, bigger than Gato Loco's, but the hoverjets seemed to take up very little of its actual space. The frame was made of the same high impact polymer that he used in his armor, so at least it was durable and lightweight. He climbed on, feeling the slight hum of engine through his thighs and hips. A large, covered switch was mounted prominently between the gauges, and it flashed bewitchingly at him. It was candy-apple red and tantalizing in its mystery. It wasn't labeled, and he cursed the genius who put such a prominent stitch on something and didn't bother to label it. In the end, he decided to trust his instincts that had served him so well in the past.

He flipped the switch.

For a long second nothing happened, and Jaccob was mildly disappointed. But when he put both hands on the handlebars, the grips snapped closed on his hands and the rest of the bike began to collapse. No, he realized after a second of initial panic, not collapse, fold. Like some intricate piece of metal origami, the hovercycle folded itself around him until he was armored in what he could only describe as the coolest battle suit he had never invented himself. It even had disintegrator beams, although he had no idea what he would want to disintegrate.

The heads-up display gave an indicator arrow and distance reading, not unlike some of his favorite video games. The floating, amber cursor was labeled "Seattle Campus," and by the time the garage door finished sliding open, he had already figured out the instinctive control systems. Within seconds, he was flying out over the lake, cutting through cotton-candy fog in the chill morning air. The handling was a bit chunkier than he would have liked, but the jets had plenty of power, easily the equal to his own armor. He didn't have the reflex amplification he was used to, which ruled our any fancy maneuvering, but servo motors provided a significant strength increase, and he had several options available when it came to weapon systems. Overall, this armor had been built as a flying tank, with little of the finesse of his original design.

But the real surprise came when he topped the ridge and looked out over Seattle and his campus. The huge university he had worked at when he had first discovered the meteorite that powered his armor was gone. In fact, everything within a mile of the school had been removed. In its place stood a medieval castle, complete with surrounding outbuildings and a high wall, constructed with reinforced concrete, glass and steel. It was like an amusement park without the rides or, for that matter, the amusement. Energy weapons topped the towers along the outer walls, and the wreckage in the cleared zone that flanked the walls showed that they weren't just for decoration. The major north-south interstate which once passed just west of the university as it crossed the narrows over the lake was now just gone, with ruined concrete pilings jutting accusingly from the murky water.

"Welcome to Camelot," the voice that should have been Elizabeth said over his internal communication suite. "I have cleared gate beta five for entry."

He checked the indicator arrow and noticed that it had turned into a targeting crosshair, which hovered over a circular portal in the side of the central building. As he passed over the outside wall, he saw armored figures that looked disturbingly like Stardust armor, but his sensors picked up no life readings and high-energy signatures. Robot sentries. Jaccob was starting to see a pattern, and it was one he was comfortable exploiting if needed. Since coming to this world, he hadn't spoken to or even seen a single real person.

As he cleared the threshold of the entry gate, the armor folded back out into a hovercycle and parked itself in a recharging dock. From the inside, the campus looked less like a castle and more like the inside of a space station designed by an early German Expressionist: stark walls, severe angles, and dark tones. He half-expected to see Dr. Caligari round the corner with a bubble-style space helmet. It wouldn't have surprised Jaccob. He didn't think anything would have surprised him anymore. He finally realized that he had figured his darker self out. Evil Jaccob never did anything by halves, he knew that now. Being a loner geek with more money than God, he was easily able to facilitate every crazy whim that came his way. He just hoped that evil Jaccob had never taken a fancy to Disney's *Beauty and the Beast*, because he knew that if he saw a singing and dancing candlestick, he was going to have to start shooting.

Through a connecting door which slid open at his approach was a sleek, modern office with several hundred square feet of polished black floors and a matching desk made of a single sheet of highly polished black glass supported by massive computer hard drives. Three computer screens were inset into the surface of the desk itself, occupying most of the surface space and tilted to optimum visibility. The keyboard had been split and placed on the armrests of the womb-like black leather chair. Jaccob had only glanced at the screens when he realized that he needed to sit and pay more attention.

Cobalt City was the subject of one report. Of all the Protectorate's evil duplicates, only Worm Queen and Mister Grey were located in Cobalt City. It couldn't be a coincidence, could it? He only read only the first few pages before giving up on it. There was no mention of Lazarus or Lenore in the report, simply a risk assessment on a business venture there and some mention of recent weather anomalies.

A second report included satellite images of a massive battle brewing in Sub-Saharan Africa, and that quickly took priority. A detailed study had been done on the two factions in the region. Jaccob recognized the leaders of the two warring nations immediately, with one being Edirin's doppelganger Sundiatta, and the other Doctor Shadow's counterpart Shade who had apparently purchased weapon systems from Deathstar less than a year ago. That would have to be the meeting place. He could go suborbital and get there in an hour or two.

But a rumbling in his stomach reminded him that he was only human, and that this body had skipped breakfast. Plus, taking time for a good meal would allow him to tidy up a few loose ends. "Elizabeth, I need a late breakfast," he said, thinking that she could recommend somewhere nearby.

"Please order when ready," the voice said. Power had its privileges, apparently.

Jaccob finally settled on chicken fried steak and eggs over easy, sourdough toast, and hashed browns with cheddar and onions. Elizabeth wouldn't have let him get away with eating it at home, and he was always a little conscious of what he ate as well. The armor didn't allow for a significant weight change, and he'd hate to re-forge the torso piece because he couldn't say no to cake. Plus, his suit was so precisely calibrated, that a few pounds here or there could have an impact on system performance. But this wasn't his body. He might even stop somewhere on the east coast for pie on his way to Africa.

While he waited for food to be delivered, by robots, no doubt, he got busy with data retrieval. There was the slim chance that any team members that had been swapped over might have tried to email or contact him in some way. His biggest concern was that Velvet, Gallows, or Archon might have been pulled over, since they had been in the conference room when the change happened. Without knowing how to find their dark reflections, it would be up to the rookies to try initiating contact. Fifteen minutes searching alleviated his concerns that he was going to miss an important message.

By then, breakfast had arrived, and he dug in, turning his search to a more personal matter. He gave his evil self the benefit of the doubt and went with the assumption that something had happened to Elizabeth to necessitate her being downloaded into the computer. But there was no record of her at all in the files, at least not on the surface level. Elizabeth began and ended as an OS and that was it. But he wasn't satisfied with that answer. He began pulling in data streams from outside his immediate network.

A bite of yolk-soaked toast almost lodged in Jaccob's throat when he finally found her. She had been institutionalized several years ago, completely tabula rasa. He did the math. It would have been less than a year after they met in college. Jaccob found that he had lost his appetite, and pushed the half-full plate away.

Jaccob sat back in the chair and wheels began to turn in his head. He looked up a few members of Elizabeth's family until he found who he was looking for and then checked visitation records at the institute where they were holding her. Within minutes, her transfer paperwork had been pushed through and a bed in a much better facility was made ready for her, paid in full for as long as she needed it. Her family was notified of the change in residence. He made sure they were notified of several other things as well. Then he contacted his own legal department and made a few changes, barely able to control his smile.

With a final keystroke, Jaccob considered that matter dealt with, and moved on to other matters. He had overcome his nausea with a bit of poetic revenge and decided to finish off his breakfast after all. He ordered up a chocolate malt with a double hit of protein powder to wash down his breakfast. He also looked up the location of a cheesecake place he and Elizabeth had gone to in New York to make sure it was still around, and pre-ordered a pumpkin-praline cheesecake to go, charging it to the company card. He knew it was petty, but every little bit helped him feel better.

Done with his meal at last, he spent a few hours doing programming. He hauled out every virus, Trojan horse, and worm he knew, and set timers to spread them out over the next month. He took time to make sure that they were deeply embedded, and that the ones lying dormant would remain hidden until they began to march through Deathstar's armor hard drive like Sherman through Atlanta.

As he left in the hovercycle armor, he turned and paused, floating high above his doppelganger's shiny toy kingdom. "4-3-2-1..." he counted to himself, then smiled as one by one, the sentry robots below began to explode in huge gouts of flame.

Stardust turned and set his sights on New York, smiling widely. All things considered, it was turning out to be an okay day. A productive morning, a nice snack waiting on the other coast, a clear sky ahead of him, and by this evening – if he was lucky – a reunion with his friends. It could be a lot worse.

And when he finally swapped back home, the stupid goatee-wearing evil Jaccob would learn what happens when you fuck with Stardust.

Chapter Eighteen

On a philosophical level, Manuel understood there was a razor thin line between the ultimate in sensual ecstasy and torture. That he should ever see the practical proof of that division was something he never expected. He should have never brought his handcuffs, he thought dully, trying to ignore the deep, burning pain in his shoulders that he knew must be spoiling for an infection.

"I am not impressed," the thing inhabiting Katherine's body told him as she licked his blood from still-extended claws.

"Too spicy?" he said. His voice sounded slurred in his head, and he was having a hard time remaining conscious. He had to fight. If he passed out, his chances went from slim to none. Manuel de la Vega had, in the past several hours, become keenly aware of his own mortality.

"The skills you boasted of," she said, pacing naked before him, just out of his reach, not that it would do any good if he could reach her, "They were...adequate. But your endurance leaves something to be desired. If I am not careful, you will be dead soon."

"Guess you have to be careful, then," he said.

A growl sounded deep in her throat, dangerous, predatory, and far, far too natural. "I don't like being careful."

After only ninety minutes, Manuel had figured out that the person he had spent the last several hours with was not Katherine Wilde. He kicked himself for not figuring it out sooner, but he had so wanted to believe. By the time she had re-cuffed him to the disturbingly load-bearing shower rod, he know there was no chance of overpowering her. Wild Kat had superhuman speed and strength, not to mention claws that could cut through a million aluminum cans and still slice a tomato. The way out of this, if there was one, was not through violence but through guile. And Manuel de la Vega was all about guile. Dozens of women would swear a statement to attest to that.

"What have you done to Katherine?" he said, letting his weight hang from his wrists, despite the pain. The pain kept him awake and reminded him that he was here. And he needed to conserve the strength that standing on the blood-slick tile required.

"I am Katherine," she said with a smile. There was more there behind her eyes. She was toying with him. He was used to that look now.

"No," he said. "You're something else."

132

"I'm...improved, but I am Katherine. I always have been."

He let the detective in him mull over the pieces. Possession or perhaps multiple personality disorder could account for the change. But was it only her that was affected? He hadn't seen or heard any of the Protectorate since entering the building, and there had been no calls to duty on the communicator Katherine had put on the bedside table. Wasn't that odd? It seemed that there was always *something* to do qwa hero in Cobalt City. Not just big stuff, but routine robberies and car thefts and day-to-day things. And there was the Blak Dawg thing she had been working on just yesterday. Surely that case hadn't been closed already. But instead she had been here, with him, for most of the day.

With the exception of when she left the room to put his leather Gato Loco costume somewhere else, Katherine hadn't left her suite. And therein lay the other problem. Without his leathers, he was just a man in a building of super humans. "The others are improved as well then," he said. It was a bluff, but he was good at bluffing, and he had to know what he was up against.

"Most of them," she said, but a look of bitterness crossed her face briefly. "Some of the newer ones...well, we will find them and deal with them."

Okay, he thought. Good, bad, and worse news. Archon, Gallows, and Velvet were the newest recruits, so that gave him some backup--if he could contact them. But the rest of the team had gone a little bit nutty, so that was bad. But the fact that she would so readily answer his question implied that she didn't intend to leave him alive for long. He felt just a little like James Bond, but not in a good way.

"And what about my clothes," he said, letting his voice fade. "Are you going to keep them as a trophy or something?"

"How well you know me," she said, raising an eyebrow. "They will be a trophy of my first kill on this soft world."

That's enough detective work for now, Manuel told himself. Just take a nap. Everything will work itself out by morning. Instead he fought to keep his eyes open, focusing on the distant pain in his shoulders. "If you're going to kill me, make it quick," he mumbled, confident that Katherine's keen senses would be able to hear him. "Let me die like a man, with some honor. Not slowly, like some caged animal."

Manuel wished he could see her face, to read her reaction, but try as he might, he couldn't force his eyes to stay focused any longer. He concentrated on the soft pad of her bare feet across the glaring white bathroom tiles, and of the occasional drip sounds of his blood in the tub and on the tiles. Please, Brer Fox, he thought. Don't go throwin' me in that there briar patch!

"If you still have breath in you when I get back, then I might see that you get your wish," she purred. Her pronouncement of a delayed death was followed by the sound of her footsteps out into the bedroom. There, he thought he heard the rustle of clothes being put on. The zip of the long, concealed side zipper in Wild Kat's leather pants. Then as he cracked his eyes back open, the sound of the suite's door sliding open and then closed.

Manuel didn't know how long she was planning to be gone, but he couldn't take a chance on a short reprieve. He managed to find inner reserves of strength and got his legs underneath him. The shower curtain rod had been more than able to support his weight, but he had noticed early on that the curtain rings had no hasps or hinges. They were solid complete rings, so there had to be some way of sliding them onto the rod. He didn't dare investigate this too much earlier for fear that Wild Kat would figure out that he was planning an escape. His gaze turned to the wall anchor and he found that his intuition had paid off. The heavy-duty bar he had been hanging on was supported in a simple U-joint. A quick push up on the bar and he was able to get the cuffs free.

His legs felt weak, but they worked well enough to let him stagger to the sink. There, he was able to inspect the damage to his back in the mirror in more detail. A quick, queasy glance into the tub allowed an estimate of how much blood he had lost. It didn't look good. He was definitely down a few pints, but they had emergency plasma up on the top floor. If he could get there, he just might live through this particular date.

The keys to the cuffs were still on the bedside table, and he quickly unlocked them. He found his shorts next to the bed and managed to slide them on. At least he wasn't going to die al-fresco, Manuel decided. He listened at the door before hitting the button to open it. "Have to gamble sometime," he whispered.

The lounge-like common area beyond was currently vacant and he was able to make it to the next suite without passing out. He prided himself on the effort. He remembered something Katherine had said about recently having neighbors move in, which he took to mean one of the new teammates. There were suites on either side, so his chances were 50-50. And he had been given full building access by Wild Kat. He doubted that she had considered that when she was torturing him, but he needed to act fast before she realized her nummy treat was gone. Once she cancelled his access, getting around the building would be impossible.

Manuel opened the door to the next suite, uttering a whispered prayer when he found it dark. He slid in and closed the door, waiting to catch his breath before he turned on the lights. After a minute, he realized that if he sat against the wall in the dark for too long, he would fall asleep. And it would most likely be a nap he wouldn't wake up from. "Lights," he said, blinking in the sudden brightness.

No effort had been made to decorate, but it was clear that the room was at least in occasional use. He pulled himself back to his feet, wincing as he felt the wounds on his back reopen slightly with the effort. The closet, when he got to it, was stocked with black t-shirts, jeans, and a few heavy, denim over shirts. Gallow's room, Manuel decided. Archon didn't strike him as the denim type. He managed to pull on a t-shirt advertising a place called Dick's Last Resort in San Diego. He would laugh at the irony later, he decided. The jeans fit well enough once they were belted. For good measure, he put on one of the over shirts, in case he bled through the thinner t-shirt and started to drip again. The boots he found tucked at the back of the closet were a no go, being a full size smaller than he typically wore. Plus, they would make more noise and sacrifice traction.

Thus outfitted, he made his way out across the lounge to the stairs and began to ascend the two floors to the garage and medical bay area. He hoped that everyone else would be using the elevators, and so far had lucked out in that regard. As long as he was in the system as authorized personnel, his presence in the stairwell wouldn't trip any alarms. He suspected that in the anonymous jeans and shirt, he would look like any other member of the support staff as long as no one knew to look for him. As long as he didn't leave a trail of blood and no one noticed that he was barefoot, that is.

It wasn't until he reached the top of the stairwell that he realized that the hangar area was considered a secure area. Manuel stared blankly at the number pad next to the heavy-gauge steel door and felt his heart sink. They were going to catch him, he realized. The crazy Wild Kat who, if he hadn't hallucinated the whole conversation, seemed to think she was from another world, was going to find him, kill him, eat his flesh, and probably make a hat out of his skin. In despair, he reached out and let his fingers graze across the security keypad housing.

The sudden arrival of the "vision" almost slid him the rest of the way into unconsciousness. Manuel never knew when they were going to hit. He tried to train the second sight, to use it as an investigative tool, but had never been able to trigger it intentionally. Psychotelemetry, the text books called it, the ability to "read" the past of an object with physical contact. Sometimes a blessing, sometimes a curse, he had been hit with images of people who used the same silverware in a restaurant before and with details of gruesome murders while at crime scenes. The visions ranged from the helpful to the annoying. The visions had sent him first to a priest and then to a handful of psychiatrists over the years, anything to explain, control, or mitigate the effects of his so-called gift.

Some people got super-powers and they could fly and catch bullets in their teeth. When the super-power fairy waved his wand over Manuel, he got mind fucked. It just wasn't fair.

But this time, at least, it saved his life.

He didn't remember entering in the security pass code, an automatic pattern to the hand that had touched the panel last. He vaguely remembered looking up and seeing the door slide open and a surprised looking panda in cargo shorts and a Sex Pistols t-shirt on the other side. The panda stared at Manuel, a monkey wrench in one hand and a stick of sugar cane tucked in the corner of his mouth like a cigarette, and uttered a string of profanities the likes of which Manuel didn't find appropriate for any animal, let alone a panda.

Manuel wanted to say, "You kiss your mother with that mouth?" but the world got all black and wiggly. The next thing he knew, he was looking at the floor, which was moving quickly towards him. This can't be good, he thought, but he didn't get a chance to voice that thought either before the floor bludgeoned him into unconsciousness.

"Next thing I know, the roof door is open and he's gone," Snowflake said, chewing on the end of his sugar cane petulantly. Wild Kat stared at him, turned her attention to the open roof door and the smears of blood, then turned back to the petulant, evolved panda.

"And he got the door open how?" she said coldly.

"Same way he got the door from the stairwell open, I guess," he said with a disinterested sigh.

"And you were in the bathroom when he opened both doors?" she said, repeating his earlier statement.

"Caffeine is a real bitch on panda physiology, but the heart wants what the heart wants," he shrugged. "I've spent more time on the toilet today than Elvis. Anyway, what does it matter where Gallows went? He'll be back soon enough, right?"

"Gallows?" Wild Kat said with a slight tilt of her head.

"Yeah," Snowflake said, confusion creeping into his voice. "I mean, he had all the codes, and all I saw was dark hair and his Dick's t-shirt, so that's him, right? I mean, who else could it have been?"

Wild Kat sniffed deeply, picking up the strong scent of blood. It was on the lift, on the keypad, on the door. Even a few big splotches on the floor near the lift controls. From a distance, with only a glimpse, Manuel could pass for the elusive teleporter. And what reason would this perversion of nature have for lying to its employer? She would find this Gato Loco. He was, after all, only a man. She only wished that there were cameras in the hangar bay to confirm the panda's story.

"He's injured," she said. "He may be confused, wandering lost. You let me know if you see him again."

Snowflake noticed that it was not a request, but a command, but let it slide this one time. "Of course," he said. "You'll be the first to know."

Wild Kat gave a final sniff, then raced out of the roof door in search of her prey, closing the door behind her as she went. Snowflake watched her go, wiping his hands on a rag. He tossed it into the small waste incinerator next to the lift and wandered into the small medical suite next to his sleeping quarters.

Standing next to one of the pod-like emergency medical cots, he flipped the lock open and slid the red, opaque case open. Manuel de la Vega looked up at the surly panda with an expectant smile. "Are we clear?"

"She's on the town, and I don't think she's alerted anyone else to her little indiscretion," Snowflake grumbled. "Your transfusion still has another ten minutes or so to go. Don't want to rush things like that."

"We have a little time if she's out looking on the streets," Manuel said, already feeling a little better. "We need to gather some supplies, like my costume, for instance. Wild Kat would have put it in some kind of trophy room by now, I'd expect."

"I'll look into it," Snowflake said, monitoring the flow of plasma and painkillers. "But first you have to tell me one thing. What the hell is going on around here?"

"I don't know," Manuel said. "But if you have a cell phone, I might be able to call someone who can explain it."

Chapter Nineteen

"They are going to start to consolidate power soon," Archon said as he eyed his hamburger suspiciously. He had eaten goat's brain in Athens, dog in Hanoi, eel in Hamburg, bugs in the Amazon basin, and God himself only knows what was in the stew in rural Scotland, but all of them paled in comparison to the burger before him. I mean, really, who put fried egg on top of a half-pound burger with bacon and cheese? He should have never let Gallows order for him when he was using the pay phone. He suspected that Gallows was smiling at his expense, but it was hard to tell under all the barbeque sauce.

"What makes you so sure of that?" Libertine said, returning from the jukebox where she had selected an eclectic mix of Hank Williams, Billie Holiday, and The Clash.

"Cobalt City has a big list of heroes, both active and semi-retired," Huntsman said. "Eventually, these heroes are going to start wondering why the Protectorate isn't out there stopping crimes. They have to act quickly, before anyone else figures out that they have been switched or they lose the element of surprise. Once word gets out, they couldn't possibly hope to take over Cobalt City, not to mention any other objectives they might have."

"And how do we get out the word?" Velvet said, having rejoined the group after taking care of her business at Starcorp.

"Warning the other heroes in a credible fashion would tip our hand to the people we're tying to warn against. It pushes them into action, both against us and towards their overall goals," Archon said. He pushed his plate away, finally deciding that he wasn't too hungry after all.

"So we're on our own," Huntsman said.

"My kind of odds," Gallows said.

"And the next time we run up against them, they're going to want to cut off our escape," Velvet said, looking pointedly at the teleporter.

"Dog pile on Gallows," Libertine said with a wicked smile, "How do you like those odds?"

"Long as it's you, cupcake," he said with a wink, pleased with the bike messenger's reaction as she turned red around the ears and became very interested in her chicken strips.

"So that leaves us with a brick, a psychic, an archer, a teleporter, and a big, walking brain," Velvet said, mulling over the possibilities.

"All we need is a Halfling rogue and we'll be a complete party," Archon said, "And I am not a big, walking brain."

"Yeah, and your Dungeon and Dragons comment proves that how?" Libertine said with a laugh.

Huntsman smiled. "He has a point though. If we had someone on the inside, we might be able to find out what they were planning. Call it what you want...Halfling rogue, Trojan horse, poison pill, something."

"And to minimize damage, perhaps, we should pick the playing field, because any big scrap is going to tear up the city pretty bad. We have a difficult enough time containing the damage Stardust does when he isn't evil," Archon said.

Velvet had been silent for a while, chewing on the remains of a chicken sandwich as she looked at all the options, trying to find an angle. "They aren't the Protectorate, so they won't think like them," she said, an idea formulating.

Archon had been thinking the same thing for a while, but was still working on a way to use it to their advantage. But now the cat was out of the bag and it was time to knock ideas around. "On their own world, they weren't a team. In fact, based on what little was in the reports, they barely knew each other, Lazarus and Lenore notwithstanding. So they won't be coordinated, not yet at least. We might get lucky and be able to separate them and pick them off one at a time."

"I don't know where we would keep them in that kind of circumstance, but at least I could procure some power shackles. Starcom Inc. was working on an upgrade. Jaccob was telling me about them just last week, so there should be prototypes available," Velvet said.

"And you think you can get some?" Gallows said, liking the odds better and better.

"I still have the all access card, and Elizabeth Stevens owes me a favor," she said simply. "I can have them in a few hours." She had yet to tell anyone about her encounter with Deathstar, and was still kicking herself for letting him get away. If she hadn't felt the need to take care of the matter alone and taken some backup, their job would be that much easier now.

"Okay, so we can contain them," Libertine said. "Now where do we stash them?"

"I can find somewhere," Gallows said.

"You have somewhere in mind already?" Archon said. "Somewhere secure?"

"Define secure. There are a lot of places to put them where they won't cause any problems as long as they remain shackled," Gallows said with a shrug. "I know some unused industrial storage tanks over in Morrison, abandoned houses and store fronts down in and around Quayside, and some nice homes over in Regency Heights that are for sale but are priced out of the market."

"Regency Heights?" Archon said.

"I was looking for a place to live," Gallows said.

"Okay, but in the Heights?" Archon said.

"You never know when you might find a great deal…you know, haunted or something."

"We won't have to keep them for long," Huntsman said. "At least I hope not. Any of those sound okay to me. Now all we have to do is draw them out."

Libertine's cell phone made a bug-like buzzing noise and she went outside the noisy café to answer. while the others discussed strategy around the food-cluttered table. "What the hell do you want?" she said into the tiny, silver phone. She hunched her shoulders against the unexpectedly cold wind coming off the river.

"Do you recall a walk we took in the park last night?" a familiar Mexican-tinged voice said.

"Where I introduced you to my boyfriend?" she said, smiling as she waved at Huntsman through the front window. He was busy and didn't notice, but Gallows did and winked at her again. Her gaze snapped back out to the street.

"The straight-shooter," Manuel confirmed.

"That would be him, but it isn't serious, you know, if you're interested…"

"I seem to have enough lady problems, thank you," he said. "Turns out one of your former employers took a dangerous liking to me."

Former employers? Staci from Parcel Express is after Manuel now? No, that couldn't be it. "Where are you now?" she said, realizing that if he was calling her cell, the Stardust armor might be monitoring the signal looking for key words. It was a lot of signals, but Jacob Stevens was the king of cell phones in Cobalt City, and Huntsman claimed that he had written filters to pick up key words and phrases in the past. Surely Gato Loco was keeping the conversation safe as well, or he wouldn't have been playing coy. She waved urgently at the table inside until she got someone's attention. This time it was Velvet, and the tough-as-nails-scrapper pushed back her chair and headed outside.

"I got stuck at the office," Gato Loco said, "Where you used to work, before getting frustrated about not getting enough assignments."

Libertine covered the mouthpiece and whispered sharply to Velvet. "Tell Archon that we have his Halfling," she said. Then she uncovered the mouthpiece and made her voice sound as conversational as possible, "Boy, do we have some catching up to do. Can I put a mutual friend on the line in a second? He has a favor to ask."

"I think I could agree to some mutual back-scratching," Manuel said. "I have a ride waiting, but we're both stuck here. We both have places we'd rather be, so anything we can do to help each other out is a step in the right direction."

Archon burst out onto the street and motioned urgently for the phone. He caught his breath and held the small phone up to his ear. "Hey, buddy. Long time no see," he said. "We have so much to talk about."

Chapter Twenty

Worm Queen quickly figured out what had happened. The incident that resulted in the Protectorate being reflected in the Mirror of Shadows the first time around had cut her deeper to the bone than anyone else. No, she knew within seconds that it was happening all over again, only this time it was worse. Getting home was the easy part, Anna quickly decided. Getting back into her body was another thing entirely. And the state Lenore had kept herself in, getting back in her own skin was imperative. A scent clung to everything Lenore wore, permeating the majestic and opulent penthouse she shared with Lazarus, the anti-Simon Floyd. It was a smell of death, and not the pleasant-by-comparison smell of something that crawled up under the porch to meet its maker on some lonely August afternoon and wasn't discovered for a few days. No, this was the smell of deliberate, planned, prolonged death. Dust and embalming fluid and rose perfume to mask another, more cloying sweetness, filled every fiber of Lenore's entirely black wardrobe.

But it was more than the wardrobe, or the smell of her skin. She felt weaker than she was used to. Anna wasn't as physically fit as most other members of the Protectorate, but she still took care of herself. Spandex was a cruel mistress, and her self-image was often less forgiving than circumstances warranted. In the middle of laying the smack down on some bank robber, there weren't that many people looking at how her ass looked. But every once and a while a camera crew might be there. So Anna endeavored to keep toned, if nothing else. Lenore made no such effort. She was slender and shapely enough under the baggy clothes, but just moving around the apartment, the muscles felt underused. Wandering from room to room for longer than a few minutes might cause her to break a sweat.

She was surprised to find herself taken aback by the sleeping arrangements. The "His and Hers" coffins in the bedrooms were an uncomfortable blend of creepy and sad, but still they seemed at home in the funeral parlor atmosphere. They had the money and influence to live like kings, and they chose, instead to be buried like them. At least Lazarus had an excuse. Like Mister Grey, he had been dead for over seventy years, but instead of being cremated, he had been granted a more traditional zombie experience and from there a more immediate chance at revenge.

But parallel world Anna Lyta had no excuses for turning all gothic. The more Worm Queen thought about it, the angrier she got.

She tried to focus on that she was only short-term tenant in this body, and that made it a little easier. But it was no means perfect.

The minor dust storm that rattled the windows of the penthouse shortly after she appeared in this dimension had increased exponentially, and Anna eventually decided to try to wait it out rather than deal with it. She had looked for some explanation of the weather on television, but the only answers the meteorologists had given was "a sudden and unusual convergence of fronts creating wind funnels that were concentrating the region's industrial air pollution."

Rather than brave the dust storm by going out into the small rooftop garden through the broad sliding doors, she instead pressed herself up against the windows over looking the Lafayette Park neighborhood. Anna had a hard time identifying the building from landmarks. She was more used to ground level than high-rise, and even better at finding her way underground. She was pretty sure that the penthouse used to be a hotel's rooftop nightclub called the Oriental, but when the hotel went condo, the nightclub and several floors beneath it had been turned into corporate office space. There was an arts foundation there now, or something like that. She was never too sure.

With the exception of the howling dust storm outside, the penthouse was quiet as a crypt. Anna summoned up a ten-foot long worm for company and managed to find the stereo, but didn't recognize any of the CD's. She settled instead on a nice, loud radio station and got to work.

First thing, she decided, was to see what was going on back home. She concentrated on the kind of worm she was looking for and summoned one up. The Worm Queen sent it through the fabric of time and space to send images of her own dimension. She wanted to send it directly to the Keep, but remembered Doctor Shadow setting up magical barriers against exactly that kind of intrusion. Instead, she was forced to settle for a view of home from a nearby rooftop. It didn't provide much information, but it was something.

Next, she decided she needed to find out where the rest of her team was. If they were here as well, it was possible that Doctor Shadow might already have a solution to getting everyone home. If she was alone in this little slice of hell, then there was probably some kind of worm she could summon to transfer her personal consciousness between the two bodies. She called up a thin, silvery worm to scan radio frequencies for any sign of Stardust, figuring that he was the fastest and most likely to use radio waves. As for the rest, she could only hope for stumbling upon some other method of contact.

That left her with the unsettling question of what had happened to Lazarus. Anna had half expected him to be here once she realized where she was, but there was no sign of the erudite zombie. Simon's body had started to turn to flesh when things got fuzzy back at The Keep, so perhaps he had been swapped as well, but that constituted a physical shift and not the mental one she had experienced. And if the bodies had been swapped, then where was Mister Grey?

She eyed the mysterious dust storm outside the windows.

It couldn't be him out there.

Could it?

Anna found that she had enough strength of will to summon forth another worm, and at her command, a long thin worm the color of dried blood slid out into this dimension. It coiled up her leg, across her back, finally coming to nest around her neck, its front section pulsing softly like a heart beat. She felt it open up the synapses in her brain, connecting itself telepathically to her, and from there out into the greater world.

She reached out with her proxy telepathy and tried to touch the clouds of dust that raged beyond the window. "Simon?" she said.

There was nothing there. No reaction. No acknowledgement. But she wasn't satisfied. Anna had felt something at the moment of contact, tenuous, maybe; brief, definitely. There was some degree of awareness to the storm. She was pretty sure that it wasn't Simon Floyd. But the coincidence was too great to ignore. She continued to prod, but the more she pushed, the more the awareness retreated.

She didn't know how to classify what it was she was contacting. She wasn't used to initiating telepathic contact with anything above the level of invertebrates. While her powers were, technically speaking, psychic in nature, this was out of her depth. Anna broke off contact and sent the brain worm back to where it had come from.

Where her worms went to, and, for that matter, came from, had been the subject of several arguments among her peers. When her abilities first manifested in graduate school, she had been part of a school club jokingly called the Society of Evil Geniuses. To her surprise, the group's name had not been a joke at all, and the two people behind it had been using the group as a pretense to steal their associates' research and use it to leapfrog to bigger, more marketable discoveries. But when things were good and it was just a bunch of naïve science geeks doing their thing, the argument had gone round and round. The popular theory was that Anna was somehow able to create these worms psychically and then control them. Anna contested that since matter could not be created or destroyed, she had to "pull" these worms from somewhere, and then compel them to do what she wanted. She was not comfortable with the idea that these worms were a product of her imagination, merely a psychosis made real. Her rivals were not comfortable with the idea of a dimension populated by worms of unimaginable size and abilities.

It was an impasse that they could never quite resolve.

In the end, Anna didn't really care where the worms came from. They came when she called, they did as she commanded, and the process was tiring. What more did she need to know? If she were to look too deeply, to understand what her powers truly were, it might give her answers she didn't really want. That way madness lies.

As Anna waited for her scouting worms to contact her, she managed to find several huge scrapbooks to entertain herself with. The black leather bindings were cracked and dusty on the earlier two volumes, with dates on the spines all the way back to 1931. "The Simon Floyd story," she said, pulling them down and retreating to a red velvet chaise lounge. No, she corrected herself. These books were the Lazarus story. It was important to keep them separate in her mind.

The scrapbooks, she discovered, were full of newspaper clippings. The first started with Simon's death. But not the obituary, as she had expected. Already things diverged from the history she knew. "Noted British Pianist Killed In Botched Bank Robbery!" read the headline. The brief article detailed how Simon had been one of five men who had tried to rob a bank branch on Lincoln Boulevard. One other robber had been killed, a black male named Dexter James. Music, alcohol, and drugs had been blamed for leading them into a life of crime. Dexter's body was being shipped back to an aunt in Harlem. Simon was to be buried in Potter's Field. The photo that accompanied the article showed Simon lying lifeless on the sidewalk in fuzzy black and white while a crowd looked on. And there, in the crowd, a face that Anna had seen only once, very briefly only the night before. Camilla. Her eyes blazed with righteous fury as she looked at a man on the other edge of the crowd, a chiseled granite monolith of a man in a dark suit who looked on with disinterested eyes.

The next page featured a brief piece from less than a week later on vandalism at the small cemetery outside of town. It was reported that in addition to paint, bottles of rum, and butchered animals being found, someone had stolen one of the bodies as well. It was no surprise to see the big man from the first picture dead from a suspicious fall on the next page. From the photo, it looked as though

145

most of his limbs might have been broken before he "fell" from the balcony of the nightclub he worked at. She looked at the photo for several minutes then reread the article.

The first retaliatory murder happened right here, at the Oriental. Simon had come back from the dead with vengeance on his mind, but he wasn't really Simon anymore. He was Lazarus. Anna found it difficult to separate the two, for the Simon she knew came back from the dead wanting revenge as well. If he hadn't been cremated, would the two Simon Floyds have differed so greatly? She liked to think so, but had to admit that there was no way to ever know for sure.

Following the "accidental" death outside the Oriental, the scrapbook began cataloguing the revenge of Lazarus. The newspaper had been diligent in covering every horrible act, every death, every mysterious fire, every search party that went looking for the missing children of some enemy or another. It was all there in black and white, and Lazarus had been as methodical about saving his clippings as he had been about eliminating everyone who ever did him harm. And when every last bit of vengeance had been exacted, the clippings became more sporadic.

The nature of the articles changed as well. It took a couple of articles for Anna to see the pattern, but then it hit her. Lazarus had spent several years systematically destroying a criminal empire in Cobalt City. But he wasn't a hero. He was a monster, even worse than those who created him. And while he was destroying one criminal empire, he was busy setting up one of his own. By 1955, Lazarus occupied a special level of the city's upper strata reserved for movie stars, politicians, and suspected mob bosses.

Pictures and stories of him began to turn up in the society pages, always accompanied by a striking, older, black woman. They went to movie premieres and concerts and clubs, and the papers loved it. By now it was public knowledge that Lazarus was a zombie. It wasn't the kind of thing that could be concealed for long. But he was articulate, even, one article admitted, surprisingly charming in a chilly way. And, the police were loath to admit, he was essentially free from prosecution.

To their frustration, an assault charge in 1948 revealed that there was no way to prosecute a dead man. His case was dismissed on the spot, and the whole world opened up to him. And there Anna saw the difference between the Lazarus and Mister Grey. While one kept to the shadows, separate from the world, the other embraced it.

But Lazarus' status as a corpse, and a British one at that,

presented a whole new range of problems. Not only could he not be prosecuted, but he could not own property. With no legal status, he couldn't even have a bank account or own a business. For all his wealth and power, he had no real assets, and in the end, everything had to be owned through Camilla.

So when Camilla finally died in 1974, she willed all of her estate, including the Oriental and tens of millions of dollars, to her assistant, Josephene Lyta. Less than a year later, she made Lazarus the executor of her will and her newborn daughter the sole beneficiary and inheritor. Her daughter's name was Anna. The picture in the scrapbook could have been taken from Worm Queen's own baby album.

Anna sat slack-jawed for a long moment, too stunned to know what to think. The worm she had summoned for companionship poked its head out from under the coffee table and looked at her like a puppy. A slimy, brown, limbless and faceless puppy that happened to be ten feet long and capable of battering a full grown man into unconsciousness...actually, it wasn't anything like a puppy, Anna had to admit. She looked back at the picture in the photo album and shook her head as she closed it. "Well, I guess that explains a few things," she said, deciding that she was in danger of stumbling into the "things man was not meant to know" section of the library if she continued.

The silver worm Anna had summoned earlier chose this moment to wiggle excitedly into the room. "I have a cheesecake on order for an afternoon pick-up," the worm hissed as he relayed Stardust's static laced transmission, "and I want to know if I can add a late lunch reservation on as well."

"Does one o'clock work for you?" the chipper hostess asked.

"The signal is isolated and locked in?" Anna whispered into the worm's mind. The worm nodded its head enthusiastically, like a puppy that...no, nothing like a puppy at all. Anna waited until Stardust had finished his lunch reservation then had the worm "call him back."

"I don't suppose you could pick a girl up for lunch, could you?" she asked him, the worm translating her thoughts into a radio signal tight-beamed onto his transceiver signal.

"Worm Queen?" he said, laughing in surprise.

"In the flesh," she said. "Well, in someone's flesh, at least."

"How did you find my radio signal?"

"A little worm told me," she said.

"Kickass! Where can I pick you up?"

"You know the Oriental in Cobalt City?"

"West side of Lafayette Park, right?" he said. It sounded like he was reading as he talked, like he was pulling up the building on Mapquest.

"That's the one," she said. "There is a garden of sorts on the roof. I'll meet you there."

"I'll be there in five."

Relieved to have made contact with at least one person, she gathered a change of clothes that seemed at least marginally multi-purpose and crammed them into a plush spider-shaped backpack. Anna was in such a rush, she didn't even stop to wonder what had happened to the worm she had sent back to spy on the Keep from her dimension.

And when she went out into the garden, she was somewhat comforted to discover that the dust storm had moved on. She was long gone before the news mentioned that the storm had swept into an abandoned apartment building in the Hollows, breaking several windows and inexplicably scouring all the paint from the walls before blowing out again.

Chapter Twenty-One

"Why are you spying on us?" Rakshasha said, her claws extending and retracting angrily, betraying the tension she would rather not show.

"It's not mine, bitch," Lenore said with a dismissive mumble. She was barely paying attention to the thinly veiled threats as she sat on the conference table staring at Lazarus. Her zombie guardian had barely moved since coming here and she was beginning to think something was wrong. He had said that he wasn't alone in there, and her brain worm had confirmed as much. But she had no idea what to do about it. As much as she hated to admit it, this was a battle that her lover would have to fight on his own.

"How many other people do you know that summon ten foot long worms?" Rakshasha countered, wishing she had a carcass to throw at the feet of the pale, death-scented annoyance, but the worm had faded away after she struck it. She had come across the spy on the roof of the building across the street, obviously watching this so-called "Keep." It might have seen Manuel de la Vega's escape, and she didn't know which possibility angered her more; the fact that Lenore might know about the missing visitor, or that Lenore's opposite was back so soon.

"What color was the worm?" Lenore sighed.

"Grey," Rakshasha said, thinking back carefully, "and there were bits of yellow."

"Yellow swirls, spirals, about mid-way down the body?"

"So it was yours," Rakshasha said, considering how to play this without showing weakness.

"It was a dimensional crawler. Someone sent it through from the other side of the looking glass," Lenore said, her lip curling in what she might have thought of as a smile. "I bet even you can figure out who sent that one."

"What do you have to hide, anyway?" Augustus Dei said from behind her. She hadn't heard him come in. She *never* heard him come in.

"Hide? Nothing," she said casually, but she couldn't bring herself to turn and meet his eyes. If she didn't look, if she remained calm, he could not possibly know about her mistake.

"You know, I can't help you if you don't help me a little bit first," he said, his voice warm, smooth. It was the voice of a friend. But she had no friends. They were a weakness she could ill afford. She

149

noticed that Lenore was watching the exchange with open interest. Even Lazarus himself seemed to have turned his eyes in her direction. She needed to establish strength here, or her position with or under these people would forever be in question.

"Rakshasha hides from no man!" she roared as she spun towards him, her claws extended. The intent was to cut him, just a little. Maybe a small scratch across the cheek would solidify her position. She knew that the smug, unassuming looking man was more than he let on. But a man with vast powers was still just a man, and she was faster than the wind.

She didn't get a chance to prove her speed however. Mid-spin, she felt something grab her wrist and hold it tight. Through a red haze she realized that her target had anticipated her attack, had most likely anticipated far more than that. Rakshasha's wrist was held tight. A look in Augustus Dei's eyes made her fight the instinct to attack with the other hand as well.

"Maybe now would be a good time for us to have an understanding, okay?" he told her. His voice was light, but his eyes were infernos that extended forever into his skull. He twisted her hand until her claws were pointing up, and placed one fingertip on the tip of a razor sharp claw. "While I don't know everything, I do know more than you ever will," he said. With that, he pushed her claw back into the sheath of her hand as if it were nothing. Not a drop of blood appeared on his finger, and she found it curious that she felt nothing.

He moved on to the next claw, "Second, hiding behind a lie is a weakness. The truth is never a weakness," he said. He pushed in the second claw. "So we will only speak truth from now on."

His finger went to the next claw, "Thirdly, do not presume to know me. If you lived to be a million, you would still be younger than me, and you would be no closer to understanding what I am," he said. He pushed the next claw in.

"Finally," he said as he began pushing the last, lethal weapon slowly back into her hand, "you would do well to remember this conversation, because I will not be so patient the next time."

Her claws completely retracted, feeling began to return to her hand as Augustus Dei released her wrist. The pain was excruciating, but she was relieved to find that it faded quickly. Rakshasha had never been afraid before. It was a new experience. She was certain, however, that she did not like it. "I brought someone back to the building. He had a communication device, and I thought he might have been one of the escaped team members at first. But he was just a friend of this body. I...he was in my quarters here for several hours, and when I left him there, he was dying. I thought he was secure, but I was wrong. He escaped and left the building."

"He didn't leave the building," Augustus Dei told her. There was no hesitation, no room for argument in his tone. She thought to question him, but her hand still stung and she thought better of it.

"The panda thing lied to me."

"And now you see why lies hurt," he said with a sad smile.

"They are nothing," she said. "I will hunt them down and kill them. They are only a wounded human and a pathetic panda who thinks he is a man."

Augustus Dei continued to look at her as if he were seeing something she couldn't understand. Finally, he shrugged, "If you say so."

His lack of confidence concerned Rakshasha for only a few seconds as she raced out of the conference room to begin her hunt anew.

In the conference room, Augustus Dei and Lenore stared at each other for a long while. "Don't you have something else to do?" he finally asked her.

"What is wrong with him?" Lenore said, her eyes flitting over to the motionless Lazarus. "And remember that a lie is a weakness."

Augustus Dei smiled, but it looked forced. He walked up to Lazarus until he could stare directly into the unblinking eyes from only inches away. "The Simon Floyd from this world had a very specific wish. He wanted to be made flesh. I had to bring your beau over in the flesh anyway, as per his arrangement with me. But that left me with two Simon Floyds and one body. It must be cozy in there."

"Then who is going to be in control and what happened to the body back home?" she said. A trace of a whimper was in her voice, but Augustus Dei pretended not to notice.

"I don't care who ends up in control. You wanted the truth; I give it to you. I'll say it again. I don't care. But if it gives you comfort, I believe Lazarus will end up on top. He's more of a fighter," he said. "As for the other body, what does it matter if you are here now?"

"But what happens if we try to go home?"

Augustus Dei pursed his lips, considering the young Goth carefully. "Such a lot of questions for one so young," he said.

Lenore's eyes grew steely, her fingernails making little red half moons in the palms of her hands. "Answer...the...question," she said. She had seen what had happened to Rakshasha. She didn't care. She wasn't afraid of pain or death. She had welcomed them since she was an infant.

"I could fit two souls in one body," he said, the amused tone gone from his voice. "But there is only ever room for one life. Your lover's body is soulless, and given some semblance of life on the other side. With no soul to direct it, I could not hope to predict what it will do. Whatever identity it retains is probably fragmented at best. A collection of recollections, maybe some kind of base compulsion directs it. I don't know. I don't particularly care. It is merely scrap…the remainder of a magical long division. And if Lazarus here doesn't shake it off and get to work, then maybe I shall see that he is left as scrap as well."

Lenore did not remove her eyes from Augustus Dei's for a long time. Neither of them budged, nor did they flinch. "Have the others already taken care of their targets?" she finally said, her jaw set.

"Sundiatta and Shade have sanitized the majority of the city," he told her. "The heroes of this city are very receptive to a friendly invitation. And trustingly, they were pinned, helpless, and sent somewhere out of the way."

"Another dimension?" she said.

"Shade knows several unpleasant planes of existence where time runs differently. It should keep the city quiet for a while."

"What about Deathstar?" she said. "I heard he got beat up by a girl."

"He is doing some work on his armor," Augustus Dei said, the slightest glimmer of a smile passing ghost-like across his face. "I believe his anger at the earlier setback will produce some spectacular results."

"So where do you want me and the boss man?" she said.

"There is a training facility south of the city," he said. "A gym, if you will, with several young heroes who learn how to use their powers there. They even share a home adjacent to the gym. While they are no threat now, today's children are tomorrow's freedom fighters. I would like it dealt with."

"Consider it done," Lazarus said, his sudden arrival in the conversation prompting a very un-Goth-like squeal of delight from Lenore.

"Didn't Huntsman train for a while in some shared facility down in Quayside?" Snowflake asked, his furry cheek pressed up against Manuel's as they watched the conference room on a tiny monitor from the safety of cramped but secure confines of the lab level maintenance crawlspace.

With the help of an occasionally confusing cell phone conversation with Archon, Manuel's limited circuitry knowledge, and

Snowflake's skill with hotwiring, they had worked some miracles. A small plasma screen monitor snatched from diagnostic equipment in the hangar served as a window into any room in the building equipped with a camera. That excluded access to living quarters and the locker rooms in the training area in the lowest level of the sub basement, and the hangar where the cameras had been damaged in a fight and not yet replaced. Since security panels and the most basic comfort functions throughout the building, things like lights and temperature, had vocal commands, they were also able to use the imbedded microphones to pick up audio signals.

To help cover their tracks, Manuel had fumigated the garage with a bug bomb, knowing that once Katherine's sensitive nose picked up his or Snowflake's scent, hunting them down would be easy.

Manuel hit the speed dial on the borrowed cell phone, and Archon picked up on the first ring. He barely had a chance to say hello before Manuel rushed ahead. "Didn't one of the guys in your group go to a trade school in town somewhere?"

"I believe so," Archon said slowly. "Is that a problem?"

"His former classmates are about to get a visit," Manuel said, trying to sound casual. He knew time was of the essence if Archon and the others were to have a chance of stopping Lazarus and Lenore before they lost themselves in the city. "I heard that an old, good friend of mine was headed that way with his girlfriend. I don't think it's a social call."

"That's not good news," Archon said, tapping madly into his mini-computer. "How are things going at work for you?"

"Well, I found out that we're not going to be able to call anyone else to work to help finish this project," Manuel said. "Seems that they are all out of town right now."

"Also not good. Do you know if any of them have been terminated?"

"I don't think so," Manuel said, "but this is all through the grapevine. Point is, we can't call them in. They might as well be in Wonderland."

"Ok. Thanks for the update. Let us know if anything changes on your end," Archon said, hanging up.

Manuel slid the phone back into a pocket, straining in the tight confines of the crawlspace.

"Do you think he knows we're here?" Snowflake said suddenly.

"Who? Archon?"

"No. Him," the panda said, nodding towards the screen where

the dark suited man who put Wild Kat in her place stood, motionless. He was looking into the camera, smiling slightly.

"Madre de dios, I hope not," Manuel said, a shiver running down his spine. It was like the man on the screen was staring straight at him, but didn't consider him enough of a threat to deal with himself. He felt beneath notice, and not in a good way. He considered that he might very well die here this evening.

There were degrees of super-hero. Without his costume, he couldn't hope to compete against any of the people who wore the skins of the Protectorate. With his costume, he might live out the night. But not if the man in the suit decided to take a personal interest, he thought.

Manuel reached out and changed the alligator clips to a different wire on the thick trunk of feeds. The view on the monitor changed to one of the labs, where Jaccob Stevens hunched over a long table strewn with circuits and molded metal. At the back of the room, tossed haphazardly over a workspace, were the leathers and helmet of Gato Loco. Snowflake had been able to identify which lab space it was.

As fate would have it, Manuel was less than ten feet away. But with one of the false Protectorate there, and on view of the cameras, it might as well have been on the moon. "Why did she have to put it in the lab?" he said.

"You said she was going to put it in the trophy room, right?" Snowflake said.

"But that's on the lobby level. I could have gotten in and out of there without having to deal with Stardust."

"It has to go to the lab first," Snowflake said. "The computer has a built-in safety program. Any tech for display has to be deactivated first. See that long, chunky object above your helmet? The one on the wall?"

Manuel looked closely and saw what could have been a rifle of some sort if it hadn't been about five feet long and over a foot thick in places. "You mean the thing that looks like a gun."

"The thing that *is* a gun," Snowflake said, his voice dripping with envy. "It happens to be a cutting laser that Wild Kat snatched from some psychotic dwarf a little less than a week ago, when they were in space. Archon got to use it once, and Knockabout told me that it did a number on Doctor Shadow before Wild Kat took the power pack out of it. She's waiting for it to get through quarantine so she can add it to her personal trophy room."

"So the gun still works?" Manuel said. A plan was beginning to form. He wasn't 100% sure that it was a good plan, but any port in a storm.

"Everyone's been too busy to neuter it," the panda told him wistfully.

"How to you feel about using guns?"

"Ah, man, I love them," Snowflake said. "I used to sleep with one under my pillow until I had an unfortunate accident shortly after watching the movie *The Ring*."

"What kind of accident?" Manuel said, fearing the worst.

Snowflake looked vaguely embarrassed, but there was nowhere to retreat to in the narrow confines of the service conduit. "I was sleeping and one of my roommates put in a video tape. I woke when I heard the VCR start to hiss, and I came up shooting."

Manuel whistled low, and wondered if he should rethink his plan.

"No one got hurt," Snowflake was quick to add. "But I had to buy a new television, and everyone moved out of the bunkroom which was fine by me, bunch of sissies. And they made me give up my guns, which is against the Constitution. There is a specific provision about the right to arm bears."

"I don't think…"

"And I'm a panda bear. Freaking B, freaking E, freaking A, freaking R," Snowflake said a little too loudly. As close as they were to the lab where Jaccob worked, Manuel was afraid that it was only a matter of time before they were heard at this rate.

"I believe it says you have a right to bear arms," Manuel said quietly, hoping that the panda would take the hint and quiet down.

"That doesn't make any sense," Snowflake hissed, much quieter.

"Um…"

"I mean think about it," Snowflake whispered harshly, "Bare arms is like bare handed, which is without a weapon. And then we're all back in the bamboo like savages. Not me, brother. I'd show you my opposable thumbs if I could get my arm free. I'm a tool user, baby."

Manuel closed his eyes and said a brief prayer. There was no other way.

"So when we get into the lab, I want you to grab the gun while I grab my leathers," Manuel said slowly. "Don't shoot it while we're in the lab. Too many things in there might explode, but if anyone follows us into the crawlspace, you can let loose a few warning shots. That should discourage them."

He stopped when he realized that the panda man had gone

silent. He swiveled his head and noticed that Snowflake was crying. Realizing that he was being watched, Snowflake sniffled and smiled. It was a frightening smile. Manuel had never looked at panda teeth up close before, and these were definitely a panda's teeth. Bits of sugarcane and bamboo were still stuck in between the row of coffee-stained but otherwise very inhuman molars. "I'm sorry," Snowflake said. "I just...I love you, man."

Manuel rolled his eyes and began crawling towards the nearest access panel. "Now is not the time or place," he said, his mind on the task ahead.

"I know," Snowflake said, his voice thick with apology and emotion. "I just wanted you to know that in case we die. But if I get to fire that baby in there just once it will be worth it."

Once Manuel had moved past and he was a little less crowded, Snowflake pointed at Jaccob on the monitor with his hand shaped like he was holding a gun. "Zap."

Chapter Twenty-Two

Doctor Shadow was reminded of a scene from Disney's *Fantasia* where a macro-encephalitic mouse chops up the broom and then it reforms into thousands of tiny brooms. He always found the whole affair preposterous and more than a little insulting. But at least the music was good.

But now he was watching the same thing happen in reverse, and it was no longer as laughable. Plus, there was no music.

The skeletons marching the worn stone of the Valley of Kings had bashed each other to pieces and then reformed into a smaller number of larger bone golems so many times that now there were only three giant figures left. He had noticed that the larger the figures got, the less they looked like skeletons. As the pieces shattered smaller and smaller with each successive battle, they were able to fill smaller and smaller gaps. The three bone warriors that circled each other now looked more like fifty foot statues covered with rough, monochromatic mosaic. He had watched enough of the combat and rebuilding to realize that they were solid now, not the fragile latticework of the original skeletons.

He was horrified to realize that they were evolving.

Watching them circle each other on the worn stone, Doctor Shadow could tell that they were developing a sense of strategy, a deliberateness that would most certainly cause trouble before too long. By the time this next battle was over, whatever grew from the cast-off carnage would be large enough to reach the balcony from which he watched. True, once he became incorporeal, they could not hope to touch him, but the rest of the Protectorate did not have that luxury. Even incorporeal, a body needed oxygen, and while Doctor Shadow had long ago forgone the need to breathe, if he were to grand the incorporeal state to the others, they would still need oxygen. There was only so long they could be expected to hold their breath.

No, the less time spent here, the better. And if he managed to find some kind of weakness in Shade's scrolls, then that would help their cause as well. Doctor Shadow retreated to the library and threw himself back into his research. He rapidly confirmed that the downside of necromancy was that virtually all applications of the craft involved actions or materials that were, at best, unsavory. And while he discovered that it was possible for him to assume control of the giant bone golem, he doubted he had the time to find thirteen infant boys and cook down their fat in an iron cauldron. It appeared that the

Protectorate would have to deal with the situation in a more traditional manner, by meeting violence with violence.

He also came to the conclusion that Shade had done nothing directly to cause the transfer between worlds. The necromancer had clearly been caught off guard, as there were too many things left unfinished here. Perhaps it was the nature of his last extended cross-dimensional jaunt, protecting the cursed mirror from the Queen of the Black Sigh that colored his theories. Try as he might, Doctor Shadow could not shake the feeling that the King in Yellow was somehow involved as well.

If not for that one, brief reflection in the double-damned Mirror of Shadows, then this might not have been possible. And it was the King's other persona, the twitchy Louis Malenfant, who had the mirror in his possession when they first encountered it. After having been lost to the sands of time for so long, once the mad occultist rediscovered the mirror in the ruins of a Blackpool hotel, powerful new forces became active in this world's supernatural circles. Too little time had passed between the reemergence of the artifact and the appearance of Augustus Dei. It all felt connected and dangerously deliberate. There were too many coincidences to rule out anyone's involvement at this point.

The Mirror of Shadows was a common denominator. So far, he had only heard from Knockabout, but he suspected that Stardust, Worm Queen, and Wild Kat had crossed over as well. There was no good way to be certain, but the ancient sorcerer suspected that the rest of the team had been left behind. In his relatively brief experience with Archon, Doctor Shadow was confident that if he and the others had been pulled through as well, the talented and resourceful hero would have made contact of some kind. In addition, Velvet had been introduced to the group through Stardust, so it was likely that she might contact him first in this world as well. When and if Jaccob showed up, he would have more answers. And Gallows had read the reports himself just the other night, so he would have been able to figure out where people were. Surely if he were here, he would have teleported to someone's location by now.

But Doctor Shadow had to admit that without the hard facts to back it up, he was taking a lot on faith. It made sense to him that everyone would seek him out, as they were all on a magical mystery tour, and no one else had the expertise to find a way home. But if there was one thing he had learned in his several millennia on Earth, it was that people rarely did what made sense. Stardust could even now be flying around fighting crime thinking that he alone was plucked from the reality he knew. Worm Queen might have headed home on her own, deciding in her impetuousness to take the fight directly to her duplicate self and figure out the rest later. And who could predict Wild Kat? She was probably on her way to the Valley of Kings, but there was no telling how or when she would get here.

Outside, the bone giants clashed, shaking dust from the walls of Shade's sanctuary. Inside, Doctor Shadow sat amid a deadfall of scrolls and books, feeling very old, and very alone.

In this introspective moment, he found something he didn't expect to see in this library of dark arts, something he could only see while sitting on the floor. Across the tops of several volumes stacked on the stone shelves, Doctor Shadow saw a thin volume, its unlabeled spine much newer than the texts supporting it. Curious, he retrieved what, at first glance, appeared to be a journal. "Please don't let it be bad poetry," he said, flipping the cover open, "I can not abide that much evil in one day."

What struck him first off was the similarity of the handwriting, a discovery that should strike a blow to handwriting analysts everywhere. He was thankful that his other self did not waste his time filling pages with painful self-reflection. The early pages were mundane: "...suffered a setback along the Tigris and was forced to devote an entire new battalion of howling dead to bolster defenses there. The new governor ensures me that he will have the insurgency smothered..." Quickly flipping through the pages, something else caught his eye and forced him to go back.

> I had the most singular experience earlier today as I was delivering commands to the troops in defense of the valley. A shimmering darkness appeared in my mind's eye, a disk composed entirely of such utter darkness that I felt a shiver of longing in what remains of my soul. This blackness expanded within me, and I found myself falling through eyes that were my own, but not my own. I was standing in a high, marble hall, and I recognized the Queen of the Black Sigh from St. Germain's scattered written accounts. She was standing before me and several other people, none of whom I recognized at the time. We were under threat, and working together.
>
> I tried to fight against this vision, this taunt of weakness, but it was to no effect. Suddenly, I was aware that this was not a taunt, nor a vision of what was to be, but instead a rare opportunity to look through the eyes

of another vibration of self. Just as there are multiple layers of reality, I had, by some miracle, been given a glimpse into the life of myself from that other reality.

It was over as unexpectedly as it began, and I found myself on my viewing walk gasping for breath. Another me, fraught with weakness, not self-reliant, his will subservient to the will of his inferiors...this knowledge possessed me to distraction. All vibrations of self are real reflections of the self. A weakness in one dimension diminishes the strength of the whole. This abomination could not be allowed to continue. I could not allow this imperfect self to drag down the purity of my potential.

If only some way exists to improve my other self, to push it to excel and become the master of the world as he deserves to be...

The section went on for a little longer, detailing Shade's efforts to gather information about his "weaker" self. Doctor Shadow was surprised by how much information had been uncovered, without the subject even realizing that he was under inter-dimensional surveillance. Doctor Shadow had made some of the same efforts on his own, but had been busy with other matters that had required his attention. In the end, Shade had won the information war, but in doing so he had also gathered some false information and drawn some erroneous conclusions. For instance, Shade had discovered that Doctor Shadow now carried a large pistol beneath his robes and assumed it was because his powers were fading. The truth was far less exciting. Doctor Shadow had realized that not all problems could be solved with magic. The timely appearance of a .45 magnum revolver could be a wonderful tool of persuasion as well, even when he didn't actually fire it.

A few pages later, however, he hit proverbial gold.

The stranger walked out of the desert in a dark suit as if he had just taken a pleasant walk in the park. What I found extraordinary was that there appeared, on the surface, to be nothing extraordinary about him. Of average size, plain of features, and displaying no weapons, he would have not seemed out of place anywhere in the civilized world. But despite the heat and the distance from any other city, there was not one bead of sweat on his head, and he did not even blink at the legions of bone soldiers surrounding him on every side.

I flew down to get a closer look and he waited patiently for my approach, a drink that I had not noticed before in his hand. The ice in the glass tumbler could not have been more than a minute old. He looked up at me as if I were an equal and said 'I heard you have a problem that I might be able to help you out with.'

He produced a slim, black piece of parchment small enough to put in a wallet and handed it up to me as I floated above him. In gold print was only his name:

Augustus Dei.

A sudden, thundering crash tore Doctor Shadow's attention away from the journal. A quick glance confirmed his worst suspicions. The bone giant reached the limits of growth and ran out of things to fight all at the same time. With one, van-sized fist, it had punched a hole through the stone wall separating the balcony from the front parlor and was now crouched slightly, peering with one eye through the hole it had created down the narrow hallway into the library.

"Damned inconvenient," Doctor Shadow said, tucking the journal into his cloak and becoming incorporeal. He had no choice but to press the attack to preserve the library and map tables beyond and anything else that might prove to be of use in Shade's suite. He flew through the giant's head and out into the eternal night of the valley.

The towering abomination was over 120 feet tall, and appeared confused, ready to reach deeper into the hole it had created in search of targets. Doctor Shadow used telekinesis and grabbed some of the larger debris that littered the ancient stones and pelted the bone giant. As it turned to focus its rage on him, Doctor Shadow was provided his first good look at what the bone shards had been trying to create.

Standing before him, ready to strike, was Shade. The primary difference between the real thing and the bone representation was the size, of course. At over twenty times the size of the original, this Shade could put a severe physical hurt on anything foolish enough to cross it. Its intelligence was also limited, animal-like, so there was no way this being could cast any kind of spells, but that didn't necessarily make it less dangerous.

A massive hand reached out and closed around the still-incorporeal Doctor Shadow, and the fingers passed harmlessly through him. There was a constant crunching sound as the bits of bone ground into smaller and smaller pieces inside each joint as it moved. With each second it evolved, its limbs better and better defined, its edges smoother, its movements more fluid. There was something wrong about the proportions of the thing, but Doctor Shadow wasn't as concerned about the specifics of its anatomy as he was about trying to stop it.

Doctor Shadow continued to fling debris, and when he ran out of stones, he switched to raw telekinetic blasts. Each hit marred the surface, which then smoothed itself out. He led the giant further away up the valley, but could not escape the fact that he was making things worse as it smoothed its movements. But still they fought, the multi-millennial mage and his giant, pale duplicate with footsteps that rang out like thunder and shook the stone walls of the valley.

"You realize how Freudian this looks, don't you," Knockabout's familiar voice sounded clearly next to his ear. A quick glance found his teammate on a levitating platform a few hundred feet behind the giant. He might never get used to Knockabout's "ventriloquism."

"Really," Doctor Shadow said as the giant tried to grab him again, "I would think this conflict was decidedly Jungian. Now, if I had been fighting a giant representation of my mother or, perhaps, an enormous penis, then I would agree with your Freudian diagnosis. This is an archetypal hero journey I am undertaking."

Edirin's rich laugh was a welcome reminder of the absurdity of the situation. "I didn't think I'd ever live to hear you say 'penis'," Knockabout said.

"I have been around quite a lot of blocks in the past few thousand years," Doctor Shadow told him. "I don't suppose you could do anything to end this could you?"

"Your friend there is well out of my mass range. I could sap some of his inertia and put up my force fields, but even then I don't want to attract too much of his attention. With more firepower, we might be able to take it apart a bit at a time."

"It regenerates," Doctor Shadow said, "And rather quickly at that, I'm afraid."

"Pleasant," Edirin said in a voice that made it clear that it wasn't actually pleasant at all. "What do you recommend?"

"I'm not certain, but we should probably deal with it before less calm heads get here."

Edirin laughed again. "I just picked up a radio transmission from Stardust. He and Worm Queen are going to be here in about twenty seconds. That should give us plenty of time. No pressure, right?"

Doctor Shadow found himself laughing along. "For today, it

would be about what I have come to expect. Tell them to hold back and we'll see if we can think up something."

Another giant hand passed through his incorporeal body, but he was still laughing and didn't notice.

Chapter Twenty-Three

Manuel grew up in a middle class neighborhood in Mexico City. He had never been in a real fight until he was fifteen, when he came to the defense of a classmate being bullied out of his bike. Manuel de la Vega was an inexperienced brawler against two older, bigger kids in a fight that didn't even concern him. When he regained consciousness, the bike was gone, he could taste blood, and his left eye was swollen closed. It was an inauspicious start for the skinny, awkward boy who would grow into the leather-clad, cycle-riding vigilante Gato Loco.

As he prepared to enter the lab and reclaim his gear, he tried in vain to push the image of that first fight out of his head. Since that sound beating on the street outside the Zapotec Cinema, he had worked hard to get his body in shape, joining the police force in Mexico City right out of college and pushing his reflexes to their limit racing motorcycles through the midnight streets. Since that time he had learned to fight. He was not that fifteen-year-old kid. And it was not the high-tech suit boosting his dexterity to superhuman levels and protecting him with hundreds of molecule-thin force fields that made him different. He could handle himself in a fight with or without the suit.

Jaccob Stevens had played football in college, and had been an all-star running back his last two years, a little voice in the back of Manuel's head told him. Jaccob Stevens, he had heard, spent a lot of spare time in the Protectorate's exercise facility. He probably took vitamins, and was more likely to drink a protein shake than coffee. Jaccob Stevens looked a lot like a bully last seen taking a bike away from a classmate sixteen years ago.

He couldn't help but feel that, despite all his experiences in the past decade plus, he was entering a fight that he could not possibly win. He was just Manuel de la Vega. Gato Loco was on a table just inside the lab. But if the two were to be reunited, he had to risk a beating.

"Time's a-wasting," Snowflake whispered tautly.

It was true and Manuel knew it. The longer they were out of the service crawlspace, the more likely that the faux-Wild Kat would find them. Like it or not, he had to move. He took a deep breath and punched in the all-access code that Archon had given him earlier. The door hissed open, revealing Jaccob's t-shirt-clad back as he hunched over his work. He must have heard the door, but who else would be here if not his teammates? He wasn't wearing the least bit of armor, every bit of the Stardust suit spread out over the table in front of him.

I could take him now, Manuel thought. While he's not looking, I could hit him over the head with something solid. He hesitated for just a second then reached for a chemical fire extinguisher on a nearby wall while Snowflake, entranced by Wild Kat's cutting laser, slipped past, headed to the back of the room.

In his haste, the oh-so-stealthy panda knocked over a small calibrating instrument on one of the workspaces. The subsequent clatter caused several things to happen at once: Jaccob Stevens turned around, curious, while Manuel snatched the fire extinguisher from its wall mount, and Snowflake uttered a very un-panda-like explicative and stood there like a deer, or in this case, panda in the headlights.

Once he had the fire extinguisher in hand, Manuel took a powerful swing at Jaccob's head. He was stunned to see the muscular scientist drop back into a martial arts stance. No one told me Jaccob Stevens knew martial arts, the little voice in his head screamed. As the momentum from his swing carried him around, he saw the end of the fire extinguisher pass within inches of his opponent's nose. Jaccob didn't even blink and waited patiently for the opening he knew was coming. When the extinguisher had cleared, Manuel found himself fully extended and more wide open than the Texas plains. He barely saw the punch that hit him in the kidney region, dropping him to the ground blinking back tears.

"I don't know who the hell you are, amigo," Jaccob said, "but I've had a disappointing day and I intend to take it out on you and your stuffed animal friend there."

"What happened, tough guy?" Manuel said, struggling to find his feet through the blinding pain, "Did a girl kick your ass or something?"

Jaccob's momentary smile of amusement faded. His neatly trimmed, kindly science teacher face turned hard and mean. Manuel thought distantly that he had seen something like it in that Pat Morita movie, the Karate one that had kids everywhere standing on one foot before getting their asses kicked. In fact, he might have even tried that himself during the bike incident. The thought moved to the back burner as he became aware of Jaccob's fist getting closer to his head. Manuel shifted enough to take most of the blow on the side of the head instead of the face, and he considered himself lucky.

His head rang, and tiny red and black spots danced before his eyes, but the skull was thicker there and was better able to absorb the impact. The same punch to his face might have hollowed out his skull. His little voice told him to lie down for a while. He had a hard time arguing. The floor, when he found it, was cool and inviting. He considered that perhaps he and Jaccob should sit down together and discuss bad days. He figured that was a competition he could win.

Through the seductive shroud of sleep that he knew was probably signs of a concussion, Manuel could tell that Jaccob had stopped beating on him for now. He was safe, but something still nagged at him.

"This is all a misunderstanding," the little voice pleaded. "We work here, and went into the wrong lab by mistake."

Manuel wondered why the little voice in his head sounded like the Protectorate's panda driver and pilot.

"If you work here, you wouldn't have tried to attack me," the voice Manuel knew as Jaccob Stevens said. "Unless you've gone crazy or something, that is. Either way, I should beat and restrain you just to be safe."

"That won't be necessary. I'll just pick my friend up and be going. Sorry for the inconvenience," the little voice said again. Manuel wasn't so sure the voice was coming from his head anymore.

No. It was Snowflake, he remembered. This wasn't some cracked, sun-baked sidewalk in Mexico City. He wasn't fifteen anymore. He wasn't just going to get beat up if he failed now. He was going to die. And Snowflake would probably die as well. Manuel clenched his teeth and blinked his eyes open. The light was bright, even from his position on the floor, but he refused to give in. The real little voice started to say something, but he tuned it out. It was time to stop listening to little voices.

It took every ounce of resolve he had left to get back on his feet, but once he had his weight centered it became easier. Even the pain went away a little bit. Snowflake was a few feet from the gun and Gato Loco suit, cowering from an anticipated blow . Jaccob once again had his back turned. Manuel took a slow breath then raised his voice, "Take your hands off the bicycle," he said with as much authority as he could muster.

Confused, Jaccob turned towards Manuel, and was more than a little surprised to see him standing. "Bicycle?"

"Panda," Manuel said, feeling his ears getting red, "I meant panda."

Jaccob spun quickly and shoved Snowflake hard over the table and into the wall. All manner of things clattered to the ground along with him, including Gato Loco's helmet, some small plastic boxes full of parts, and the gun. "You mean that panda?" Jaccob said. Manuel liked Jaccob's sneer. It reminded him of a very early James Spader

166

beneath the beard.

"That would be the panda," Manuel said, "And now you've gone and done it."

Jaccob took a quick hop-thrust at Manuel, trying to spook him. If his reflexes were responding the way they were supposed to, it might have worked. Instead, Manuel just blinked at him, focusing on keeping his feet under him and not swaying. It was working. He was feeling more focused by the second, but he knew he didn't have forever to get his head back together.

"Do you have any idea who I am, fruit-picker?" Jaccob said, advancing slowly.

"I know exactly who you are," Manuel said. I have to drag this out, he though. I have to buy some time, but not too much. He couldn't risk Rakshasha stumbling onto them.

"Do you know that in my junior year at college, I beat two bums to death with my bare hands? I was on my way home from a bar and one of them had the nerve to ask me for change. Then the other one threw up on my new Doc Martins," Jaccob said with a trace of anger over the incident still lingering in his voice. He advanced several more steps forward, doing efficient katas with each step. Manuel fought the urge to stand up on one foot like a crane. "That's the kind of guy you're dealing with, Paco. I'm the kind of guy who beats people to death for messing with what's his."

"Don't sell yourself short, 'ese," Manuel told him with a smile. "You could also be the kind of guy who gets cored out from behind by a ticked-off panda."

"I'm not afraid of a panda," Jaccob said.

Manuel's smile did not falter. "No? Then how about that cannon he's holding? Does that scare you, tough guy?"

Jaccob froze, his smile a lot less certain now. He seemed to remember the gun mounted on the wall for the first time. "I could kill you before he fires a shot."

"Maybe," Manuel said. "But you can't kill *him* before he fires a shot. And he's the one you should really be worried about. In nature, pandas kill more people in their environment than any other animal. And that's without alien mining lasers. Kill me and he'd still burn a few grapefruit sized holes straight through you."

The air was torn by the sudden hum of a thousand bees as Snowflake fired off a short burst over Jaccob's shoulder, melting the security camera and eight inches of blast shielding before he remembered to take his finger off the trigger. Manuel couldn't help but yelp in surprise. His plan of getting their stuff and moving on without firing any shots was now dead. By now, the building's alarm systems would have detected the weapon discharge, and the faux-Wild Kat would be on her way. That didn't leave them any time for Stardust.

Not unless they killed him. And Manuel wasn't about to take that step. From the look in Snowflake's eyes, he wasn't so sure about the panda's respect for life right about now. "I'd be hitting the ground about now, macho man," he told Jaccob as he walked quickly past to gather his leathers and helmet.

Jaccob turned his head, fixing the two of them with a cold stare as he slowly got to his knees. He didn't need to say anything. His anger was apparent as they left the lab with their bounty, closing the door behind them. He was barely on his feet again when Rakshasha raced into the room.

One of the first things she noticed was the smell of fear and sweat, mingled with the smell of slagged metal, electronics, and ozone. Manuel had been here, less than a minute ago. And from the looks of things, he had bested Deathstar as well, although there appeared to have been no blood spilled. Even more frustrating, she discovered that her trophy was missing.

"Where did he go, pig!" she said. She swung around behind Jaccob and lifted him off the ground with one strong hand at the base of his neck. His feet kicked wildly.

"Which one?" he said, trying to sound calm. This had promised to be such a good day, and lately, well, lately he had been wishing that he had never come along for the ride. "Are you looking for the panda or that crazy Mex bastard?"

"They are together?" she said, sniffing the air more closely. Yes. The panda had been here as well. It was hard to pick up anything over the smell of the melted security camera, but he had definitely been here.

"As near as I can tell. They came through the door and left the same way, less than a minute ago," he told her, deciding that there was no point in hiding anything from her. Hell, she'd probably do them all a favor and hunt the thugs down, kill them, and eat them.

"I didn't hear them on the stairs when I came up, and the elevators have been locked down," she said.

"I'm just telling you what I saw," he said. "There are a few more labs on this level, and if they got in here, they could have gotten into one of them."

Rakshasha released him, and he went straight back to his worktable. It was time to quit screwing around with trying to improve the armor. He needed it working, and soon. Rakshasha went to the door and looked out into the empty hallway and closed doors, sniffing for a scent trail.

"Oh, I should probably warn you," Jaccob said as he started plugging pieces back together, "They took that leather body suit you brought in. I suppose you noticed that. But they also grabbed an entertaining little gun that you might want to keep an eye out for. Happy hunting, and close the door on your way out."

Rakshasha didn't hear him. She was long gone.

Chapter Twenty-Four

"I still think it's too risky," Libertine said.

"I'm not arguing that, but don't rule it out," Huntsman said.

"Not to mention sheer lunacy," Archon said.

"Which is why they won't expect it," Gallows said.

"It doesn't matter. I think the idea is irresponsible," Velvet said.

"And it's also the best chance we have at stopping them," Huntsman said. They stared at him as they stood on the edge of the easternmost bridge connecting downtown to Quayside—and the Dixon Gymnasium. Archon's computer had notified them when Lenore checked a car out of the motor pool minutes ago, and the GPS locater in the car showed it approaching fast.

They were out of time. And they needed to bolster their ranks. But in a city of secret identities, it was difficult at best to contact any given hero on short notice, and the counterfeit Protectorate had already removed most from play. That left them needing someone useful who could be found immediately. No one liked the name Huntsman had come up with, least of all Huntsman.

"We don't have time to argue," Archon said. He looked at his computer to gauge Lazarus and Lenore's ETA. "Huntsman, since this is your idea, you go with Gallows and Libertine to get him."

"Are you and Velvet going to be able to handle the gruesome twosome?" Gallows said.

"We have the benefit of surprise," Velvet said, plotting her hiding place and trajectory already. "We might not take them. I don't know what Simon will be like now that he has a body. But we can at least hold them until you bring in the cavalry."

"But only if you hurry," Archon said, looking pointedly at the tattooed teleporter.

Gallows had already taken his passengers and was gone, looking like a night full of stars as he folded space around himself. Libertine and Huntsman had become used to the effect in the past few hours and no longer felt the few seconds of blurry disorientation. But as they stared up at the imposing brick façade of the Fermi Mental Institute, they felt a different kind of discomfort.

"I can't believe we're actually going to break someone out," Gallows said under his breath.

"Not someone," Libertine corrected him, "Jeremy Red. I can keep him somewhat muted, at least get his telepathy to a tolerable level."

"But don't trust him," Huntsman said as he headed inside, "and don't turn your back on him for a second."

The first people were at the reception desk. As they asked what the heroes were doing there at such a late hour, Libertine reached easily into the guard's heads and found the images of several staff members.

The main guard stopped in mid-sentence and shook his head. He wondered for a second if maybe two years of working at the asylum had started to make him see things as well, for clearly he wasn't seeing three of the city's super-heroes. He waved Doctor Gelner and the two orderlies through the checkpoint, then promptly forgot that he had seen them at all.

At the entrance to the extreme ward, the two guards thought they saw the doctor and two orderlies vanish on one side of the secure door to appear suddenly on the other side, but then they remembered Dr. Gelner buzzing them all through with his pass card. And then they too forgot all about the late night visit.

By the time they reached the dim hallway of the extreme ward, less than ten minutes had passed, and no cries of alarm had gone out. "Remind me to write a letter to the director about their security," Huntsman said. At least now he understood a little better how people kept breaking out of the Fermi Institue to terrorize Cobalt City time and time again.

The section they finally found themselves in reminded Gallows a little of the nocturnal house of a zoo. The prisoners were behind heavily reinforced Plexiglas windows, and had created a homey environment to the best of their ability. The hall outside was kept dark to allow visitors to look in, but difficult for the patients to see out.

The far end of the hall belonged to Jeremy Red. Early on, the doctors hit upon the idea of keeping people as far away from Jeremy as possible. They kept him pumped full of psi-dampening drugs, and his room was outfitted with state-of-the-art power draining devices, but even then, they couldn't shut Jeremy's telepathy down completely. Anyone within ten feet of Jeremy could feel it. The probing, nauseating waves of ego that rolled of the young psychic were a constant violation. And they bothered Jeremy as much as anyone else.

Less than a year ago, the Mysterious Five had captured a member of the Society of Evil Geniuses named Nicodemeus Candledark who took pride in his evil. Anna Lyta's former associate worked on the cutting edge of virology. His hatred from the slings and arrows of society caused him to infect himself with numerous deadly and constantly mutating viruses. Instead of dying, he found that his years of work with diseases had made him immune. Overnight, Nicodemus had become a walking hot zone. When Mister Grey helped bring him in, there was no denying that the once-brilliant scientist had gone completely insane.

With space at the Fermi Institute being limited, Candledark became Jeremy Red's new next-door neighbor. It was one of those expedient, temporary solutions that threatened to become permanent. But space was still limited. Since the current trend in the courts was to declare anyone who put on a clown mask to commit a crime criminally insane, there was no sign of things getting easier.

As the three stood in the darkened hall, surrounded by killers and madmen, even the most jaded had difficulty denying the existence of pure evil. Even unable to see them through the Plexiglas barrier, Candledark sat in the semi-darkness of his own room, staring in their direction, his eyes burning with white-hot fury. Shadow fell heavily in his eye sockets and the hollows of his cheeks. His smile was wide, his teeth gleaming in a smile that would send most sane men scampering for the trees.

"He doesn't know you're here," Jeremy Red said from his room. The skinny young man stood facing the back corner of his room, his bare, bony back twitching as he scribbled something on the wall. Every flat surface had been covered with tiny, precise writing. Even the Plexiglas itself had been victim to Jeremy's writing, the words and symbols scratched in by some sharp instrument. It was difficult to follow Jeremy's movements for long through the marred barrier. It was as though the dangerous psychopath was swimming in words, afloat in ideas.

"Who doesn't know we're here?" Huntsman said.

"Nico," Jeremy said, rolling his head on his long neck to indicate Candledark in the next cell. "He doesn't even try to see what's on the other side of the glass. He is much happier with the pictures in his head. You're much happier alone, aren't you, Nico!" he said, his voice climbing to a shout. "Aren't you!"

In the next cell, Candledark started giggling and rocking back and forth, his eyes and smile wide. His skin stretched tight, giving him the appearance of a grinning skull with a shock of fine, blonde hair dusting the top of his head.

"You have to get me out of here," Jeremy said, his shoulders slumped. He was still in the corner, but Libertine could tell that he knew exactly where his visitors were, and, more frighteningly, who they were. "He's always like that, grinning and giggling, imagining what he'll do when he gets out and to whom. He has a certain fascination with your friend Anna Lyta. They knew each other before he became a total basket case. Some of his fantasies, well, they would make de Sade queasy. And I can't shut them out. I can't. I've tried and I've tried, but they still creep in around the edges. Sometimes I have a hard time telling where he ends and where I begin. If I stay here much longer, I think that I might go insane."

"You aren't the only one," Gallows said under his breath.

"Oh now, please let us not forget our manners. Remember that it is you who need me," Jeremy said, turning to face them for the first time since their arrival. His long, dark hair framed an angelic face. He was shirtless and rail thin. At first glance, he was an innocent young man in his early twenties, the victim of mistaken identity. But then the mental probes he could not control washed over them, like huge, invisible tentacles trying to pry open their skulls to lay eggs in their brains. This was no angel. This was Jeremy Red. And although an argument could be made that his unfortunate condition drove him to brutally murder over a hundred people in cold blood, it was readily apparent on the video evidence at his hearing that he enjoyed every single violent death.

"We made a mistake coming here," Huntsman said.

"No, you did the right thing," Jeremy said, pressing up against the Plexiglas. "Please, Marcus, believe me when I tell you that you did the right thing. I can help you. I want to help you."

Huntsman masked his alarm at the eastern seaboard's most prolific murderers knowing his identity. He didn't know why he was surprised. "I believe that you are thinking of someone else," he told the psychic.

Jeremy pouted and began distractedly tracing some of his writing on the marred barrier between them. "Oh, I thought we were past all that nonsense. You know, the whole black hat, white hat thing. Now that you're here to break me out, it puts you decidedly into the gray area, doesn't it? And if I can help you then that makes me a shade of gray as well."

"We're wasting time here," Gallows said thinking of Archon and Velvet back at the bridge. "Do I grab him or not?"

Huntsman took his eyes off Jeremy, who was busy playing pensive, pretending not to listen when in fact he could hear the words forming in their heads before they were even spoken. "What do you think, Libertine?" Huntsman said. "Can you keep him on a short leash?"

"I've read the specs on the psi-drainers they use here, and I'm graded a few degrees above them, at least for the short term," she said. "I can keep him leashed."

"I'll be your bitch any day," Jeremy said, smiling wolfishly. "Your teleporter has other doggie ideas, but I won't sully your virgin ears by repeating them. I'd slap him if I were you."

"He's trying to distract us," Gallows said. "Maybe we should leave him."

"We'll take this up later," Libertine said to Gallows.

"How long are you thinking for short term?" Huntsman said.

"Depends on when he took his last meds," she told him. "Duty nurse down the hall dispensed them two hours ago, next dose in six hours. I can keep him under my thumb until then, but I can't promise you longer."

"That's good enough, isn't it chief? You have a whole bunch of powerful friends with someone else in their head, and you need a way to get the upper hand. Disorient them with detailed, broad area illusions, maybe even track their locations for the ones that go invisible, or predict their strategy, right? I understand. I see it all. Your girl Libertine here is good, but she's no Doctor Shadow, is she? Trust me when I tell you that I'm your man," Jeremy said. "You need me. You know it, and because you know it, I know it as well. Can't you see the symmetry?"

"Six hours, no more, and then you're back in here with your pal Candledark," Huntsman said.

"Any vacation is good vacation," Jeremy said, stifling an excited giggle. Just to be safe, he wiped the memory of the giggle from his liberator's minds. He couldn't have them see his joy. Soon they would be gone, and only minutes before the ward nurse sent in his dose of psi-dampening drugs, too. It had been so easy to plant the false med schedule in Libertine's mind, distracted as she had been by Gallows' lewd thoughts. He watched Huntsman call his companion Archon for an update and waited patiently. Soon he would be face to face with Anna Lyta, and he could have his revenge on her for abandoning him here. He knew the memories he had of Anna were not his own. Neither were his memories of Mister Grey capturing him. But it didn't matter anymore. He had lived with their torment long enough that they might as well have been his own defeats, his own betrayals.

Nicodemeus Candledark had an itch to scratch. And with a psyche as fragile as Jeremy Red's, that itch had become, like everything else he touched, contagious.

His plotting was interrupted as Gallows teleported them away. The sensors in his room at the Institute noted his sudden absence and a blaring alarm went off. Security scrambled, grabbing dart rifles loaded with psychotropic drugs and sedatives. Steel doors and shutters slammed shut all over the facility. But it was too late. Jeremy Red was long gone.

In the noise of sirens and clomping of running boots, there was no one to hear Candledark as he rocked in place, giggling. No one but madmen. And having been rudely awakened by the suddenness of the late night alarms, none of them saw what was so funny.

Chapter Twenty-Five

A steady progression of cars made their way across the bridge in the Cobalt City night. Archon stood in the shadows beside one of the huge supports for the suspension bridge and watched the detailed map on his small, handheld computer. "They're almost here," he said to Velvet, who crouched even deeper in the shadows.

"They made good time," she said, watching the moving cars for the Lincoln Continental checked out of the motor pool. The others had been gone for only a few minutes, and depending on what kind of resistance they met, it might take a while before reinforcements showed up. "Guess we have to take them down ourselves."

"Think you're up to it?" Archon said, with a smile.

"Leave Lazarus to me," she said. "If you're not still standing when I'm done, I'll take care of Lenore as well."

Archon set his cell phone to voice activation and tucked his mini computer into its hip sheath. "Lenore is easy," he told her, seeing their target cruise towards them at a smooth thirty miles an hour. "It's the worms that I'm worried about. I might be able to predict what our Worm Queen would summon up, but I have no idea what is going on in her evil twin's head."

"I see them," Velvet said, her muscles tightening. They were in the close lane, which made her job a little easier. At least this way she didn't have to dodge a lane of traffic.

"Attack pattern twelve," he told her, muscles tensing as he waited for his part. The car was twenty feet away when Velvet passed by, low to the ground. A small tire-killing charge from her belt was tossed with unerring precision beneath the front tire of the long black car. A loud bang sounded as the tire shredded and the car swerved into the guardrail separating the street from the pedestrian path. In a spray of sparks and blaring horns, their target ground to a halt five feet from where Archon hid.

Archon considered himself fortunate that neither of the car's passengers had seen Velvet or had considered the blown tire the first strike in a coordinated attack. He was able to get right up against the side of the car, an automated program in his computer telling the car to roll down the windows. While Lenore watched, confused by the crash and sudden contraction of the glass, Archon lashed out with a swift, decisive strike to her temple. The attack could knock a normal person unconscious if done properly, and Archon wasn't trained to miss. The blow struck home and Lenore slumped forward in her seat.

The driver's side door flew open, and was sheared from the Continental by a speeding cab dodging through the next lane's traffic. Lazarus stepped out onto the bridge surface as calm and collected as if he were waiting for a valet to take his keys. He looked at Archon across the top of the car, his dead face contorting horribly in a broad smile. "I think it's time someone taught you some manners," he said, his flat voice carrying easily over the growl of the bridge traffic.

"Funny," Velvet said, emerging from behind the wrecked car, "but I was going to say the same thing to you." Without waiting for a response, she flipped up onto the car's roof and spun a foot out at the zombie's head.

Rather than knocking him sprawling, the powerful blow only caused his head to turn slightly. She didn't pause long enough for him to react, and retreated to just out of his reach until another opening presented itself. Archon took the opportunity to unbuckle the Lenore and drag her from the car to the relative safety of the walkway. He propped the unconscious body up against the concrete support and reached for the power-dampening restraints Velvet had procured from Starcorp, Inc.

A sudden crunching of steel accompanied an inhuman roar. Archon looked up as Velvet tumbled over his head towards the edge of the bridge. Lazarus was not far behind, stopping in a crouch on the steel and concrete divider, his eyes never straying from Velvet. Archon couldn't watch everyone at once, and decided his best course of action was to keep an eye on the dead man crouching only a few feet away and above him. He would have to trust Velvet's abilities to get out of this situation herself. With deft, almost automatic motions, Archon reached for Lenore's wrists, fitting one into the opening of the high tech cuff, while he watched Lazarus track Velvet's trajectory. It didn't look good.

They were on the extreme north end of the bridge, still high above the docks and warehouses of Cannonade, not over the relatively safer landing place of the Cambrian River.

Lazarus shifted his focus onto Archon. His smile faded. "Get your hands off my girl, fancy pants," he said. His voice, while flat, had the sound of two gravestones rubbing together. Archon took a second to wonder if he had time to whip up some zombie repellant, then sidetracked himself wondering how one went about making something to repel zombies. They used sea salt in legends, he recalled, something about the property of the salt reminding the zombies that they were dead, but he wasn't sure if that worked in reality. It was effective in *I Walked with a Zombie*, he remembered. What a great movie. He would have to track that down on DVD sometime. If he lived through the night, he reminded himself.

As Lazarus cracked his undead knuckles, something Archon didn't know a corpse could do, a thin, microfilament cable fitted with a sharp, three-pronged hook snaked past Lazarus' head. As it neared its apex, the line snapped tight and pulled the dangerous little hook back, snagging the back of the zombie's head, pulling him over Archon to the far rail. To his credit, Lazarus didn't cry out in pain. Maybe he didn't even really feel the pain, Archon thought, not gaining any real comfort from the idea. But he was comforted that Velvet had a few tricks of her own tucked away beneath her cloak.

Lazarus braced himself against the far rail with one hand and managed to get his feet beneath himself again. But by the time he pulled the grappling hook out of his scalp, Velvet had already swung to a stop somewhere below. As the well-dressed zombie tossed the hook and line over the edge, he looked over the rail to see where it was falling. Velvet's dark blue boots shot up over the edge, her ankles locking behind Lazarus' head. In one, smooth motion, she pulled and flipped him over the edge towards the warehouses forty feet below. Seconds later, Velvet hopped back up onto the walkway, her grapple-gun on her belt, the line already fully retracted.

"Miss me?" she said with a wry smile.

"That isn't going to stop him," Archon said. He put Lenore's other hand into the remaining cuff and flipped the switch. Nothing happened. He had expected lights or a hum or something. Jaccob was really slipping on the aesthetic end of the design process, he thought.

"No," she admitted, sparing a look over the rail to the rooftops below. "But it looks like it made him angry. Ooh…and he missed the roof. That's going to subtract a full half point from his dismount. If he wants to compete at this level, he's going to have to learn to nail those dismounts."

"And we want him angry?" Archon said, hoisting Lenore over his shoulder as he stood.

"We want him careless," she said. "He's solid. He looks like he's made of foam rubber, but he's more like stone than the rotting flesh you usually get out of movie zombies. He's a lot faster than the Simon we've all come to love, and he's a lot stronger. Moreso than me, even," she added, stepping back from the rail as her eyes tracked something below Archon's line of sight.

"How much stronger?" Archon said.

A 1974 Pontiac Le Mans station wagon arched up over the edge of the rail, like some fantastic, improbable whale breaching the surface. It didn't take long for Archon's knowledge of physics and geometry to kick in and tell him to get the hell out of the way. A diving roll, made even more difficult with the unconscious Lenore on his shoulder, carried him well out of the way of the hurled car. All the while, he calculated the listed factory weight of the '74 Le Mans and the distance thrown. He didn't like the strength rating he came up with. It was no fault of the math, he knew. He didn't make mistakes in the math and physics area. He just didn't like what the answers meant. "Okay," he said to Velvet. "A lot stronger. Still think you can take him?"

"I'm not letting one of these bastards get away from me again," she said, her jaw set.

Again? Archon found himself thinking. He had the sinking suspicion that Velvet hadn't told him everything about her earlier errands. But now was not the time . Later, if she didn't get turned into a broken and discarded toy, he could ask a few pointed questions.

Archon kept moving away from the scene of destruction towards the north side of the bridge, where he could take the time to drug Lenore into a deeper and, for his needs, much safer state of unconsciousness. Velvet stayed near the rail, looking back over the edge to track Lazarus. "He's coming," she warned. "He's climbing the support like a big, scary monkey. I give him less than half a minute before he's on us again."

"No pressure," Archon said under his breath as he lowered Lenore to the ground. He pulled a leather-lined, metal case the size of a paperback out of one pocket. He thumbed the catch and it flipped open to reveal a pre-loaded hypo, already prepped for Lenore's weight and physiology. When he looked down at his patient, however, he saw her hands and wrists covered by fat, writhing grubs. "This does not bode well," he said loudly enough for Velvet to hear.

Archon leveled another knockout punch at Lenore's head, and was unpleasantly not surprised when it skidded off an invisible field of force a scant half-inch before impact. Lenore's eyes snapped open, completely aware, and more than a little angry. The grubs at her wrists had done their job, and the melted and apparently defective prototype restraint cuffs fell away. The odds against Velvet and himself just got exponentially worse.

"How's the patient, doc," Velvet said loudly over the blare of traffic.

"Awake," Archon said, standing and backing off to consider the best course of action. His eyes were drawn to a Protectorate communicator at her throat. Her eyes followed his gaze. A slight smile played across her lips and he knew then, in that instant, that things were much worse than he could have expected. "Hey, Velvet?" he said as he backed towards her.

"Need a hand over there?" she said distractedly as she leaned over the rail watching Lazarus get closer and closer. She counted the seconds in her head before he would be on the bridge deck again.

"She hit the panic button," he said as calmly as he could. "We have company coming."

"How is our back-up looking?" she said. Twenty, nineteen, eighteen, she counted to herself.

"No word," Archon said. He watched a flood of red, writhing worms pour forth from some unseen dimension at Lenore's feet. They knitted together, the ember-like glow of barely contained fire igniting when they touched each other. "Tactical retreat time."

He felt Velvet's arm around his waist as she held his body tight against her side. "Hang tight," she told him. Velvet carried him over the side of the bridge as a column of flame erupted where they had stood seconds ago. With practiced precision, she launched out the grapple to snag the underside of the bridge as wind whipped past his face. The line kept spooling out, the ground getting closer and closer with each second. Ten feet above the pitted asphalt, the line slowed their fall, swinging them at an angle towards the side of an anonymous warehouse. Velvet's feet found purchase on the corrugated metal as she ran along the side, killing their momentum. A click on her grapple released the line above while they were still a dozen feet from the ground. An acrobatic flip and roll, and they were on the ground as smoothly as if they had stepped off a bus. "Think they're going to follow us?" she said.

"That's what I'm hoping for," he told her, his eyes falling on a parked vintage Mustang. "Keep an eye peeled. I'm going to get us a ride."

Archon raced over to the parked car and whipped out his multi-tool. As Velvet tracked their two opponents, the Protectorate's resident thievery expert selected a small, thin, flexible piece of metal from the dozens of options in his folding, pocket-sized device. A quick jab into the keyhole and a little jiggle, and the door popped open. He reached beneath the steering column and yanked out the ignition wires, getting a spark and a quickly hotwired car in just under fifteen seconds. Degrees from some of the finest universities in the world, he thought to himself, and here I am hotwiring cars at the docks. How the mighty have fallen.

"They're coming," Velvet said, strapping thick, black pads onto the bottom of her shoes. "I can get us a little protection, but it won't help if we don't have somewhere to run to."

"If the others can get the help we need, I know just the place," Archon said sparing a look over Velvet's shoulder at their pursuit. Coming down off the bridge was a forty foot worm the color of old cheese, crawling and undulating through the air with Lenore riding regally upon its back. Lazarus sat behind her, holding on tightly to God only knows what. Despite all he had seen in his travels before and since joining the Protectorate, it was a chilling sight. A bright flash in the sky gave him warning that new hunters had joined the pursuit. A barrage of energy blasts rained down near them, and Velvet deflected the one headed for the car back in the direction it came from. Archon didn't need to be told that if they were going to run, they had better do it now.

As Archon threw the car into drive, spinning its tires on the scarred Cannonade asphalt, Velvet hopped up onto the roof of the car, her newly applied electro-magnets holding her securely. The Mustang screeched out of the lot, fishtailing slightly as Archon aimed it towards Adams Street. Deathstar rained destruction down from above, but Velvet was able to keep the worst of it from hitting the car. The street around them was not so lucky; screeching bolts of energy tore out tire-eating potholes with every miss.

With Deathstar firing from above, Archon had to rely on Velvet to keep him safe. From the angle of attack, there was no way to anticipate where the shots might be coming from or where they might hit. So instead, Archon became very Zen, blocking out the destruction around him and feeling the flow of traffic and terrain, reacting with finely honed instinct and informed choices as they sped their way towards Earl's Court to the north.

On the roof, Velvet kept her eyes on the glow of Deathstar's boot jets and the devastating star bolts that originated from above. She had lost sight of the monstrous worm and its passengers once Archon had started out through the narrow Cannonade streets. When they hit Adams Street, Lenore and her pet were nowhere in sight. But Velvet had been doing this for far too long to be optimistic and believe that they had lost their pursuers. With each volley of star bolts she deflected back up into the night sky with her cloak, she hoped that maybe, just maybe, she would hit a giant, invisible flying worm, or at the very least, Deathstar.

This wasn't Jaccob Stevens. Not really, and she knew that. Even if she hadn't completely believed the early theories by Archon, she knew the man she had beaten and been so heartbreakingly close to capturing was not the Jaccob Stevens who had employed her to protect his wife and children earlier in the year. The Jaccob Stevens that wore the armor now was little more than an animal. And she would put an end to his charade if it took her last breath to do so.

Ahead of the car, a great worm rounded the corner, and the air before it shimmered. Spreading outwards from the head of the worm, the glass on either side of the street buckled and exploded in a wave of carnage that rippled down the narrow street towards them. Archon snapped up the emergency brake as he cranked the wheel tightly, hoping that Velvet's grip up top was secure.

The two-week intensive driving course in which Archon had participated in Munich began overtaking his reflexes, as his breathing became deep and regular. Panic led to mistakes, sensei Takashi had taught him. Trust your training and live in the state of No Mind. The cars around him became as nothing, and it didn't matter that the last time he had performed a bootlegger reverse like this had been on an empty test track three years ago. The rear of the car whipped around in an angry screech of rubber until the car faced the other direction, clipping the side mirror off a parked Honda Civic and setting off two car alarms. Nothing else on the street was even scratched.

Archon stomped on the accelerator again, and slid around a corner into a narrow, litter-cluttered alley as the wave of sonic destruction blew past behind him. The Mustang sent discarded newspapers and bottles flying as he tore through the alley, the speedometer climbing towards forty. He clipped a tin trashcan, sending the lid flying over the hood.

The spinning trashcan lid raced towards Velvet, who neatly crouched and caught it as it skimmed over her head. She tucked it under her left arm. When fate provides, don't question it, she thought. She glimpsed the flow of traffic at the mouth of the alley and recognized it as the busy 23rd Street. It was usually pretty heavy with traffic at this time of night, and she wondered how Archon would deal with it. Slowing down, she realized, was not part of the plan. The car's horn sounded as Archon leaned into it, and startled pedestrians jumped aside.

Seconds later, the borrowed red Mustang shot out into the busy street between a bus and VW Bug painted like a soccer-ball. Horns sounded, brakes were slammed on, and several minor collisions jammed up the road around them. Archon saw a break in the traffic and went for it, fender benders following in his wake. As they neared the Franklin Street intersection, the great worm appeared again.

This time, Velvet was waiting for them, and she hurled the garbage can lid with every bit of her considerable strength. It wasn't enough to destroy the worm, but it was more than enough to distract it and send the massive sonic blast up into the sky where it couldn't hurt anyone but Deathstar. As luck would have it, the misfire caused Deathstar to change course, and he missed a few clean shots at the Mustang as it shot past beneath him. She watched as he raced a few blocks ahead of the speeding car.

A deep red beam blazed out of Deathstar's breastplate to hit the street half a block ahead of them. It was new weapon, something that neither Archon nor Velvet had seen the armor do before, and a sinking feeling settled into Velvet's stomach. From her higher vantage point, she could see the street disintegrate into nothingness. And their borrowed ride was going far too fast to stop in time.

Archon couldn't identify precisely what the red beam was doing to the road ahead, but every instinct he had told him it couldn't be good. He doubted that this Deathstar had incorporated a Hugs and Puppies beam into the armor. His eyes surveyed the terrain while his brain hummed with possibilities. As he rapidly approached what he could now see was a deep pit, he angled the car to the right, towards one edge of the street. There wasn't room for a car to get by, he knew that, not even if he drove on the sidewalk. But the handicapped ramp out in front of the Delaware Building gave him one chance, however small.

As the car's tires hit the angle of the ramp, Archon popped the car to the side then maneuvered it up onto the two driver's side wheels. He was rewarded by a spectacular and very close view of the fifteen-foot deep pit in the middle of the street out his side window as they cruised past. His cell phone started ringing, and he dropped the car back onto all four wheels just past the pit. "Answer," he told the phone.

"We have the package," Huntsman said on the other end, "How busy are you on your end?"

"We're playing Fox and Hound right now," Archon said lightly, "Guess which ones we are?"

"How many are in pursuit?" Huntsman said.

"Three that we know of," Archon said. "Shade and Rakshasha may be en-route, though, so that would make it a full house."

"Where do you want us to meet you?"

"I'm leading them to Earl's Court," Archon said. "I figure I should be there in about five minutes at this rate. Why don't we surprise our friends there?"

"We're on our way," Huntsman said. "Are you sure you don't need a hand?"

"I'll call if something comes up, but so far so good. Meet you at the Plaza. I should probably get off the phone, though. It's not really safe to talk on cell phones while driving," Archon said, popping the car up on two wheels again, this time on the passenger side. He hoped that Velvet was still holding on up top.

Outside, Velvet kept her eyes peeled for more pursuit. Well, at least if we crash it will be over soon, she thought to herself. But she could hardly wait to ask Archon which Duke brother had taught him how to drive in the first place.

Chapter Twenty-Six

Katherine Wilde had traveled extensively in her life, a benefit of having been born into money. But her travels had never taken her to the Middle East. Her father, the instigator of most family vacations, associated the region with what he called "the unpleasantness of the Crusades." This attitude had flavored her childhood so much so that the closest she had come to Jerusalem was a five-day sojourn to Istanbul where she soaked up the wonders of the Hagia Sophia. So it was with a sense of wonder and vague disappointment that she found herself headed towards Jerusalem to meet with Shade's regional governor.

A military escort had picked her up somewhere in Jordan after her SUV had been disabled by a land mine. At first, she considered fighting the thirty well-armed undead soldiers and their living commander, taking their vehicle and making a go of it, but she still had a fair distance to travel and she couldn't be certain of eluding pursuit forever. An added wrinkle came when it turned out that the squad commander knew who she was and decided to parlay rather than fight. He wanted to take her to his boss, and from that officer all the way up the chain of command to the governor. Safe and quick travel through tough territory, with the possibility of an even speedier end to her travels was too good of an opportunity to pass up.

But she hadn't taken quite everything into account. It didn't take long for her to tire of the smell of the overripe undead soldiers, for instance. To reduce the olfactory distress, she was forced to revert to her Katherine Wilde identity. The change was subtle but undeniable, and while such an action would compromise her secret identity at home, she didn't give a damn for how it might affect Rakshasha. Her ears lost their fur and slid back down the side of her head to where they belonged. Her pronounced brow receded into her skull. The fangs pulled back into her head. Katherine also spontaneously shed enough fur to fill a shopping bag—she was decidedly hairier here than back home. The gold and black hairs pin-wheeled behind her in the wind as she sat in the back of the personnel transport.

To her disappointment, the hot, dry air did little to improve the scent of her escort, but she was at least able to distract herself by watching the sun-baked rocks and date palms roll by through the open canvas flap. They were moving fast, she had to admit, but not as quickly as she would have been driving had a landmine not interfered.

Stupid landmines, Katherine sulked. More often then not, they injured, killed, or (in her case) inconvenienced the wrong people. Most importantly, once they were planted, they were left, armed and ready to maim until they were triggered, sometimes years after the relevant conflict had been resolved. Children tended to mistake them for toys when they found them, abandoned in an overgrown field. Here, in a world where evil and dark intentions were the order of the day, it was not surprising to find landmines in use. But they were still used in her world as well. This sobering thought occupied her mind the rest of the way to Jerusalem.

The streets of the city had been abandoned for some time. With no traffic to contend with, the military convoy reached its heavily fortified destination almost before Katherine knew where she was. The transport rocked to a stop on the dusty street and the engine was turned off. Her undead traveling companions made no move to disembark, but Katherine, at least, needed to stretch her legs a little. She hopped down and took in a glorious, red sun setting behind the high steeple of a sand colored temple across the courtyard. The uneven cobblestones beneath her feet felt warm, and solid, and Katherine was glad to be done with travel for at least a little while, even if she was inside a walled compound where zombies hunkered down behind sandbags with heavy machine guns.

The squad commander crossed the courtyard and began talking to someone just inside the door of the church in a language she didn't know but which sounded distantly like Hebrew. A brief exchange took place, and even if she couldn't understand what was being said, she could sense that the squad commander who had brought her here was explaining the same thing again and again, his patience getting thinner with each telling. Finally, the commander spun on his heel and crossed over to her as the door opened behind him.

"They will not let me enter into the audience chamber, but you will tell them that it was I who brought you, yes?" he said, his head bobbing energetically. "You will tell them Ibrahim Mossul brought you, my friend?"

Considering that they had exchanged little more than a dozen sentences since he came across her on the roadside early in the day, she doubted that "friend" was really appropriate. But, despite the use of undead troops, this organization was like others she was familiar with. If you didn't push to get the credit for your own ideas, then you would be lost in the shuffle, passed over. In an organization where you didn't get fired, you got killed and reanimated as a drone, publicizing your own accomplishments would be key to survival. "Ibrahim Mossul," she said, watching his face break into a wide, broken-toothed smile.

She doubted Ibrahim would be so enthusiastic if he knew her reason for agreeing to this meeting.

Shade ruled in the Valley of the Kings, a land of perpetual shadow. Even before the sun set forever there, maps of the region were scarce to nonexistent. To find him and the others quickly, she would need more detailed directions. What better way to find accurate directions than in the company of one of Shade's trusted governors?

With unhurried strides, Katherine crossed the courtyard towards the modest church where she assumed her meeting was to take place. The zombie machine gunners eyed her warily, but their .50 caliber guns were pointed out, to the silent streets beyond. She was reasonably confident that she could avoid being shot if an alarm was raised, but it would be even better if no shots were fired. All it took was one stray ricochet, one unlucky twist of fate, and things could turn very ugly very fast.

Katherine reminded herself that she was alone here. There were no allies one quick communicator shout away, no Protectorate available to step in if she got in over her head. It felt strange. She had never seen that emotional twist coming. Until the Tesla twins broke into the Oriental during renovations to become her headquarters, until they accidentally woke up Simon, Wild Kat had been a solo act. And she had been happy going it alone, proud of her self-sufficiency in a world of super teams. She convinced herself from time to time that the Mysterious Five was not a team, not really. She had been a den mother of sorts, keeping the twins and, at times, Simon out of trouble, helping them adjust to the role of being heroes. And they had relied on each other, gaining strengths as a group that they could never have realized on their own. And for all the frustrations her caretaker role had brought, honestly, she had to admit that the Mysterious Five had been a team.

She could hardly wait to get home and rub Manuel's face in the fact that he had been, at least nominally, a team player. Mister not-a-team-player had a lecture coming. The thought put a spring in her step as she crossed the threshold of the church into a much cooler interior space. The robed guard stepped outside and closed the door behind him.

The first thing that caught her eye were the crutches, a plethora of crutches, some crude and wooden, some modern and metal, all of them lining the walls on either side of the church. Layer upon layer, no free space was spared. The rough wooden pews were stacked along the back, near the door where she had entered, and their haphazard mass was an unexpected darkness of angles and shadows, looming in her peripheral vision as she made her way into the room. At the far end, she saw no governor, merely a statue tucked into a darkened alcove of a seated man, his right hand held up as if giving a blessing.

"You wonder about the crutches," a voice said. It seemed to come from the statue, but the echoes made her uncertain that the voice originated from anywhere in particular. The timbre of the voice was deep and rich, thickly accented. It reminded her in some inexplicable way of James Earl Jones crossed with Anthony Quinn.

"Yes," she said. She wondered if her mind was being scanned, her secrets peeled away.

"Everyone wonders about the crutches their first time here," the voice said. There was a trace of amusement in his voice, but she was no closer to pinning down where it was coming from. She triggered the change, and felt her Wild Kat form materialize. "In fourteen-ninety-one, a pilgrim came to this church to seek help for his people in Andalusia. He had been told in a vision to come here and prey for his people, and being one to believe visions, he had undergone an arduous trek across the north of the African continent. By the time he reached the church here, almost a year had passed, and his people were gone from this world, but he did not know. He kneeled at the foot of the altar here and prayed for a vision. What the vision was, no one knows, for he would tell no one of it. Perhaps it was of the death of his people, for he stayed kneeling there and cried, his tears pooling in a low spot on the floor. Long after the pilgrim himself was gone, those tears remained. They never dried, never went away. The foolish and weak of heart believe that to touch the tears of the pilgrim will cure lameness. And so word spread. With each person who relinquishes crutches at the door, the myth grows. So it was and so it shall be."

"But is any of it true?" Katherine said. She approached the altar where the small circle of muddy water was pooled on the worn stone. The statue in the shadowed alcove seemed to stare down at her through closed stone eyes, but the cracked stone of its legs revealed it to be a statue and nothing more.

"I have seen stranger things proven true," the voice said. "Are those the tears of the pilgrim? Who can say? Are those who wet their fingers there cured of their lameness? True, many have tossed their crutches aside never to need them again, but is that a miracle of the tears or of their own mind, their own body? Only God himself has those answers, and he has been suspiciously silent on the matter."

Katherine stared into the small pool, and watched her breath cause ripples on its surface. She was finding it difficult to turn away, difficult to remember why she was here in the first place. The reflection, she said, but her mouth wasn't moving. I'm dreaming, she thought to herself. This is all a dream. None of this is real. Her attention got pulled deeper and deeper into the reflection. No, she wanted to shout, not *this* reflection. The Mirror of Shadows, the shadow world, that was what brought her here. Not this muddy reflection of her own face and the inverted body of the statue. This was not why she was here. But was she really here at all?

She kept getting closer to the water. The small pool of tears seemed to encompass her entire field of vision. Her hair felt heavy, wet, the weight of it pulling her downward. The tip of her nose touched water and she couldn't bring herself to pull back. It was all beyond her. It was a dream. None of this mattered. Just let the water take you in, she thought.

The reflection, some part of her brain screamed at her. And she realized at that moment it wasn't the shadow world reflection that she needed to concern herself with. Reflected in the pool of tears she could see the statue above her. And the statue had opened its eyes.

Katherine recoiled quickly from the pool of water she had been so ready to drown herself in. Less than an inch of water, and it would have been so easy to just succumb. Someone less observant, or someone of weaker will, perhaps someone who really wanted to believe, would have been doomed. She advanced upon the statue, still wreathed in the shadow of the alcove. "How many people came here to be cured only to have you prey on them?" she said. She reached out and tapped one claw hard against what proved to be a stone chest.

"They were all cured," the statue said. Now that she was closer, the acoustics of the alcove couldn't hide where the voice came from. "No one who came seeking help left here on crutches. They kneeled before me, I baptized them, and they were lame no longer. Even the pilgrim who created the pool left this place cured, after a fashion. I never thanked him for the constant stream of faithful that his tears brought. It was worth the effort of arranging his arrival here in the first place."

"You've been here for over five hundred years?" she said. The chest had been proven to be stone. The arms were melded with the chest and with the chair. But the eyes that stared out at her, they looked human enough. A creeping sensation that she should know who this was crawled up the base of her spine.

"I've been here much longer than that, child," he said. "But you have survived the test and did not take my baptism, not unlike the one they call Shade. Of course, he is much older than myself and not generally taken in by such trickeries. You will be of great use to me.

You were wise to seek me out. Together there is much we can do."

"I'm looking for Shade. I want directions and passage to the Valley of Kings from you, nothing else," Katherine said. Her eyes had adjusted to the shadows, making the place where the severed head sat upon the decapitated statue easier to see. Its skin looked smooth, but with the toughness of old leather. She could easily believe that he had been around for a few thousand years. As he himself had said, there had been stranger things. For instance, he looked almost exactly like she had imagined the head of John the Baptist when she first read about it as a child.

"Shade will destroy you," John said, "But I can give you direction, purpose. Stay with me and be my right hand. Your reputation precedes you, Rakshasha. I know that I can be good to you. I know I can provide a rewarding outlet for your unique skills."

"You drowned countless people, and for what? So you could gather dust in the desert? You can't even scratch your own nose. I don't think there's anything you can do for me," she said, an outstretched claw hovering inches from his left eye. "All I want from you is how to find the Valley of Kings."

"I have reasons for what I have done. I didn't get this old by eating broccoli and doing push-ups," he spat. "If you are so anxious to go to your doom, then by all means, leave. Any one of my officers or my pilots can give you the coordinates. But you are wasting your time. No one who still breathes comes back from the dark valley."

Wild Kat curled her fingers in John's ancient hair and lifted his head from its resting place. "I get it," she said, raising the gruesome trophy to eye level. "You get to live forever. You drown people and in exchange you get to live forever." She could detect more than a trace of fear in her subject's eyes. It had been a long time since anyone had not been afraid of him, had not fallen victim to his suggestions.

"You know nothing," he said, but there was a quaver in his voice that told Katherine that she was close. "It is infinitely more complicated than that."

"I don't know magic like some of my friends do," she said, pausing for a second to realize that, yes, they were friends, not just associates, "but I do know one thing. There is a balance in everything. Big magic means big costs. Nothing comes free, right? So are you really as immortal as you think you are or does fate have a sense of irony?"

John tried to struggle, tried to bite her wrist, but it was to no avail. She had gone toe to toe with Blak Dawg. And John was, after all, just a head. There was nothing he could do to prevent her placing him face down in the Pilgrim's Tears.

Wild Kat held him there for a long time as she thought it over. John had said pilots. That meant there were planes for the taking nearby. It was much better than driving: no risk of land mines. And she could be rejoined with Doctor Shadow within an hour or two. Minutes passed as she planned her next course of action. When she lifted the head of John the Baptist from the small, muddy pool, she discovered that he hadn't been immortal after all.

Chapter Twenty-Seven

The conference was held four hundred feet above the ground. Doctor Shadow's previous experience with the bone giant determined that perfect altitude to be out of reach of the monstrosity while still affording them a good view of its rampage. Worm Queen and Knockabout were glad to be able to see anything, having been subjected to total darkness for the first few miles of their travels into Shade's inner domain. Stardust had relied on his onboard instrument panels and had not even seemed to notice the absolute absence of light, and Knockabout's traveling companion Emil al-Aswan had apparently been able to see as well in the darkness as he had in daylight. The five of them stood upon the hovering platform Knockabout had brought with him across the desert, and watched and discussed strategy.

"And you can't lift him?" Stardust said to Knockabout.

"Too big and too dense," Knockabout said. It was the third time he had given Stardust the same explanation.

"But you did it with Brimstone," Stardust insisted.

"When he was a third of the size and mass of that thing down there, yes, I did lift him, and, might I add, you weren't there," Knockabout said. He closed his eyes and rubbed his temples with one hand. "When Brimstone went rampaging through that town in Canada, he was roughly the size of Doctor Shadow's friend down there, and, I must point out again, he was too big to be lifted."

"Shade's friend," Doctor Shadow said.

"Pardon?" Knockabout said, giving the dark-clad mage a sidelong glance.

"I claim no responsibility for the thing down there," Doctor Shadow said. "I was absent the day they taught necromantic arts."

Knockabout smiled slightly. "Of course. I apologize for the mistake."

"How fast does he regenerate damage?" Worm Queen said. She was leaning on the rail, watching the giant below them wave ineffectually at them from the ground. She knew she could call forth a worm to shrink herself, but again, the bone giant was likely too massive for her to make a significant difference.

"The process begins almost immediately," Doctor Shadow said. "The damaged bone fragments begin to knit back together, making the whole stronger."

"Using whatever bone is lying around, right?" she said, not taking her eyes off the creature below. She thought she saw something, but was uncertain from this distance. An idea came to her. "Worms! To me!" she said.

A translucent, amber-tinted worm slid out of thin air onto the platform. Or at least to those standing on the platform, it looked like it was right there before them and only five feet long. But with a blink, the worm looked to those watching that it might be fifty feet long and floating in space off in the distance, and the uncertainty of perspective hurt Knockabout's head to look at it for too long. Only when is slithered up Worm Queen's leg and across her back to peer over her shoulder did they get any idea of its actual size. "Telescopic vision," she said with a wink to Doctor Shadow. She patted the worm on the head as it peered over her shoulder down at the bone giant stomping four hundred feet beneath them.

"I've never seen that one before," Stardust said, trying to reconcile the distance readings from his sensors as he looked at the amber worm.

"A girl has to have some secrets. This one comes from a place where distance is relative. One foot is the same as one hundred feet to it. Try not to look directly at it if it bothers you," she said, studying the giant below with the aid of her slithery sidekick. Finally she saw what she was looking for. "Good job," she said to the worm, patting it on the head again before it blinked out of existence.

"The lady has a plan," Emil said. He was smiling, and these were his first words since being introduced to the others.

"It would seem so," Knockabout said. He raised an eyebrow, glad that the team's biologist was finally putting forth a theory. He hoped it was something other than the "blast it to pieces" tactic that Stardust had been putting forth for the past ten minutes.

"I know how to beat it," Anna said. "The giant down there isn't symmetrical. It isn't even close. I'm surprised that I didn't notice earlier. For instance, the left leg is smaller than the right. Close to the same length, otherwise it couldn't stand, of course, but not as muscular, not as well defined."

"But what does that mean to us?" Stardust said.

"That means that the regeneration the bone monsters use is non-distributive, probably because it has no circulatory system. When it gets broken, it needs the same or similar material applied to the affected area to regenerate," she said, waiting for the others to come to the same conclusions she had.

"We know that," Stardust said. "Just not in so many words."

Anna sighed and tried to break down the implications of the obvious in ways the hardware people would understand. "But if we were able to chip away at it and remove those chips before they could re-attach, then we can reduce the overall mass."

"Ok, that would work, but it would take forever," Stardust said.

"You've never cut down a tree in your life, have you, city boy?" she said.

A smile appeared on the faces of the other four people on the platform. It was crazy and would require precision teamwork, not exactly the strengths of everyone involved, but it could work. If Stardust and Worm Queen could manage to coordinate damage to a specific area, Doctor Shadow could push the debris clear with telekinesis. Once the material was removed, Knockabout could release it from gravity and put it into the increasingly crowded orbit.

"Stardust, I have video displays here," Knockabout said, pointing to the left of the command platform's control systems. He moved the platform lower and to the side where he could better observe the impending combat. "Can you patch in to give me a visual feed from your helmet?"

"You can do this through remote viewing now?" Stardust asked as his armor's computer began a signal uplink sub-routine.

"I've never tried," Knockabout said, "but it will at least help me see when pieces get broken free. I'll get a little closer to grab hold of the pieces, but the better the information, the faster I can react."

"Hey, anything that helps," Stardust said. The sub-routine finished in record time and the command platform was wired in and crystal clear.

Worm Queen stepped to the edge of the platform and raised her arms high above her head. "Worms! To me!" she called. Seconds passed and no one saw any worms appear.

"Are you not getting a response?" Doctor Shadow said as he floated off the edge of the platform.

"They're here," she said. She favored him with a sly look. "Just be ready to do your part, old man. We might not get many chances at this."

"Old man?" the mage laughed. "I'll have you know that in geological terms, I am scarcely an infant."

"Left leg?" Stardust said, powering up the suit's disintegrator beams. He had been curious about them for some time. He would never use weaponry like that at home. The potential for accidental property damage and the resulting lawsuits was astronomical. But this place had all the requirements of perfect a test range, and his target had already damaged just about anything worth protecting.

"Let's start at the left ankle," Worm Queen said. "The worms could probably climb up the leg to the knee, but they might get noticed and destroyed before they did any good."

"Left ankle it is," Stardust said. He took to the air with Doctor Shadow close behind him.

The giant swung a clumsy punch at them with a fist the size of a drive-through espresso stand. It was easy enough to dodge. The targeting system locked onto the left ankle just as five milky-colored worms burst up from the ground around the giant's foot. Each worm was close to ten feet in length, and when they hit the ankle, they bored through it like it was soft cheese. "And the new tricks just keep on coming, don't they," Stardust said through the helmet link to the people on the platform.

"Corrosive worms," Anna said into the microphone on the control panel. "I generally frown on destroying something that might be used as evidence back home, so I haven't used them before."

Not to be outdone, Stardust lined up a clean shot and let fly. A screeching red bolt of energy that surprised even him lanced out of his gloves. When the dust cleared seconds later, a clean hole six feet across had been burned straight through to the stone behind it. As he watched, two worms poked through the wall of the hole, looking at each other as if confused.

Already, the ankle was starting to regenerate. "Okay," Stardust said. "This part is not my fault. Doctor Shadow was supposed to clear out the debris."

"There was nothing to clear," Doctor Shadow said, flying along side the armored hero. "Whatever that attack did, it didn't leave matter behind to be moved."

"Disintegrator beam," Stardust said. "I figured it might leave dust or something behind. I wasn't expecting total matter elimination."

"Don't worry," Worm Queen said. "It gets the job done without the others having to sweep up. This thing might be regenerating shape, but without the material to fill it out it has to honeycomb. It might look solid on the outside, but it won't be able to support its own weight before too long."

"I'll make another pass then," Stardust said. He executed a pinpoint turn and targeted the same leg ten feet higher up. He might not know much about biology, but structural integrity was right up his alley. This time he was able to sweep the shot a little, making for a wider impact area. Below the long, deep score he put in the giant's leg, Anna's worms zipped in and out through the huge bone ankle, destroying anything they touched and digesting it. They honeycomb effect was visible now as the giant's regeneration struggled to keep up.

Down below, Doctor Shadow levitated the remains of a ruined stone column off the valley floor. As the webbing of bone particles rushed to fix the damage done by Stardust and Worm Queen, the ankle and lower shin looked smaller, more fragile than ever. It was no match for the chunk of stone the ancient mage used as a focus for his improvised telekinetic battering ram.

Stardust was so focused on watching the giant fall that he didn't even see the left foot and a significant portion of shin shoot up into the upper atmosphere. But by focusing on the toppling monstrosity, he was the first to see the left arm snap under the weight as it made a feeble attempt to catch itself. "Knockabout! Left arm!"

"Good eye," Knockabout said. Seconds later, it was following after the broken leg and foot.

"From the shouting, I take it that you're playing Twister," Wild Kat's voice broke onto the radio channel.

"Glad you could make it," Knockabout said. "I thought we were going to have to send out a search party."

"I ran into a delay," she said, "but I should be there in a few seconds."

"We have a big problem on the ground, Wild Kat," Stardust said. "You might want to hold back until we finish mopping up." Down below, the bone golem was mutating, the damage having come so quickly that it had to improvise. What it was growing into down below could barely be called humanoid.

"I could give you a hand with that," Wild Kat said.

"Sorry, but I don't think your claws could do much against the hundred foot undead bone monster," Stardust said as he hovered just out of what he predicted its reach to be, readying another shot.

"Too bad," Wild Kat said. "I'll just have to use the Soviet surplus MIG fighter I'm in instead."

On the command platform, the others started laughing at Stardust's stunned silence. "Where did you get a MIG?" Emil said.

"Who is that?" Wild Kat said.

"He is an ally," Knockabout said, "And where *did* you get a fighter jet?"

"I borrowed it from Shade's head guy in Jerusalem," she said as the jet sliced through the dark sky, waving its wings in salute. "I know this thing is armed, but I don't know what it's armed with. I'd hate to drop a nuke on all of you, especially now that I've just found you and everything."

"The Jerusalem MIG units are armed with conventional

warheads missiles," Emil told her. "None of Shade's forces use nuclear arms because of his aversion to light. And the Jerusalem forces use too many human officers to make biological weapons practical."

"After I get down, you're going to have to tell me how you know all this," she said.

Stardust fired off several more disintegration blasts into what he could only call the creature's back, while the corrosion worms continued to eat away at whatever they could touch. Tentacles of bone grew in the place of limbs, the torso collapsed and reformed several times, curling in a ball as if it were consuming itself. In a way, Stardust supposed, it *was* eating itself. It was difficult to make sense of what he was seeing, but it looked like the middle of the creature was stretching thinner as more and more honeycombs filled the interior.

"You know, I don't remember seeing a landing strip anywhere around here."

"I believe the runway was destroyed by the bone giants when there were several of them and they were much more comical," Doctor Shadow said.

"Don't worry about it," Wild Kat said. "I'll take care of it, but everyone might want to get clear of the crash site." She armed the missiles under the wings and nosed the plane towards the huge bone abomination on the valley floor. She could see Stardust and a floating platform back away to a safe distance. With a few flipped switches, she turned the autopilot on then yanked the eject lever. The exploding bolts in the canopy blew and she was safely clear before the borrowed jet hit.

A fireball erupted in the heart of the bone golem, sending huge chunks of the creature flying as the honeycomb structure created by Worm Queen and Stardust's constant assault channeled the force of the explosion. Each piece sent flying tried to change into some reflection of itself as it soared through the dark sky, only to be caught by Knockabout. It was the opportunity he had been waiting for. With the giant reduced to pieces, sending it away was child's play. All through the Valley of Kings, any piece of animated bone he could sense moving was released form Earth's gravity. By the time Wild Kat's parachute landed, there was peace in the valley again.

The exiled members of the Protectorate were reunited at last.

Chapter Twenty-Eight

The library and map room survived the worst of the damage, but the balcony and lounge were a total loss. Doctor Shadow was most saddened to see a wonderful leather chair with mahogany claw feet gone. True, it was too dark for most rooms, but it worked well in Shade's quarters, and the leather had been butter-soft with age. Half of it had been consumed in a short-lived firestorm that had ripped what remained of the balcony and surrounding outside wall free from the rest of the tomb.

There was enough room for everyone in the library to reconvene, but since Shade had never been one for entertaining, seating was at a premium. Thankfully, most people were so worked up at being reunited that the only person interested in sitting was Edirin's new friend, the mercenary al-Aswan. Emil found a comfortable, overstuffed library chair finished in red velvet and settled in with a book while the others discussed.

"So there is no connection between them," Anna said. "There is no anti-Protectorate, so to speak."

"Apparently not," Doctor Shadow said, indicating the journal that Wild Kat was speed-reading as Stardust glanced at the pages from over her shoulder. "Shade and Sundiatta were at war with each other. Shade purchased some military hardware from Deathstar's company, landmines and missiles mostly, but the arrangement was strictly business."

"So the landmines all over, let's say Jordan, hypothetically were provided by Starcom or whatever your business over here is called," Wild Kat said.

"At great cost, I wouldn't doubt," Doctor Shadow said.

Wild Kat tapped a long claw on Stardust's helmet. "Evil Jaccob just made my list," she said.

"I think evil Jaccob supplied Lazarus and Lenore's crew in Cobalt City as well," he said. "Evil Jaccob is an equal opportunity war profiteer."

"You don't make landmines in any of your subsidiaries, do you?" Wild Kat said. "In our world, I mean."

"Restraint devices, containment systems and such, but no offensive weapons," he said. "And cell phones and communications of course. Those are my bread and butter."

"Ah, now you made my list," Knockabout said with a smile.

Worm Queen tried to stay focused as the others wandered on

and off topic. It wasn't always easy with this group, and she had to admit that she frequently sidetracked the conversation herself. But this wasn't the end of their journey, merely a rest stop. There were miles to go before they got to Mordor -- or wherever this particular adventure was taking them. "What I don't understand is, why us?" she said.

"Isn't it because we were reflected in the Mirror of Shadows or whatever?" Jaccob said.

Anna shook her head, turning it all around. Doctor Shadow didn't seem willing to buy this theory either. It had to be more complicated than that.

"Augustus Dei approached Camilla decades ago," she said. "Didn't Simon tell us that before everything happened?"

"He did," Katherine said. She didn't like where this course of inquiry was taking them.

"And we're here, but Simon isn't," Doctor Shadow said. "In fact, when we dealt with the Mirror of Shadows the first time, Simon was the first one there. He had been held by it for an unknown period of time, and there is no telling what that kind of exposure could have on a human mind."

"His motes of ash can absorb magic," Katherine said. It had been a recent discovery, but a significant one. She had begun thinking of the ash as magical nanites ever since. "That might have made him a danger to the mirror's owner, so she would have wanted to remove him from the equation early. I believe we established that sufficiently at the time. Her main focus was trying to get to you, Anna, because she believed you to be her mother."

"And she and others thought Simon was her father," Anna said, "which is clearly impossible. It would make more sense if Lazarus and Lenore were her parents."

"But that isn't even the point," Doctor Shadow. "The Mirror of Shadows is safe in the possession of the Yellow King. We have no sign of its owner making an effort against us. But it is suspicious that Simon is mysteriously absent once again."

"I'm not sure that he's absent, exactly," Anna said. "He wanted to be made flesh, right? I mean, that was what he told us his deal with Augustus Dei was for. We have no reason to suspect that Augustus Dei didn't live up to his end of the agreement. He turned to flesh before us, but it looked, well, dead. It looked like Lazarus. And Lazarus wasn't there in the penthouse in Cobalt City."

"So maybe Simon swapped physically, while we were swapped mentally, caught in the undertow or whatever?" Katherine ventured.

"It would explain a lot. And an effect of that scale does tend to put out ripples which might have consequences we couldn't even imagine," Doctor Shadow said.

"And there was a massive dust storm that hit Cobalt City not long after we shifted over. You were there longer than me, Anna. I was just passing through, but it made news on the west coast. What do you think?"

Anna shrugged to mask a shiver that coursed through her body. "The dust storm is...I don't want to say alive, but I'm pretty sure it has some kind of consciousness. I don't know how to say this. Maybe Doctor Shadow could get more information than I could, but I don't think it was Simon. But I can't rule out that it wasn't Mister Grey."

"You lost me," Stardust said.

"It is possible that there is a psychological break between Simon Floyd and Mister Grey," Doctor Shadow said. "One is his sense of identity prior to his death, and the other was formed by seventy years in a jar in the room in which he was killed. Some mystics would suggest that Simon is the soul, but Mister Grey is everything else. A hungry ghost."

"So we need to go to Cobalt City?" Wild Kat said.

"We may have to anyway," Doctor Shadow said. "I can get us back to our world, but I can't get us back in our own bodies. I need to look elsewhere for answers."

"The King in Yellow," Knockabout said.

"And more importantly, the artifact he protects," Doctor Shadow said.

"Do you think the King in Yellow is involved in this somehow?" Katherine said. With her enhanced senses, being around him was more difficult for her than the others. The last time she had to schedule a full-body sea salt scrub to remove the scent of decay from her skin.

"Augustus Dei is a unique entity," the ancient mage said. "What little I was able to gather from the King in Yellow suggested that the two of them are similar entities...perhaps from the same race, somewhere outside of the normal continuum. Neither of them reflects in the mirror. That is not to say that I think the King in Yellow is involved, but the connection is clear and I think it merits further investigation."

"And how sure are we that the others didn't get pulled through here as well?" Anna said. "You know, Velvet and Gallows..."

"I'd put the chances that this only happened to us at about ninety-nine percent. Archon is a smart guy and he would have contacted us within an hour, and Gallows could have probably tracked us down physically long before them," Stardust said.

"I agree," Knockabout said. "Simon is the only loose end. And he and the King in Yellow's anchor are both in Cobalt City."

"And what do we do about him?" Stardust said, pointing towards Emil who was deeply immersed in an Arabic translation of early Greek tragedies.

"I shall stay here," Emil said. He did not bother to look up. "I have business with the one called Shade. It is long past time that I tended to it."

"He might not return here," Knockabout said.

"He will," Emil said, waving away the concern with a flip of his wrist, still reading. "He always has before, he will again, he will forever. Until I stop him, that is. This is his base of power. Without it, all he has done is for nothing. So you go and I will wait."

"There could be any number of dangerous magical texts stored here. I'm still not sure why we should trust you, or for that matter, who you are," Katherine said.

"You trust me, do you not?" Knockabout said. "I trust him, and that should be enough."

"He is from our world," Doctor Shadow said. "He has an interest in helping us return there."

"But why, exactly?" Worm Queen said. "And why don't you want to come back with us?"

"See, that's the part that bothers me as well," Wild Kat said.

"My work is here, so here I must stay," Emil said, smiling slightly and nodding as if her were explaining to a child.

"That explanation doesn't exactly make me comfortable about leaving you alone with a library of magic books," Stardust said.

Emil closed the book and folded his hands on top of his lap. He pursed his lips while he looked down at his hands. Finally, he looked up and stared intently at Stardust's visor. "First, let me assure you that even if I were to be able to use any of the magic here, it is anathema to me. Secondly, let me answer you with a question of my own. Why do you seek so fervently to return home?"

"Because my wife and kids are there, my company, my whole life is in that world," he said quickly.

"And if you had no family," Emil said. "If you had no friends, no business, nothing to hold you there, you would still want to go back, wouldn't you?"

"Of course," Stardust said, sensing that he was walking into a trap somehow but not seeing a way out of it.

"Why? You have nothing there, no…connection. Why go back to a world that would not miss you, would not mourn your loss?" Emil said.

"Because there are still criminals there, still evil. People might not be there to miss me personally, but I make an impact. I make the world a better place," Stardust said. "I may not need anything in that world anymore, but they still need me."

"There are other heroes, are there not?" Emil said with a shrug.

"Not enough."

"Not enough to do what, exactly?" Emil said.

"To get rid of all the evil, to make the world a better place, to make it safe," Stardust said. His voice was starting to climb. He was getting tired of going around and around with this chatty little mystery man.

"And you think that this goal is possible? Why is that?"

"Because we're so close," Stardust said. "I mean, there's still crime, and people still exploit other people for money or power or whatever. But we're making a difference. *I'm* making a difference. There is more good than bad in our world, and if we keep trying…"

Emil cut him off with a waive of his hand, "…more good than bad. And this world, it is more bad than good, would you not agree?"

"Without a doubt."

"So it would be hopeless to try to eliminate crime, and hate, and evil here," Emil said. "It would be hopeless. A fool's crusade to make this world a better place, you would say."

"Yes," Stardust said.

"And that," Emil said with a flourish of his hands, "is why I must stay. I must stay because someone has to. Because I believe there is light in the deepest dark if we only strive to find it. It is my calling; my crusade. It is why I came here."

Stardust opened his mouth to reply and found he had nothing to say. Emil al-Aswan was a madman. He was fighting a battle he could never hope to win. Based on what little he had seen of this world, there was no way one man could make a difference here. But at the same time, he was right. Someone had to try. He looked around and noticed that the others had come to the same conclusion. Doctor Shadow was actually smiling.

"He did the same thing to me on the ride up," Edirin whispered to Jaccob.

"Thanks for the warning," Jaccob said.

"Think nothing of it," Edirin said. "Anyway, he explains it

better than I could."

"I find it fascinating that we have not met before," Doctor Shadow said to Emil.

The seated mercenary shrugged and resumed his book with a mischievous grin. "Well, I have been here for many years," he said. "But we will meet again."

"You are certain of this?" Doctor Shadow said.

"As certain as one can be in this uncertain time," he said, "We will meet again, sooner than you expect. But you will not know me, and I will not remember you."

"Then we might as well not have met again at all," Doctor Shadow said.

"Oh, it will be significant, never fear," Emil said. "You will save the life of someone very close to me. Look into my mind if you do not believe me."

Doctor Shadow smiled and briefly scanned Emil al-Aswan's surface thoughts. He saw himself clearly, as though he was upside down. He was outside, with a man-made waterfall behind him, water cascading down ridged concrete into a pool. It was night, and there was a look of wonder upon his own face. But then the image was gone, and Doctor Shadow was again in the ruined home. "Good luck on your crusade," he said to Emil.

"And you on yours," Emil said with a polite nod. He returned to his book.

"There doesn't appear to be any food or water here," Knockabout said as they prepared to leave inside a force field while being made weightless by Knockabout. Stardust would pull them at supersonic speeds in a sub-orbital arc that would get them back in less than an hour.

"I have no need of food or water," Emil said. "Allah will provide."

"I'm not certain that there is any God or Allah here," Knockabout said.

"They are the same, and He is here," Emil said, tapping his own chest with two fingers. Then he reached up and tapped Knockabout over his own heart. "And He is here as well. Do well to remember that."

"I'm not certain I..." Knockabout began.

"You don't have to believe in Him," Emil said. "It is enough to know that He believes in you."

"I'm not comfortable leaving you here alone to face down Shade when he gets back," Knockabout said.

Emil smiled. "But you will. You already have. You just don't know it yet."

And strangely, Emil was right about that as well.

Chapter Twenty-Nine

Deathstar recognized the woman on the roof of the speeding Mustang the second he responded to Lenore's request for help. But it had proven next to impossible to predict the actions of the car's driver. Between that and his target's annoying ability to deflect even the most precise of shots, he had done little more than scratch the red Mustang. At least he had made several major roads around Cobalt City completely unusable. That was a minor consolation.

He had been forced to pause on a downtown rooftop and make some quick recalibrations to the gauntlet blasters. This...Velvet...could deflect narrow beams, but if he dialed up the output and shifted the focusing element back, he could change the shape of his beams to a cone-like area. The final adjustment made, he snapped the housing closed. "Deflect this, bitch," he thought as he took to the air again.

Lenore, her giant, milky worm, and its passenger had moved in behind the fleeing vehicle again and were sweeping the street with a massive sonic barrage. The sound wave, pushing a wall of broken glass, twisted metal, and crumbled concrete and asphalt closed on the tail pipe of the darting car, its roaring engine muted by the destruction ready to overtake it as it neared a large office plaza near the heart of downtown. Deathstar zipped ahead and let loose with a wide-beamed assault of his own.

Through the annoyingly gold, sparkling glow of his blast, Deathstar saw the Mustang and its passengers caught between the twin engines of destruction, the sound and the fury that he and Lenore had unleashed. He had to admit, there was something to be said for teamwork. Velvet collapsed over the roof of the car just as the two waves collided, her cloak spread over the top of the car like the wings of a dying bird. The dust settled, and the car, dented beyond recognition, rolled into the plaza on little more than shredded tires and a prayer.

The driver's side door flew open and fell to the ground spinning listlessly, and the battered driver helped the limping and broken-looking caped annoyance off the roof. They broke into a shuffling run towards the heart of the plaza, looking for somewhere to hide in the empty acres of concrete, steel, and installation art. There was nowhere to run, and Deathstar didn't even bother to suppress a chuckle at the pleasure he was going to take in running them into the ground.

Lenore flew over their target's heads, and Lazarus jumped from the worm, his forty foot fall crushing the concrete around him into a crater as he landed, unharmed, ten feet ahead of Velvet and her companion.

That was when their targets turned into twenty-foot tall chrome praying mantises.

"Tell me I didn't just see that," Deathstar said over his radio to Lenore and Lazarus.

Lenore dove and swung her worm mount around for a look, but mid-turn a pair of arrows hit the worm in its side and exploded. The worm blinked out of existence, back to wherever it was called from to begin with, and Lenore dropped and skidded into a bronze pyramid sculpture twelve feet high. Her force field absorbed the damage from the fall, but she came to her feet angry.

Lenore surveyed the battleground and didn't completely understand what she saw. At the edge of the plaza, Lazarus threw double-fisted blows at the nearest giant mantis, while Deathstar rained down a fiery barrage from the air. Something was wrong here, Lenore could feel it. There was a psychic presence here that she sensed like oily water on her skin, but she couldn't pinpoint it. The feeling came from all around her. As she tried to locate its source, her mouth went dry. The plaza was breaking free of the rest of the city and rising high into the air as she watched. They needed backup. "All active units converge on my location," she said over the communicator, "Major offensive underway."

The Shade responded immediately. "I am bringing Sundiatta and will be there in twenty seconds."

"What about Rakshasha?" Deathstar said as he fired off another barrage of shots. The reflective nature of the chrome praying mantises made this a futile exercise, but at least it kept one of them distracted while Lazarus pounded on the other one.

"She is dealing with an infiltration," Sundiatta said. "I believe you know of whom I speak."

"That's okay then," Deathstar said, switching to the disintegrator beam, hoping that the bug's chrome carapace was an armor of some kind and not organic so that the ray would have an effect.

From the near edge of the plaza, two more arrows sizzled through the air, hitting Deathstar in the back with an electric jolt that almost overloaded his sensors. When he turned in that direction, however, there was no one to be seen. "Damn it all to hell!" he shouted. "Where the fuck are all these arrows coming from?"

Near the center of the plaza, Velvet chuckled, making her broken rib hurt all the more. Archon crouched over her, bleeding from several cuts along his face and arms, although the worst had been dealt with already. They were tucked into a giant steel pipe painted orange and welded to several more in a large installation piece in Earl's Court. Libertine sat lotus position near them, her back turned to Archon, her full attention on the skinny, shirtless youth standing in the mouth of the pipe, his long, dark hair matted to his bony shoulder blades as he concentrated on the illusion that enveloped the whole block.

They had been there since limping out of the car, and Archon had played doctor since. Jeremy Red had made an illusionary overlay, and Gallows had popped the real Archon and Velvet to the safety of the pipe. Archon was actually a bit surprised at how lucky they had been that Lenore and Deathstar hadn't coordinated their attacks earlier.

Archon had turned his communicator back on, and it was set to receive only so that this command post could listen in. A quick verbal command had been programmed in to allow him to broadcast hands free if he needed to, but he hoped he wouldn't have to use it. He favored Velvet with a small smile about Deathstar's frustration. Even now, Huntsman had changed position to far across the plaza, with Gallows acting as his transport. It would not win the battle, but it would at least buy Archon the time he needed to patch Velvet up. Without her, their offensive abilities were greatly diminished. Without her, they would either be forced to flee or die this very night in Earl's Court. There were worse places to die, Archon had to admit. At least this place had some tradition of heroes sacrificing themselves for the greater good. The original Libertine, for instance, had died not thirty feet from where they now hid. Archon wondered if this Libertine possessed the memories of the one who came before her or merely his powers. A topic for another day, perhaps. If there was another day.

"That was some pretty fancy driving you did there, Mister Smooth," Velvet said, trying to regulate her breathing through the pain. Archon's medication had already taken most of the edge off, but she couldn't shake the feeling that something was grinding in her chest when she inhaled.

"Mister Smooth is my brother," Archon said. He applied a quick-setting plaster composite to her side as an improvised brace for the broken rib. It was a new technique he had read about in a Singapore medical journal and had intended to research more thoroughly before putting it into practice, but there were simply no other options.

"You have a brother?" she said.

"No. I'm just humoring you," he said, binding the chest with tape. "Mercedes offered a course in defensive driving and I happened to hear about it…"

"And you had to take the class," she said.

"Oh, no," he said, shaking his head. "I had to teach it. I learned to drive from Hank Bacca in Los Angeles. He was a stunt driver in Hollywood in the seventies and eighties. He needed work after a director damn near blew him up by changing a stunt without running through safety protocol, and I needed to learn. It was a mutually beneficial arrangement. But the Mercedes thing a few years ago gave me a chance to brush up."

"You're a pretty impressive guy, Archon," Velvet said.

"I know," Archon said, patting down the end of the tape. "But the name Mister Impressive was too big to put on the action figure."

"Everyone's a comedian," Velvet said. She stood and tested her range of motion. She didn't have full flexibility, and it hurt a bit, but at least pain meant she was alive. Time to settle some scores. She went to the end of the pipe and looked out past their borrowed illusionist, a little nervous despite herself to be so close to the mass murderer.

Out in the plaza, Deathstar had switched from golden star bolts to the wide, red disintegrator beam with little effect. Little effect on the illusionary mantis things, but not to no effect on the plaza itself. Lazarus was merely punching air, and not a threat to anything, and Lenore had summoned five ten-foot long worms glowing the color of embers. Fire worms, most likely, contending with illusory crows with six foot wing spans. But the only real threat came from Huntsman's explosive arrows, which removed any worm they hit. With their numbers dropping and their burning heads pointed skyward, the property damage there was minimal as well.

At the edge of the plaza, only night sky showed, as if the area was suspended a thousand feet above the city. Also an illusion, she knew, but it still unnerved her. And when Shade and Sundiatta pierced the outer edge of the illusion and saw the plaza, they would have a clearer idea about what was going on than their companions. Shade might have some ability to see through to only what was real, and that was a concern. And with Sundiatta's ability to sense sound and motion, he might also have a better chance to ignore the illusions. She had to act fast.

From a temporary perch high atop of the large pipe sculpture, Huntsman and Gallows saw Velvet emerge from hiding. Huntsman saw her sweeping out to the side, in line to get a flanking position on Deathstar. "Get me a good line of sight on the tin can," Huntsman asked Gallows. The teleporter nodded and ported them next to a series of concrete steps where water cascaded past their feet.

Huntsman spotted Deathstar, with Velvet on the far side of the armored menace. With practiced precision, he grabbed two arrows, nocking one and letting fly. The second arrow was nocked and released before the first even hit. Gallows ported them back to the top of the sculpture just as the second arrow left the bow.

The first arrow hit Deathstar directly in the middle of his disintegrator beam projector and exploded. Before he could react, however, the second arrow hit home, striking the boot jets with a high strength adhesive polymer that all but smothered the boots in a gob of pale, rapidly hardening plastics. Huntsman didn't know the design specs on the boots, and wasn't sure if there were intakes to clog up like on a jet engine, but he was at least reasonably certain that it would present some kind of navigation hazard.

Huntsman had his answer as the hardening polymer changed the direction of thrust and spun Deathstar wildly out of control. The fake Jaccob was forced to shut off the boot thrusters entirely and try to shoot the adhesive off with his regular gauntlet blasters. Deathstar knew that the armor would easily sustain the fifty-foot drop, to the plaza surface, and, if lucky, he would have the thrusters clear before then anyway.

Deathstar was right that he wouldn't hit the concrete. Velvet connected with a double-fisted swinging punch three feet before the impact, sending him flying into the last of Lenore's worms, bowling them over and scorching Deathstar in the process. As Deathstar blasted free the last of the restraining adhesive, he fired the thrusters and skimmed across the battle-scarred concrete of Earl's Court with Velvet in his sights.

At this point, Sundiatta, wearing black Armani dress pants, a lion's skull for a helmet, and a lion-skin pelt for a cape, stepped out into the edge of the plaza, with Shade right behind him. They would have been there sooner, but had made a stop for supplies first—at the circus. Sundiatta got his battle attire, much to the dismay of a Belgian lion tamer, and Shade had spell components. Seven children between the age of three and ten were roped together and followed the necromancer with blank looks on their faces. Some still clutched their balloons and cotton candy tight in grubby little fists.

With reinforcements here, and her most recent batch of worms destroyed, Lenore was forced to summon forth more, even though the effort was starting to tire her. Under the circumstances, she decided on economy of scale, and created hundreds of small, putrid green worms that hissed and popped as they hit the concrete before her. A fifty-foot hedge five feet tall and five feet wide, composed entirely of chemical acid worms only a few inches long now at her command, she ordered them to disperse and attack her enemies.

Since the battle she saw was before her, she didn't bother to look in any other direction. And so her worms didn't think to look anywhere but before her. If they had, they might have seen the skinny, shirtless man walking silently towards her from behind, something in his hand.

"Where the hell is Jeremy Red," Archon said, shaking Libertine slightly in the confines of the steel pipe.

"He's standing right here," she said, but her voice faltered. To the untrained eye, to the eye expecting to see Jeremy Red at the end of the pipe, he was there. But he wasn't casting a shadow. Libertine's heart sank as she saw what Archon had just noticed. Jeremy himself was an illusion. The false Protectorate was not the only group being fed a lie.

Archon and Velvet peered out the end of the pipe and surveyed the battle before them. A pair of explosive arrows hit an impervious wall of force inches away from Sundiatta. The flames and force from the blow flowed harmlessly around him, and he barely seemed to notice.

The train of children seemed to flicker for a moment, as if Gallows were attempting to teleport them away, but then the rope binding them glowed brightly and the children were still there. Shade waved a finger in the air and glowing symbols appeared in space before him, seeming to dance and shimmer. For all his studies and research, Archon had never seen the symbols before, something that bode about as well as the necromancer playing babysitter.

Meanwhile, Velvet and Deathstar clashed amid craters and pits caused by the indiscriminate blasts of the Stardust armor weapons. She had been able to avoid Deathstar's first charge much like a matador, but her follow-through punch to his side had missed, and put her out of position to block his blaster shot as he turned for another charge.

Nearby, Lenore stood amid an expanding arc-shaped crawling swarm. The concrete sizzled and smoked at the passing of the worms. A wide area attack. This Lenore was full of unpleasant tricks, Archon thought. But behind her, and out of sight of everyone else, Jeremy approached. In his hand, he had the shattered half of one of Huntsman's arrows. Tall grass grew up around him where he walked, and for the briefest of seconds, Archon had the impression of a lioness hunting her prey.

His view was obscured when the mass murderer Jeremy Red was only a few feet away from Lenore. Not Lenore, Archon reminded himself. Lenore wearing Anna's body. Anna's very human and vulnerable body. He would have wanted to see more, but a shadow had suddenly covered the mouth of the pipe as Lazarus swung down into the opening. "Boo," the super-strong zombie gangster said as he grabbed Libertine's head in both of his cold, dead hands and squeezed.

Chapter Thirty

"Is anyone else cold?" Anna said as they walked through the disturbingly empty and silent streets of the mirror universe Cobalt City.

"The rest of us aren't dressed like we're going to a rave," Jaccob said as he accessed news feeds from his helmet. There had to be some explanation for the dust storm. But there was nothing definitive, merely dozens of web log posts about a feeling of doom; of the end of the world.

"Hey, I did what I could with Lenore's wardrobe," Anna said. "I didn't have a lot of options. I don't see Wild Kat complaining, and she's dressed like Jeannie."

"Except for the puffy pants," Katherine said. "And the silly hat. The fur keeps me warm. That must be why Rakshasha doesn't wear confining clothes."

"Oh, is that why?" Jaccob said, smiling beneath his visor.

"So what's up with the lack of people?" Anna said in a desperate attempt to change the subject. "They were all here earlier when Stardust came and picked me up."

"They sense something is happening," Doctor Shadow said. He looked through the walls of the buildings as they passed as if the concrete and steel were no more substantial than air.

"And they see us," Katherine said. "I don't think anyone ever imagined all of us in one place at the same time. Like Adolph Hitler, Attila the Hun, Genghis Khan, Vlad Teppes, and Michael Eisner all on the same hockey team."

"Those are all heroes here, most likely," Edirin said. He had listened to the hushed whispers behind the walls as word of mouth spread of their approach. Communication had been mostly by phone and person to person, he figured. People in the buildings nearby had turned off computers and televisions, afraid that the Big-Brother reputation that Deathstar had cultivated was more than rumor. He found it odd that for all Jaccob's effort to get good media spin in their own world, the boogieman tales here had inspired such effect.

Far off down the street, the wind howled, and a storm of ash scoured the paint from every car parked near Earl's Court. Anna remembered her earlier attempts to communicate with the storm and shuddered. She couldn't see it from here, but it sounded larger, fiercer than before. "Where are we going to try to contact the King in Yellow?" she asked, looking around for some shelter should the storm sweep their way. None of the buildings looked substantial enough to weather her mental image of the coming storm.

"If the King in Yellow truly is a singularity, then there should be no manifestation of him here," Doctor Shadow said. "So we are going to have to seek him in a different plane. His host seems fond of where we call home, but I want to talk to the King himself, so I have to look elsewhere."

"The big, dead stone city he took us to?" Stardust said.

"Carcosa," Doctor Shadow said.

"I didn't know you knew the city's name," Katherine said.

Doctor Shadow shrugged, looking down the wide, empty boulevard towards the howling wind and ash. "It is possible that there are many ancient cities overlooking many cold, dark lakes as deep as the universe is old. I could not say. But one is known as Carcosa, and there are legends of this place that have bled into our world as half-remembered nightmares and the ravings of madmen. I have only been there twice, both times at the whim of the King in Yellow. I suspect that it is the same place, but it does not matter if I am right or not. It is just a name, same as any other."

"And you can find the place again," Knockabout said with certainty.

"It is not a place one soon forgets," Doctor Shadow said, a wry smile on his pale face.

"All right then," Stardust said, tilting his visor open, "Let's get going."

"I am going alone," Doctor Shadow said.

"Like hell," Stardust said. "You're going to talk to the creepy magic guy who might or might not be able to fix this. We don't know much…hell, *anything* about him except what he told us. If things go pear-shaped, you're going to need backup."

"I hate to admit it, but he's right," Katherine said.

"Someone needs to stay behind and try to communicate with the storm," Doctor Shadow said.

"I can do that," Katherine said. "Mister Grey knows me better than anyone else here. I'll need Anna here to be the telepathic conduit, but I can do it."

"And I'll stay behind to keep them safe," Knockabout said. "You and Stardust can watch each other's backs and come get us when you have the return ticket home."

Doctor Shadow looked at his companions intently for a few long moments and realized that they had made up their minds, although Anna was obviously torn between the lesser of two evils. "Well then," he said, turning to Jaccob, "I guess it is just you and me

213

on the magical mystery tour."

"Koo-koo-ka-joo," Jaccob said with a smile.

"Be careful," Anna said as Doctor Shadow put his hand on Jaccob's shoulder, preparing to make the shift to Carcosa.

"Same to you," Jaccob said, "But don't sweat it. We'll be back soon."

And then reality folded around them like a rancid piece of cheese and they were gone, with the others afforded a brief glimpse into the cyclopean city of Carcosa at night with the vast lake beyond and alien stars above.

On the motionless streets of the reflected Cobalt City, the three remaining exiled members of the Protectorate started walking towards the sound of the storm.

Anna dreaded the prospect of dealing with the storm again, but Katherine was right. Someone needed to provide the conduit, and the only other person who could do that was also the only person who could find Carcosa on his own. She didn't like being in the mirror universe at all. Things were so similar, but at the same time so different. She saw a shoe store where she bought a pair of sneakers three weeks ago, but while the store was still there, the name of the place had changed and they only sold knee-high lace up boots. How could a shoe store make any money only selling knee-high lace up boots? Then again, they did have a lovely pair of rich blue leather boots with platform heels. Not that she could afford it on an academic's salary. "Does anyone else feel kind of...you know...over the rainbow?" she said.

"I resent the implication," Knockabout said. "Since Wild Kat would obviously have to be the Cowardly Lion in that scenario, that would make me the Scarecrow with no brains, or the Tin Man who is clearly Stardust anyway."

"I didn't mean..." Anna began.

"You could be Toto," Katherine told Edirin.

He laughed a deep, rich laugh. "I'd rather be a flying monkey."

"Ok," Katherine said. "Anyway, I would be Dorothy. I look great in red shoes and blue gingham."

Anna joined in the laughter. It almost made her forget the storm of ash, which seemed to sense their approach and had started up the street towards them. It was bigger than anyone could have imagined. All the paint chewed off cars and houses, all the brick and concrete it had eroded, all the smog and dust and grime it had come into contact with had swelled its size exponentially. A funnel cloud that touched both sides of the street bore down on them from several blocks away. Katherine's very un-ladylike curses were torn from her mouth by the wind that accompanied the storm.

Knockabout stood between the two women and squared his jaw. A force field formed around him; with considerable force of will, he stretched it out to cover Anna and Katherine as well. Inside the field, he was able to mitigate the sound of the storm a bit as well. "Well, if this is Oz, I guess we don't have to guess who the tornado is, do we?"

Another world away, Stardust and Doctor Shadow flew to the rooftop of one of Carcosa's vast buildings and tried to get their bearings. "Do you know which way we're going?" Stardust asked, looking at the yellow stars twinkling above in unknown constellations.

"I've been here exactly twice," Doctor Shadow said, "And I didn't exactly get a AAA road map."

"This should be fun," Stardust said.

"You didn't have to come, you know," Doctor Shadow told him.

Stardust flipped up the visor on his helmet, having determined that there were no radio signals to pick up here. He was smiling. "What, and miss the Carcosa tourist season? Come visit our moon-bathed beaches, the ad said. Who could pass that up."

"You truly are a madman, aren't you," Doctor Shadow said. He was surprised to realize that he was smiling as well. "Anyway, I thought you hated magic."

It was Stardust's turn to shrug. "I don't hate it," he said, turning again to look at the stars with his naked eye, "I just don't understand it. And I have a hard time trusting something I can't understand, measure or quantify."

"Then why did you insist on coming?"

"I told you," Jaccob told him, still looking up. "You might need help. Plus, there's always the stars. Man, but they're amazing here."

Doctor Shadow had been to dozens, if not hundreds of worlds in his several millennia of travel. And after such a long time, one gets jaded by wonder, he supposed. How long had it been since he had bothered to look up and wonder "What if?"

He tilted his head back and looked at the stars. He looked at them with Jaccob's eyes. And he realized for the first time how truly magical they were. Strange, he thought, the simple wisdom of a mortal teaching essential truths to his immortal self. Magic wasn't just dusty tomes and arcane artifacts. It was looking at alien stars and opening your mind and heart to possibilities.

"You mortals," Doctor Shadow said, his voice small against the infinite canopy of night, "You never cease to amaze me."

"It gets better," Stardust said. "I know how to find King in Yellow."

This startled Doctor Shadow and his head snapped back down. Stardust was still smiling, still looking at the stars for another long moment.

"And how is that?"

Jaccob lowered his head and looked at his companion. "Well, this is a dead city, right? No one here but the King in Yellow?"

"As I understand it, yes."

"Bet he doesn't get many visitors," Stardust said.

"I don't see…" he began, but then he *did* see. "Would you like the honors?"

Jaccob flipped down his visor. "I thought you'd never ask." He raised his arms over his head, clasping his hands together. The bright, golden glow of his star bolts infused his armor, then shone outward like a beacon, illuminating the permanent night of Carcosa. "All we need is a little symbol of the King in Yellow, you know, shine it up like a Bat-signal."

"A what?" Doctor Shadow said, mystified by the reference.

"I'll let you borrow some books when we get home," Stardust laughed. "I'll educate you some for a change."

It only took a few minutes for the King in Yellow to make his appearance known. A thunderous shout of "ENOUGH!" shook centuries of dust from the walls of the buildings around them, and the tall, yellow-cloaked ruler of the dead city appeared, walking out of the air behind them as if on an invisible staircase.

Stardust didn't need to be told twice, and doused the light immediately. He felt like an insect under the King in Yellow's gaze. Just like Gallows described, he thought. What a perfect analogy.

"What has brought you uninvited to my realm?" he intoned.

"The one we spoke of previously, the one known as Augustus Dei, has worked…"

"I have never spoken to you before! Do not lie to the likes of angels and devils, foolish mage!" King in Yellow said.

"Look deeper," Doctor Shadow said with a bow. Stardust, surprised at first, quickly followed suit, although his was made more awkward for the armor.

The King in Yellow stood above them, all of his imposing height bearing down on them, as if he were inspecting them both on the molecular level. Finally, he stepped back, and Stardust felt as if the weight of a hundred lifetimes had suddenly lifted from his back.

"You have my ear, timeless one of a hundred names," the King in Yellow said.

"As you can now see, those of us who have been reflected in the black mirror you guard have had our souls switched with those of our reflections," Doctor Shadow said.

"This is none of my doing," the King said, "And the mirror has not once left my custody since you relinquished it to me."

"We would be fools to doubt you," Doctor Shadow said, "but you cannot deny what has been done. We have reason to suspect it was the one known as Mister Infamy."

"Ah," the King in Yellow said, "A mere mote, an insignificant speck, but like an unwelcome guest, he is impossible to eliminate entirely. However, we have rules, and I cannot interfere with his contracts."

"We don't have a contract with him," Stardust said, wishing immediately that he had kept his mouth closed.

"You have no contract, yet you have fallen under his spell? Do you take me for a fool?"

"He meant no offense," Doctor Shadow said, "But what he says is true. We have no contract with him, no bargain, no discussion of any kind took place between us. One of our member did make a contract with him, but that contract, as I understand it, pertained to him and only him alone."

"And did he get what he wished for in the contract?" the King in Yellow said, his voice now quieter, a sense of curiosity evident in his tone.

"In a manner of speaking…" Doctor Shadow began.

Back in the reflected Cobalt City, a ferocious storm tried in vain to find some kind of purchase on the force field separating it from the others, but to no avail. One of the women, one he knew on some level to be the Worm Queen had a slender, red-black worm around her throat and her hand was on the back of the head of Katherine Wilde, but he could not be certain where any of this knowledge came from. The tall, thin black man with them was named Edirin Okoloko or Knockabout, or maybe both, and somewhere, deep inside, buried amid a few hundred pounds of dust and rubble, there was a voice telling him to stop. He thought that he recognized that voice, that maybe, at some time, it was his own voice. But listening to that voice brought back too much rage, too much pain. And somehow, Katherine was speaking to this voice, calling to it, trying to reason with it.

He drove harder against the invisible field of force that separated them. He wanted them to join him, wanted them to feel what it was like to have everything and lose it, not all at once, but gradually, like the wind erodes the mountain, like 70 years in a jar erodes a sense of self. He wanted them to share his pain, as he shredded their skin from their muscles, as he crawled into their lungs, their heart, their bowels, filling them from within, then leaving them as empty as he was. He wanted to reduce them to bone, and then remove the bone, until there was nothing left but the memory of what they once had been, what they would never be again. What *he* would never be again. How dare they try to reason with him! How could they ever hope to understand, unless they shared this unending hell, this hell that was made even worse because he was condemned here by love.

The little voice that called itself Mister Grey shouted and railed, but the storm swept the voice away. These people had lives, and they wasted them. Life wasted on the living! How hellishly appropriate! Katherine, he knew, had someone in her life, a suitor who wanted her as much as she wanted him, but did they act on this? Of course not! And this Worm Queen, young, lovely, intelligent, wasting her life on bugs. Bugs! She lived in her tiny office, re-heating food on a hotplate as often as not. And Knockabout, with his exotic accent, his nice clothes, his skeletons in the closet. He had to have skeletons, didn't he? How could a man with so much raw potential not have stories, not have regrets? But did anyone know anything about him other than that he was from Africa? No. Three people gifted with more power in their lives than anyone could hope to see in a thousand lifetimes, and they were, to a man, afraid to live. Better to end it now. Let them reflect on what they had once it was taken from them.

Like it was taken from him.

Maybe then they would appreciate what had been within reach all along.

And then, suddenly the voice was silent, and the three people he knew but did not know were gone, as if the world had denied their existence. He wondered for a moment who they had been. He had just known a moment ago, hadn't he? And he had been angry. But he could not remember about what.

The winds died down slowly, concrete and brick dust and paint chips settling like gray snow on a summer Christmas. He had been angry, hadn't he? Of course. Of course he had been angry. But what was his name again, he found himself asking. What was its name, it found itself asking. The ash and dust and detritus fell in drifts, and the questions stopped forming.

When the rains and winds came off the river, all that was left of the storm washed into the gutters, then the sewers, then the bay. And then it was over.

Chapter Thirty-One

"We're never going to see the sun again," Snowflake whispered. All hope was gone from his voice. They had gotten to the hangar bay access panel and found it sealed shut, a development that made Manuel more than a little nervous. The fact that the trigger-happy panda was stuck behind him with a gigantic cutting laser and was starting to feel claustrophobic didn't exactly make him want to dance with joy either. If there was room to dance in the tight maintenance crawlspace, which of course there wasn't. He had at least found enough room in the junction between this floor and the lab floor below to change out of the borrowed clothes and into his Gato Loco costume. Now they were making the long crawl down towards the last exit really open to them.

Snowflake had considered cutting through the access panel with the laser, but was unable to get it aimed properly in the narrow confines. Plus, he had to consider all the equipment in the bay that might get hit when he cut through, not the least of which was the reserve jet fuel or the shelves of chemical batteries.

Cutting their way out from just anywhere also wasn't an option. The building's sensors would give away their location immediately, and Rakshasha would undoubtedly be there in seconds. They were lucky to have avoided her when she rushed to the lab where Snowflake had melted the camera. They might not be so lucky again. The crawlspace was confining, but that was also an advantage. With no room to move, Rakshasha could not hope to dodge the laser.

Things were bound to get dicey soon, Manuel realized. If Rakshasha had gone to the effort of sealing the access panel, then she knew they were in the service conduits. He doubted that she would come crawling after them. She had to be as aware of her limitations as he was. No, she would most likely wait somewhere, watching the only open access panel. Or even worse, she could be waiting in one of the few open spaces this route forced them to cross on their way to a safe exit.

He hadn't spent much time in the cramped crawlspace, but he had realized that they were limited to the horizontal spokes through each of the upper few floors that branched off a vertical shaft running parallel to the elevator shaft. None of the horizontal spokes got very near to the outside wall of the building, making cutting straight through to the outside wall risky at best. They lacked the blueprints, and had no reliable way to access them. There could be worse than jet fuel on the other side of any wall.

Snowflake knew there were two other access panels near an exit. One was on the second floor, opening into the communications suite, but from there it was a long way down two hallways and a set of stairs just to get within view of the front door—which would be locked at this time of night anyway. They could get through the door with the all-access codes from Archon, but there was too much open area to cross, and the door would still take precious seconds to unlock. That left them with the sub-basement.

The biggest problem Manuel and Snowflake saw with the sub-basement was the necessity of using the elevator shaft to transition from second floor to the sub-basement sixty feet below. No floors between those two points needed the kind of tech infrastructure that the service conduit provided. With the basement systems being more insulated and secure, the least visible means of getting there was alongside the building's two elevators. It was significantly less cramped, and on the off chance that the elevators descended below lobby level, there was still room between the side and the moving car if they were careful. At least that's what Snowflake said.

"We're almost to the elevators," Manuel whispered.

"She's in here with us," Snowflake whispered back.

Manuel stopped moving, the grate to the elevator shaft directly before his outstretched, leather-clad fingertips. He paused, listening to his breathing, listening for any sound of Wild Kat beyond the grate or behind Snowflake. "I don't think she's out there," he said after a long minute of relative silence.

"How do you know?" Snowflake whispered. "Trust me, man. I'm a prey animal. You get a sixth sense about things like this when tigers routinely eat your people. We're the entrée portions of the circle of life."

"You have people?" Manuel whispered. "I thought you were the only one of your kind?"

"Yeah, maybe, but I got roots. Panda pride. And right now my roots are telling me to curl into a ball and play dead."

"Somehow, I don't think that's going to work on her," Manuel whispered. He pushed out on the grate and watched as it swung open easily to the side. He inched forward and glanced out into the elevator shaft. No sign of Rakshasha. One elevator was three floors up; the other was far below in the darkness. The total lack of elevator cables was unnerving, but Snowflake had told him to expect that. Both cabs ran on a magnetic track with pneumatic brakes that switched on automatically in the case of a power failure. A narrow power strip

marked clearly as hazardous ran alongside the rail, supplying electricity
for the lights and intercom inside the elevator. It was a very smooth
system, very fast, and very quiet. But from the outside looking in, it
didn't look secure at all.

Manuel pulled himself out by the ladder above and below the
grate and climbed up enough for Snowflake to pull himself out as well.
They'd decided to let the panda take the lead down the ladder, and his
descent was slower than Manuel wished. Snowflake might have been
right about Rakshasha. As long as the elevators were stopped, there
was ample space to move around, she had the dark to work with, and
both of her targets were virtually guaranteed to pass through. It was,
Manuel thought, too good of an ambush for her to pass up.

As Snowflake climbed down slowly hand over hand with the
cutting laser slung across his back, Gato Loco activated the low-light
filters in his helmet. She would want to be above them for the tactical
advantage of a pounce, so he started by looking up. His helmet allowed
him to see in near total darkness, peering between the molded plastic
cat jaws that framed his visor, but his vision was only in imperfect gray-
scale. Seeing details over distance was a little more difficult, but not
impossible. He was almost ready to give up when he saw a shadow
shift and become softer, more organic.

Rakshasha *was* in there with them. She crouched on the roof
of the elevator three floors above, carefully selecting her target, while
Manuel bent his knees and tensed. It took her no time at all to realize
that Manuel had seen her. And then her choice was made.

With terrifying swiftness, Rakshasha raced headlong down the
wall of the elevator shaft opposite Gato Loco. Seconds later, ten feet
above him, she leapt across the intervening distance, claws extended to
their full length. As soon as Rakshasha's feet left the far wall, Manuel
kicked off and flipped over her head and claws to the opposite wall.
"Run!" he shouted down the shaft as his knees absorbed the impact
and tensed for another leap. He hoped with all his might that the
panda wouldn't just curl up in a ball and play dead.

When he looked back at the ladder, he realized that Rakshasha
was already on her way to the bottom to deal with the lesser of two
threats. Snowflake had the gun, but Manuel didn't take the panda for a
confident marksman. Rumor had it that Wild Kat had snatched that
gun from the hands of a skilled mercenary as he shot it at her. Taking
the gun from the panda would be a piece of cake. And then Gato Loco
would lose his only advantage.

Rather than jump back across, Manuel instead let himself fall,
his body a perfect line, toes pointing to a landing atop the edge of the

lower elevator. As he got closer, he realized that Snowflake had fallen also, but far less intentionally and only fifteen or so feet. Manuel watched as the panda slid beneath the elevator a split second before Rakshasha landed. A quick, sweeping discharge of the laser pierced the darkness, causing her to dodge by flipping back onto the ladder. Thus discouraged, she had to consider other avenues of attack.

Gato Loco provided that avenue, falling smoothly and nailing his landing on the edge of the elevator without making a sound only ten feet away. "I don't want to hurt you, Katherine," he said, his voice modulated and masked by the helmet.

"Big words for a dead man," she said as she pounced. At her best, she could make a thirty-foot vertical leap from a standstill, so clearing the distance from her to Gato Loco was no problem. He twisted with her attack, but her claws still drew blood, raking him hotly across the stomach. Without the force field, he would have been disemboweled. With it, he was looking at a nasty infection and a colorful scar to impress the ladies with.

The little glowing dial projected on the bottom right corner of Gato Loco's visor showed his protective field integrity drop to 92%. Not an auspicious start, but with the exception of the first hour or so with the possessed Katherine Wilde, this whole day had been pretty much a do-over. And even that brief amount of time he would be willing to give up if it meant having a Katherine Wilde around who didn't want to kill him and eat him. "Was it something I said?" he asked as he fired off a sharp kick to the back of her knee, missing completely. "Does this mean you want to start seeing other people?"

Rakshasha responded with swift swipes of her claws. Gato Loco blocked both swings with only minor scratches, but his field integrity dropped to 84%. He couldn't keep this up forever. He began coordinating his steps and kicks and dodges to move him into a better position. With his back facing the wall, he would stand a chance.

"Be proud, human," Rakshasha said, "After I kill you and make a feast of your entrails, I will wear what remains of your skin as a mask." She growled, putting all her strength into a powerful swing. But by sacrificing precision for power, she ended up telegraphing the blow enough for Gato Loco to dodge it entirely.

"I don't think we're at the skin mask stage of this relationship. Maybe I could just give you a drawer at my apartment," he said. His quick jab grazed the hair on the back of her head, but that was all. He was actually impressed that he had made any contact at all. The Wild Kat he knew had the uncanny ability to sense attacks and react instinctively, and this one appeared to be no different. With her reflexes, it was rare that anything touched her. He was so caught up with having almost hit Rakshasha that he didn't see her back kick coming.

Her foot caught him high in the inside of the thigh, and he was immediately glad that she didn't have claws on her feet. The field took the brunt of the damage, but the impact still shifted him out of position and made him reflexively bend a bit at the waist. Her follow-up attack hit him high on the back, her claws making a cross hatch with the wounds from earlier in the day. In sympathy, those wounds felt like they were opening up again as well. "No more jokes!" she roared as she flicked his blood off the end of her razor sharp claws.

His field integrity readings were down to 65%. He knew that once it dropped to around fifty or so, it was over. If he was going to act, it had to be now. "Remember the Alamo," he whispered into the helmet microphone. The computer heard the vocal command and shut down the multi-stage protection field, but began putting all the available energy into the capacitors. A small bar on the bottom left of his visor went from green to orange immediately.

Gato Loco managed to keep his feet while he checked his position. Good, he thought, still in the right place. Rakshasha licked Manuel's blood off a fingertip, sensing that the game was about up. Kat and mouse to the end, Manuel thought, but we are both cats here, are we not? "What happened to you, Katherine?" he said, his stance relaxed, as non-threatening as possible. "How did you get to be such a bitch?"

With a roar of rage, she lashed out and grabbed Gato Loco by the throat. He could feel her claws poking into the side of his neck, but they were thankfully only superficial wounds. She didn't intend to rip his throat out -- her grip was all wrong for that, and that would be too easy. But Manuel still hoped he wasn't making a mistake here, realizing that she could easily snap his neck . "You do not speak to me like that!" she growled. "I am better than you, and you should fear me. You are nothing! A skinny man in a fancy leather suit. You have saved no one. You are not a hero. I am stronger and faster! I am better than you, better than all of them!"

"But I'm smarter," he said with considerable effort. The little bar on the left had hit red, showing the capacitors close to overloading. "Pow," he told the helmet.

The stage-field generator fired out its hundreds of tiny force fields in a wide arc. With her hand on his throat, there was no way for Rakshasha to get out of the way of the invisibly targeted area. Hundreds of tiny sequenced impacts hit every square inch of her body,

224

coursed past her ear canal, and caused several amusing physiological effects to happen. Manuel had seen it drop a 350-pound lineman on PCP like a sack of potatoes. He hoped it was enough to stop Rakshasha. He was relieved when her grip released and he felt all of his weight on his feet again.

But she wasn't down for the count, merely staggered. "I never claimed to be a hero," he said as a quick knee to her solar plexus doubled her over. "I'm just a damn good detective," he said as the subsequent uppercut to her jaw sent her backwards into the power strip next to the magnetic track. Sparks flew and Rakshasha was thrown from the roof of the elevator.

Manuel leapt over to her. She still had a pulse, he was happy to find. She was going to hurt a lot when she woke up in an hour or so, but by then she would be restrained in the power draining cuffs the Protectorate kept near the elevator on this floor. If she wasn't herself by the time someone found and released her, he planned on being long gone. Fiji was nice this time of year, he had heard, and he had vacation time coming from the department.

"How is she?" Snowflake said, poking his head out from under the elevator.

"She'll live," Manuel said, offering a hand up to the panda. "But if she asks, you're the one who kicked her ass, right?"

"Not on your life," Snowflake said. He looked down at the unconscious Rakshasha, tilting his head to the side slightly as he considered her. He looked back up at Gato Loco. "You slept with her, right?"

"A gentleman never tells," Manuel said, his eyes already searching for the access panel to get them out of the elevator shaft.

"I'll bet she's a tiger in the sack," Snowflake said with a sigh.

"My friend," Manuel said, the exit he sought in sight, "you have no idea."

Chapter Thirty-Two

Spending several months confined to a cell with Candledark as your neighbor would be difficult under any circumstances. But when you couldn't keep the bio-terrorist's dark thoughts from leaking into your own dreams and those rare moments when the powers came close to the surface, it was hell. As Jeremy Red prowled through the high grass of an imaginary savannah towards Lenore, he couldn't be certain if he knew her or if these memories belonged to Candledark. It was confusing, as the echo of Candledark which looked through his eyes told him it was Anna Lyta, but in *her* mind, she was someone else entirely, named Lenore. Jeremy curled his hand tighter around the shaft of the broken arrow, knowing that at least *it* was real. Not a real weapon, he knew, but the can opener hadn't been a real weapon either, and he had made that blunt, crooked piece of metal work for him last time.

Fifteen feet away, moving one silent, shifting step after another, and his memories of Anna/Lenore grew stronger. He was seated with her in some downtown club, with several fellow students from the Hanover Technical Institute. The others snubbed him, thought he was crazy. Only Anna showed him any kindness, offering him a smile and…

Jeremy had no classmates, had never even gone to college. He knew that, deep down. His eyes avoided the reflection in the mirrors of the club, because he knew it wouldn't be him that he saw there. But if he made his own memories of Anna/Lenore, memories of her hot blood pulsing over his hand as he plunged the broken piece of wood into her throat, then he would have something real. And then, maybe, he could get Candledark out of his head. And maybe, just maybe, if he killed her, she would settle into being one entity instead of a duality vibrating between two extremes in his mind.

Seven feet away, and he sent out soothing images plucked from her mind, images of a pampered childhood with her friend, surrogate father, guardian, and eventual lover, the cold flesh of the man she knew as Lazarus. He felt her relax. She felt protected, but a little nervous. He could see her controlling the expanding wave of acidic worms, and could feel the worm that had provided her body with a force field atrophy and slip back to wherever it had come from. Jeremy could tell that she was vulnerable, and predicted each move of her head before she knew she was making it, masking himself behind tall grass each time she threatened to catch him in her peripheral vision.

The seven feet slowly grew to only two as battle raged across Earl's Court, and Jeremy allowed himself a quiet moment to take it all in, knowing that no one could stop him now that he was so close.

The young archer had launched every kind of arrow in his arsenal at the black man with the lion skull helmet, as the teleporter moved him from place to place to avoid a retaliatory strike.

The albino necromancer had shielded himself and several children within a glowing red bubble of force, and was preparing some kind of ritual.

The wounded woman in the cloak scrapped with the flying man in armor, his fist glowing with power as he attacked, each punch deflected, but at a high cost, and Jeremy didn't think the woman would last much longer.

In the pipe where Jeremy had hidden only minutes before, the dead man from this Anna/Lenore's memories held the psychic he had duped by the head and squeezed, while the genius in the torn suit watched Jeremy's steady advance with a look of horror in his eyes, knowing that he could not get there in time to stop the inevitable.

Even a novice psychic could pick up Jeremy's delight as he closed in on his kill, intent to close a loop in a memory that wasn't his own. And Libertine was no novice. As Lazarus tried in vain to crush her force field protected head, she received the images of what Jeremy saw and felt the improvised weapon in his hand. She could not resist the pressure Lazarus was putting on her defenses for long. A little bit had already started to filter through, and she felt her skull throbbing and a tiny trickle of blood from her nose run across her upper lip. Libertine decided she couldn't stop Lazarus and try to control Jeremy Red at the same time, so she shifted her tactics and combined the two endeavors. With a slight mental shift, she transmitted what Jeremy was seeing directly into the cold, dead brain of Lazarus. The pressure on her head vanished immediately, but she felt her knees wobble as blood returned to her scalp.

Jeremy raised the broken, wooden shaft high over his head as he stood behind his unaware target, and swiftly drove it down into her throat, oblivious to the sudden shadow. A spray of scarlet splattered the concrete of Earl's Court, and a stunned Lenore fell to her knees, her hands fluttering up towards her throat. Jeremy sensed an almost overwhelming explosion of rage from above him. He turned his eyes skyward just in time to see Lazarus land on him with both feet, driving him into the cracked concrete.

"Gallows," Archon shouted, "Med evac now! Libertine, you're on Sundiatta. Get behind the wheel and have him lock the place down."

Libertine struck at Sundiatta with her mind, and found him stronger willed than she expected. Her fingernails drew blood from her palms as she concentrated on breaking down his defenses.

Meanwhile, it took Gallows only a few seconds to lock onto the fallen Lenore and port her inside the pipe. She came to rest, motionless, where Velvet had been only minutes before. She was already pale from shock and loss of blood, and Archon hoped that the wound was not as severe as it looked at first glance.

Velvet had prepared herself for Sundiatta's eventual arrival, and had activated a gravity-equalizer attached to her belt, so his attempts at weighing her down or flinging her into space had met with no success, but he had been able to completely sap her kinetic potential. Each punch she threw at Deathstar was as weak as a kitten's, and she had been forced to fight a purely defensive battle, feeling the soreness in her ribs with each block and dodge. She had sparred with both Jaccob and the squatter who now occupied his body, so she knew he could fight, but had forgotten just how good he was when the chips were down. Even masters make mistakes, she reminded herself, and she kept mitigating the damage he did against her, hoping that she could hold out long enough to capitalize on one of his mistakes.

Suddenly, she saw an obvious kill punch coming and moved to evade, only to realize that he had pulled her in with a feint. The punch she had moved to block stopped short, and the other fist was already inches from her head. She had committed her body to action too completely, and found herself out of position to defend. But strangely, the punch didn't pack the impact of previous blows, and it was only the energy field around the gauntlet that she felt. It was enough, however, and as she slipped into unconsciousness, Velvet wondered why Deathstar's punch hadn't taken her head off at the shoulders like it was been supposed to.

Deathstar wondered the same thing. It was as if he had no force behind the blow all of a sudden. His eyes grew huge as he figured it out, but it was too late. Already Libertine had taken over Sundiatta and used his powers to snare both man and armor in a heavy gravity well. Deathstar strained against the crushing gravity, but found that he was virtually incapable of movement. Even shifting his gauntlets in a more tactical direction was beyond his abilities. Unable to fire at anything except empty courtyard, he was reduced to merely watching as the battle continued on around him.

The area immediately around Lazarus and Jeremy Red was a riot of illusions. Children's book images walked alongside supermodels, images of heaven shimmered into portrayals of hell itself. The cracked and bloodied concrete played host to more themes and characters than could be comprehended before they were replaced. But through it all, one constant remained: Lazarus reducing Jeremy Red to a skin sack of broken bones and ruptured organs. The undead mobster was single-minded in his punishment of the disturbed psychic, and didn't acknowledge the flickering images around him or the growing number of arrows sprouting from his back, arms, and legs. It wasn't until the illusions flickered out entirely that he even slowed down to look around for his missing companion. "Lenore!" he bellowed, his voice raw and animal-like.

The subject of Lazarus' search groaned, blood bubbling in her mouth, but did not move. Archon crouched over Lenore, his mini-computer switched to voice activation in an effort to coordinate the battle that was rapidly getting away from them. In the poor light and less-than-ideal conditions he had difficulty seeing the wound clearly enough to stitch it closed. The blood loss had slowed considerably, but he attributed most of that to shock. "Computer, give me Protectorate communicator audio feed, receive only, Doctor Shadow's channel only," he said. He processed the ancient language automatically as he operated on the unconscious Lenore. He didn't like what he heard. "Open channel to Gallows," he said, then paused. "You there, Gallows?"

"For the moment," the teleporter said. "Need another evac?"

"Any luck on getting the kids from Shade yet?" Archon asked, as he threaded a small, curved needle.

"Negative," Gallows said. "He has them under an energy dome of some kind, and earlier they were bound by some glowing rope that seemed to bind them to him or something."

"Are they still tied?"

"No, they're loose, but they aren't running," Gallows said. "I don't think they can get through the field. And they're probably too scared to try. Any idea what kind of hoodoo tall, dark and spooky is pulling in there?"

"Well, my ancient Sumerian is a bit rusty, but he seems to be invoking the sprits of the dead," Archon said, trying to remain calm. Anna's vitals were falling, and he wasn't sure he could prevent that with what he had here. "If I understand correctly, for every child sacrificed, he brings forth angry spirits."

"How many angry spirits are we talking here?"

"The prayer to the Sumerian death god asks for every spirit within approximately a hundred feet. That's for the first child. It grows exponentially from there. Death gods like to deal in bulk, apparently," Archon said grimly. "But it gets worse. There was a major battle here in the days after the Revolutionary War. Hundreds died. Gallows, we don't have a way to deal with ghosts if they happen to show up. If he completes the spell, they've won. It's as simple as that. Now, can you get them out?"

"Or die trying," Gallows said shifting himself to the inside of Shade's force bubble. The seven children looked up at him with blank eyes and the ancient necromancer stumbled over his incantations and stopped. "Didn't anyone tell you to pick on someone your own size?" the teleporter said.

Shade's lip curled in an approximation of a grin, and Gallows felt a chill. A small, placid child pressed up against Shade's legs, and the necromancer had one hand on the boy's fragile-looking shoulder.

With a blink, Gallows took the six children not in contact with Shade to the relative safety of a nearby public library's front steps and then blinked back inside the energy field. Getting hold of the kids from the outside had met with all kinds of interference, but other than a tingle as he appeared in the area, teleporting in and out, even with kids, had required no effort at all. The remaining boy was under Shade's control, and that posed a problem. It was unlikely that tall, pale, and spooky was willing to part with his sacrifice so easily, but Gallows wasn't ready to give up quite yet.

Before Gallows could launch a teleport-assisted barrage of punches and kicks at the mage, Shade waved his hand and spoke three inhuman sounding words. At first, Gallows thought he had managed to dodge whatever effect Shade had planned for him. But midway through his full-bore teleport attack, a painful burning sensation in his stomach and lungs bent him over double. He fell into the small, square pool of the waterfall fountain behind Shade, with the uncomfortable feeling of something moving around inside him. He hacked and gagged and was horrified when a pair of small beetles wet with blood fell out of his mouth into the clear water around his knees. He wanted to scream, but found that his lungs and stomach had become bustling nests, and there was no room for the air he needed to cry out.

Shade ignored the gasping and choking teleporter and began his incantations again. His shield of force glowed slightly as the possessed Sundiatta tried to work his vile jungle technology based powers on him. The advantage of trusting no one, he supposed, was that you were prepared for attack from anyone. Without missing a syllable, he knelt and grasped the small boy by the ankle and raised him high. A small, thin blade emerged from his sleeve, and he continued chanting, wishing for the hundredth time that the Sumerian death rituals were more abbreviated.

"I need a situation report," Archon's voice crackled over Gallow's communicator. "Are you there?"

When Archon got no response from his teleporting teammate, he turned instead to Huntsman and Libertine, asking for their status.

"I've put everything I have into Lazarus and he's not even slowing down," Huntsman said. "I have to keep moving on foot to keep out of hand-to-hand range. Gallows got all but one of the kids out, but he's been taken down inside the bubble."

"He's down, but he's still moving," Libertine said. "He's been infected with something, I think. He's writhing in the water in a lot of pain. I can't tell more without letting go of Sundiatta. I've been trying to lock down Lazarus, but he's too strong, and Shade's force bubble is blocking any attempts I make to get to him."

"Have you tried removing Lazarus from the Earth's gravity? Knockabout does it all the time." Archon said.

"He's making handholds in the concrete," Huntsman said. "Seems he's little smarter than I gave him credit for. He's making his way towards Sundiatta now. I give him less than a minute before he gets there."

"Can you outpace him, Libertine?" Archon said.

"Not if I want to keep a grip on Sundiatta," she said grimly. "He's a willful guy. Guess he would have to be, wouldn't he?"

"Ok, hang in there, and we'll get you some help," Archon said, looking at his options. He didn't have many left. Too many pieces had been removed from the board or were locked up. "Gallows, I know you can hear me. You have to listen. This is important. Whatever Shade did to you, you have to fight your way past it. You said it yourself. Do it or die trying. I'm sorry, buddy, but we don't have any other choices."

Gallows managed to lift his head, as he spit out a stream of blood and squirming insects into the water of the fountain, already swimming with things he didn't want to look at too closely.

"The only thing we have going for us know is that Libertine has Sundiatta under her control and that's keeping Deathstar out of the fight. Velvet is down, Jeremy Red is probably dead, and Huntsman has hit the wall," Archon said. He had known Gallows longer than the others. They joined the team together, and he knew what he was asking. And he knew that Gallows could do it. He wished there was another choice. But there wasn't. No one knew that more than him. "Gallows. This is the line in the sand. If we lose here, we don't get another chance."

Gallows focused through eyes blurred by tears of pain. Archon was right. Damn him, but he was always right. Gallows focused on the crawling sensation inside him and tried to isolate it as best as he could. He had never tried anything like this before, and it occurred to him that if he screwed up, he was as good as dead. But looking around him, he realized that he was dead if he didn't try. He imagined a big, invisible hand, but instead of reaching out and touching a visible target, he imagined it inside, touching all the bugs within his torso. He closed his eyes and flexed, and found himself stunned by the inner emptiness he felt. Several feet away, his dinner and a cubic foot of crawling beetles splashed down in the already filthy waters of the fountain.

Blinking back relief, and not sure if he accidentally removed any organs that might prove to be important later, Gallows reached out with his mind and teleported Lazarus somewhere else. He didn't know where. He hadn't even thought about it. The world turned dark and opened up to swallow him.

As Gallows slid into unconsciousness, he was aware that Shade had stopped his incantations. The knife's edge touched the throat of the small child. It had all been for nothing. If Archon's concerns were valid, in one stroke, all of their hard work and sacrifice would be washed away. And then Cobalt City would be lost.

Chapter Thirty-Three

The black waters of ancient lake Hali spread out for miles beyond the pallid walls of Carcosa, and beneath those cold waters, something enormous and timeless lay waiting to be born. Doctor Shadow had watched the horizon of the lake distractedly from the high windows of one of Carcosa's empty and tomblike grand halls since pulling Katherine, Anna, and Edirin out of the mirror world. The other exiled members of the Protectorate had spent the last half hour pacing and pondering beneath the high, vaulted ceiling, listening with growing unease to the sounds the echoes made in the all but stifling silence.

Katherine Wilde came to a stop before Doctor Shadow and tried to read his expression. "Do you trust him?" she said.

"That is a complicated question," he said eventually.

"No, it is a simple question, Doctor," she said. "Do you trust him or don't you?"

"I trust that the King in Yellow is bound by certain laws," he said. "Everything is bound by certain laws, and he is no exception. But what those laws are, I cannot say with any certainty. Does he want to help us? Possibly, but perhaps not for the reasons we believe. Can he help us? Yes. But I believe him when he says he cannot help Simon. Do I trust him? I trust him enough to listen to his offer if he makes one, but I will evaluate it as shrewdly as a deal with the devil himself."

"If only Simon had been as careful," Katherine said, hating herself for saying it as soon as the words were out of her mouth. "I'm sorry. I don't mean that."

"No," Doctor Shadow said, turning his eyes again to the vast lake. "You did mean it. And you are not the only one to have had that thought. But I also know that you meant no harm in thinking it. A more careful consideration of the consequences his deal might bring about would have been ideal. But not everyone is perfect. We all have moments where, in a flash of doubt or weakness or self-delusional glory, we do something foolish. It is human nature. Perhaps we should take this as a sign that, for all that has happened to him, Simon is more human even now than he ever realized."

"Everyone makes foolish mistakes?" she said. "Even you?"

The shadow of sadness that passed across Doctor Shadow's face vanished as quickly as it appeared. "Like Simon, my immortality was not something I asked for. But I would rather not think about it now. It will not help us here."

"Of course," Katherine said.

Deeper in the room, Knockabout had released gravity on himself just enough to recline, several inches off the ground. It had been a long day, and he had no way of knowing when it would be over. At this point, any rest was welcome. He just had to remain awake enough to remember not to fall. He was in no danger of falling asleep with Jaccob and Anna talking near him, however.

"Why do you think Augustus Dei went after Simon?" Jaccob said. He had his helmet off and was tinkering with some of the sensor arrays inside.

"Who would you rather have had him go after?" Anna said.

"That's not what I meant," he said. "It's just that I always thought of Simon as perceptive and really strong willed. If I was trying to con someone I'd look for someone more suggestible or impulsive."

"Like you, you mean," Edirin said, cracking one eye open to look at Jaccob, a sly smile on his face.

"Or Anna or Katherine, hell, especially Katherine," he said.

"What makes you think that Katherine is suggestible or impulsive?" Edirin said.

Jaccob shrugged. "She always reacts so quickly to stuff…faster than me even."

Edirin chuckled. "Do not confuse reflexes with impulsiveness," he said.

"Anyway, Augustus Dei was interested in Simon long before any of us were born," Anna said. "Well, except for Doctor Shadow, that is."

"Instead of asking why it was Simon was targeted, I see a bigger picture," Edirin said.

"What is that?" Jaccob said.

"Not 'Why Simon' but instead, what could Augustus Dei only get from Simon that he couldn't get from making a deal with us?" Edirin said.

"And you think that is a factor?" Jaccob said.

"I think it's the most important factor," Edirin said. "What did Augustus Dei get out of it? Was it entertainment? If so, and he was setting this up decades ago, that's…well, that's a long time to wait for entertainment, don't you think?"

"So why do you think he did it?" Anna said.

"Because he already knew what Simon would ask for and what would happen because of it, maybe?" Jaccob said. "I mean, what if he isn't linear? If he's extra dimensional, which we have reason to believe he is, then maybe he already knows what is going to happen. Like everything is a big chain of dominoes and he's just setting them up piece by piece."

"So you think he has precognition," Anna said.

"No," Jaccob said. "It's bigger than that. He doesn't so much look into the future as live in the future, like he's outside of time. What if, rather than experiencing events one at a time, everything happens at once?"

"So he experiences his entire life all the time?" Ediin said.

"It's a theory," Jaccob said.

"And isn't he immortal or something?" Anna said.

"Really, really old at any rate. I would suggest even eternal instead of immortal," Edirin said.

"So it's possible that this is just another piece to something much bigger," Anna said.

"It's entirely possible that we may never see the end result of what Augustus Dei set in motion with Simon," Jaccob said.

"Am I the only one bothered by that?" Edirin said, thinking so hard about the quantum angle that gravity grabbed hold of him and caused him to sit in the dust.

"Hey, you're the one who asked the big question," Jaccob said. He pretended not to notice Edirin picking himself up off the ground and dusting himself off. "This might just be the grain of sand to make a really big pearl."

"A pearl of evil," Anna said.

"I have made a decision," said the booming voice of the King in Yellow as he floated into the room, his feet invisible beneath the voluminous yellow robes leaving a wake in the dust behind him. The gathered members of the Protectorate stopped their individual conversations immediately and turned towards him, bunching together for the perceived safety of numbers. His white, ageless eyes stared down at them from above the veil drawn across the lower half of his face. The small, unidentifiable charms suspended on the cord that connected the veil to the tip of the sweeping, carved bone helmet jingled in the heavy air and failed to bring any cheer whatsoever. The King in Yellow waited, breathless, motionless, drawing out their anticipation, until there was absolute silence. "I can help you and ask nothing for this uncharacteristic kindness save that you do not seek me out for something so trivial again."

"What about Simon?" Katherine said. All eyes turned to her, but she did not flinch or lower her eyes.

A heartbeat passed. Then another.

"He is beyond my help," the King in Yellow said, his voice

sounding like gravestones grinding the bones of old men to dust. It was not a voice to be questioned. "You will follow me to the mirror," he said, turning and gliding back the way he had come.

The exiled members of the Protectorate fell in step behind him. Jaccob adjusted his speed to walk along Katherine. "Anna said you were able to contact the dust storm in Cobalt City," he said, his voice low so as not to anger their host. "Could you tell if it was Simon or not?"

Katherine shook her head. "Part of Simon was there, I'm sure. He recognized us, I could feel it. But…it was so angry. I've known Simon for well over a year now, and I've never seen him angry like that before. And sad, too. That didn't really surprise me too much, I guess."

"So part of Simon is still there, in the alternate Cobalt City?" Jaccob said.

"Do you believe in ghosts?" she said so suddenly he almost tripped.

"What? I don't know," he said, trying to take the scientific position. "You think Doctor Shadow was right, about him being a hungry ghost?"

"Well, Simon died but he's still around, right? He believes, and I trust him on this, that Voodoo magic animated him. So, in a way, he's a zombie, but not like any other zombie because of certain circumstances," she said.

"Okay, but what about ghosts?" Jaccob said.

"I'm no expert, but certain members of my family have had extensive…well, experience with ghosts," she began.

"Right…most of them still live in England, don't they?" Jaccob said. "Whole damn island is haunted, the way I hear it. Go ahead."

"Well, the theory is that ghosts are just the manifestation of strong emotions, usually perceived as an energy signature," she said. "Doctor Shadow suggested that maybe the Mister Grey we know is part of a fragmented personality, but what if it's more than that? In the end, a ghost is just an energy signature, not necessarily the soul of the person who died."

"An energy signature," Jaccob said, starting to make sense of it. Simon did have a specific energy signature. That was what Jaccob had ended up using as his security access trigger.

"More or less," she said with a shrug. "What if Simon, still a zombie in a non-traditional sense, also had some fragment of ghost caught up in his ash? I mean, the circumstances around his death would lend themselves to a haunting."

"So the ghost of Simon was somehow tied to the rest of him. But which part was Mister Grey? Which part have we have been fighting crime with for the past year?"

"The zombie part," Katherine said. "If ghosts are just energy signatures, little bits of tragedy and heartbreak and anger playing themselves out over and over again, then that doesn't describe Simon at all, does it? But it does help to explain why he is prone to fits of melancholy. He's been dead for seventy years, but he's been haunted by his past the entire time. In this case, really haunted."

"So when the hoodoo went down, the ghost got sent to the mirror world..." Jaccob said.

"But Simon never left. His deal was to be made flesh again, so why would he be sent here and turned to ash again? It would violate the contract. Doctor Shadow said there are always rules to magic. Rules and costs. He wanted to be flesh, so he's flesh. But maybe he's trapped in the same head as Lazarus all this time," Katherine said.

"Damn. So how do you think he's handling having a roommate in his head?" Jaccob said.

"Not good, I'd bet. He's been driven for so long by these strong emotions that might not have even really been his. And now he doesn't have those around anymore. Then we get taken away from him. All he has left is a darker version of his own personality and a few teammates he doesn't really know that well. Who, might I add, are probably being hunted into the ground if they haven't been caught and killed by now."

"Then we need to get back," Jaccob said.

"You shall be going home soon enough, mortal," the King in Yellow said, his deep voice echoing off the high stone walls of the Hall of the Lens. "At least one of you will be going home," he said.

"Wait. Only one of us?" Anna said. "This wasn't part of the deal!"

On the far wall, the Mirror of Shadows seemed to sink into the fabric of space, as if its density had created a gravity well not unlike a black hole. Katherine could almost feel her soul being tugged towards it, like water down a drain. "Do you feel that?" she said to Edirin and Jaccob.

"It isn't me," Edirin said, "And, yes. I do feel it."

"I said I would help," the King in Yellow said. "Even now, in your world the necromancer is prepared to sacrifice the life of a child and bring about an unstoppable force. Make your decision or you will be too late. Who do you send?"

"Doctor Shadow, you have to go," Edirin said. There was something about the way the mirror pulled on him that he found vaguely familiar. Time and space began to stretch like taffy, making everything look strange, like funhouse mirrors. He didn't much care for funhouse mirrors and closed his eyes to keep his stomach from doing flips. Somehow not being able to see made the motion worse.

"I will find a way and come back for you," Doctor Shadow said.

"Just as nature abhors a vacuum, the Mirror of Shadows abhors a dimensional aberration," the King in Yellow said, as if he were reading the directions on the back of the box. "I merely have to let nature take its course. I expect that you will find the transition…unpleasant. I hope you remember it the next time you bring your petty concerns to my doorstep."

This is all wrong, Katherine thought. If only one person is allowed through, then where are the rest of us going? And why was Edirin smiling?

Stardust experienced a drunken, uncontrolled fall into darkness. When the lights came back on, he found himself flat on the ground, too weak to stand. Something had gone terribly, terribly wrong. He tried to lift his hand to his face, to see if he was somehow in yet another different body, but found that his hand, in fact, his entire body, weighed several tons. Above him, he could see only a thin cover of clouds and the tall, vertical lines of a strangely familiar office building at night. "This had better be the right Cobalt City," he grumbled under his breath.

Worm Queen's eyelids fluttered open and then closed again. As unpleasant as the trip had been, the final arrival was worse. She was numb and groggy, but when she tried to regain focus, she found that the distant sensation was preferable to the pain it masked. She saw Archon kneeling over her, a small flashlight tucked behind his ear, a concerned look on his face. She wanted to tell him that it was all going to be okay, and that she had come back to help, but found that she couldn't speak. And when she breathed, there was a gurgling sound she didn't like.

"Go to sleep," Archon told her, voice soft, his hands in blood-slick latex surgery gloves.

Wild Kat rode out the twisting, gut-churning transition with good humor and faith in Edirin's confidence. When the blackness of the journey gave way to another kind of darkness, she wondered if it was possible that the worst was not entirely behind them. Her hands were in Protectorate high-rating restraint cuffs, and she had a bruise growing on her chin. She could tell that her hair was wildly unkempt, and decided that the lingering smell of ozone might explain that mystery. Her eyes adjusted to the dark slowly and she realized that she was at the bottom of the elevator shaft back at The Keep. "Well," she said to the indifferent dark, "this is just typical."

Knockabout found himself drifting suddenly into focus, realizing that this was his own body, but that he was no longer in control of it. He wondered if his gamble had paid off after all. When Augustus Dei had played Three Card Monty with their identities the first time, only Simon had been the real target of the transition. The others had been pulled along because they were close enough to the area of effect, and attuned to the Mirror of Shadows. If the King in Yellow had only wanted to send one person through, then why bring everyone into the presence of the lens and tell them that it abhorred abnormalities? Perhaps the King knew, but the rules prohibited him from sending multiple people through intentionally.

He looked about and realized that he was in Earl's Court. Velvet and Stardust lay flat on the ground fifteen feet away, and a badly beaten body sprawled fifteen feet beyond that, its features unrecognizable from here. Up in one of the installation art pieces (a Raymond Earle from 1957 entitled Orange in December, he recalled) was the somewhat familiar figure of Libertine. From the damage done to the plaza, it appeared a huge fight had been in progress.

"Welcome back, handsome," a female voice in his head said, and then Edirin felt what he assumed to be Libertine's mental hold over him release.

Doctor Shadow, used to a wide variety of dimensional travel, had no difficulties in the transition home. But he was not expecting what would await him. He felt a great surge of magical potential swirling around him, the tremors of a powerful spell just awaiting completion. In one hand was a long, thin knife. In the other, he was holding a small child by the ankle, a placid, wide eyed-boy, with a knife at his neck. The image was too hauntingly familiar, as though...he shook his head. It was too unlikely, he thought. He looked at the scene through the eyes of the child and saw himself, a bewildered look on his face while a waterfall cascaded over ridged concrete behind him. He quickly retreated back to his own head and lowered the child to the ground. The magical potential that had permeated the air only seconds ago was gone, and he had some suspicion as to where it went. "Well, Emil," he said to the boy, "I imagine that you shall remember this evening for a very long time indeed."

Then, after taking quick stock of the damage around him,

Doctor Shadow began assisting Archon in caring for the wounded.

Chapter Thirty-Four

From the rooftop of an abandoned warehouse in the West End, Lazarus saw the golden glow of power armor as Stardust, no, Deathstar took to the sky. A mixture of emotion flooded the cold, undead brain, suspicion and hate and, strangely, relief. Why did he care if the self-obsessed inventor lived or died? The welfare of such men did not concern Lazarus. But Simon...

There it is again, Lazarus thought, as he leapt from rooftop to rooftop, the light of the power armor his north star. That *voice*. Simon was nothing, merely the shell from which Lazarus hatched. And once hatched, Simon was discarded. Or was he? The black-suited benefactor who had brought him here had told him. There were two souls, two minds, two separate and by no means equal purposes, but only one body between them. Lazarus, however, was strong. Lazarus ruled over lesser, weaker men. This frail wisp of a memory that was Simon was nothing to him.

But it concerned him that he couldn't seem to eradicate Simon entirely. While there were times he thought he was alone in his head, at other times Simon had almost gained control. They had both been affected by the attack on Anna, and those emotions, while somewhat different, had been equally strong. When Lazarus had tried to beat Anna's skinny, shirtless assassin to death, Simon had been able to put the enormous strength in check, and in the end, they had let him live. Broken, Lazarus comforted himself by thinking. Broken and useless was worse than death.

Lazarus kept jumping, not letting the glow of the armor out of his sight except for the several seconds it took to run beneath the highway and get atop a roof again. He remembered that he had been given a communicator at some point, but not where he put it. Then he realized the memory of receiving the small ear-bud was not his own, but Simon's, and the thought shook him slightly. He caught a fire escape ladder in one hand to steady himself. What could it mean if he was experiencing memories that were not his own?

He paused and watched the Stardust armor and realized that it was not going in a direct line. It was, in fact turning back his way. An unconscious impulse drove him into the shadows near a cluster of smokestacks as the glowing armor passed within a few hundred feet, then turned again and swooped to the north. It was a patrol, he knew deep in his gut, but he didn't want to admit how he knew.

Deathstar would never patrol Cobalt City, Lazarus knew. He

would search, possibly, but what could he be looking for so far away from the recent battle? And then it hit him. "He's looking for me," Lazarus said, and the idea chilled him. If it was Deathstar in the armor, then he couldn't be looking for Lazarus to help. Deathstar didn't help anyone but himself.

"Or maybe he's looking for the teleporter," Lazarus realized. That made more sense. Gallows ran and took a few of his allies with him. And the thought of Gallows and some of the others escaping made him, no, Simon, happy. Lazarus shook the thought loose. He set his sights on the high towers near Earl's Court and took off through downtown again. They would have some answers there, he decided.

It took several minutes to traverse the traffic-clogged streets. With everyone forced to detour around the destruction caused to several of the major arterials, it was difficult to get to his destination unseen by bystanders or the still-searching Stardust armor, even at this time of night. Eventually, he got within a block of the earlier fight and discovered that emergency vehicles had already pulled up onto the pitted concrete of the plaza itself. Lazarus crouched behind the rotating icon of some anonymous nightclub and watched the scene play out before him.

Doctor Shadow was loading Anna onto a stretcher, while an archer dressed in deep blue and gold talked with police. The woman from the pipe whose head he had tried to crush was nearby, crouching near the inert body of Anna's assailant. As he watched, the Stardust armor touched down near the others. Gallows appeared next to Doctor Shadow suddenly, and no fight broke out between them. It was all too friendly to make Lazarus comfortable.

His allies were gone. Not that Lazarus had really trusted them to begin with, but this was a dangerous world to be a criminal in. Too many people with hero complexes had the urge to put on a mask and cape in this world. It was unnerving. It was probably caused by something in the water or a product of bad parenting. The human and, in his opinion, admirable quality of looking out for number one seemed to be suppressed in a high percentage of people here.

And worse than losing his allies, he had lost Lenore as well. True, there was an Anna here, but he doubted that they would be able to work out their differences. He wasn't going to get less dead anytime soon. But he couldn't just give up. He would still be stuck here, for some reason, while the only person who had even tried to understand him in the past twenty years was gone.

The only people who could conceivably send him home were more likely to arrest him or kill him if he darkened their doorstep. He couldn't really blame the Protectorate. Not only did he beat the hell out of a few people, but he also caused this whole mess to begin with. No, Lazarus thought, this feeling of guilt isn't mine. Simon caused this to happen, not me.

No, Simon thought in reply, Augustus Dei made this happen. And last we checked, he was back at The Keep.

It occurred to him suddenly that there was one person here who might just understand him. And this ally was in the most unexpected of places: inside his own head.

"I want to go home," Lazarus said as he watched Anna being loaded into an ambulance. The others watched her as the doors closed. Archon had joined her in the back. Even from here, Lazarus could see the concern on his face.

Augustus Dei, Simon thought, he can send you home.

"The others won't be happy to see me," Lazarus said as he jumped to the street and began heading to The Keep in bounding, fifty-foot leaps.

They won't be happy to see either of us, Simon thought.

Two minds in one body moved steadily through the tangle of wrecked cars and ruined streets towards the heart of the city. Neither one said or thought anything for a long while. Eventually, the silence in his head, once a source of great comfort, started to wear on Lazarus. "Why did you do it?" he said.

Well, I spent seventy years in a jar, Simon thought, so the prospect of getting some part of my old life back was very attractive.

"And you didn't read the fine print or something?" Lazarus said, laughing deeply as he leapfrogged off a stranded bus to the roof of an apartment building.

I had a sworn testimonial from someone I trusted, Simon thought.

"Who was that?" Lazarus said, "Because I would begin to question whether they were worthy of trust."

Silence filled his head for a while, and Lazarus began to wonder if he had gotten rid of Simon for good.

It was Camilla, Simon thought suddenly.

"That bitch," Lazarus said, spitting although he had no saliva in his eternally dry mouth. He could feel Simon's shock and almost laughed again. "She's the one who got us killed, idiot!"

Peppermint Nick is the one who killed me, Simon thought, despite what happened in your world.

"Did she have a taste for smack?" Lazarus said evenly, climbing to a rooftop overlooking The Keep.

Yes, Simon thought, but that is neither here nor there.

"You see, with me, baby needed her candy, so I went out to get the money to pay for it," Lazarus said. Overhead, the Protectorate flew towards the roof door of The Keep. Lazarus crouched low in the shadows. He wasn't ready to be seen. Not yet. "I hit the bank with a few mates, thinking it would be easy and where else was I going to get the money to support her habit? Jobs didn't just fall into my lap, you know?"

Nothing of the sort happened to me, Simon thought, I had gone to the club early to get some arrangements done and witnessed a killing.

"Why were you at the club early?" Lazarus said, watching the rooftop across the way carefully.

Camilla had just taken a large quantity of heroin and I didn't want to see her like that, Simon thought.

"So if it wasn't for her habit, you wouldn't have been in the club at that particular time, am I right?"

The voice in his head had gone silent again. Lazarus wondered if he should continue, and decided that until the Protectorate went down into the damn building, there was nothing better to do. "And to make matters worse, just when you finally get your eternal rest, she calls you back from the dead. Why did she do that, you ask yourself. Was it to apologize? No, my friend, it was because she was an addict, and she was selfish and weak and needed you to take care of her. That is why she called you back. Not out of love, but out of weakness."

Camilla loved me, Simon thought, and I loved her. We were going to be together forever, she and I.

"Then where is she now?" Lazarus said. Across the way, the last of the Protectorate had vanished into the light of the hangar bay door, and Lazarus leapt from the nearby rooftop onto the grounds of The Keep. The sensors allowed him in without any of the usual protocol and merely acknowledged his presence.

You can't twist her love and make it something horrible, Simon thought.

"I'm not twisting anything," Lazarus said. He bounded to the front door, pressed the access panel and smiled as it hissed open. "My Camilla loved me too, and she was around for decades. But nothing lasts forever. Nothing except you and me, that is."

What did Augustus Dei promise you, Simon thought.

"Interesting you should ask," Lazarus said. "One night, I'm shaking down a warehouse owner for money he owes me, and I get this strong, mental image of this group of people I've never seen before, but they all look familiar somehow. Then I realize Lenore is with them, but she's wearing this body stocking with thick, wiggly lines, white and blue and red, like her worms, you know? There's this big, black disk floating there, and this beautiful mummified woman crawling with bugs stands in front of everyone, threatening them. She's real interested in Lenore, but I can't hear what they're talking about. Suddenly, I'm back in my body again, and it turns out I was zoned out for a few minutes and the warehouse owner made a break for it. I had to kill him for that when I finally caught him.

"So I couldn't get this vision out of my head, right? Then a day or so later, this man in a black suit walks right up to me as I'm stepping off the elevator. He says he can explain what the vision is about. I have to admit that I'm curious. Turns out Lenore had a similar vision, and I'm getting a little concerned about what it all could mean. So I tell him, 'Sure, why the hell don't you show me what that crazy crap meant' and next thing I know we're shaking hands and then he's gone, like it never happened. Time goes by, I almost forget about the vision and the strange guy, then one minute I'm at home, the next I'm in your little clubhouse and the guy in the suit is smiling at us. And you're in my head, which, I have to say, has taken some getting used to."

What a charming story, Simon thought.

"Hey, you asked," Lazarus said. "Computer, locate any guests or personnel on property."

"Reservist Libertine is in the hallway of sub-basement level one in presence of Knockabout, Huntsman, Stardust, Velvet, and Gallows. Wild Kat and Doctor Shadow are in the elevator shaft at sub-basement level one. Unidentified guest in secure conference room on sub-basement one," the vaguely feminine voice of the computer said from a nearby speaker.

Well, seems we are running late for the party, Simon thought. Libertine and the others will be confronting Augustus Dei any second. Not that they could stop him.

"So we're of the same mind on this Augustus Dei, right?" Lazarus said. "We get him to send me home."

Even if it means our deaths, Simon thought.

Lazarus laughed as he hit the elevator call button. The door opened in mere seconds and he stepped in. "It takes more than a little death to stop me," he said. The doors closed and they began their descent towards whatever fate awaited them.

Chapter Thirty-Five

Jeremy Red and Anna Lyta would both live, thanks in no small part to the magical re-knitting of bones and tissue that Doctor Shadow had performed upon his arrival. Archon had already sewn up the worst of the damage on Anna's throat, his needlework so deft that he doubted there would be a visible scar, but the magical touch-up alleviated any concerns about possible infections from his improvised surgical suite. Jeremy was still out cold, but at least the ruptured organs and broken bones had been magically repaired under Doctor Shadow's ministrations. Libertine still wanted to accompany Jeremy Red to the hospital to keep him under control should he unexpectedly wake up. Doctor Shadow assured her that was unlikely to happen for some time. Jeremy had retreated to a near comatose state from shock, and might not wake up for some time. Given the circumstances of his disappearance from Providence Asylum, it was for the best if the Protectorate had nothing further to do with the unconscious psychic killer. In the end, the asylum sent a retrieval team loaded down with drugs and power-dampening restraints mounted on a gurney.

The EMTs on scene wanted to take Anna to the nearest hospital for observation, but since her condition was no longer dire, a compromise was reached where they would deliver her to The Keep's medical facilities. Archon even agreed to ride along to make them less nervous about not heading directly to a hospital. With all that had happened in Cobalt City in the past day, there were other people who needed the assistance of the EMTs more. Especially with the roads around the downtown core badly damaged, they were all happier with the relatively quick trip to The Keep.

Stardust had patrolled an inward spiral pattern over the downtown core looking for some sign of Lazarus, but with no luck. Gallows was little help in narrowing down the search parameters. He had merely been trying to send the eminent threat "away," and not somewhere specific. He could at least say that it was on a rooftop with a view of downtown, which addressed several people's unspoken concern that Lazarus had been sent to the bottom of the ocean or straight down into the bedrock.

In the back of the ambulance, Archon remembered Gato Loco and his potential problems with Rakshasha. He pulled out his cell phone and dialed the number they had been using to coordinate efforts earlier. He was only a little surprised when Snowflake answered a few rings later. "You have reached the mobile office of Gato Loco," the panda said in a relaxed voice. "Who may I say is calling?"

"Snowflake, it's Archon. Where are you guys?"

"We just pulled off the east bridge into Quayside," Snowflake said. "And you can call me Sancho Panda now. I'm Gato's new sidekick."

"I never said that," Manuel said, taking the phone from Snowflake. "How are things on your end? You save the world yet?"

"Things are wrapped up downtown and we're on our way back to base. Everyone reverted back to their primary selves," Archon said. "Glad to hear you made it out okay. Guess Rakshasha never managed to find you?"

There was silence on the other end, and Archon wondered if he had lost the connection. Finally Gato Loco answered, "Yeah, about that…when you get back to base, I left Katherine cuffed in the elevator pit. She's probably crazy angry now if she's awake. Good luck with that."

"You stopped Rakshasha?" Archon said.

Anna lifted her head from her stretcher with extreme effort. The EMT whose nametag said Harris tried gently to hold her down and was awarded a withering glare. "Snowflake took out Rakshasha?" she mumbled. Archon mouthed the name Gato Loco to her and she smiled wide, and let herself be pushed back onto her pillow.

"I didn't stop her," Gato Loco said, "and don't ever say that again. To anybody. I took out someone piloting her body, that's all. I paid a blood price for it too."

"Do you need an ambulance?"

"The way traffic looks, I'm better off heading out to get help on my own. I'm only a pint or two low. We slapped some gauze on the worst of it and Snowflake and I are heading to a discreet doctor. Give me a call when things quiet down and let me know how things end up."

"I will," Archon said. "Thanks."

But Gato Loco had already hung up.

"How is that crazy cat doing?" Anna said, her voice soft in an effort to not put too much strain on her throat.

"He lost some blood, but not enough to keep him off his cycle. He should be alright. Snowflake is with him."

"I meant, how is he emotionally?" Anna said with an exacerbated sigh. "He and Wild Kat were kind of an item. Beating up your girlfriend only works if you live in a trailer park and work at the Piggly Wiggly."

"The two of them are dating?" Archon said.

"For a genius, you sure can be dumb sometimes," Anna said. She smiled and closed her eyes, enjoying the slow crawl of the ambulance back home. It was the first chance she had had to relax in some time.

I guess it's true, Archon thought, you really do learn something every day. He activated his communicator and tried to raise Wild Kat, but she had apparently turned hers off, or more likely, Gato Loco had it taken from her so she couldn't call for help. He widened the channel and contacted the rest of the Protectorate. "Be advised, Wild Kat is restrained in the elevator pit back at The Keep. Possibly unconscious, but use your best judgment when approaching. We're at least twenty minutes away where we are, so please get the med suite warmed up for us."

"We're on our way," Stardust said. "I'll fly ahead and unlock her."

"By all means," Doctor Shadow said. "I'm certain she will be in high spirits to be released."

"Are you kidding?" Huntsman said, laughing. "Fiercely independent, tough as nails, she's one of the scariest scrappers I've ever seen, and I've seen a lot. She's going to *love* being rescued."

Stardust kept flying ahead without saying anything, while Libertine and Doctor Shadow carried Huntsman, Knockabout, Velvet, and Gallows, who was feeling reluctant to teleport. Finally, Stardust slowed down and allowed the others to pull alongside. "Maybe I'll just wait for you guys. I can get the med suite warmed up, and Doctor Shadow can unlock her when we get back."

"And why do you think I am the candidate for this endeavor?" the mage asked, one eyebrow arched.

"Because you can do it while you're invisible. She'll never know we were there," Stardust said. The group landed on the roof of The Keep, and the hangar bay door slid open for them.

Stardust had his helmet sync up with the base computer and almost immediately discovered an anomaly on the sensor grid. He checked and re-checked, but the computer still showed someone in the secure sub-basement conference room, but when he checked the monitor feeds, the signal got crossed. The two cameras in that room only showed a clip from an old black-and-white musical. A smiling chorus line kicked and stepped while they twirled umbrellas and glitter fell from above. "I think we might have a problem here," he told the rest of the group. "I'm getting an unusual signal from conference room B-1. The computer says someone is there but isn't saying who, and the video feed won't give me any more information."

"What are you getting on the video feed?" Huntsman asked.

"If I'm not mistaken, it's *Gold-Diggers of Broadway*. I've checked to see if the signal could be coming from somewhere else or corrupted along the way, but everything comes up negative."

"It would appear that Augustus Dei is still here," Doctor Shadow said. "I will gather Katherine. I suggest that the rest of you follow close behind."

"Conference room?" Huntsman said as he restrung his bow.

"I believe I can get us all there fastest," Gallows said. To their credit, none of them backed down from the fight. "Hang tight and I'll set us down outside the door."

As the others blinked out, Doctor Shadow shifted into his incorporeal self and flew quickly towards the bound Wild Kat, deciding against turning invisible along the way. He found her easily, and she didn't look as angry as he had expected. Despite the beginning of a bruise on her chin and frizzed-out hair, she looked none the worse for wear as she waited patiently for someone to find her.

"Not that I wouldn't have tied Rakshasha up myself given the chance... I trust that someone will explain to me what happened here?" she said to Doctor Shadow as he unlocked the restraints. Freed of the power-dampening cuffs, she immediately shifted to her Wild Kat persona and wrinkled her nose. "Panda musk, blood, and ozone, and...was Gato Loco here?" she said, looking at the blood on the floor of the pit and on her hands in a whole new way. Doctor Shadow watched as her concern changed to sudden realization. "He knocked out Rakshasha, didn't he!"

"Perhaps he should explain that part himself," Doctor Shadow said. "In the meantime, we don't want to keep the others waiting. Augustus Dei is still here."

"And do you think we can beat him?" she asked, prying open the doors to the hallway.

"No," he said. He followed her down the hall towards the cluster of friends and teammates waiting outside the conference room door.

Katharine was more than a little surprised to see Libertine and Huntsman with the others. "But we're going in anyway," she said.

"Yes," Doctor Shadow said. "We are going in *because* we cannot defeat him. If he had wanted to destroy us, he could have done so anywhere along the way. Yet he did not. And now that we are back in our own bodies, he could have easily fled The Keep, and I have no doubt, this entire world. Yet once again, he did not. What more can he have planned for us?"

"It could be a trap," she said joining the others at the end of the hall before the ominously dark, closed doors of the conference room.

"I know," Doctor Shadow said with a twinkle in his ancient eyes. "Fascinating, isn't it?"

Wild Kat looked over the assembled heroes, ready to join in a fight they couldn't possibly hope to win. Her eyes finally settled on Huntsman. "Glad to see you finally made it in to work," she said, knowing that if he had been at the morning meeting, he would have been switched with his doppelganger as well.

"I know," Huntsman said. "I had something else going on."

"Doesn't matter," Velvet said. "You're on the reserve now anyway."

"I can live with that," Huntsman said.

"And you," Wild Kat said, turning to Libertine, "Keep away from older men."

"Or?" Libertine said, defiance evident in her voice.

Katherine said nothing but the icy cold stare she fixed Libertine with said volumes. It was hard not to notice the blood that still flecked the leather of her costume. Dead silence filled the hallway. Libertine took one, long look at the claws. "I see."

"Glad we agree on this," Katherine said. "Stardust, the door please."

"Finally," the armored inventor said. He raised both arms before him and blew the doors off the hinges with a double-fisted energy blast. The metal doors slammed to the floor a few feet inside the room to reveal an unassuming, dark suited man sitting on the edge of the conference table with a martini in one hand and a remote control in the other. He was watching cartoon mice beat up on cartoon cats on the main display screen. Dynamite was involved in the plot somehow, but they were unable to see exactly how as Augustus Dei turned off the screen.

"For the record," Augustus Dei said, "The door was unlocked." He stood to straighten his pants and jacket. Stardust, true to his nature, didn't waste time talking. Once he saw an opening, he fired another double-fisted blast at the erudite mastermind. Before the bolt reached him however, Augustus Dei lifted one palm, catching the full fury as easily as one would catch a tossed ball. The energy flickered, changed color and shape, and became a rose, which he tossed to Libertine.

Knockabout tried to get some kind of feel for Augustus Dei's personal gravity to contain the situation, but it seemed to fluctuate between nothingness and the mass of a black hole. His sense of motion when watching Augustus Dei transmute Stardust's attack made no sense either. Their target's hand didn't move from point A to point B. It was as if it were always at point B to begin with. Something about his earlier discussion with Jaccob and Anna about quantum state physics started to tickle the back of his mind. He only wished he knew enough about the theory to help him here.

Libertine had flexed at Augustus Dei and then gone stiff as a board and fallen over. Stardust had launched several more shots in a quick barrage at their black suited target, but each one was effortlessly diverted. Two of the deflected shots hit Huntsman, sending him to the ground in the hallway, two arrows still clutched in his fingers. Velvet had jumped in and was hitting him with everything she had, but he didn't seem to even notice her.

Gallows started flickering in and out of existence for a few seconds, and then came to a stop, his skin smoking slightly as he stood in the doorway. "Okay," he said, "I'm out of ideas."

"You too?" Stardust said.

"He won't budge, and he sent me somewhere really bad last time I tried to move him," Gallows said. The look in his eyes did not invite debate.

"You can't hurt me," Augustus Dei said. "You can't even touch me. I am so much more than any of you will ever understand."

"Then why even waste your time with us?" Wild Kat said.

"Because I don't want any of you to harbor the illusion that you have gained a victory here," he said calmly. "Did you think I didn't know about your spy in the crawlspace here? Do you honestly believe that I didn't know where you were each and every moment since you first left here?"

"Then why..." Stardust began.

"Because you imagine yourselves heroes," Augustus Dei said. "And perhaps you are. In a world of insects, you are insect heroes. In a world of pale reflections, you shine more brightly than the others. But do not ever forget just how insignificant you really are."

"There are rules, even for the likes of you," Doctor Shadow said. "You cannot act directly, can you? In fact, you can barely act at all, you can only react. You haven't initiated any attacks against us since we arrived. Not because you don't want to, but because you can't."

"Do not be so sure, twice-cursed pawn of dead gods," Augustus Dei said. The very air around them seemed to ripple with unseen but undeniable waves of power.

The Protectorate were thrown back against the walls, as they felt reality roil around them. They saw the room flicker at unimaginable speeds, thousands upon thousands of realities. In all of them, there was only one constant: Augustus Dei stood unique among them.

And then through the tempest, Lazarus stepped from the hallway into the conference room. With a casual, measured gait, he walked directly up to Augustus Dei. "But the mage was right, wasn't he? There are rules, there are laws," Lazarus / Simon said. He stood before Augustus Dei, who at least had the good grace to look surprised. A cold, dead, hand reached into the inside breast pocket of the impeccable, black jacket and returned with a crisply folded piece of paper. The undead fingers unfolded it with surprising delicacy. "This is the contract for Simon Floyd, isn't it?"

"Of course it is, but possession of that paper will do you no good," Augustus Dei sneered. "These people do not want back the so-called friend who betrayed them. And I suspect that you know what happens to you if you return home."

"I have a pretty good guess," Lazarus said. His eyes met Augustus Dei's while the disorienting flickers of universes ripped cries of protest from the mouths of the Protectorate. "I want to go home. And, for the record, I don't care what the cost is," Lazarus said. With one, sudden flick of his hands, he tore the contract in half.

The world settled back into place as the two pieces of paper fell towards the ground, turning to ash as they went. Lazarus himself dissolved into ash in the space of seconds, collapsing and filling the center of the room with an impenetrable cloud of grey haze. When the cloud reformed into the familiar form of Mister Grey, Augustus Dei was nowhere to be seen.

Chapter Thirty-Six

The man once known as Deathstar woke up alone in a nest of black satin sheets, listening to rain. The last thing he remembered was being pinned under his own weight in some public plaza surrounded by office buildings. We must have won, he thought, or I would be dead or in prison. But something about the sheets and the sound of the rain was uncomfortably familiar. Slowly he opened his eyes, already prepared for what he would see. The room he was in was dimly illuminated, the shades of the window across the room from him open to reveal a pine tree, lit from behind by low patio lights. He was home again. And he had to admit that he was a little relieved.

Too many capes and cowls, and that had been just the one city. Sure, he could probably take over in much the same way that he had here, but it would have taken a lot of work. It just wasn't cost effective. And the other Jaccob had given up running the company himself and instead let his wife run the whole affair. Straightening that out and wrestling control away would have been a nightmare, one he was glad to avoid.

He turned on the television while he got dressed and brushed his teeth. He was surprised to see a picture of his main development compound on the screen when he wandered out, toothbrush clamped tightly between his perfect teeth. He found the remote and zipped back to the beginning of the news piece.

"In a surprise move yesterday, communication and weapons system billionaire Jaccob Stevens signed over controlling interest in his financial empire to the estate of Elizabeth Barquist," the perky cable news talking head said. "In a written statement released through his lawyers, Stevens claimed to have met Ms. Barquist while undergoing therapy to overcome a lifetime sexual attraction to kitchen appliances. He said that he was so impressed with her strength that he thought she would be the perfect person to take control of the company he had built from the ground up. Ms. Barquist was unavailable to answer our questions, but her lawyer said that, while the gift was a surprise, they are already prepared to begin looking into the series of unexplained equipment malfunctions that led to multiple explosions and structure fires at the company's main research campus yesterday afternoon."

Jaccob didn't know when the toothbrush had dropped from his mouth, but he figured it was either when he started wailing or when he threw the chair through the plasma television screen.

Then the first of the viruses hit, and the fire safety system detected a false positive. All through the house, the sprinklers turned on, sending Jaccob scampering. Three more separate computer surprises lay in wait on the off chance he was able to get the water turned off. It was going to be a long day.

All the way across the world and some time later, Rakshasha awoke on the jungle floor with the sun low in the sky. The strong scent of banana groves told her that she had been screwed. That little Mexican bastard had cheated her somehow, and now she was back in her old body. She relished the return of her fangs and the thin layer of fur, but what she really wanted was revenge. He hadn't killed her, she acknowledged, but she was divided on whether that was a good or bad thing. Now she would live, but with the constant memory of her defeat. At least she had left him with some scars. The thought comforted her somewhat.

She was able to determine the direction to her estate well enough by starlight once she stopped focusing on her rage. Rakshasha sighted on the corner gun tower of one of her exterior walls, and ran at a reckless pace to get there. She was a quarter mile away before she realized that something was wrong.

There was no smell of smoke from cook fires, no diesel fumes from the generator, no rattle and shuffle of servants who should be active at this time of night. The compound was deserted. She could tell by the sound and smell before she came within sight of the unmanned guard towers and wide-open front gate. She walked into the courtyard, stunned by the evidence of looting. Every car gone from the garage, the generator ripped from its moorings. They had even stripped the copper power cables from the walls leading into the house.

It was worse inside. Her only remaining valuables were a handful of portfolios that her semi-literate servants could not understand as being rare. How could Jerry have let this happen? She raged. Had he betrayed her as well? It was only a matter of time, she figured, but she had always thought that she would be the one to kill him for treachery.

But when she got to her quarters, she discovered that the other Katherine Wilde had taken care of that as well. The bull man's carcass slumped against the window seat, body already swarming with fat, black flies. It was just one more reason on a rapidly growing list for Rakshasha to find a way back to Cobalt City.

There had to be a way back, she thought. This Augustus Dei didn't strike her as a science geek like that pathetic Deathstar, but he was able to make the transition for them easily enough. And if it was magic, then she knew the perfect place to start.

Who knows, she thought as she left the shell of her home, Shade may be looking for payback as well.

She was not incorrect in that assumption. He had checked the map tables for an update upon awakening on the floor of the command room. The skeleton army was gone. Gravas Tet Amon had vanished and the troops he had commanded had been destroyed. His all-but immortal governor in Jerusalem had mysteriously drowned, but no one admitted to knowing what had happened. Shade was not happy.

He strolled out into the parlor and found that the wall was missing, along with the balcony, and a small portion of the lounge itself. An enormous blow from outside, most likely, but he was hard-pressed to come up with what could have done so much damage.

A flicker of light from the library caught his eye, and he went to investigate, his frustration with this Augustus Dei growing by the second. Someone had set up a small table in the center of the library floor and on it burned a large candle behind a wire screen. The flame intrigued him. Perhaps something left behind by his body's temporary squatter, some key to how he had been dragged back here. He could feel magic radiating from it, and he was unable to magically snuff the flame. He approached carefully, and removed the wire screen, regretting his decision immediately.

Sitting in the middle of the table was a human hand, propped upright on its stump. The hand was waxy and sallow. The fingers were spread, and each blazed with a white light that hurt to look directly at, but was impossible to turn away from as well.

"I assume you recognize it," a cultured voice said to him in Arabic from the corner behind him. Shade was so taken in by the light that he hadn't bothered to check if he were alone. Why would he? With the exception of his skeletal servants, he was always alone here. No one dared venture into Shade's realm uninvited. "The hand of a man hanged at a crossroad, properly prepared, of course," the voice continued.

Shade tried to tear his eyes away with every ounce of his being, tried to turn invisible or incorporeal or teleport away, but he was frozen so completely that he found it impossible to speak, let alone cast magic.

"When used properly," the voice continued, "it allows a mage to remain awake for as long as the flame burns, usually several days, while absorbing the knowledge from books. A useful study aid, don't you think? But the Hand of Glory has a risk associated with it, which I am certain you are aware of, if not before then certainly now. By looking directly at the candle at any time, a person becomes transfixed by the flames. It is a small price to pay for a little mistake, a little embarrassing perhaps to be so careless. But you are not just any person, are you?"

The grotesque candle allowed Shade a moment's distraction imagining what he would do to the person who had visited such an indignity upon him. He heard footsteps on the stone behind him, as his tormenter headed out towards the gaping hole that had been the balcony. He could feel warmth on his back, and saw shadows forming before him in his peripheral vision. An unexpected chill went down his spine.

"You have made some powerful enemies in your time," the voice said, "but the two you offended most were the first, were they not? I have given you a great gift, oh immortal one. I have pled your case to the two gods who cursed you those thousands of years ago. Their squabbles are at an end. Anubis has decided to forgive and forget. You have done so much in his name in years past, that you are now welcome in the lands of the dead as an honored guest. Sadly, Ra would like a few words with you."

The light from behind him grew stronger as the stranger stepped to the side and let the sun blaze into the library. But it was more than merely sunlight. So very much more, and it burned what it touched.

When Emil returned to the library, he was careful to avert his eyes from the Hand of Glory, on the off chance it had survived the fury of Ra, Egyptian God of the sun. But the room was bare of everything but dust. The ancient stone walls were blackened everywhere except for a silhouette in negative of a powerful necromancer who had, in a moment of weakness, made a very bad decision a long, long time ago.

To the south, Sundiatta was too busy to notice that the permanent darkness over the Valley of Kings had been lifted. He had awoken seated on the Antelope Throne to the sounds of chaos in the streets. Sundiatta shouted for the steward who, bowing and scraping, hastily stumbled through the throne room doors in less than a minute. His fly was still unzipped and his shirttails were untucked, but he seemed unaware. Confusion and surprise played across his face as though the devil himself had just interrupted his revels.

"Your Majesty," the steward fumbled, "I had not been alerted to your return."

"And where had I gone to reduce the city to such chaos?" Sundiatta boomed, coming to his feet.

"You led our troops into battle with the foul army of ghosts who walk, north in the Vale of Golden Sun," the steward said, trying to be as subtle as possible as he tucked in his wine-stained shirt. "And after defeating the Shade's army, we were told that you went alone into the Valley of Kings to confront and destroy him."

"And why have my generals not restored order?" Sundiatta said, his fist tight around the Spear of Kings.

The steward looked confused, as if he feared his king were going mad. It was only a matter of time, really, he thought. In time, the ancient whispers rumored to come from the Antelope Throne drove all who sat in it to some kind of insanity. "Your majesty?" he said. "They are all dead, killed in the battle at your side. All who marched into the Vale of the Golden Sun perished or vanished after the battle. The people are already calling it the Battle of Ghosts."

Sundiatta killed the steward with a pure blast of kinetic force, and regretted it almost before the body hit the floor. He wasn't sure who was still around to clean up the mess for him. He certainly wasn't going to do it himself, and in the heat of the throne room, it would begin to smell soon. He went to the window and looked out over the high walls of the palace as the fires continued to blaze, listening to the explosions and shouts of a city descended into chaos. He reached to turn on the command board, but thought better of it. By now, word had certainly spread. The conqueror king had vanished into the night of the Valley of Kings, from where no one returned. His generals were dead, his army reduced to the point where they could no longer maintain order. He didn't need the computer to tell him what he already knew. His reign in D'habu was at an end.

But with the burden of kingship removed, it freed him up to pursue something new. For instance, revenge had a particularly nice sound to it at the moment.

Far across the Atlantic Ocean in Cobalt City, Lenore had begun making calls looking for Lazarus. She started with his three lieutenants, hoping that he was with one of them on business, but they hadn't seen him for days. Next she tried some of his favorite clubs and front businesses, but he had been a no-show there as well. She had even gone the extra, desperate step to summon up a Hell Maggot, a worm which had an uncanny ability to sense the undead. She knew that she could send it away before it started to consume her lover and protector. But even that had come to nothing.

Two things slowly became apparent to her. One, Lazarus was not anywhere close by and might not have even been sent back at all, and, two, that the more she looked for him, the more she unraveled his power structure as button men began to sense the power vacuum. She realized the pathetic irony of it all. She had been raised in a gangster lifestyle, but knew nothing about running the organization. Lazarus had done all of that, while she had simply enjoyed the extravagant trappings of power.

As she sat on the red chaise lounge, something out on the patio caught her eye, a flapping of cloth caught by the wind. Lenore opened the door to the broad rooftop patio with its potted trees and flower garden crowded with nightshade and calla lilies. Out next to the flowerbox was a pile of clothes, which she quickly identified as Lazarus' vintage tuxedo. She picked up the jacket, and a fine, gray ash fell from both sleeves. Ash had piled in and around the shoes as well. The removal of the jacket exposed it all to the wind which had come howling up over the edge of the building, and before Lenore fully realized what was happening, the ash was gone, carried dancing by the indifferent wind until it scattered over the rooftops with all the soot and grime the city had become accustomed to.

For the first time in her life, Lenore understood what it was to be alone.

Chapter Thirty-Seven

A surprisingly warm breeze blew up from Cannonade and stirred the ruby-colored cape that had gathered around Libertine's legs. The breeze carried with it the sounds of road crews jackhammering and patching sections of nearby Madison Street. Already, those who had to drive around downtown had adjusted to the detours and delays. For the average Cobalt City citizen, life had returned to normal in the past two weeks. She looked down at Huntsman, crouched near the edge, watching the sky where the Protectorate's hover-jet was coming in for a soft landing on the roof of The Keep after another successful mission. "Do you miss it?" Libertine said.

Huntsman shrugged. It was complicated, but he could never explain it to her. She had not been a member of the team, not like he had. When he got back from his soul searching, there was nothing he wanted more than to make a break of it and try something different. A smaller team, maybe going it solo. Or, heaven forbid, he could focus on his studies and spend more time with the classmates he had neglected in the past year. But something about being there in the pinch and saving the city, about just being there with Katherine and Edirin and Anna and Jaccob... It had felt like a family again, like it had at the beginning. But it couldn't last. Nothing ever did. "I miss parts of it," he was finally able to say. "And there's nothing wrong with being on the reserve. It's still a big city. We need all the heroes we can get."

"Well, I'm off the clock," she said. She took off her communicator and turned on her pager, tucked beneath the folds of her cape. "Can I buy you a beer? We can kick it at my place, maybe put on some Marley..."

Huntsman stood and removed his own communicator. They would know where to find him when...if they needed him. "Thanks, but no. I don't drink. You know that."

Libertine's smile was revealed as her costume dissolved as the illusion it was, leaving her in a Ramones T-shirt and bike shorts. "Yeah, I know. How about ice cream sandwiches and Playstation?"

Marcus pulled off his cowl and ran a finger through his shaggy red hair. He grimaced against the setting sun as he looked at her, but there was a wry smile on his face. "You know I'll destroy you, right?"

"Whatever you say, milquetoast," she said. She cast an illusion to make him look just like any other guy on the street, in the same way she created an image of her costume. "One full game of basketball, you pick the teams, and loser buys pizza."

"Hope you like crow with your pizza," he said as they climbed down the fire escape to the street. "Because you get the Clippers."

"Bastard."

To the north, the Protectorate disembarked from the plane while pneumatic lifts lowered it into the hangar. Knockabout was one of the first out, hopping off the lift before it had reached the hangar floor. Velvet and Worm Queen were not far behind. "Are you sure you don't mind monitor duty tonight?" Stardust asked Mister Grey as he stepped off the lift next.

"I have something I've been meaning to do in the West End, but I will be back for this evening's shift," Mister Grey said.

"Hey, if you're heading west, do you mind dropping me by my place?" Velvet said, but a quick look over Mister Grey's shoulder to Wild Kat shaking her head made her think better of it. "Actually, I was going to hit the whirlpool tub downstairs first, so never mind, I'll cab over."

"No, I don't mind," Simon said, but something in Wild Kat's eyes made Velvet side with the downstairs tub.

"Don't sweat it," Velvet said. "I've got to soak out the muscles, and you don't need to wait."

"Wait up, Velvet," Worm Queen said. "I could use a soak too after getting hammered by that robot. I think I pulled something."

"You should both be checked out in the med suite, but of course you won't listen to me," Archon said. As the last one off the plane, he keyed in his security code and locked it up tight.

"You want to join us in the tub?" Velvet said with a wink.

"I, uh, I have to finish inputting my report," Archon said. With perfect control of his body chemistry, he was able to confine his blush to the tips of his ears.

"Okay, but then you're joining us for daiquiris at the Arctic Club after," Worm Queen said.

While the banter continued upstairs, Gallows shared an elevator with Knockabout and Mister Grey, getting off at the quarters level. A quick shower and a change of clothes later, and he was ready to spend a little downtime playing pool at a hole-in-the-wall in Quayside. It was an especially nice night, and he decided to walk a part of the way and enjoy it. The elevator took him to the lobby, and he was only a little surprised to see Snowflake loitering just outside the front door smoking a cigarette. Gallows stepped out and rocked on his heels for a bit, breathing in the smells of the city at sunset, mixed with Snowflake's Turkish tobacco smoke. "Nice night," he said to the panda.

"I was almost a sidekick, damn it," Snowflake said, taking an unhappy drag on his cigarette.

Gallows shrugged, and folded a stick of Blackjack gum into his mouth. "I had over a cubic foot of beetles conjured into my lungs and stomach."

Snowflake thought it over with another drag, "You win."

"Sorry about the sidekick thing though," Gallows said.

"Ah, what you gonna do, you know? Sorry about the bugs," he said.

"Yeah, well, you move on, I guess," Gallows said.

"Cigarette?" Snowflake said offering the pack to the teleporter.

"Nah...those things will kill you," Gallows said. He chewed his gum and rocked on his heels some more. "You play pool?"

"Only for money," Snowflake said.

Gallows smiled and put his arm around the panda, "Okay, but when they ask, you've never even seen the game before. You're new to the city and I'm just showing you around."

"You talk like I've never done this before," Snowflake said, sounding hurt. "Lead on, my brother." In an instant, the front step was empty but for the scent of smoke and intrigue.

Inside, Edirin sat in the communications lounge with a headset on. His back was straight and formal, and his hands kept picking invisible threads off of his jacket sleeves and pant legs. "No, everything is fine here," he was saying into the mouthpiece. "We just got back from a mission and we haven't spoken in a while."

He waited, listening to the questions coming from the other end, a smile on his face, his posture relaxing. "Yes the rebuilding is faster than I had expected. I was thinking it would take a month, but it looks like most of the streets will be opening again next week. I'm sure the news reports made it look far worse than it actually was."

Edirin laughed and shook his head, "Yes, father, I'm getting plenty to eat, but thank you for your concern. I was wondering..." he paused, and noticed that Jaccob had come in behind him, dressed in a flannel camp shirt and jeans. Edirin smiled and motioned for him to wait. "I was just wondering how things were doing in D'habu. The last time I was back, I never got out of the city. It would be nice to get out and see the old house and you and the rest of the family."

Edirin paused, listening to the comforting voice of his father. "I understand, father. Get to work and we will speak again tomorrow. Of course. Love you too," he said, then reached out and flipped off the transmitter. "My father, he doesn't believe in having a phone because all he gets are people calling to bother him and sell him things he doesn't need," he said to Jaccob.

"Wow," Jaccob said, "there are telemarketers in D'habu?"

"They are everywhere," Edirin said. "The plague of our times. So, I see you are ready to go?"

Jaccob lifted his arms and modeled the blue flannel shirt. "Four days, no communicator, no cell phone, just me, Elizabeth, the kids, and a cabin in the Wharton State Forest."

"No technology for four days," Edirin said. "How will you ever survive?"

"Elizabeth's idea," Jaccob said, "But it could be fun. I might even get some fishing in. She packed a pair of poles and a tackle box. I just wanted you to see the ensemble before I left."

"Very stylish," Edirin said. "Not everyone could pull it off, but it's a very dad look. Have fun."

"I will," Jaccob said as he headed for the door. "Thanks for keeping the city safe while I'm gone."

Far overhead, Doctor Shadow floated and watched Cobalt City roll on beneath him. He could tell them, of course, but who would listen. Augustus Dei was gone, but he had put his fingerprint on the city. One of his preplanned events could pop up at any moment, another domino ready to fall. But this time things were different. This time he had encountered not one, but two people who would live as long as himself. Doctor Shadow doubted that Simon would forget the black suited manipulator anytime soon, just has he himself would endeavor never to forget.

And the next time Augustus Dei came calling, they would be waiting.

Over near the northeast corner of Lafayette Park, Katherine Wilde checked her appearance in the window of a bookstore one more time. She checked her watch, trying to time this just right. Can't be too early, she thought, have to set the right tone. At least the bruise on her chin had faded completely. That had made for an awkward moment with the gallery committee, and she had been reduced to claiming that someone had tried to mug her. Better the rumors and snide suspicions masked behind gushing sympathy of her social peers than the truth. A week avoiding society functions and it had been forgotten by all but the cattiest socialites, and no one paid them much mind anyway.

"I have to do this," she said under her breath. She smoothed the pleats of her red plaid skirt and straightened the two inches of white stocking above her knee high black leather boots. She took a deep breath and let it out slowly, then got the walk signal and crossed the street to Schrodinger's Cup.

Manuel was already there, fetching two tall paper cups from the barista at the end of the counter. He was all in long sleeves, but she had heard from Simon that the scars were pretty dramatic. Katherine tried to imagine them for perhaps the hundredth time, and was stopped by remembering the amount of blood that she had cleaned up in her quarters. She had burned the sheets, despite their extravagant thread count. She waited by the door and let him approach. It gave her a chance to get her pulse back under control.

"I got you your favorite," he said, a nervous smile flickering across his face, ghostlike.

"Macadamia mocha, extra hot…" she began.

"…triple shot with nonfat whip," he finished. He held out a cup for her. "For the lady."

"A lady wouldn't have flayed you alive," she said, jumping right to the point. He was taken aback and froze, not sure what to say next. Katherine's taking the mocha from his hand seemed to stir him back into motion. "Let's walk, okay? I feel like walking."

Manuel led her out the door and began walking in the direction of the nearby Cobalt City University campus. Katherine quickly fell into step beside him. "I don't know what you've been told or pieced together, but…your out of town friend…was not a lady, so I don't hold you responsible," he said.

"Manuel, you wouldn't have gotten into that situation in the first place if you hadn't thought it was me," she said. "And I'm the one who cleaned up the mess, so I have some idea of what she put you through."

"It wasn't all bad," he said tentatively. *That* stopped her in her tracks. "Or did you not know that?"

"I suspected, of course," she said, her voice sounding smaller than her body, "No, I guess I knew, actually, but I didn't want it to be true. It's just that it felt like…like you were cheating on me."

"So are we dating now?" he said, looking at her over the white plastic lid of his coffee cup.

"I don't know," she said. "Are we?"

"I'd like to think so," Manuel said, taking a sip of his coffee. She looked hesitant, so he bent in and kissed her softly on the upper lip. She didn't stop him.

When he pulled back, she was smiling. "I don't know if I can trust you," she said. "You did sleep with my evil twin."

"God," he said, "We sound like a Mexican soap opera!"

Cobalt City Blues

"I wouldn't know," she said, "I've never seen one."

Manuel offered Katherine his arm, and after a second she took it as he led her towards the nearest monorail station. "I have four hours saved up on my TIVO, if you'd like to come back to my place?" he said.

She laughed and allowed herself to be tugged along. "I haven't eaten yet," she said, "Dinner first?"

"I know a great sushi place down on Adams near the Cannonade," he said.

"Deal," she agreed, "but we go by cab. Katherine Wilde can't be seen on a monorail with handsome Latin strangers. The society pages would have a field day."

As they hailed a cab, miles away in the south end of Karlsburgh, Simon stood at the front of the car he had taken out of the car pool. A bouquet of lilies was in one hand as he steeled himself. The potter's field stretched out before him, unkempt and desolate. He had considered having Camilla moved when he found out where she was buried, but he didn't have the legal status. In the end, he had been forced to leave her where she lay. And perhaps that was for the best.

Simon walked out among the small, anonymous headstones and crosses until he came to the grave he had come to know by heart. The sorrow and rage he used to feel had faded since the last time. He figured the incident with Augustus Dei had something to do with it, but didn't want to look too closely. Dwelling on the matter would not help anything.

A lonely wind stirred the grass around his feet as he looked down at the sad little grave marker. Simon knelt and carefully placed the white flowers, his head lowered. "I can't stay, Camilla," he said. "I have work to do. I'm sure you understand. Anyway, I wanted to come by and leave you your flowers. I know how much you liked them."

He stood and turned his back on the flowers and marker, and looked at the lights of the city out over the rooftops and treetops of the West End. "I've been busy. I have a new life now, new friends, new family. What I'm trying to say is that…well, I think it's time I let this go. I'll still come to visit you from time to time. I'll still miss you, of course. But I can't hide anymore. It's time I got a life."

Minutes later he was back in the car, headed home. And it didn't hurt anymore.

Epilogue

"What did you really hope to accomplish?" the King in Yellow said as he viewed the scene through the lens.

Augustus Dei stood silently next to him, arms crossed, his eyes on the lens.

"I mean, really," the King in Yellow said as he turned his back on the view. He led his companion out of the room to an adjacent hall where a large chessboard sat beneath cloudy light. The pieces on the board looked a little like the knights and pawns of a conventional set. A minotaur lay on its side, while another piece that looked broken, as though only the head remained, lay off to one side of the board. "Your contract was canceled, and your clients are now aware of your presence. Aside from some entertainment in where you chose to return the one set of pieces, I saw very little gained."

"Yes," Augustus Dei said with a tilt of his head. A crooked smile spread across his face. "But there were other compensations. The amount of chaos alone was worth it."

"Perhaps," the King in Yellow said. "And you uncovered and removed two of my pieces."

Augustus Dei smiled slyly. "True, both the bull and the Baptist removed from play, both taken by the tiger-in-disguise. Plus I have a new piece on the board."

"The Lion of the Atlas," the King in Yellow said, with a nod of his head. "Well played on that. I particularly liked how you closed the loop. I never saw it coming and will have to plan accordingly going forward. But I think I still come out ahead in the end, cousin."

"How so?" Augustus Dei said, cocking an eyebrow.

"While you were busy making power plays, I was able to promote a few hidden pawns to larger roles," the King in Yellow said. His dead white eyes looked as though he were smiling as well.

"I suppose you won't tell me who, will you," Augustus Dei said.

"Have I ever?"

Augustus Dei stuffed his hands into his pockets, not bothered at the moment by how it ruined the line of his pants. "So the game goes on."

"You concede the round so quickly. Do not pretend that you did not plant a few seeds of your own as well," the King in Yellow said.

"Anything is possible," Augustus Dei said with a distracted

smile. He eyed the board and planned his strategy as he stood next to the King in Yellow. Madness and Chaos, shoulder to shoulder in a dead city by an ancient lake. There was no rush, no pressure for Augustus Dei to make his next move. The board was enormous and stretched across infinite dimensions. A good move was expected to take a little while, and he did have forever, after all. And truly, anything was possible.

Other adventures in the Cobalt City Universe:

Chanson Noir

Greetings from Buena Rosa

Ride Like the Devil

Cobalt City Christmas

Cobalt City Timeslip

Revised Editions of the first four coming in 2011.

www.ingramcontent.com/pod-product-compliance
Lightning Source LLC
Chambersburg PA
CBHW020614260626
47157CB00003B/1016